The Short Fiction
of D. H. Lawrence

THE SHORT FICTION
OF D. H. LAWRENCE

JANICE HUBBARD HARRIS

Rutgers University Press
New Brunswick, New Jersey

1984

Publication of this book has been aided by a grant from the National Endowment for the Humanities.

Library of Congress Cataloging in Publication Data

Harris, Janice Hubbard, 1943–
    The short fiction of D. H. Lawrence.

    Bibliography: p.
    Includes index.
    1. Lawrence, D. H. (David Herbert), 1885–1930—Criticism and interpretation. I. Title.
PR6023.A93Z63124   1984   823'.912   83–23055
ISBN 0–8135–1046–5

To My Parents
and
Duncan, Adam, and Joshua Harris

Contents

Preface

This book has been a long time in the making. It originated in a conversation years ago with Mark Spilka, one of the first critics to help secure ground claimed for Lawrence by F. R. Leavis in the 1950s. Leavis had asserted the value, quite simply, of reading Lawrence as a thinker *and* an artist. Lawrence may have been a prophet, but Leavis's series in *Scrutiny* beautifully demonstrated that he was also a magnificent craftsman.[1] Leavis's "formalist-moralist" readings opened the way for a large body of scholarly criticism published in America and England throughout the 1950s, 1960s, and 1970s. Never again would Lawrence be read only as an inspired, wacky genius. Spilka's point to me in the late 1960s, however, was that a surprising gap existed in the critical literature on Lawrence. There were of course many studies of his novels; the emphasis was predictable and justifiable. The novels are Lawrence's large works; in form and content they challenge readers in ways none of his other writings can. There were also studies of his poetry, life, travels, essays, philosophy, and painting. But where were the studies of his short stories? Where were the analyses of that lively body of fiction capable, as Julian Moynahan says, of bringing light back into the eyes of the reader exhausted by *The Plumed Serpent* or fainting amid the incremental repetitions of *The Rainbow?*[2]

There was and still is only one full-length study of Lawrence's entire corpus of short fiction, Kingsley Widmer's *The Art of Perversity: D. H. Lawrence's Shorter Fictions*, published in 1962. Widmer's is a fascinating book. Starting from the premise that Lawrence was covertly attracted to extreme, self-annihilating modes of experience, Widmer gathers Lawrence's tales into clusters of perversity, ranging from tales that explore the attraction of the destructive woman to those that celebrate the death throes standing at the extreme of eros. His readings are often subtle, giving the lie to saccharin interpretations of Lawrence. But Widmer's approach is highly restrictive. Inevitably, he minimizes or fails to recognize the many aspects of Lawrence that do not fit his thesis. As Spilka has argued in a different context, criticism that finds Lawrence ultimately perverse—ultimately drawn to pain, death, and dissolution—often concentrates on particular images in a work while ignoring the work's dramatic conflicts and progressions.[3] That concentration is clear in Widmer. Further, by organizing the stories thematically, Widmer makes it impossible for a reader to discern any development in Lawrence's thinking or craft. One ends up with a peculiarly static view of this extraordinarily dynamic artist.

The majority of studies of Lawrence's short fiction resides within literary journals and within the array of books devoted mainly to the novels. Ranging from the *D. H. Lawrence Review* to *Lettore di Provincia* to *Mostovi*, periodicals in this country and across the globe have published a steady and valuable stream of criticism and scholarship. The books that now comprise the classic criticism on Lawrence's fiction frequently contain a chapter or section on his tales. These include, for example, F. R. Leavis's *D. H. Lawrence: Novelist*; George Ford's *Double Measure*; E. W. Tedlock's *D. H. Lawrence: Artist and Rebel*; Julian Moynahan's *The Deed of Life*; Eliseo Vivas's *D. H. Lawrence: The Failure and the Triumph of Art*; James C. Cowan's *D. H. Lawrence's American Journey*; R. E. Pritchard's *D. H. Lawrence: Body of Darkness*; Keith Sagar's *The Art of D. H. Lawrence*; R. P. Draper's *D. H. Lawrence*;

Graham Hough's *The Dark Sun*; and Mark Spilka's *The Love Ethic of D. H. Lawrence*. The list could go on. As with the criticism published in the periodicals, much of this latter commentary is essential reading. But in each instance the limitations are inevitable. The very form of the analysis militates against a full exploration of the entire body of Lawrence's short fiction. Even the most discerning article or chapter does not have the scope to discuss Lawrence's stories as a creative endeavor extending over twenty years, a creation interesting in its own terms and in its relationship to the art of modern short fiction.

A still different kind of restriction marks the approach to Lawrence's short fiction taken by Keith Cushman in *D. H. Lawrence at Work: The Emergence of the Prussian Officer Stories*. A carefully researched study, Cushman's book traces the creative process that gave birth to five of Lawrence's early stories. One watches Lawrence writing out an original version and then returning to it, often in draft after draft, year after year, as he revises and reforms his vision. Cushman's book is also essential reading; yet, again, the very conception of his study prevents a wide-ranging critique.

Why the gap? Why have we not had a study of Lawrence's short fiction that honors it as a distinct *oeuvre*, traces its particular turns and counterturns, assesses its strengths and weaknesses, and evaluates its ties and contributions to the modern short story? One reason may be the sheer quantity of tales. Another, the lack, until recently, of a sufficiently detailed chronology.[4] A further reason may be the power of the novels. But a similar discrepancy appears whenever one compares works of differing genres; short stories and novels, like sonnets and epics, have different latitudes, limits, potentials, demands. Still another reason may be the marvelous variety of subject and form found among the tales. Having decided to tackle the entire *oeuvre*, one is tempted to move along list fashion, letting variety be the theme. That listing may avoid the contortions of the grand thesis, but it produces a book that is all trees, no forest.

In the study that follows, I have sought to analyze trees and forest, interpreting the critical issues raised by a particular tale and seeing those issues as they relate to the short fiction as a whole. I am especially interested in providing a sense of Lawrence's progress within the genre. A roughly chronological scheme is followed; each chapter opens with a brief biographical and critical overview. I should state here, however, that readers not familiar with Lawrence's life will want to consult the several biographies cited in the notes. Information on his life—and a remarkable life it was—is readily available. Correspondingly, I include discussion of early versions only when Lawrence's revisions were significant.[5] Upon finishing a tale, Lawrence would usually send it to be typed and, through his agent, circulate it among small magazines in England and America. Most of his tales appeared in current periodicals within a year or two of composition. Often as much as six or eight years later, Lawrence would then return to a particular group of stories and, working with either the magazine texts or original manuscripts in front of him, revise the works for one of the three volumes of collected stories published during his lifetime. Major revisions were often made at any stage during this process. In some cases, Lawrence's developing ideas and techniques correlate neatly with his work in the long fiction, but in many instances the long and short fiction dramatically part ways. And here one makes an important discovery.

For too long, critics have seen the tales as bits of material left over from the novels, as spinoffs or holidays from the major work of the long fiction.[6] The truth is more various. In general, novels and short stories are more like first cousins than brothers and sisters. They have much in common, employing many of the same literary elements, but they are also distinct in fundamental ways. They make different demands on the author and create different expectations in the reader. Poe understood those differences, and his insistence that the short story have, above all else, a unified effect was shared, until recently, by great practitioners of the art. Furthermore, the short story and novel have separate histories, are often written for different audiences and for different reasons.[7] Faulkner said that writers who cannot write poetry write short stories; if they fail at short stories, they write novels.[8] But one can also say that novels resemble a painter's large canvases, short stories his or her small ones. The large may take years of work, the small only months or weeks. For that very reason, an artist may feel a degree of insouciance toward the smaller work, and that casual attitude can lead to surprising developments, such as the paradoxical situation of freedom of expression in a highly contained form.

Faulkner's comment aside, all of the above pertains to Lawrence: to his skills and attitude toward his novels and stories, to the models he followed and discarded, to the field of short fiction as he found and left it. To see his short stories as leftovers is to miss all that is interesting in the relationship between his long and short fiction.

Thinking about that relationship raises issues of nomenclature and genre. From the eighteenth century on, short fiction has distinguished itself through a variety of names: short story, tale, sketch, nouvelle. In our own century, Russian formalists such as Victor Shklovski, B. J. Ejxenbaum, and Tzvetan Todorov have introduced a different set, based on their work on the linguistic and narrative patterns that distinguish novels from short stories and the various kinds of short stories from each other.[9] At various points in writing this book, I adopted a strict system of nomenclature following either my own or one of the critics' schemes. I found however that the schematizing tended to impede a particular discussion rather than clarify it. Emphasis gravitated away from Lawrence's writing toward the terminology. Thus I have chosen to adopt the pattern most common to current critics as well as to Lawrence and his contemporaries; tale and short story will be used interchangeably, reserving sketch (*skaz* in Ejxenbaum's theory) for special use.

Many readers encounter Lawrence for the first time through his short fiction. No respectable anthology excludes him. At the very least, it is my hope that these new readers will find here the information and critical insights they need to begin exploring Lawrence's thought and art. Lawrence is a demanding author; an exciting journey awaits them. For the reader who knows Lawrence well, I hope this book captures the character of Lawrence's short fiction as an *oeuvre*, reveals his development in the genre, challenges accepted readings of particular tales, and helps define his place in the art. One knows that it is a high and mighty place, and that without Lawrence the genre would be, in Frost's words, a diminished thing. But what is the nature of his accomplishment? What did he do to reshape that marvelous vehicle of twentieth-century sensibility, the modern short story? My examination proceeds along two fronts: Lawrence's vision of human experience and the ways he articulated that vision through his short stories.

Returning to my conversation with Mark Spilka, I thought about his comments and bought Viking Press's three-volume set as a first step in acquainting myself with the full range of Lawrence's short stories. Sometimes fate gives us the right books to read and also the right context in which to read them. On a late-summer drive from California to Rhode Island, beneath magnificent skies and between acres of ripening wheat, I read to myself and my companion four books: Lawrence's three volumes and Betty Friedan's *The Feminine Mystique*. How the wealth of impressions, from within and without, would come together I neither imagined nor cared. It was, it remains, a rich, extended moment. I hope this book manages to convey a glimmer of that richness.

Acknowledgments

From the outset, Lawrence was a controversial writer. Criticism of his work is voluminous, combative, and exciting. My debt to Lawrence scholars and critics is too great to be acknowledged adequately here. My discussions and notes partly indicate the extent of that indebtedness. To Mark Spilka and Keith Cushman I owe special thanks, the former for introducing me to Lawrence, the latter for his encouragement and extensive criticisms of an early draft of this book. For their guidance at various stages in my research and writing, I am also grateful to Julian Moynahan, Robert Scholes, Charles Rossman, and Morris Beja.

Portions of this book appeared in different form in *Philological Quarterly, Modern Language Quarterly, D. H. Lawrence Review,* and *Modern Language Studies.* I thank the editors for permission to reprint material from these periodicals.

In doing research for this study, I required the assistance of library staffs throughout America and in England. I am grateful to the following libraries and institutions for making available their Lawrence manuscripts and for allowing me to quote from unpublished material in their collections: the Humanities Research Center, University of Texas at Austin; the Bancroft Library, University of California at Berkeley; the Department of Special Collections, Stanford University Libraries; the Henry W. and Albert A. Berg Collection of the New York Public Library and the Astor, Lenox and Tilden Foundations; Manuscripts Department, University of Nottingham Library; the Beinecke Rare Book and Manuscript Library, Yale University Library; Department of Special Collections, University Research Library, University of California at Los Angeles; McFarlin Library, University of Tulsa; and the Ellen Clarke Bertrand Library, Bucknell University. In addition, I am grateful for support given to me by the University of Wyoming: kind assistance from the staff of Coe Library; three indefatigable typists, Eugenia Manuelito, Patti Martin, and Barbara Kissack; and grants of time and money from the College of Arts and Sciences and from the University.

I wish to thank Laurence Pollinger Ltd. and the Estate of the late Mrs. Frieda Lawrence Ravagli for permission to quote from the published and unpublished works of D. H. Lawrence. My sincere thanks also to Leslie Silko for permission to quote the opening stanza of her poem, "Ceremony," which introduces her novel of the same name.

Finally, let me express my gratitude to my husband, Duncan S. Harris, and my children, Adam and Joshua. Just as Lawrence has enriched my understanding of them, so they have enriched my understanding of Lawrence.

THE SHORT FICTION
OF D. H. LAWRENCE

Ceremony

I will tell you something about stories
[he said]
They aren't just entertainment.
Don't be fooled.
They are all we have, you see,
all we have to fight off
illness and death.

You don't have anything
if you don't have the stories.

. . .

Leslie Silko
Ceremony

Introduction

Ahead lies a range of stories written under the most diverse circumstances. Neatly penned in Lawrence's clear script, they were conceived over a period of twenty-three years in England, the Bavarian Alps, Germany, Italy, Ceylon, Australia, Mexico, and New Mexico. One does not want to romanticize their genesis: sometimes they were written out of spite, sometimes to keep bread on the board. At times, in his letters, Lawrence moans in exasperation as he sweats away at revising them. Often he does not mention them at all or scratches out a quick line telling an agent or typist when a tale will be finished and sent. This relative silence is in contrast to the situation with the novels, which he frequently writes about, discussing their progress and design with a variety of correspondents. If the tales came more easily than the novels, they also came more steadily. During dry periods, when Lawrence's despair dammed the energy and faith he needed to write novels (well disciplined, he was, nevertheless, no Trollope), the short stories are often the only vehicles through which his narrative imagination continued to flow. During these periods, they stand as flowers in a desert, wonderful in their very existence but also in their vibrancy, in the love and hope they betray. At other times, they remind one more of leeches, that is, as leeches were once thought to function, drawing off bad spirits and poisoned blood. These cathartic tales are sometimes full of wit and power, sometimes full of mere sound and fury. Often the tales exist as participants in a rich dialogue of theme and technique with each other and with whatever else Lawrence was writing at the time. At other times they seem to come out of nowhere.

The problem for the critic who wants to examine this diverse creation is to find a way to describe the whole and, at the same time, analyze the constituent parts. I have tried a variety of approaches, from thematic clusters (tales of the revivifying stranger, tales of exile) to clusters that emphasize the contrast between the exploratory and conservative tales in a certain period. In most cases, the schemes obscured Lawrence's development in his short fiction, or gave a falsely neat picture of his real but fluid progress in the genre.

I knew from the beginning that the progress followed a movement away from conventional, nineteenth-century tales toward realism, visionary short stories, and eventually fabulation.[1] But that scheme alone did not always indicate the special nature of the short fiction, especially as it compares and contrasts to the long. Further, the stories too easily became mere examples to prove the scheme. A summer recently spent visiting the museums of the hilltop towns of Orvieto, Perugia, Arezzo, Assisi, Siena—country Lawrence loved—provided a possible solution, not in the form of a new scheme but of an image that helps convey the particular quality of Lawrence's work in the short story. A common motif in medieval and Renaissance painting, especially in Italy and the Netherlands, is the dance of life and death. In dignified procession or raucous parade, figures garbed in satins and homespun dance their way toward life, death, heaven, hell, spring, winter. The principle of composition is often a series of small circles—characters turn in toward each other—moving along in an inevitable, linear progression. Even under the brush of painters as different as Mantegna or Brueghel, the motif tends to capture our sense of life as both a series of intense moments and a general movement forward through time.

Looking at Lawrence's fiction in general, critics have often employed metaphors related to dance: Mark Schorer likens the structure of *Women in Love* to a Morris dance; Regina Fadiman writes of Lawrence's choreography in "The Blind Man."[2] The language allows one to talk about structure without tying oneself to static, architectural imagery: choreographers and architects invite different kinds of examination. Useful as the metaphor has proved to be for specific analyses, it may be equally useful for grasping the character of Lawrence's entire corpus of short fiction, especially if one lets the metaphor suggest a progressive dance of life and death.

By virtue of their quantity, frequency, capacity to tease, undercut, complement, and reverse each other, the individual short stories continually create local circles. Far more clearly than his successive novels which were written over years, Lawrence's tales, written over weeks or months, speak to each other with respect to theme and technique. A story written in realistic mode will be answered by one in visionary or fabulistic style. Characters from one story force characters from another to pause, listen. They challenge each other, ask for reconsiderations, raise alternative possibilities about the issues at hand. The hero in a story written in August looks very much like a villain in a story written in October; the martyr in an early tale sails back in a subsequent work with her head high, sword drawn. An intense spirit of exploration and adventure rules these conversations. There is an openness to conflict and contradiction, a willingness to let everyone, from collier to fairy princess, have his or her moment.[3]

At the same time, the localized tensions and parallels are part of a steady progress. There is a shape to the whole event. The going forth is different from the fare-thee-well, and the change comes very much from the experiences that have transpired along the way.

In brief, in seeking an appropriate scheme, I have chosen to trace a linear, chronological progress of developing themes and techniques, which simultaneously emphasizes the frequent and highly exploratory conversational circles that form as story addresses story.

Setting the Scene

Lawrence published his first short story in 1907. He was twenty-two. Had he been a young French, Russian, or Italian author, he

3

would have been entering a field already well populated with modern masters of the art. In the second half of the nineteenth century, the *conte* in France was being transformed into a vehicle of compressed, intense observation by Flaubert and Maupassant. In Russia, Gogol had opened wide his great overcoat. Out of its ample folds had come Turgenev, Tolstoy, Dostoevsky, Chekov. In Italy, Giovanni Verga was publishing *Cavalleria Rusticana,* a starkly beautiful series of tales of peasant life in Sicily. This continental flowering, still flourishing at the end of the century, produced various blooms, but in general it was marked by a concern with the lives of ordinary men and women. Drawing on conventions broadly called "realistic," these stories progressed by way of sharp observations of the mundane.[4] They avoided the drum-rolling climax and replaced the lively voice of the storyteller, carried over from oral tradition, with a transparent, omniscient narrator and a series of significant images. As more than one surprised reader noted, these odd stories began and ended, but one could not always say exactly what had happened, at least not in conventional terms.[5]

By comparison, the modern short story in England blossomed late. Up to the last decade of the century, English readers were still spending a quiet hour with fables, legends, anecdotes, and tall tales. In these works, the story-teller is usually an important presence. The plot, the key structural element, is often intricate or exotic; the climax is notable, the point of the story clear. Robert Louis Stevenson and Rudyard Kipling offer fine examples. The writers who would take the discoveries of Turgenev, Chekov, or Verga and make them their own—Joyce, Mansfield, Woolf, Lawrence—were still schoolchildren. Their season would come in the first quarter of the twentieth century. Of them, Lawrence is clearly the leader in range, sheer quantity of masterpieces, and, something harder to define, in stretching the conventions of the genre to include a variety of new possibilities.

Early Realism

In his own brief, brilliant season, Lawrence speedily recapitulated the development of the nineteenth-century short story and then altered several of its premises to serve his own talent. His first tales, written while he was studying at Nottingham University in

1907 and 1908, are relatively traditional fare, consisting of legends and anecdotes. They tend to be heavily plotted and strive for atmosphere. Interest in character is minimal; the power of the modern short story to imply the depth and complexity of ordinary experience through precise details and radiating images is barely suggested. Each of these early tales, "Legend," "The Vicar's Garden," "The White Stocking," and "A Prelude," contains within it, however, the promise of a later, far more interesting story, thoroughly reconceived and reworked.

In December, 1908, now teaching in Croydon, Lawrence picked up the first issue of the *English Review*. In its iconoclastic editorials and exciting contents (publishing Hardy, James, Conrad, Galsworthy, William Hudson, Tolstoy, and H. G. Wells), he discovered what he and others termed "the exciting new school of realism."[6] He adopted its curriculum at once—at least in his short fiction. In his long fiction, he struggled for three more years to rid himself of a variety of romantic, nineteenth-century notions about the novel. "Odour of Chrysanthemums" and an early version of "A Modern Lover" are the first of a cluster of tales to focus on the familiar rather than the fantastic and to develop a style appropriate to that change. The early realistic stories, written between 1909 and 1912, are important for several reasons. They taught Lawrence the tools of his trade, the craft of writing a short story. Later, when he began to write his visionary tales, the early work he had done in realism provided him with that "toe in Liverpool" which Woolf saw as essential to all fiction. The grounding toe makes itself felt in the best of his visionary tales by way of sharp observation of character and place and the willingness to allow human contingency to enter even his most stringently designed visions. The early realistic tales are also important because they lead, quite clearly, to *Sons and Lovers*. They point the way to his first great novel as neither *The White Peacock* nor *The Saga of Siegmund* (published as *The Trespasser*) could.

But Lawrence's early realistic stories are also significant for reasons beyond his own development. As Ford Madox Ford noted, they showed English readers a world they knew next to nothing about. The tombs of the pharoahs were more familiar to them than the streets, markets, and cottages of the workers in their own land.[7] Ford's editorial in the first *English Review* is literally a cry to the writers of England to hold up a mirror to contemporary England, to show her what she was and where she stood in the first decade of the twentieth century. Lawrence responded to that cry, heart and mind. In particular, he held up a mirror to the daily routines, the loves, hatreds, injustices, and miracles of the miners and farmers of the English midlands. And most important, he wrote of those communities from within. Raymond Williams, pointing out the genuine innovation in British fiction that Lawrence's early realism represents, emphasizes the change in language inherent in Lawrence's stance as an insider. Williams is speaking of *Sons and Lovers*, but he notes that in fact one sees the identification between narrator and community even more clearly and consistently in contemporaneous short stories such as "Odour of Chrysanthemums."[8] It is a breakthrough that eventually leads to any number of contemporary works which locate themselves within the community of a people whose voices have previously been framed by an outside narrator. Thinking of Lawrence's immediate predecessors on the continent, one realizes that Lawrence chose not to employ the distant, often ironic voice of Flaubert and Maupassant; rather he adapted the voices of Chekov, Verga, and Tolstoy to English material, voices that similarly draw no apparent distinction between the perspectives of narrator, character, and community. When Katherine Mansfield played variations on Chekov's stories, she changed them in important ways. The early Lawrence, more simply, shared Chekov's basic stance.

Lawrence would lose that firm identity with the community he was writing about; indeed he would lose all certainty that a knowable, nurturing community is possible. In compensation he would gain and give radical insight into the terrors of alienation and the uncertainties of identity that lie at the heart of much modern art. But the points to be made here are, first, that Lawrence's early realistic fiction was fundamental to his own development; second that in England it represented a genuine break with the past; and third that the qualities which made it revolutionary can be seen with particular clarity in the short stories.

The Visionary Stories

In 1912, Lawrence left England in a blaze of expectation. He had found his mate, Frieda von Richthofen Weekley, and his métier, writing. Having published several very good short stories and poems and two novels of mixed quality, he was on his way to a

final rewriting of *Sons and Lovers.* The stories he wrote upon land-
ing on the continent look back in some ways toward England and
realism. But in June of 1913, he wrote "The Prussian Officer," his
first fully realized visionary work. It is a landmark in his own development and in the art of short fiction. Lawrence was eager—as
were Kafka, Joyce, Woolf, and others—to stretch the realistic
short story in ways that would allow an author to light up areas of
the human psyche which realism had left dark. (In the previous
century, Melville, Hawthorne, and Poe had lit up those areas but
by means quite uncongenial to these moderns.) Kafka wrote
dreamscapes with highly realistic surfaces. Woolf employed a
stream of consciousness technique. Joyce extended Flaubert's art
of implication as he combined a style of scrupulous meanness with
a structure of complex, hidden allusions. But Lawrence did something different.

In his visionary tales, Lawrence discovered what turned out
to be a highly flexible way to retain what he needed from the realistic short story while he reshaped it to his own continually changing sense of human experience. Basically, he fused the conventions and philosophies of the realistic short story with those of the
religious exemplum. It was a fruitful marriage. I will say more
about that union below, but as Frank Amon and Mark Spilka
noted years ago, the key to the structure of Lawrence's visionary
tales is ritual form: these tales are built around rites of baptism,
communion, sacrifice, resurrection. The key to his tone, however,
is the literalness of his belief that human experience is sacred. The
apocalyptic pulses in the quotidian, not elevating the quotidian to
a plane outside time and place but investing it where it lies, in
kitchens, bedrooms, and gardens, with immense significance. Setting, plot, image, character, and point of view endeavor to present the world as it is, but from the perspective of a passionately
religious man. The impulse is mimetic; but the world to be imi-
tated is infused with theos, mana, godhead.

The flexibility of the adaptation of realistic short story to visionary perspective becomes apparent when one realizes that, between 1913 and 1925, Lawrence's visionary tales saw him through
great changes in his thinking. His first visionary tales, "The Prussian Officer" and "Vin Ordinaire" (the original version of "The
Thorn in the Flesh"), are among those that capture the terror and
eventual death of the individual who leaves his community for an
intense relationship, overtly or covertly sexual. With the onset of

the war, Lawrence sees the potential of intense, personal engagements differently, now viewing them as resurrecting, bringing new life to people and societies gone dead. The sensual, heart-felt love between a woman and a man or between two men stands during these years as a vivid alternative to the mechanical, mass movements of modern warfare, patriotism, and technology. In these visionary tales of individual resurrection, community exists but no longer in the form of neighbors and co-workers. Rather, community exists primarily in the distant, abstract form of Western culture. Lovers and friends such as those one finds in "The Thimble," "The Horse Dealer's Daughter," or "The Blind Man" are, by implication, redeeming Western culture as they redeem themselves.

With the Armistice and the decadence and fascism which followed, Lawrence joined others in thinking that democracy was a flawed concept, that what Western culture truly needed was a properly recognized aristocracy. There follows a highly chauvinistic period in Lawrence's thinking as his aristocracy becomes more and more exclusively masculine. Women, often the sharpest eyes and most courageous seekers in his fiction, are asked repeatedly to go to sleep, submitting their wills and desires to a male leader. Out of this period and frame of mind come "The Fox," "You Touched Me," and "The Border Line," for example. By 1924, "The Overtone" and "St. Mawr" mark an end to that masculine vision; Lawrence's last visionary tales are written from a perspective that once again honors all its voices, male and female alike.

In looking at the visionary stories Lawrence wrote during his middle years, one notes, in brief, an extensive range of themes, attitudes, settings, and characters. One also notes the steadiness of output and general high quality. There are some failures, but in the difficult decade between *Women in Love* and *Lady Chatterley's Lover*, it is the short stories that bear witness time and again to Lawrence's talents as a writer of fiction. If one wants to confront a well-realized, carefully balanced fiction on masculine power, one must go to "The Captain's Doll" rather than to *Aaron's Rod*. If one wants to trace Lawrence's growing awareness of the solipsism implicit in his vision of male dominance, one goes first to the curious, brief story, "The Overtone," and then to "St. Mawr" and "The Man Who Loved Islands." Far more than *Kangaroo* or *The Plumed Serpent*, these point toward Lawrence's last great novel, *Lady Chatterley's Lover*.

Fabulation

Turning to Lawrence's late short stories—those written between 1925 and his death in 1930—one observes many interests and directions, but the dominant and most interesting is his movement toward fable and satire. Said another way, the balance he maintained in his visionary short stories between realism and exemplum now shifts toward the latter. The shift inspired him to write some of his best-known and most provocative stories—"The Rocking-Horse Winner," "The Man Who Loved Islands," "The Man Who Died" (always called "The Escaped Cock" by Lawrence)—and anticipates contemporary writers' interest in fabulation. Further, the shift toward fabulation reveals aspects of the relationship between his long and short fiction from 1916 on. A word of background may be helpful.

As many critics have noted, *Lady Chatterley's Lover* represents a return and reconciliation in Lawrence's thinking. But the novel also represents a sharp contrast to the kind of short stories Lawrence wrote during his late years. Both points are important. Years earlier, defending *The Rainbow*, Lawrence had condemned novels that fit all the characters into one moral scheme. Elsewhere he called the tendency to rigid, ethical design "putting one's thumb into the balance." The novel so skewed is a dead thing.[9] One should observe that these comments assume that the novel is inherently mimetic; if life is full of contingency and flux, then the novel must be also. Now, Williams and others have argued that the three novels, *Aaron's Rod*, *Kangaroo*, and *The Plumed Serpent*—which Lawrence wrote between *Women in Love* and *Lady Chatterley's Lover*—suffer precisely from Lawrence's having fit everything into an abstract, rigid, moral scheme, that of sacred patriarchy.[10] By contrast, for all the clarity of its ethical design, *Lady Chatterley's Lover* represents a rejection of abstraction, a return to flux, contingency, and openness, to what Alan Friedman nicely calls a "stream of conscience."[11] Looking strictly at *Lady Chatterley's Lover* and the three novels that precede it, one might initially agree with Williams's point. But looking also at the excellent work Lawrence did in short fiction in his late years, one sees a different picture.

Aaron's Rod, *Kangaroo*, and *The Plumed Serpent* suffer from two unreconciled impulses in Lawrence, one to abstract his material, the other to remain true to his idea of the novel as open form, open forum. Far from being tight or rigid, those novels wander, contradict themselves, contain unincorporated material. They read neither as realistic novels nor as fables. With important qualifications, *Lady Chatterley's Lover* does very much represent the return to realism Williams describes.[12] But one must ask what happened to the opposing impulse toward abstraction; in Lawrence's case, the desire of a fierce and dying man to prophesy, sum up, *assess* the world he is leaving rather than *present* or imitate it.[13] In fact, the impulse did not lapse. Far from it. The movement toward closed form finds expression in Lawrence's late topical essays, epigrams, barbed poems, and, far more interestingly, in his fabulistic short stories.

In his late satires and fables, the world as we know it is wonderfully distorted, simplified, and abstracted as Lawrence creates ethically controlled fantasies. Character is stylized, landscape becomes mindscape, plot is clearly an argument, and the narrator often takes on the role of opaque story-teller. It is an exciting new field of expression for Lawrence's talents. Unlike his enthusiastic conversion in 1908 to the realistic short story and unlike the dramatic break into visionary short fiction which he made in "The Prussian Officer" in 1913, Lawrence's movement to fabulation consists of stages and experiments. Looking both at what the stories are about and how Lawrence chooses to tell them, one notices again a fine flexibility in the mode as Lawrence employed it. In theme, the fabulistic tales range from proclamations on the need for absolute patriarchy to satires on the patriarch. Moreover, they encompass tales that demand the reader's willingness to accept ghosts and ESP to tales that carefully analyze the difference between mystery and mystification.

The rewards of fabulistic fiction are many, and one senses that Lawrence and his readers were especially ready to appreciate them after the strong emphasis during the previous two decades on realistic fare. Among the rewards is an escape from what Frank O'Connor sees as an inevitable limit to all short fiction. Because of its scope, he argues, short fiction cannot deal directly with large, normative, social issues. It must focus on lonely souls wandering at the fringes of society, presenting general issues only by implication.[14] O'Connor's strictures assume a realistic short story which works primarily through the techniques of representation. But O'Connor fails to account for fabulation, which, eschewing representation, can directly present every kind of social issue, from materialism to idealism, to conformism, the women's movement, and traditional Christianity. The energy, wit, and formal beauty of Lawrence's late fables and satires suggest his delight in his dying years in moving beyond all the regulations of realism. In a sense, he returns in a late work, such as "The Man Who Died," to the land of legendary events he had visited in "Legend" in 1907. The utter contrast in the two works bears witness to the nature of the interval that separates them—twenty-three years of work, thought, love, life.

The above overview has many generalizations, and obviously the questions asked in the preface have received only the promise of answers. What did Lawrence accomplish in his short fiction? What are the shape and character of his *oeuvre*? How did the genre change beneath his hand and how did it help him formulate his vision of life?

Yeats said that out of the quarrel with others we make rhetoric; out of the quarrel with ourselves, poetry. Yeats means to elevate the nature of poetry, but, in each of its elements, the statement provides an apt introduction to Lawrence, one of the most quarrelsome and creative writers of any time. As relentless toward himself as toward others, Lawrence continually challenged his ideas, perceptions, feelings, and those of the world around him. The quarrel, and the rhetoric and poetry he made out of it, are apparent in all of his work but they are especially clear in his short stories.

A Halting Commencement

1

When D. H. Lawrence wrote about his debut as a publishing author, he recalled Ford Madox Ford, then editor of the *English Review,* accepting some early poems in 1909. So easy a launching, Lawrence reminisced, was almost magical.[1] In fact, Lawrence had had an earlier, humbler debut. In the fall of 1907, a local newspaper, the *Nottinghamshire Guardian,* had sponsored a short story contest. The categories were "An Amusing Adventure," "A Legend," and "An Enjoyable Christmas." Contestants could submit a tale for any one category. Winners would receive three pounds and have their tale published. Encouraged by friends to enter, Lawrence bent the rules and sent in a tale for each category. Under his own name, he submitted the legend entry. His entry for an amusing adventure, "The White Stocking," was sent in by Louisa Burrows, a young woman to whom he eventually became engaged; and his "A Prelude to a Happy Christmas" was submitted under the name of Rosalind by Jessie Chambers, his long-time adolescent sweetheart. "A Prelude" won and was published on December 7, 1907. Jessie signed the check and gave the money to the young author.[2]

If the *Nottinghamshire Guardian's* motive was to encourage local talent, it amply succeeded. In that Christmas issue, it introduced its readers to an author who would go on to write over sixty short stories, many of them classics of the genre, not to mention a rich collection of novels, poems, and essays. But that was years later. The Lawrence who wrote "Legend" (later revised and retitled "A Fragment of Stained Glass"), "The White Stocking" (revised several times), "A Prelude," and, early in 1908, "The Vicar's Garden" (revised and retitled "The Shadow in the Rose Garden"), was living at home in Eastwood, planning a career as a teacher, and approaching and avoiding marriage to Jessie Chambers. Like many other sensitive young souls, he was struggling away at a novel. *The White Peacock* was begun in 1906 and published in 1911.

Taken together, Lawrence's first four short stories appear a mixed and timid lot. Had Lawrence not gone on to become a major twentieth-century author, one might allow this quartet to lie undisturbed in the vast fields of literary obscurity. But Lawrence did go on; and readers curious about his beginnings as a short story writer do well to examine these youthful productions on the chance that they contain hints of things to come.

Both elements of this chapter's title deserve emphasis: Lawrence's first tales constitute a commencement, but it is halting. Let me begin with the halting.

The categories set up by the *Nottinghamshire Guardian* reveal an important fact about British short fiction. That is, in general, it remained relatively traditional up to the turn of the century. Indeed, in the view of some people, it remained hidebound by nineteenth-century constraints through the first decade of the twentieth century.[3] "Relatively" here refers to the contrasting situation in America and on the continent; "traditional" refers to a cluster of assumptions influencing the practice of English short fiction from the latter half of the eighteenth century on. Those assumptions and practices can be summarized briefly. A work of short fiction could be a rambling, diffuse sketch, perhaps of a travel adventure in the mountains of Italy. The principle of the narration, to use Shklovski's term, is accumulative. Incident is added to incident. There is no closure. A short story could also be a frenetically paced, compressed novel. Here, an attempt at closed design—a loop perhaps or a figure eight—might be made, but the overall effect is one of shallowess, of rich material being wasted. A third kind of short story, quite common and definitely closed in design, is represented by the cleverly plotted legend, tall tale, exemplum, ghost story, or satire. As Wendell V. Harris points out in his excellent survey of English short fiction in the nineteenth century, examples of each of these types are easily found in the pages of *Blackwood's, Household Words, Cornhill, The Ladies' Magazine,* and a host of other nineteenth-century periodicals.[4] An important element in the third mode is an emphasis on the extraordinary. Setting and atmosphere tend to be exotic. Plot centers around the remarkable, fantastic, or supernatural incident. Crises are well marked; endings are often comprised of a sudden twist, a surprise of the kind O. Henry made famous. If endings were power-packed, however, openings were often slow and awkward. Many a dusty manuscript or hoary crone is dragged forth to serve as informant to the first-person narrator. Underlying most of the traditional practices is the assumption that short fiction is not a genuine or serious art. Because the aim of a short story is mainly to entertain, it need not and should not have thematic significance; a writer with commitments will voice his or her ideas in a novel or poem. Stories are holidays, for the English reader and writer alike.

As Harris indicates, however, some writers in England during the 1880s and 1890s had challenged this view of short fiction. In avant garde, fin de siècle magazines such as the *Yellow Book* and *Savoy,* one would have encountered the winds of change. But Lawrence, not surprisingly, shows little awareness of those challenges. It is not simply that he was a child, distant from London, when those magazines briefly flourished. His unawareness seems also a function of the general reception those avant garde writers received. Often political radicals, often women, generally hardbitten realists able to out-Zola Zola, their genuinely innovative work seems only indirectly to have altered the climate. Ford Madox Ford, launching the *English Review* in December 1908, for example, sends out a call for realistic short fiction. He makes no mention of the work of the *Yellow Book* or *Savoy,* yet his call itself may come partly from the shift in expectations that the stories in those magazines inspired. In any case, in 1907 and early 1908, Lawrence steps onto the field of English short fiction with very traditional notions about short stories. "The White Stocking" is an anecdote; the nature of "Legend" is self-explanatory; "A Prelude" is a sentimental love story; and "The Vicar's Garden" is a vaguely eerie antiromance.

The germ of "The White Stocking" was apparently an incident that occurred to Lawrence's mother in her salad days. Jessie Chambers saw the heroine as an idealized portrait of Mrs. Lawrence.[5] This is surely a misreading, for Prissy Gant is vain, shallow, posturing. In the first version, the tale opens with her peering into a small looking glass, delighted with her face and hair, irritated that she cannot see the rest of herself.[6] She is getting ready to go to a Christmas party. Prissy's preparations are a prelude to the tale's main action, which takes place at a dance given by her employer, Sam Osborne. There, Prissy shows off the lovely silk outfit she has bought with money Mr. Osborne gave her, basks in his attention and the attention of his nephew, and proudly dances with her boss. On the sidelines, her decent beau, George Whiston, stands glowering. The climax occurs when she and Mr. Osborne take the lead position in a line dance. Conscious that all eyes are on her, she regally draws her handkerchief from her pocket to dab her lips. To her dismay, she finds that she has brought out a long white stocking instead. Mr. Osborne collapses in mirth while throughout the room waves of laughter surge around her. She flings the stocking at her boss and runs from the house. Whiston snatches the stocking, runs after her, comforts her, and takes her home.

Humor is clearly the intended effect. In the early party scenes, Lawrence unsuccessfully attempts to create gay, diverting prattle. Midway through the evening, Whiston spills coffee on Osborne to everyone's amusement but Osborne's. And Prissy's mishap is followed by "'He He's'" and "'Ha Ha's'" cascading down the page. But the comedy is forced. The dialogues are stilted, and the physical humor is silly. The plot is a series of accidents taking place almost independent of character. Nothing is made of Prissy's vanity or pleasure in masculine attention. The setting—an industrial town in the 1880s—works only to create a nostalgic atmosphere. All this Lawrence will change, change utterly, when he returns to the story several years later. What is now the key event, the stocking blunder, will become part of the background to an intense dramatization of the marriage of Prissy and George, rechristened Elsie and Ted.

"The Vicar's Garden" is an equally stock item in the storehouse of traditional short fiction.[7] The tale combines two main movements, the second undercutting the first. Most of the story follows the progress of a pair of would-be lovers as they walk toward a holiday spot near the sea, pause for a rhapsodic visit to the garden of the local vicar, then move on to the boarding house where they will chastely spend the night. The story ends with a conversation between them and the landlady at the boarding house. She tells them that the vicar's garden hides a gloomy tale. The vicar had two sons. One died of thirst in Australia; the other went mad and now paces the halls of the vicarage. He may have even been watching the lovers as they strolled in the garden, observes the girl with a pleasurable shiver. Lawrence closes with a presumably wry comment: "The honeymoon will not, I fear, be spent by that bonny northern bay."[8] Although different in mood, "The Vicar's Garden" resembles "The White Stocking" in its reliance on incident and a surprise ending. Again, character development is minimal. Who these young lovers may be and what future awaits them are questions Lawrence will tackle only in revising the story years later. Transforming "The Vicar's Garden" into "The Shadow in the Rose Garden," Lawrence pursued the same lines he laid down in revising "The White Stocking." He joins his young lovers in tension-filled matrimony, sets them at the center of the work, and shows them fighting their way through to new understanding.

Two more couples move uncertainly across the field of Lawrence's imagination in "Legend" and "A Prelude." Packed with incident, "Legend" opens with a group of astonished medieval monks staring up at "the evil one" who has just broken a stained glass window in their monastery and is laughing down at them.[9] As their annals record the event, St. Bardolf saved them and thenceforth his broken statue has "'vertue for to heal and bless.'" The second, opposing, and much longer movement reveals the very human identity of "the evil one." It is Scarlatte, serf, participant in the peasants' revolt. His comrades have been caught and hanged. Along with Mattie, the daughter of the local miller, he is on the run, homeless, hungry, and cold. Pausing in the forest, Scarlatte climbs the statue set against the wall of the monastery in hopes of breaking off a piece of glowing red "faery" glass. The statue breaks, he falls and cuts himself, and he and Mattie continue on to a cave hoping soon to join a band of robbers. The medieval setting, the ancient annals, the natural explanation of an apparently supernatural incident, the contrast between the meek Christian monks and the pagan lovers, and the mannered, "archaic" language are all elements to be found in similar tales throughout the previous century. Incident vies with atmosphere as the tale's carrying force; theme, character, and significant patterns of imagery exist only as hidden treasures which Lawrence will later uncover.

"A Prelude" is the one tale of the four that relies on a change of character rather than on accident or incident to shape plot.[10] Sentimental the story undoubtedly is, yet the initial distance between Fred and Nell, their hesitant rapprochement, and their eventual declaration of mutual love rest entirely on Nell's gradual awareness of Fred's worth. In this story alone, the familiar—love's old sweet song—is the focus. Although a change of pace from Lawrence's other tales, "A Prelude" does not constitute a departure from typical short fiction of the time. With the exception of one outstanding scene, one finds approximately the same tale told over and over, if not in *Blackwood's* or *Cornhill,* then in the volumes of Christmas annuals that lay on Victorian coffee tables from 1820 on.

So where is the promised commencement? It leaps out from a variety of places, here in setting, there in characterization, elsewhere in the tale's imagery or story line. In "The White Stocking," Lawrence's demon—his genuine, vibrant voice, his particular perspective—slips out in the tale's opening scene as Prissy prepares herself for the party. In that scene, Lawrence captures, quickly and surely, this young working girl's sensuality, first from her own sense of herself, then from a male's perspective. Alone in her room, Prissy caresses her face, plays with her hair, and lovingly runs her hands over her breasts, waist, and hips as she puts on her silk party dress. One thinks ahead to the scene in *Lady Chatterley's Lover* when Connie gazes at herself naked in the mirror, keenly aware of herself as a sensory being with sensual longings. In "The White Stocking," Lawrence switches narrative point of view from Prissy's perspective to that of a man outside her window. The first males to watch her are some rowdy young boys, but they are chased off by a working man who stands gazing up appreciatively at the young woman. With respect to the story, the man's attention foreshadows the masculine attention she will later enjoy at Sam's party. With respect to Lawrence's imagination, the two perspectives combine in an otherwise conventional story, to suggest the bisensuality of Lawrence's demon. Comparison with

18

Keats is not farfetched. The scene in "The Eve of St. Agnes," when Madeline removes her scented bodice and warmed jewels while Porphyro stands watching, loving, and feeling with her, captures the same kind of androgynous, physical sympathy Lawrence felt and would eventually beautifully express. Here, in "The White Stocking," the expression is brief, but it is there.

An altogether different entry into the landscape of Lawrence's sensual imagination is provided by the contrasting images and patterns of response in the opening sections of "The Vicar's Garden." Anticipating his ending, Lawrence builds a mood of threat throughout the tale. But the specifically sensual, indeed sexual, quality of the threat peers out occasionally from behind the explicit story line. One notices that the girl urges the boy to enter the garden; he would rather not. Once she has persuaded him, she demands a level of response he is reluctant to give. At one point he says complainingly, "I must stroke with my finger the velvet smoothness of the darkest crimson blossoms."[11] The garden and its surging roses are, for moments, terrifying. For moments, his ecstatic companion is equally terrifying. The young man repeatedly looks out beyond the garden to the sea, which he sees as blessedly aloof and distant. The contrast—not sustained, only hinted at—is between a calm, unengaged stance and a passionate, intense stance toward love and experience. As in many of Lawrence's fictions, the passionate stance promises great joy but also threatens madness; insanity haunts this rose garden. It is not until quite late in his writing, in "The Man Who Loved Islands" for example, that Lawrence pursues the opposite tack, the possibility that withdrawal, hermitage, and distance carry their own seeds of insanity.

In "The Vicar's Garden," it is the male who is threatened by the almost surreal life in the garden. The female, at home in this bower, tempts him to enter, holds out the ancient apple. But one greatly simplifies Lawrence if one sees that opposition of male/female identity and role as Lawrence's only position. It is one of many positions he takes, often depending on how his own tempestuous life is faring.[12] In his early fiction, females can be equally threatened by a beseeching male. This second pattern gives rise to precisely the opposite simplification, that Lawrence ceaselessly retells the tale of Sleeping Beauty.[13] "Legend" and "A Prelude" are the first of many stories that challenge both simplifications.

In "Legend," Scarlatte knocks on the door of Mattie's heart.

Willingly she opens, enthusiastically she agrees to join him in his flight. In the forest, it is she who sees the stained glass window and urges him to climb up and snatch a piece of that glowing light. When he falls, clutching what is now simply dark, rough glass, she loudly rues her decision to come on this journey. Scarlatte, in turn, grumbles and swears as they trudge off together. One suspects Lawrence had decided not only to rob the monks' explanation of its supernatural cast but also to rob the love story of romantic tone. A mild form of Punch and Judy drama ensues, as irritability reigns. But the point to be made here is the balance struck. Mattie is as active, critical, and disgruntled as Scarlatte. She is no Sleeping Beauty, he is no dashing prince. Nor is she Eve playing to an innocent Adam. Our closing view of them—together in a cave, warmed by fire, wrapped in animal skins, far from the monks and masters of civilization, clearly about to make love—is almost quintessential Lawrence. What is missing is some link between the antiromantic characterizations and the sexual resolution. What is present is, again, the sense of two rebels, male and female, poised and equal on the edge of the unknown.

In the flight of the two lovers, "Legend" gives us what will become a classic Lawrentian situation. In providing each with the spirit of combativeness and rebellion, as well as the potential for sensuality, Lawrence's young demon hints at the complex figures his characters will trace in the many sexual dances to come. In "A Prelude" Lawrence's demon sets Nell and Fred a slightly different figure to dance, but one equally promising with respect to complexity and balance. Initially the tale traces out a fairly conventional pattern: rustic woos scornful lady, lady spurns rustic. That pattern is countermanded however in the brief scene that comprises the tale's crisis. Fred and his brothers have departed Nell's house in anger, leaving behind the branch of holly they had brought over as a Christmas gift. Nell discovers the holly, regrets her rudeness to Fred, realizes her love for him. What shall I do, she wails. Go to him, her friend replies. What if he is out? Wait for him. There follows a fine scene, the like of which nineteenth-century writers had almost dropped from fiction's repertoire. Nell and Blanche struggle through the dark, mud, and cold to Fred's family's house. Together they stand outside the window singing Christmas carols, serenading. They do what Jane Eyre and her modest sisters could never do: they woo a potent male, risk rebuff, and win their suit. Furthermore, unlike Jane's forward rivals, they retain the approbation of the fiction. Nell Wycherley is, in brief, first in a train of bold Lawrentian ladies, figures such as Louisa Durant, Ursula Brangwen, and Lady Chatterley. Wide-awake, resourceful, and energetic, these so-called Sleeping Beauties are as quick as their male counterparts to discern the obstacles which would deflect the course of true love; they are as active if not more so in working to remove those obstacles.[14]

There is no need to go beyond Lawrence's own powers of perception and tendency to identify with women to find cause for early portraits like Nell's. But his youthful relationship with the feminist movement in Eastwood is too often ignored.[15] Time and again in Lawrence's early letters and fiction, one is reminded that the British women's suffrage movement was in full force between 1900 and 1914, during Lawrence's adolescence and young manhood. The movement contributed much to the political and intellectual atmosphere of the community that he, Jessie Chambers, Louisa Burrows, and their close friends grew up in. Through Alice Dax, for example, he would have had indirect acquaintance with radicals such as the Pankhursts and Alice Kenny.[16] In letters to Louie Burrows, written from Croydon in 1909, Lawrence speaks sympathetically of a group of suffragists he has just seen being hounded and harrassed; he urges her to read Olive Schreiner's *Women and Labor* and George Gissing's *The Odd Women*, both important feminist books.[17] Further, among the many issues Lawrence raises in *The White Peacock* and *Sons and Lovers* is the need for women to become self-responsible.[18]

Lawrence was not a young feminist. His feelings toward women, as well as toward politics and causes in general, escape label. The feminist movement in England, however, was a force in Lawrence's Eastwood youth and influenced much of the fiction he wrote up until the First World War. He himself pledged in 1912, "I shall do my work for women, better than the Suffrage" (*Collected Lettters of D. H. Lawrence*, 171).* When one weighs the value of the vote against the value of genuinely complex images of female experience in literature, Lawrence's boast is at least worth noticing.[19]

"A Prelude" raises a last point about the intimations of things to come in Lawrence's earliest short fictions. In "Legend," Lawrence hints at the ordinary, human qualities of Scarlatte and

---

* Further references to this title will be indicated by the abbreviation CL.

Mattie: for a moment he is asserting realistic qualities in the subject matter of this generally fantastic tale. In "A Prelude," Lawrence not only focuses on relatively realistic subject matter—that is, the tale is set close to home in time and place; the characters are ordinary; the plot line steers clear of the supernatural or legendary—but he also tells much of the tale using the techniques of realism. This is especially true in the opening scene, set in the kitchen of the farmer's home. An omniscient narrator draws the reader into the story with no awkward opening paraphernalia. Tone, atmosphere, background, and characterization are established through ordinary dialogue and the accretion of simple, clear detail. The narrator is more a sensitive photographer and recorder of sounds than an actively performing story-teller. The reader must discover, on his or her own, the significance of these details, this conversation. And significance is there. The warmth, color, and love captured in this kitchen scene will later contrast with the dark, cold, scornful atmosphere of Nell's kitchen, arguing implicitly for the wisdom of her leaving her house for Fred's. These techniques become central to work Lawrence will soon be doing.[20]

To summarize, although these four early tales constitute a genuine commencement, they are traditional in conception and style. To borrow a phrase from Walter Allen, they are "manifestations of the romance."[21] "A Prelude" aside, all take place in some vaguely distant spot; plot dominates character, and atmosphere takes the place of concrete, realizable setting. Further, whole sections of each are awkward, stilted, or pointless. One senses that Lawrence was learning from masters of the traditional tale such as Stevenson and Kipling, but even within their mode of story-telling, he was far from accomplished. Eventually Lawrence returned to three of these tales. Two of them emerge as powerful creations. In rewriting "The White Stocking" and "The Vicar's Garden" ("The Shadow in the Rose Garden"), he got rid of superfluous material, found the buried subject, and through the techniques of realism, dramatized that subject with economy and verve. By contrast, in rewriting "Legend" as "A Fragment of Stained Glass," he kept adding material, ending up with an unwieldy, though intriguing, construct. Lawrence never returned to "A Prelude" explicitly, perhaps because he returned to it in various forms all of his life.

Awarded his teaching certificate from Nottingham University in June 1908, Lawrence began applying for jobs. The months went by and nothing showed up until, in October, he received an offer from the Davidson Road School, Croydon, South London. He accepted and bade farewell to Eastwood, friends, and family. Except in imagination and memory, he would return only for visits.

The New Young School of Realism 2

In his first few months in Croydon, Lawrence discovered home-sickness, the strain of teaching in a public school system, a circle of interesting colleagues and friends, and, most important for our purposes, an exciting new periodical, the *English Review*.[1] As he wrote to Louisa Burrows in October 1909: "You ask me first of all what kind of 'paper' is the *English Review*: It is a half-crown maga-zine, which has only been out some twelve months. It is very fine, and very 'new.' There you will meet the new spirit at its best. . . . It is the best possible way to get into touch with the new young school of realism, to take the *English Review*."[2] Any time an artist makes a sharp break with his previous work, critics seek causes. In the present instance, the break is between "The Vicar's Garden" and "Odour of Chrysanthemums," a clear shift of technique and vision by any standard of measurement. The causes were undoubt-edly many, but clearly a major one was the call for realistic short fiction sounded by the *Review*.

Under the editorship of Ford Madox Ford, the first issue of the *English Review* appeared in December 1908. One of its aims, Ford announced, was to encourage the writing of English short fiction as sophisticated as on the Continent; to foster that, it encouraged submissions in the mode of what was popularly called "the new realism." Give us, Ford demanded, a picture of life as it is. Enough of rehashed romances and tiresome, hackneyed, historical literature:

> The common superstition of the English writer that to take any old story—the history of the fall of Troy, that of the Prodigal Son, or an episode from Richard of Gloucester's chronicles—and to use it as if it were a framework round which to mold a sculptor's fabric of poeticized atmospheres and studies of character, this singular *heresia Anglicana* is probably as much as anything responsible for the extremely small hold which imaginative literature has upon the English people.[3]

The goal of the *Review* would be "to discover where Great Britain stands, if the discovery can be made."[4] Where, for example, do the workers stand? Where stand the poor? "Of knowledge of the lives and aspirations of the poor man how little we have. We are barred off from him by the invisible barriers: we have no records of his views of literature. It is astonishing how little literature has to show of the life of the poor."[5] In essence Ford was asking for two things: more examples of the high craft of short fiction and more insights into the lives of contemporary British folk, insights such as Chekov, Maupassant, Flaubert, Verga, and Crane had been providing in Russia, France, Italy, and America. Lawrence, home for his first Christmas holiday, rushed up to the Chambers's household to share that first issue with Jessie. He saw Ford's challenge as an invitation.

"Odour of Chrysanthemums" was the first fruit of Lawrence's conversion to "the new young school of realism." Following close upon it came "A Modern Lover," "Second Best," "The Soiled Rose"/"The Shades of Spring," "The Old Adam," "The Witch à la Mode," and "Two Marriages"/"Daughters of the Vicar." "Goose Fair," also from this period is something of an anomaly, written as it was by Louisa Burrows.[6] These are the Croydon stories, written between 1909 and 1911. Realistic in subject and technique, set

squarely in the English Midlands and suburbs of London, and pulsing with autobiographical significance, they clearly reveal for the
first time Lawrence's talents as a writer of short fiction. They are
the main focus of this chapter. But as will be true from these years
forward, there is activity elsewhere, a local development off to one
side, a brief squabble off to the other. At this point, the most interesting sidelight consists of Lawrence's continued interest in
nonrealistic short stories, especially as that interest shows up in aspects of "Two Marriages" and its revision into "Daughters of the
Vicar." A second sidelight comes from Lawrence's returning to
"Legend," retitling it "A Fragment of Stained Glass." In both
cases, though in different ways, these subsidiary projects eventually reveal themselves to be rehearsals for major acts to come.

What do the Croydon stories have that nothing Lawrence
had written so far could claim? What do they have that
caused Ford to open the pages of the *Review* to this unknown
from Nottingham?

Craft and a unified effect are a beginning. As Ford recognized, from opening to closing word, these Croydon stories show a
commitment to the demand for single effect made first by Poe and
then by nearly all critics of modern short fiction. I emphasize commitment because these stories did not come perfect from Lawrence's pen. One watches him write, then revise and revise again,
seeking the true lines of his figure. The difference between Lawrence's revisions of these stories and of his earlier Eastwood tales is
that here, in the Croydon work, he seems far surer from the outset
of the basic direction the true lines will take.[7]

Within the issue of unified effect, one sees Lawrence wrestling with the same challenge faced by the writers in the *Yellow
Book* and *Savoy*, indeed by Chekov, Verga, Flaubert, Turgenev:
how to create a short story, unified, concise, and taut, about relatively ordinary events. Kipling had told many a tale about an incident in India and had made the story hang together on the anecdote itself and the underlying theme of British superiority. Robert
Louis Stevenson, named alongside Kipling at this time as a master
of the art of short fiction, told beautifully crafted tales, but they
cohere around extraordinary events and explicit moral conflict.
The *Review* was asking for a unified short story that would give
readers the same sense of ordinary, fluctuating human experience
captured years before in long fiction. Using the language of the
Russian formalists, we can say that the *Review* wanted stories that

appeared merely cumulative in shape yet had all the artifice of closed design.

For Lawrence, as for many writers of modern short fiction in England, the key strategies for drawing the two effects together lay in selection and implication. Following the techniques of the Continentals, Lawrence constructed his early realistic stories around a carefully limited set of significant scenes and images. If complexity and the flow of human experience could not be dramatized through the gradual accumulation of information and effects, they must be implied through scenes that convey several kinds of information at once. Images must reverberate with meaning. The flowers in "Odour of Chrysanthemums," for example, are a highly loaded image cluster. The chrysanthemums suggest both hope and disappointment, past and current experience. They serve as a way for Elizabeth Bates to communicate the ritual and emotional calendar of her marriage to Walter; they give the reader a powerful sensory image—a funereal smell—to associate with the laying out of Walter Bates. They convey a sense of autumn turning toward winter. Stuck in the waist of Elizabeth's apron, a sprig of ragged carnations adds to the cluster, capturing her ambivalence toward her coming child. Inevitably, with these associations and others, the flower imagery implies the complexity of Elizabeth's life and at the same time reinforces the unified effect of the story. One need only look back at "The White Stocking," "Legend," or a host of similar nineteenth-century stories to see how new this carefully wrought unity and complexity is, created out of the stuff of ordinary lives.

A further strategy, also leading to an artful account of the ordinary, is the effacing of the story-teller. An important presence in oral literature, the active raconteur disappears in most modern short stories. The burden of drawing connections and discerning significance falls to the reader. The story is less a speech act, more a series of visual and auditory images. Lawrence's early realistic work readily adopts the practice of giving the reader a series of concise scenes and reverberating images. But a curious modification of the general strategy of effacing occurs, for he has trouble releasing the story without a clear denouement. He wants to sum up significance, to dispense rewards and punishments. In the Croydon stories, the desire for clear closure frequently takes the form of a soliloquy. Barred from openly entering the story, he slips in at the end disguised as one of the characters. However, this modification gives Lawrence trouble, for his closing summaries often do not fit his preceding scenes and images. Indeed, many of his subsequent revisions consist of rewriting the denouement. What one sees here is a tension, ever present in Lawrence. As the stories discussed in this chapter will demonstrate, Lawrence can be an extraordinarily shrewd and tolerant observer; he also shows a tendency to be biased, to be overly interested in convincing the reader that virtue lies here, not there. Far more than in *The White Peacock,* however, the didacticism of the stories' initial denouements declares itself because the preceding dramatizations have been so open and balanced.

Getting rid of the raconteur and depending instead on scene and summary lead naturally to complex possibilities for manipulating point of view. Henry James saw that; James was fascinated with locating point of view in a particular mind in order to dramatize both a world and a mind. Lawrence, with a temperament and talent entirely different from James's, rid himself of the raconteur in order to take on the invisible stance of the omniscient narrator. That stance is so familiar to readers that seeing it as an authorial choice may take a moment's effort. It clearly was a choice for Lawrence, and an important one at this stage. To demonstrate the importance, let me return to the question of what these realistic stories have that is new to Lawrence and/or English short fiction. I have spoken of a unified effect and, within that, of Lawrence's ability to overcome the difficulty of constructing an artful short story about common experiences. When we look at point of view, two additional innovations become apparent. The first relates to Lawrence, the second to English fiction in general.

In *The White Peacock,* Lawrence did not adopt the stance of omniscient narrator. Instead, he located point of view in Cyril Beardsall, a self-conscious, first-person narrator who limits the novel to a pastoral, lyrical view of experience. Beardsall's world is a land without workers, class, guilt, death, or sex. Only the bitter Annabel strikes an intermittent, contrasting note. Lawrence knew Beardsall was a liability and often expressed in his letters the desire to kick him out. Nethermere was not Lawrence's view of the world: it was his view of the proper world of a novel. In writing *Sons and Lovers,* Lawrence had come a long way. The novel is told in third person and is set in a world amply endowed with post-Edenic realities. Yet even here, point of view constricts and distorts. Too often the reader is trapped in Paul Morel's point of view. Far more insightful than Beardsall, Paul still had blind spots and psychological territory to defend. Certain characters—Mr. Morel and Miriam Lievers for example—have trouble remaining quick and intricate once Paul's perspective takes over a scene or analysis. This is true of the final version, written in 1912; it is all the truer of Lawrence's earlier drafts, written alongside the Croydon stories.[8]

By contrast, turning toward those Croydon stories, one notices at once that only rarely is there a Cyril or Paul. Instead, Lawrence employs a wide spectrum of human perspectives: there are the farmers, the miners, the poor—the very voices Ford had asked to hear. There are the guilt-ridden, the class-embittered, the sexually frank; and there are the mothers, fathers, and girlfriends of the self-conscious young men. In each case, characters who serve as foils to Cyril or the early Paul come forth in the Croydon stories, state their view of life, and show us sides to Lawrence only hinted at in his contemporaneous long fiction.

The flexible point of view Lawrence uses in the Croydon tales, then, is an innovation for him. Williams cites another innovative quality in the point of view Lawrence adopts in these early tales, a quality not seen in English fiction since Jane Austen. In Lawrence's early work, writes Williams, "the language of the writer is at one with the language of his characters, in a way that hadn't happened, though George Eliot and Hardy had tried, since the earlier, smaller community of the novel [here he refers to Austen] had been extended and changed."[9] Williams argues that Austen's voice, as narrator or as main character, is at one with the community she writes about. In particular, neither as narrator nor character does she frame her fictional world within an opposing class perspective. The great social changes of the nineteenth century destroy that social identity between writers and their chosen subjects, leaving the Brontës, Dickens, Thackeray, Eliot, even Hardy, to approach their material—their characters and communities—from a step removed. They frame their material, exploring their workers, rustics, philanthropists, and doomed dreamers from the perspective of a different class, focusing on characters who themselves break out of communities and sever ties with their native class.

In his early short fiction and in sections of *Sons and Lovers*, Lawrence does something different. It is not merely that he is one of the first great English writers to emerge from the working class;

more, especially in the early stories, he chooses not to emerge. Further, he writes about characters who also choose not to emerge. Both the narrator and the characters speak from within a communal perspective. Narrative commentary—whether it be on the Midlands dialect; on the routine activities of the women, children, menfolk; or on the central conflict of the story—tends to be minimal. When commentary comes, it generally comes directly from the perspective of one of the participants. For example, when Lawrence employs the Midlands dialect, one never feels it is framed by a literary norm; this is in contrast to writers like Mark Twain, Joel Chandler Harris, Stevenson, or Kipling. Similarly, in contrast to Arnold Bennett, Lawrence does not have his narrator "visiting" Bestwood or Hagg's farm in the person of a garrulous researcher from the British Museum. We are instead kept to the perspective and voice of a people previously assumed to be inarticulate or naive. Telling their story from within demands that the writer know their story from within and have the eye, ear, and desire to deliver it in all its eloquent, normal, human complexity.

As Williams notes, Lawrence not only lost that sense of community with his characters, but also lost the conviction that they themselves—his miners, farmers, homemakers, shopkeepers— enjoyed authentic community. He became one of the century's visionaries of alienation. But to skip over the early stories and see them merely as preparation for the terrible visions to come is to ignore the genuinely innovative quality of the Croydon tales. Lawrence may have traveled a different road, but others—England's workers, America's blacks, Jews, chicanos, and native Americans—took the direction he initially pointed out. And they have created some of our culture's most distinctive contemporary fiction.

The above overview is intended to give a general frame of reference with respect to the techniques and spirit of the "new" realism of the early 1900s. In turning to the specific stories of this period, I will be pointing out tendencies but also noting moments when Lawrence anticipates the future or returns to his past.

As indicated above, the Croydon stories are far more autobiographical than anything Lawrence had yet written. No more medieval serfs or mad sons of vicars. In general, the tales cluster around two topics, family life and young love. Following one of the current conventions of realism, the image of family life tends toward bitterness and disappointment, the image of love toward frustra-

tion. All take place in the environs of Eastwood or Croydon. Because these stories constitute such an important breakthrough into
Lawrence's own experiences, a word about distancing is essential.

On the simplest level, the small distance Lawrence had traveled out of Eastwood into Croydon freed him to begin writing
about the people and the land he had left. Other events helped to
create a different kind of distance. In December 1910, Lawrence's
mother died of cancer. Before her death, much of Lawrence's writing is deeply colored by her view. Often, it seems, she is the primary audience. Apart from her actual character—so important in
forming Lawrence's own—her powerful influence kept Lawrence
from trying out other voices or imagining other slants on a
fictional situation, especially a situation touching on the Lawrences' family life. Through 1911, her perspective still haunts
some of his writing; but with his own near-death at the end of that
year and subsequent recovery in early 1912, a real and permanent
release occurs. A still different kind of distance is implied by the
very techniques of realism. In adopting them, Lawrence was approaching charged, personal experiences from a stance that encouraged narrative objectivity. Scenes and materialistic descriptions are among the basic elements of realistic short fiction; they
are also the material of Lawrence's best early insights into his own
life. Beginning with the major study of family life, "Odour of
Chrysanthemums," I will then move to the stories of young love,
concluding with "Two Marriages"/"Daughters of the Vicar" which
draws the two interests together and lays the groundwork for further innovations in Lawrence's short fiction.

Jessie Chambers remembers "Odour of Chrysanthemums" as
one of the first stories she saw after Lawrence moved to Croydon.[10] Lawrence apparently sent it to Ford in December 1909.
Ford accepted it at once, had it in proofs by March 1910, but
asked for revisions. Lawrence made the revisions, though not until
April of 1911. One suspects that the delay was caused partly by
his mother's illness and death, extending from August through
December of 1910. The *English Review* published the story in June
1911. Lawrence returned to it twice more, once in July of 1914
and again in the autumn of that year. The several revisions give a
clear view of Lawrence's growing understanding of his own childhood home and demonstrate his corresponding development as a
creator of realistic short stories.

Alongside "Two Marriages"/"Daughters of the Vicar," "Odour

of Chrysanthemums" has received more critical attention than any of Lawrence's other early stories. Particularly valuable are the addresses of Boulton, Cushman, Littlewood, Kalnins, and Moynahan.[11] The first four contain analyses of the changes Lawrence made in his revisions, particularly the changes related to the nature of Mrs. Bates. Boulton's essay is especially useful in that it prints the entire first version, based on the 1910 proofs, and describes the changes made in the 1911 revisions. Moynahan's discussion consists of an analysis of the theme and style of the final version. My own discussion builds on these but will locate the tale within the Croydon cluster and within the context of the times, especially as that context is revealed by the *English Review*.

"Odour of Chrysanthemums" opens with a carefully detailed image of a small, dirty mining village late in the afternoon of a raw autumn day. It is a "shot," an image of the kind Wendell Harris indicates replaced the voice of the traditional story-teller. As Moynahan notes, the organizing principle of the image is contrast; the atmosphere conveys "diminishment and decline."[12] With superb economy, it foretells the ruined love of Elizabeth and Walter Bates and implies the desecration of this once pastoral countryside. Lawrence left this image virtually untouched through his revisions of the tale.

In each version we move from the initial wide-angle view directly down to Elizabeth's cottage where we first see her, stooping out of her tarred fowl house. Through a succession of brief scenes, we learn that Elizabeth is a condemning woman, but with some cause; her husband has begun to stay away from home, sneaking off to the pub after work to drink with his collier friends. He is eventually carried home this evening, not from the pub but the mine, not drunk but dead. The story closes with Elizabeth and her mother-in-law washing his body, laying him out for burial, trying to understand what has happened to him and to them. Up to this last moment—when Elizabeth's soliloquy fades into narrative summary—all is dramatized, all events and responses rendered from within the perspective of the Bates family and their community.

As Ford read the first version in late 1909 or early 1910, he felt that English fiction had gained its first portrait of the working class, rendered poignantly and skillfully from within that class's own world. As for Lawrence, we may note that for the first time in his writing he is showing in a sustained fashion the rare gift for the perfect detail, the sound or line of dialogue that will communicate an entire personality or culture. Only two flaws weaken the initial version: several pages of extraneous material on the Bates children and the story's ending. Ford commented on the first problem, asking Lawrence to delete much of the children's parts so the story might work more quickly to a climax. In 1911, Lawrence complied. The cuts not only streamlined the story, but they also reduced the occasional tone of sentimentality and, most important, gave Lawrence the chance to present Elizabeth less as a mother and more as a wife. On his own, Lawrence also reworked the ending in 1911. However, while the deletions strengthen the story, Lawrence's revised conclusion only made an existing problem worse.

In the first version, Elizabeth closes the tale with a clear, unadmitted, and shocking confession of pleasure in Walter's death. She is literally happier to have him home dead than drunk. "'Think,'" she muses, "'how he might have come home—not white and beautiful, gently smiling . . . Ugly, befouled, with hateful words on an evil breath, reeking with disgust.'"[13] Lying there on the parlor floor, he is "beautiful," "gentle," "helpless." He is a baby, an infant. Elizabeth is now mother to all her family, children and husband alike. One feels that Walter's sexuality in particular is now just what she would like it to be. She can respond to it because she risks no engagement. Indeed, Lawrence tells us that as she and her mother wash his naked body, "they forgot it was death, and the touch of the man's body gave them strange thrills that made them turn one from the other, and left them with a keen sadness."[14]

The mother-in-law's mourning song is less grotesque than Elizabeth's, but it comes to the same thing. She celebrates in a voice of "rapture" how much Walter looks like the baby he once was. The only way these women can love this man is dead or infantilized; neither they nor the tale recognize the high price of their love.

In revising the proofs for the *Review,* Lawrence eliminated some grotesque details and, as noted above, cut several of the children's scenes. In looking at the ending, he recognizes that emphasis should fall on Elizabeth as wife. The shift in focus, however, yields no real insight. If anything, Lawrence underlined the tale's closing judgment on the fortunateness of Walter's death. Elizabeth now casts herself into the role of a fair maiden. Once she had

loved and believed in her young knight. But that knight had wandered down the evil path of drink. Now he is back again, fresh and
lovely. As if Elizabeth's rapture were not enough, the narrator
then steps in and delivers a sermon on the virtues of temperance.
The fine balance, the complex inner view of a community's life, is
destroyed by the closing sentimentality and oversimplifications.
The writer has put his thumb onto the scale.

By the time Lawrence revised the tale in 1914, much had
happened to him. The magazine text had been written in April
1911, four months after his mother's death, but by 1914 he had
been living with Frieda von Richthofen for two years, finished
Sons and Lovers, and written three drafts of *The Rainbow*. In his
final version, Lawrence has not entirely conquered the difficulties
that mar the conclusion of the magazine text, but he has recognized most of them. This last Elizabeth seems to have talked with
her earlier avatars in some imaginary margin of the tale. She expresses embarrassment and shame at her previous self-righteous-
ness and bathos. Taking off the martyr's robes she has worn so
fondly, she studies again her dead husband and their failure to
love each other. The blame falls on them both. Her marriage to
Walter was one long, mutual denial. He had never seen her, she
had never seen him. In the other texts, Elizabeth thanks death for
giving her a husband she can control. In the last version, Lawrence makes Elizabeth grateful to death for clarifying Walter's essential separateness and for forcing her to see her own separate existence as awesome, frightening, and never again to be denied. As
in so many of the 1914 revisions, here genuine awareness of the
existence of others leads to a rebirth of the self.[15]

In contrast to the earlier endings, the last very nearly brings
to culmination all of the dramatic action that precedes it. It reinforces the images of Walter and Elizabeth as equally trapped, suffocating, isolated in their own minds, or mines. It fits with our very
sense of Walter's absence throughout the tale; and it beautifully
captures the general tone of life being lived more intensely when
an awareness of death intrudes on routine. The one difficulty to
remain resides in the form of the ending. Descending into Elizabeth's mind, Lawrence still has trouble with stridency and abstraction. The language feels inflated. As I see it, the problem is this.
By 1914 Lawrence has expanded his repertoire to include visionary fictions like "The Prussian Officer" or *The Rainbow*. In them he
had found the dense language rhythms, the scenes, the patterns of

imagery to dramatize aspects of human identity not grasped by more straightforward realism. From start to finish, these fictions have the integrity of moving within one mode, of being governed by one intention. By contrast, "Odour of Chrysanthemums" is an exquisite, realistic tale until the end, when a new mode—foreign in spirit—interrupts its rhythms. Usually in realistic fiction, diction as high as that which closes the Bates's story is inserted in the midst and is undercut, deflated. Here that high diction has the last word.

Problematic as the last movement of the story may be, in general "Odour of Chrysanthemums" is an admirable pioneer in the art of realistic short fiction in England; within Lawrence's own work it speaks to *Sons and Lovers* in important ways, exploring and correcting problems raised by and in that novel. Between 1909 and 1911, the story by its very subject allows Lawrence to work with material he knew from the inside out, material he was still avoiding in his long fiction. (Jessie Chambers recalled Lawrence's first draft of *Paul Morel/Sons and Lovers* as one more exercise in avoidance.)[16] In 1914, two years after completing *Sons and Lovers*, the revised ending of "Odour of Chrysanthemums" allows him to express an alternative view on the Morels' bitter marriage. The story had asked all along what would happen if the miner were to die and the disappointed wife to write his epitaph. Until 1914, Mrs. Bates responds much as Mrs. Morel might have; by the final version she expresses a more complex understanding.

"Odour of Chyrsanthemums" draws upon a vein of experiences and memories crucial to all of Lawrence's writing. But another vein lay close beside that familial gold, a vein equally rich in material, equally in need of mining, understanding. That second vein relates to Lawrence's uneasy development as a sexual being. In these early stories, he works the veins separately. "Odour of Chrysanthemums" is much about family, little about adolescent love or sex. By contrast, "A Modern Lover," "Second Best," "The Soiled Rose," "The Old Adam," and "The Witch à la Mode" are much about adolescent love and sex, and little about family.

Lawrence's early love stories fall into two groups. The first explores Lawrence's relationship with Jessie Chambers. These are "A Modern Lover," "Second Best," and "The Soiled Rose"/"The Shades of Spring." The second examines a variety of relationships he formed in Croydon: included here are "The Old Adam" and "The Witch à la Mode." Different in setting and cast, the two groups are most interesting, however, in the different attitude they take toward the Lawrentian character, the self-conscious young man in each tale. In the first trio, the intellectual hero is occasionally viewed with irony, but in none of the early versions is that irony consistent. In the latter pair of stories, from the outset Lawrence sees the young hero's flaws and deals with them within the basic design of the tale.

The cast of the first group consists in each case of an intellectual hero, a home girl, and a rival for the home girl's affections. The hero has jilted the girl, the rival steps into the vacuum, and the girl is left assessing her losses and gains. In "Second Best" and "The Soiled Rose," the hero has gotten himself engaged or married to another, but in neither is his new relationship imagined in any detail. One has the sense in all three that the young writer is casting about trying to imagine a compensatory future for the jilted girl within the conventions of realistic short fiction.

The variations Lawrence plays on the central situation are notable in themselves, but also important is the dramatic structure inherent in the situation. In these tales Lawrence places his key characters at the points of a triangle. A vulnerable character stands at the apex and the dramatic action primarily traces that character wrestling with his or her choices. This is a structure Lawrence will use for the rest of his career. In later works, the resolution almost always implies a victory: Ursula will give up Skrebensky for Birkin; Birkin will escape Hermione for Ursula; Connie Chatterley will leave Clifford for Mellors. By contrast, in the Croydon stories the heroine's choice implies some loss, some compromise. Her choice is not really between two suitors, but between accepting or not accepting the one who remains, between yearning or refusing to yearn after the one who has left. It is clear that each of the Jessie Chambers stories, quite apart from whatever personal anxieties lie beneath them, are being written from within the general tone of disillusionment that marks nearly all of the realistic love stories of this period.

A second feature of the central situation slightly modifies that sense of loss however. As he did in "Legend"/"A Fragment of Stained Glass" and "A Prelude," in this trio of Croydon stories Lawrence mates a working-class man with a somewhat superior woman. In *Sons and Lovers*, that pairing in the Morel marriage spells disaster. In the tales however, Lawrence urges some genuine gains, for both the man and woman, in the cross-class romance.

The three home girls here may be compromised by losing their intellectual beaux, but, by throwing in their lot with a lower-class suitor, they are promised some compensation in vitality.

Jessie Chambers believed that Lawrence never intended to publish the version of "A Modern Lover" that she saw in 1909.[17] That may be true, but Lawrence revised it in 1912 with the intention of publishing it (CL, 102). The tale was not published in his lifetime but was collected in the posthumous volume of tales that bears its title. The fact that it did not receive the benefit of his revisions in 1914—revisions which greatly improved many of the tales—may help to explain its weaknesses. Of the three tales, it is the least controlled, the least balanced. In many ways it offers an extreme example of the warp that appears when Lawrence's planned analysis does not fit his dramatic scenes.

Cyril Mersham, the tale's hero, is frequently designated by himself and the narrator as sensitive, passionate, intelligent. He comes to visit the girl he has left behind and meets her new suitor; after the newcomer leaves, he urges her to make love with him, but she turns him down. His response offers a fair illustration of his view of himself and her: he sees himself as doomed to cast pearls before swine.

The scenes, however, imply a less complimentary view of Cyril and his relationship to Muriel. Told that he has a wonderful nonchalance, we see him fairly humming with tension. His inability to imagine Muriel's feelings demonstrates little intelligence or sensitivity. If he is passionate, it is a theoretical passion. Never does Cyril simply touch Muriel, want her. Also, Cyril sees her new friend Vickers in the most condescending of terms. Vickers may be beautiful, but he is a child in simplicity and will prove an unending disappointment to the woman he marries. Perhaps he is, perhaps he will; one sees little of him apart from Cyril's view and thus has a hard time judging.

However, this may be conscious irony on Lawrence's part. Sagar notes the juxtaposition of Cyril's looking up at Orion as he wades through the mud in the opening scene.[18] Cyril's last name, Mersham (meer sham), may be a tip-off.[19] If so, then the tale is an amusing alternative to some of the more confusing scenes in *Sons and Lovers*, scenes where Paul's actions seem strangely at odds with the narrator's explanations.[20] But I am not convinced that the irony is more than momentary. Ultimately it is a question of tone. I do not discern, for example, any sustained tension between Cyril's self-pity at the end of the story and the views of the implied narrator. In my view, "A Modern Lover" duplicates rather than corrects some of the more confusing aspects of *Sons and Lovers.*

To understand the confusions in both novel and tale, one might argue that Lawrence was not capable yet of criticizing a young man like Paul or Cyril; that he could not yet identify with a lover like Clara or Tom Vickers; that he was too close to the home girl he had jilted to see her without defensiveness. In fact he was capable of all three perceptions. "Second Best" and "The Soiled Rose"/"The Shades of Spring" have weaknesses and fail, as does "A Modern Lover," to sustain implied ironies (by the time he revises "The Soiled Rose" into "The Shades of Spring," Lawrence solves the latter problem), but from the beginning both analyze the break up of a strained adolescent love affair with a surprising increase in insight and coherence.

In "Second Best," the young intellectual, Jimmy Barrass, has gone off to Liverpool and gotten engaged. Frances, the home girl, must adjust herself to his defection. Wooing her in Jimmy's stead is Tom Smedley, a slow farmer lad. The tale closes with her acceptance of Tom's proposal. Tracing many of the same tensions as "A Modern Lover," Lawrence makes two important decisions in "Second Best." He keeps his intellectual hero off-stage and organizes the story around a powerful central image, a blind, lively mole. As will *Sons and Lovers,* "Second Best" measures the vitality of the main characters according to their capacity to perceive the distinct, alien vitality of the natural world around them. Spilka is right when he decribes *Sons and Lovers* as Lawrence's "first ambitious attempt . . . to place his major characters in active relation with a live and responsive universe."[21] But one needs to see that Lawrence first began to explore that "active relation" in the early tales.[22]

The mole enters "Second Best" as Frances sits on a bank with her sister Anne, relaying the news of Jimmy's recent engagement. Silently nosing its way over the warm, red soil, the mole shuffles up, brisk, quick, "a very ghost of *joie de vivre*" (*Complete Short Stories of D. H. Lawrence,* 214).* Anne traps it in a handkerchief, causing Frances to suffer greatly as she watches its intense struggle to free itself. The mole bites Anne; she drops and kills it. Law-

---

* Further references to this title will be indicated by the abbreviation CSS.

rence explicitly draws together the two events: Frances's confession that she has lost Jimmy and the death of the mole; a flashing quickness has gone out of her world. Jimmy's view of nature as glamor can be Frances's no more. She must face life as it comes: moles must die ("'They do us a lot of damage,'" says Tom); and she must redirect her own life away from the man who could have been a pioneer to her soul toward good-humored, easy Tom. A day later she seals her pact with Tom and the view he represents by taking him a mole she herself has killed.

Hanging on the tiny carcasses of two dead moles, the story has economy and depth, despite occasional moments of awkwardness. Like the flowers in "Odour of Chrysanthemums," the mole is a specific, memorable image, able quickly to imply a whole nexus of ideas and attitudes about nature, privilege, sacrifice, even sexuality. In *John Thomas and Lady Jane*, the second version of *Lady Chatterley's Lover*, Lawrence has Lady Chatterley refer to Mellor's phallus as a mole: "Sightless, it seemed to look around, like a mole risen from the depths of the earth."[23] The language here as well as in "Second Best" also creates echoes with the language Lawrence uses to describe the sightless existence of the sexually vital hero in "The Blind Man." There is no need to construct an argument around these widely separated references, but it is legitimate to suggest that, even as a young writer, Lawrence identified the living, mysterious forces of nature with the living, mysterious forces of sex, especially the phallus. In contrast to an early novel such as *The White Peacock*, in his earliest tales he felt free to explore and dramatize that identification.

Further, as the mole weaves its way through the story, one is impressed by the tale's approach to a unified design. That it is an approach rather than accomplishment is the result of the story's ambivalent attitude toward Tom and, consequently, ambivalent judgment on Frances's future. On the one hand, Tom is "second best." He has some of the same denseness as Muriel's suitor in "A Modern Lover." But with his intellectual hero offstage, Lawrence develops more fully Tom's potential as an earthy, passionate man. Echoing Hardy's *Tess of the D'Urbervilles*, Lawrence creates a powerful moment when he shows Frances, dressed in white, slowly, almost ritualistically, approach Tom as he stands waiting for her in a field of barley. The beauty of the land, the young man's shy stirrings of passion, the woman's simple advance look to some of the finest scenes in *The Rainbow*. Lawrence quickly backs off, assuring himself and the reader that Jimmy Barrass really is the magical one. But the language of denial is affected and stilted; the image Lawrence has just created rings with too much conviction to be gainsaid.

It is important to see that the fall into ambivalence here is a fortunate one. It shows, for a moment, a side to class and love which Lawrence will develop later. Equally significant, it promises an important break with the general tone of pessimism Lawrence's short fiction has displayed thus far.

The last of the three Jessie Chambers stories comes even closer to breaking that tone, especially in its final version. In "The Soiled Rose"/"The Shades of Spring," Lawrence returns to the basic situation of "A Modern Lover," bringing his restless intellectual hero back to his home country.[24] Again one encounters a future for the spurned home girl. From the outset, however, "The Soiled Rose" promises a gain in perspective over "A Modern Lover." After more than six years away, John Addington Syson comes back to the land of his youth. He is now a successful businessman in London, unhappily married, and still emotionally tied to the girl he left behind. As he walks through the woods toward her house, he feels like an emigrant "on a visit to the country of his past, to make comparisons" (*Forum*, March 1913, 324).[25] The comparisons turn out to be initially reassuring. But suddenly a new keeper comes across the path, barring the way toward Hilda's place. Syson successfully talks his way through, learning as he does that this ruddy and comely man is Hilda's lover and has been since the day Syson got married. It seems that the keeper cannot, however, convince Hilda to marry him. In scenes that read like remarkable preludes to *Lady Chatterley's Lover*, Hilda eventually walks Syson through her woods and shows him the flower-decked hut she shares with her lover.[26] The keeper appears, the three of them walk toward the gate by which Syson will leave, and, in a typical scene in this early fiction, Syson ends up alone with his rival for a moment. Syson says he will stop writing to Hilda, the keeper promises to let Syson know what happens to him and Hilda, and they part. Syson goes up the hillside, lies down among the gorse bushes, soliloquizes, and counts his losses. He is not regretful but unutterably wretched. As he lies there, he becomes an inadvertent voyeur to a scene between Hilda and the keeper. On the other side of the bushes, Hilda stands crying. The keeper attempts to comfort her but is ineffectual and awkward. As he stands in misery crushing bees in his hand, one stings him on the shoulder. Hilda pulls out the stinger and sucks the poison. She laughs at the mark she has made, saying "'This is the reddest kiss you will ever have'" (Forum, 340).[27] The keeper embraces her, she promises to marry him, but as he leaves, her tear-stained face is turned toward Syson's new territory. She stands "looking south over the sunny countries toward London, far away" (Forum, 340).

At this stage, the logic of the tale is unclear. Lawrence sets up a series of ironies but then undercuts them. The opening actions and imagery, for example, promise an alternative to "A Modern Lover," "Second Best," and Sons and Lovers: Syson, complacent about his place in Hilda's unchanging world, is in fact a trespasser. The rival is powerful and happily established. But Lawrence contradicts this view almost at once.[28] The keeper is labeled a "poor chap" with a grudge against Syson because Hilda will not marry him. Moving on to introduce Hilda, Lawrence reintroduces the ironies with which he began.

Like her world, Hilda is quite other than Syson had realized. She is critical, aware, brilliant, alive. Syson is abashed as she takes him on a walk through the woods, showing him the new buds and nests; in fact, she enacts Paul Morel's gesture in Sons and Lovers as she counts the five tiny eggs in a jinty's nest. This young lady, who even has the courage to mock Syson's youthful, sexual timidity, is a far cry from Muriel and Miriam. But as he did with the keeper, Lawrence eventually backs down from his positive characterization of an independent Hilda. We learn that Hilda still yearns for Syson. Her agreeing to marry the keeper at the end is simply acquiescence. Like "Odour of Chrysanthemums," this story closes with a soliloquy that contradicts much of what has gone before. Great as her loss has been, Syson feels his loss is greater. He no longer has someone to idealize him. "'I have destroyed the beautiful "me,"'" he grieves (Forum, 339). One understands now that he is the soiled rose! But all of this is unsupported and contradicts much of the previous tale. In fact, it even contradicts the story's final image. Turned away from the keeper, Hilda stands weeping, looking off toward Syson's country. She hardly seems disillusioned with him.

Revising the tale in 1914 and retitling it "The Shades of Spring," Lawrence brings the entire work into line with the opening scene.[29] The keeper's perspective is proven to be true, and, through a series of illuminations, Syson comes to share it. Syson's soliloquy becomes the culmination of those illuminations. He is a trespasser and, further, a trespasser in a land he never really knew. It is he who has idealized Hilda. Syson realizes that he had wanted to keep writing to Hilda "like Dante to some Beatrice who had never existed save in the man's own brain" (CSS, 209). The one way in which this bright spring is similar to the bright springs of the past is that both possessed and possess shades—spirits and shadows—that Syson had never taken into account. Under similar circumstances, the possibility that he has grandly misread his own adolescence never occurs to Cyril Mersham; in *Sons and Lovers*, Paul entertains the possibility of having misread Miriam but concludes by feeling that Miriam has lied to him.

The gain to Syson's character is clear, but Lawrence also makes Hilda more coherent. Most interesting, she chooses in the end not to marry the keeper; at least, she says, not yet. She likes things as they are. It is possible, I suppose, to see in her refusal one more example of Lawrence's disinclination to let this home girl commit herself to anyone other than the intellectual hero. But Hilda has readily admitted what Syson's departure cost her; she is not avoiding anything. Further, the result of her admissions is neither bitterness nor defeat, but real independence. She feels she is self-sufficient, alive in her world. As she sees it, if Syson's leaving cost her a great deal, his staying would have crippled her. The closing scene shows her simply "looking over the sunny country" (CSS, 211).

If one learns nothing more from the three Croydon tales that deal with the Jessie Chambers motif, one should see that Paul and Miriam in *Sons and Lovers* constitute only one interpretation of the difficulties Lawrence and Jessie went through. "A Modern Lover" may essentially repeat the blind spots in the Miriam sections of *Sons and Lovers*, but "Second Best" and "The Soiled Rose" offer alternatives to the novel. Frances moves toward a potentially satisfying relationship with Tom, and Hilda, far from turning into the prematurely old hag that Miriam becomes, retains all her beauty and allure. Even at this stage, Lawrence could and did imagine contrasting analyses of the deadly attraction of an overly spiritual love and the decision to reject it.

The picture drawn thus far of Lawrence's work in Croydon shows a young writer enthusiastically working with the conventions of realism, new to him and his literary colleagues as those conventions apply to short fiction. Skilled in their use, Lawrence is nonetheless employing the conventions to help him explore material he does not yet fully understand. Thus in the Croydon versions of each tale we have looked at so far, there has been a wrinkle in the logic; a denouement has contradicted the previous drama; a powerful image has been undercut by the narrator's hesitancy; a pattern of irony has not been sustained.

In the two subsequent stories of young love, written during the summer of 1911, Lawrence examines a somewhat different area of his life. Shifting the scene to Croydon, he focuses on experiences less shadowed by ambivalence, experiences he could evaluate with clarity and authority. Before turning to "The Old Adam" and "The Witch à la Mode," however, I want to carry this discussion of Lawrence's early ambivalence and its effect on his early tales a step further, into an issue implied by the wrinkles mentioned above. The issue is revealed by his revision of "Legend."

Once Lawrence had tackled the revision of "Odour of Chrysanthemums" at the end of March 1911, he moved on at once to revise "Legend" and "The White Stocking." It is the former that I want to look at here. Retitled "A Fragment of Stained Glass," the story was published by the *English Review* in September 1911. In nearly all respects, Lawrence retained this version for *The Prussian Officer* volume; it is the version we currently read. A flawed performance, creaky in structure and confusing in characterization, it initially follows then stangely breaks loose from the traditional formulas for writing legendary tales. Suddenly in a scene in the woods, those formulas get tossed aside as Lawrence writes out a very curious sexual encounter. Unprepared for, unexplained, the encounter is left hanging at the end of the tale, ready for many retellings in the tales to come.

Saving for later the astonished monks who open "Legend," Lawrence introduces "A Fragment of Stained Glass" with a wide view of a romantic, rural landscape. He then quickly directs the reader's gaze down to the ruins of an old abbey. Typical of the legendary tale, the initial sentences in the first paragraph read much like a painting. Lawrence concludes the paragraph with an arrow forward meant to provide narrative suspense: "This is the window in question" (*English Review*, 242). Lawrence then introduces a young, first-person narrator, a middle-aged vicar, and a dusty old manuscript. These paragraphs read as superstructure, intended to add patina to the tale's atmosphere and to establish a source for the account of the serf's adventure. That account is now the vicar's "gloss" on the manuscript, his admitted fabrication.

In the vicar we meet a stock figure of the ghost tale genre: he is a bachelor, shrewd, sad, ironic. An amateur archeologist, Mr. Colbran is compiling a bible of the English people. On the evening of the tale, the young narrator is treated to a look at a fifteenth-century monk's exclamation at the devil's attempt to break into the monastery. The vicar then dims the lights, arranges himself so that he is no more than a voice, and proceeds to gloss the monk's account by imagining the incident as told by the devil figure. In a "sing-song, sardonic" tone, he reads a tale of flight similar to the one described in "Legend."

Although more ambitious than the earlier version, the revised tale has obvious weaknesses.[30] Its mood rests upon shopworn, gothic gimmicks; the narrative structure is awkward and unnecessary as one moves from narrator to vicar to manuscript to gloss on that manuscript. The vicar (or narrator, or Lawrence) has trouble finding an authentic and consistent voice for the serf. But one difficulty may be less obvious and is related to Lawrence's attempts to develop the tale beyond its original anecdotal quality. This difficulty occurs in the last scene.

Apart from the excellent images of the sounds and appearance of the frozen woods, the most interesting feature in the story is the conjunction of four elements in the last scene: the serf's reluctance to relinquish the piece of stained glass which he calls his life- and bloodstone; his and the girl's love-making; its probable attendant pain (Lawrence has made much of the serf's wounds and bruises); and the arrival of the wolves. Also intriguing are the complex contradictions in the roles played by girl and serf. Because it introduces issues basic to Lawrence's fiction, a portion of the dialogue bears quoting. As the serf tells it, waking in the woods after the night's flight, he stood cutting bread for the girl. She fell at his feet, while he cried "'Nay'" and began to weep. In the next moment, he recalled the piece of glass, broken from the monastery window.

> "Tis magic," I said, "let me throw it from us." But nay, she held my arm.

45

"It is red and shining," she cried.

"It is a bloodstone, it cut my face," I answered. "It will hurt us, we shall die in blood."

"But give it to me," she answered.

"It is red with my blood," I said.

"Ah, give it to me," she called.

"It is my blood," I said.

"Give it," she commanded, low.

"It is my life-stone," I said.

"Mine," she pleaded.

"Yours," I said, and I gave it. She smiled in my face, lifting her arms to me. I sought her out with my mouth, found her mouth, her white throat. Nor she ever shrank, but trembled with happiness.

What woke us, when the woods were filling again with shadow, when the fire was out, when we opened our eyes and looked up as if drowned, into the light which stood bright and thick on the tree-tops, what woke us was the sound of wolves. . . .   (*English Review*, 251)

We are a far cry in this scene from the bickering and coziness of "Legend," but never is this highly charged material controlled or sorted out.

For example, the way this frightened serf is initiated into love is through the girl's advances. Yet importantly, those advances are a peculiar blend of imperious command and feet-kissing submission. She is on her knees before him but demanding, it would seem, his very potency. The castration symbolism is obvious in the blood- and life-stone. However, after the serf has capitulated and given up his stone, he suddenly turns to her with power and desire.[31] He now sees himself as the bold one and seems surprised that she does not shrink from his passion. Following the conventions of the time, a curtain is drawn over their love-making; waking them is the sound of their avengers, the howling, hungry wolves.

What Lawrence expresses here, however confusedly, is the sexual ambivalence that lies near the heart of much of his fiction. Sexual relationships carry allure but also constitute real threats to the very existence of many of Lawrence's characters.[32] In "A Fragment," the relationship represents a way for the serf to express

46

his power but also an occasion for him to capitulate into a devotee, a dog at one point. If one imagines story speaking to story—if one traces the interrelationships between "A Prelude," "A Fragment of Stained Glass," and "Two Marriages" (written in June or July of 1911)—Lawrence's ambivalence becomes even clearer. In "A Prelude" and "Two Marriages," the aggressive female wins a victory for all: Nell and Fred are rewarded by Nell's courage; Louisa and Alfred are saved by Louisa's. By contrast, Martha's passionate persistence in "A Fragment of Stained Glass" threatens the serf's very life, at least for a moment. This difference in attitude relates of course to the fictional context of each character, but it also characterizes Lawrence's tales throughout his career. If his heroes are at times afraid of being consumed by a strong woman, at other times they seek out that embrace for the release into selfhood which it brings. When Millett and others exclaim about Lawrence's fear of strong women and of sexual relationships in general, one can understand their surprise as a reaction to his having been hailed champion of strong women and sexual freedom. His fiction, however, demonstrates that either view of Lawrence is reductive. Millett's portrait of the wily, terrified, puritanical chauvinist is no more correct than the earlier portrait. Lawrence tapped the ranges of his sexual self and needs with extraordinary insight and sensitivity; and the self and needs he tapped seem endowed with all of the complexity of the norm. Among the many insights the feminist movement has fostered, one of the most helpful for reading Lawrence is the reminder that most people and most cultures approach sexual relationships with some ambivalence: joy, yearning, fear. Discovering the ambivalence in Lawrence's work is less surprising than realizing how early in his short fiction he allowed it to express itself.

The wolves, who have the last word in the scene, raise a different issue, one also central to much of Lawrence's later fiction. One could see them as poised to punish the serf for giving in to Martha, for giving up his prowess. It seems more likely, however, that the wolves are there to punish both Martha and the serf for their mutual transgression. The couple's most immediate transgression is of course their illicit sexual passion, but, also, both have outlawed themselves from normal society: he by his barn burning; she by her aid and comfort; and both by their "attack" on the church. Physically both are on the edge of collapse. He is starving, badly beaten, bleeding; both are freezing and exhausted.

Pushed to the limits of society and physical endurance, the two characters are, in brief, in a state of extremity. In "A Fragment of Stained Glass," Lawrence renders a fairly conventional judgment on the two exiles. The howling of the wolves suggests that the couple's flight will cost them their lives. In later tales, Lawrence will greatly modify that judgment as he examines the insights and freedom that flight can bring.

Recent criticism has explored this recurring interest in Lawrence, arguing for the fascination and elemental attraction that outlaws, pain, death, corruption, and perversity held for him.[33] Lawrence doubtless felt that attraction, but it is important to see how his understanding of corrupt, perverse, extreme experience changes. The way in which the swoon into nonbeing, the dissolution of identity, the degradation of self may or may not lead to social relations and responsibility, wholeness of being, or the resurrection of the self is a problem Lawrence wrestles with throughout his fiction. As I have suggested, in "A Fragment of Stained Glass," Lawrence seems inclined to punish his emigrés, to kill them for their radical departure. In other tales, Lawrence will indicate that only through exile, dissolution, and crucifixion, can one establish a real or natural identity and, from thence, valuable social and sexual relationships. In still other tales, one gets conflicting messages as Lawrence presents exiles who are vilified, mocked, and admired by the narrator of the tale. The subject will come up continually in this analysis.

If ambivalence—toward dying fathers, men of the land, intellectual heroes, and strong women—may be said to characterize aspects of Lawrence's work thus far, then the next two tales should be recognized as minor but important accomplishments. The third, while consistent in its attitude toward its material, raises different issues.

As Lawrence continued to publish his tales in the *English Review* and elsewhere, various people suggested that he bring out a volume. Impressed by "Odour of Chrysanthemums," Martin Secker in particular invited Lawrence to consider the possibility. The Secker volume never materialized but the invitation kept Lawrence hard at work. The summer of 1911 was especially fruitful for his short fiction. "The Old Adam" was mailed to Austin Harrison, new editor of the *English Review,* in August; and Lawrence sent "The Witch à la Mode" and a draft of "Two Marriages"

("Daughters of the Vicar") to Edward Garnett in September. The first two are accomplished short stories, although neither was accepted for magazine publication. Both appeared posthumously in *A Modern Lover*.[34] "Two Marriages" also received no takers, apparently because of its length but equally I suspect because of its initial narrative awkwardness. That story, however, rewritten as "Daughters of the Vicar," becomes one of Lawrence's first forays out of realism into visionary short fiction.

"The Old Adam" and "The Witch à la Mode" give us two more self-conscious, sensitive heroes caught up in love's difficulties. In "The Old Adam," Lawrence situates his hero in lodgings very like the ones he took in Croydon. In "The Witch à la Mode," he is apparently sorting out his relationships with his fiancée Louie Burrows and a woman whom he met and saw often in Croydon, Helen Corke. In both tales, the young hero moves with a slightly smug air. (Lawrence will always create posturing heroes, but soon—with the advent of Frieda—he will incorporate a critic in the wings to challenge and tease his protagonists.) Nevertheless, in both stories Lawrence presents a surprisingly honest picture of the young hero's repressions.

While in Croydon, Lawrence stayed with the Jones family and was apparently enchanted with their baby daughter Hilda Mary. In "The Old Adam," Lawrence places his hero, Edward Severn, in a similar family and then moves him with admirable economy through a variety of semisexual encounters. The tale takes place inside the Thomas's middle-class home in a suburb of London. Outside, a storm gathers, breaks, and subsides. The tension between the thunder and lightning outside and the civilized codes inside mirrors in reverse the hero's state. We come to see that there is an anarchic, stormy Old Adam inside Severn who is being contained by the codes of propriety. That this containment is precisely what Severn wants is one of the tale's surprising insights.

Severn's first encounter is in many ways the tale's riskiest. Having returned to the Thomas's house at eight in the evening, he is let in by the maid and goes out into the garden to play a quick game of chase with their daughter. The child is delighted; "wild and defiant as a bacchanal," she is a baby Eve in this garden. Fully aware of her infant sexuality, she teases Severn, asks that he be the one to undress her for bed, and gives him upon retiring not a kiss but a quick lick with her tongue. Severn is also aware of her sexuality, but the gentle tone of his awareness is critical to understanding the story.

> She was a beautiful girl, a bacchanal with her wild, dull-gold hair tossing about like a loose chaplet, her hazel eyes shining daringly, her small spaced teeth glistening in little passions of laughter within her red, small mouth. The young man loved her. She was such a little bright wave of willfulness, so abandoned to her impulses, so white and smooth as she lay at rest, so startling as she flashed her naked limbs about. But she was growing too old for a young man to undress. (CSS, 26)

Severn is sexually aware of her, but, as the above paragraph suggests, his awareness of her is as healthy as hers is of him. He is sensual, tender, playful with her. As it turns out, he is more comfortable with her off-limits sexuality than he is with her mother's more possible passion. The code that ultimately protects the child's sexuality frees Severn to respond to her.

The story's middle scene shows Severn and Mrs. Thomas sitting in the dining room as the storm builds up around them. Severn's desire for her is intense. In turn, she yearns for Severn and expresses her weariness with her own boorish, tiresome husband. But it soon becomes clear that Severn at least is incapable of acting on his desire. He may pant for "someone," but he will not recognize that the available someone is Mrs. Thomas. The Old Adam in him can leap out only in safer territory. Soon it will.

Thomas comes in at eleven, has a bit of supper, loses an argument with Severn over the Women's Bill, and then the two of them climb a narrow stairway to the third floor to bring down the maid's trunk. She is being dismissed from the household.[35] Mr. Thomas will take the front end, Severn the back. Toward the bottom, Severn slips and the trunk comes crashing down on Thomas. He is not hurt but is enraged. He delivers two blows to Severn, who in turn leaps on him and nearly chokes him to death. The maid, Kate, breaks up the fight. Both men are amazed at themselves; and out of their confrontation comes a tenderness and abiding closeness. In violence they have met each other as they have met no other. By the tale's end, a parallel has emerged between Severn's opening and closing encounters, his contacts with child and husband: both offer a highly sensual or intense relationship that releases joy or passion in Severn but does not ask him for any direct or continuing sexual involvement.[36] With respect to Severn and Mr. Thomas, Lawrence implies a homosexual attraction, but again Severn seems able to feel the attraction partly because the taboo against a homosexual affair protects him from genuine engagement.

The same is true, I would suggest, of Paul Morel's fight and subsequent closeness to Baxter Dawes in *Sons and Lovers*. Paul enjoys contact with Baxter precisely because it does not ask what he cannot give. Miriam and Clara, by contrast, ask the impossible: a steady, adult, sexual relationship. As will be noted below, Alfred in "Two Marriages"/"Daughters of the Vicar" and Geoffrey in "Love Among the Haystacks" are like Severn in their inability to reach out and form adult sexual ties. Both solve the problem, but at first Alfred relies on his mother, Geoffrey on his brother—two different but similarly safe bonds.

Homosexuality plays no role in "The Witch à la Mode," but here too Lawrence seems able and generally willing to see his intellectual young man as repressed, self-conscious, sexually ill at ease. Nor is that ability and willingness a result of later revisions. Writing the tale three separate times, Lawrence improved the style on each occasion but kept the central intention and dynamics of the tale intact.[37] In all versions, Bernard Coutts is wandering without any clear direction. Having drifted into an engagement with a girl named Connie, Coutts enjoys idealizing her from a distance but "vaguely he knew she would bore him" (CSS, 65).

As the tale opens, Coutts has just stepped off a train taking him toward Yorkshire and Connie. He is allowing himself a stopover in East Croydon, the home of his former lover, Winifred Varley. Seeing her is an exciting risk. As the Croydon tram carries him toward Winifred, he notices the blue sparks of the car's electrical connection. They arouse and intrigue him. Walking toward his old boarding house, he forgets he is tired. His spirit exults, and he notices "the pale fluttering of the daffodils," the blue and white of the alyssum, hyacinths, and crocuses (CSS, 55). Winifred, dressed in white, comes to his former rooming house for a musical evening. Lawrence develops an analogy between her and a statue of Venus on the mantle. Winifred's body is strong and powerful; she bows toward the piano "richly," and Coutts marvels at the "rich solidity" of her back and shoulders (CSS, 65). Like the statue, her posture is one of anticipation. Throughout the tale, she is associated with images of brilliance and luster, of fires, candles, crystal, orchids, crocuses. The key adjectives in Coutts's response to her are aroused, keen, fascinated, intense, exulting, fervid.

Especially in the early versions, the tale's diction is often stilted and clumsy, but the tense ambivalence Lawrence maintains in these images and adjectives is consistently good. Compared to being bored or nailed on a cross, to being "polite and formal, gentlemanly" (CSS, 64)—all associations Coutts makes with his engagement to Connie—the arousal, keenness, and fiery intensity he associates with Winifred are tempting, attractive. At the same time, however, such white-hot intensity is deadly. Between Coutts and Winifred there is only electric, intellectual heat friction; there is no simple, life-giving warmth. In contrast to the love represented by Venus, their love is lustrous, shining, but cold to the touch. The yellow sparks and blue flames which had intrigued and stimulated Coutts on the tram as it sped him toward Winifred burst into a real fire in the last scene, burning them both. As with much of Lawrence's later imagery—particularly of mountains, water, and the moon—the heat and light images in "The Witch à la Mode" assert that the attractive and destructive are often one and the same.

The density of the image patterns in this tale raises a second point: Lawrence's growing understanding of and desire to talk about linguistic strategies. In "The Witch à la Mode," Lawrence only briefly directs our attention to the kind of art he is practicing (in *Women in Love*, discussions on art are a major part of the novel), but among the things one learns in Coutts's and Winifred's discussions of language is that Lawrence is already questioning some of the tenets of the "new school of realism."

Lawrence indicates that Winifred in particular cannot speak out directly. She speaks in the "'foggy weather of symbolism'" (CSS, 62). If the matter were dropped here, one might see Lawrence as advocating straight, referential language for any real facing of issues. But the matter keeps coming up, and always in the context of how these two people are to speak to each other, of each other. Coutts and Winifred need to reach some truth, some understanding; but the only language that can get them there—and does in fact—is one laden with imagery, simile, and metaphor, a language that continually points in several directions, toward the immediate object, toward the speaker, and beyond them both. The outcome of their conversations argues for the value of symbolic language and structures, when they are used to reveal rather than avoid an issue, when they keep a toe in Liverpool.

Although the relationship between Winifred and Coutts forms the major conflict in "The Witch à la Mode," Lawrence enriches the tale with a secondary conflict. In a brief conversation between Coutts, his former landlady, and her father, Lawrence runs up a small flag alerting us to the theme of determinism and free will. In both overt and covert ways, the tale asks why do people do things; why in particular is Coutts about to marry Connie and why does he keep returning to Winifred. Lawrence gives Coutts two answers, both of which avoid a simple distinction between determinism and free will.

Coutts is marrying Connie because nothing matters to him one way or another. His plans for the future are to "'just go on.'" Coutts drifts toward death, unable to call upon his energies. By contrast, Coutts returns to Winifred—to love and to hate her —for the opposite reason. Far from indifferent, he is compelled, as a moth to a candle. In either case—Coutts's drift toward death or his fascination with Winifred—free will or determinism is by the way. The landlady's father ends the initial conversation by repeating "'Why do we do things?'" and answering himself, "'I suppose . . . it's because we can't help it—eh? What?'" (CSS, 57). Given the rest of the tale, the father's line suggests that human actions are often motivated by forces deep within the psyche. While not a major concern in this tale, those forces will soon become a key interest in Lawrence's fiction.

As a study of frustrated young love, "The Witch à la Mode" shows the same balance Lawrence eventually achieved in "The Soiled Rose"/"The Shades of Spring." Like Hilda, Winifred remains attractive in spite of the young hero's ultimate desertion. Further, in each of these tales Lawrence is willing to apportion responsibility and blame. For example, Winifred is seen as tense and cool, but the tale consistently admits that Coutts is equally unable to relax and lose himself. On both sides there is an awareness of the obstacles that keep them from realizing a fulfilling relationship. "'You know, Winifred, we should only drive each other into insanity, you and I: become abormal,'" says Coutts at one point (CSS, 66). "'Yes,'" agrees Winifred, "'if we were linked together we should only destroy each other'" (CSS, 68). Lawrence emphasizes that they hurt each other, often even hate each

the "each other" that is important, for it elevates Win-
⸗d the role of victim, Coutts beyond the role of reluc-
⸗er.

last image from "The Witch à la Mode" shows Coutts
running from Winifred's house, his burnt hands held out in front
of him in pain. Suffering more obviously than other lovers in the
Eastwood and Croydon stories, Coutts nevertheless represents
those lovers well. Most of the tales discussed thus far follow the assumption laid down by realistic short fiction at the turn of the
century by rehearsing the failure of relationships. In the Croydon
tales, where character becomes important, one sees Lawrence continually exploring the way people fail to respond, fail to commit
themselves to others. "Two Marriages"/"Daughters of the Vicar"
brings something new.

I spoke above of Lawrence's previous cautious breaks with the
pessimism associated with the realistic short fiction of his time. To
feel the newness of his stance one must think of Chekov, Zola,
and Maupassant, of the English realists of the 1890s, of Wells,
Bennett, Galsworthy, and of Lawrence's own contemporaries,
Joyce and Mansfield. As Wendell Harris explains, "realism as a
method" was associated with "pessimism as a world view."[38] In
1895, Hubert Crackanthorpe, a realist contributor to the *Yellow
Book*, cried out, "some day a man will arise who will give us a study
of human happiness, as fine, as vital as anything we owe to Guy de
Maupassant or to Ibsen. That man will have accomplished the
infinitely difficult, and in admiration and awe shall we bow down
our heads before him."[39] Recipient of little admiration and awe at
least within his own lifetime, Lawrence nevertheless accomplished
the apparently impossible: he gave joy, passion, and love the same
dramatic weight and authenticity as grief, disappointment, and
loneliness. Yet, interestingly, the moment he began to dramatize
joy in his fiction he also began to move away from some of the basic conventions of realism. While in its original form it is not the
"fine" and "vital" art work Crackanthorpe called for, "Two Marriages" is the first of Lawrence's fictions to imagine deep happiness
for its main characters; simultaneously, it is the first to suggest
Lawrence's eventual movement out of the school of realism.

In "Two Marriages"/"Daughters of the Vicar," Lawrence re-
turns to Eastwood country, to the land he had been exploring in
"Odour of Chrysanthemums," the territory Ford saw as foreign to
English readers.[40] As with that earlier tale, excellent work has

been done on this story. Kalnins and Cushman are particularly worth consulting.[41] Both critics look carefully at Lawrence's revisions; both relate the final version to the important work Lawrence was doing on *The Rainbow*. Cushman in particular marshals the texts of 1911, 1913, and 1914, published and unpublished, and highlights the major changes. As he demonstrates, progressively, from initial draft to final version, Lawrence irons out his contradictory attitudes toward the class barriers that Louisa and Alfred challenge. In fact, Lawrence tends eventually to dismiss class as the central concern, focusing instead on conflicts more deeply embedded in his characters' psyches. For example, Alfred's debilitating ties to his mother become especially clear. Further, by the last version Lawrence is keenly interested in finding the language to express the centrality of sensual experience to human salvation. In looking at that language, Cushman finally finds it so abstract and theoretical as occasionally to mar the work. Kalnins, by contrast, judges Lawrence's language, especially as it expresses Louisa's unverbalizable awakening to the beauty of Alfred, as highly successful, a true linguistic breakthrough. I must agree with Kalnins. "Odour of Chrysanthemums" does betray the shift in diction and awkward jump into metaphysic that Cushman regrets here. But "Daughters of the Vicar" has a different history of revision from "Odour of Chrysanthemums." Lawrence altered "Two Marriages" throughout as he gradually reformed it into a more visionary, less realistic piece of fiction. Hinted at in "Two Marriages," the final version of "Daughters of the Vicar" bears the promise of a new mode of short story in English. I will return to this issue below. Rather than rehearse the discussions of Cushman and Kalnins, let me turn to basic issues of craft and then to a major thematic motif in the tale, the Sleeping Beauty motif.

In both versions, the story is constructed on a clear narrative principle, comparison and contrast. Poised in opposition to each other are a series of antinomies: the daughters of the vicar, Mary and Louisa Lindley; Edward Massy and Alfred Durant; the households of the Lindleys and the Durants; the middle and working classes; the impulse toward self-sacrifice and the impulse toward love and self-fulfillment. Working in concert are the cluster of characters and attitudes represented by the former terms set against those represented by the latter. Like *Women in Love* in miniature, "Two Marriages"/"Daughters of the Vicar" traces the courtship and marriage of the two very different sisters: Mary weds the Reverend Mr. Massy and marches determinedly toward perdition; Louisa marries Alfred and flies toward salvation. The central irony is that the doomed sister follows the narrow path of textbook Christianity while the saved sister scorns the letter to honor the spirit. Even in the early version, by virtue of these sustained contrasts and comparisons, Lawrence at once fulfills the expectations of editors hungry for glimpses of "real life," hungry for "love stories" that admit of bitterness and failure, while he also introduces his own distinctive note of sensual, sexual celebration, of resurrection and vitality. As a result, he avoids both the unrelieved grimness of the typical new love story and the sentimentality of traditional love stories, of his own "Prelude" for example.

"Two Marriages" however is a case study in narrative clumsiness. The first information one receives is that Miss Louisa, daughter of the vicar, hates her brother-in-law Mr. Massy. The narrator then steps back in time and delivers background information on the vicar's arrival in Aldecar. A scene follows, as the vicar goes to visit the Durants. Through it, Lawrence is establishing the conflicting values of the two families and acquainting us with the characters of Mrs. Durant and her son Alfred, the latter of whom remains offstage. We then return to the vicar's family and have more paragraphs of exposition related to the Lindley family fortunes. Soon we are back in the Durant house. This shuffling back and forth in time and space not only has little rationale, but leads to Lawrence's throwing away scenes. For example, Lawrence constructs a scene between Mary Lindley, Mr. Massy, and the three Durants, that is, Alfred and his parents. Among other things, the scene gets Alfred onstage and shows us the difference between Mr. Massy and Alfred. But Louisa is not present to record or respond. Instead, Alfred's tenderness and energy are conveyed to us by Mary, who can do little with the information. If one aspect of writing short fiction is thrift, Lawrence is being profligate here. In his revisions he will bring Louisa into the scene.

It is not until midway through the first version that Lawrence finds the thread that will allow him to draw all of these lives together into an orderly, rhythmic pattern of narrative and drama. He maintains the thread well throughout the scenes showing Louisa nursing Mrs. Durant and falling in love with Alfred. But, at the story's conclusion, he once again lapses into his tendency to wrap up his early stories with a neat and contradictory denouement. Here the very horror of Mr. Massy's character—his lack of development, his resemblance to an infant, a fetus—is repeated in Alfred, though obviously in positive terms. Alfred is a child, Louisa a mother; with a tone of sentimentality and condescension, Lawrence undercuts the break into vitality promised throughout the tale. Further, the closing contradicts the story's earlier critique of class prejudice, as it repeats that prejudice in Louisa's attitude toward the working class. Finally in its form—a tidy, old-fashioned glimpse into the sunny futures of the main characters—it denies the complexity of love and experience caught, for moments, in earlier scenes.

One recognizes that Lawrence, for the first time, is trying here to see how family experience meshes with sexual awakening and adult love; the relationships between Alfred and his mother, between the Lindley parents and daughters, are central to the work. But the intricacies of those relationships are neither developed nor clear. Why Lawrence had so much trouble constructing the story is subject for speculation, but it may owe partly to his attempt to trace two separate movements here, one toward death, one toward life, and partly to his having broken out of his love triangle structure. When Cushman says that "Two Marriages" is Lawrence's first fiction to follow the two sisters motif, he is also saying that it is the first to follow George Eliot's scheme of two contrasting couples, for each sister implies a suitor. With the possible alliances, choices, and conflicts having multiplied significantly, Lawrence is groping—but, again, toward a new mode of short story.

Late in her life, Frieda complained, perhaps half in jest, that Lawrence's solid talents as a craftsman were appreciated too little.[42] The image of him as untutored genius was all too common. One point of reviewing the technical problems of "Two Marriages" is to emphasize how great a role craft plays in any fiction, but especially in the taut form of the short story. Turning to "Daughters of the Vicar," one sees that Lawrence has solved virtually every difficulty mentioned above. The opening is direct, we meet characters precisely when their appearance will further the story, all scenes and dialogue reveal character in the most economical way. The relationship between family ties and sexual commitment is richly established and, finally, the closing—tentative, open, a mixture of hope and fear—perfectly caps all that has come before.[43] The joy Alfred and Louisa experience has been earned and, in spite of the fact that the couple will leave classbound England for Canada, their joy promises to be tested by the contingencies of normal experience.

In brief, on this level, the craft is amply apparent. But another issue related to technique raises a different question, one that leads us beyond Lawrence's competence to his eventual restlessness with realistic fiction. Ford and his colleagues had asked for short fiction that reflected the normal contingencies of living. How to organize those contingencies into art was the challenge. I have spoken of the strategies adopted by Lawrence and his contemporaries of constructing scenes that do many things at once, developing a pattern of imagery that suggests complexity and creates an impression of unity, and getting rid of the voice of the story-teller and relying on a series of discreet "shots" that imply the tale's argument or theme. With "Daughters of the Vicar" Lawrence does not forego these strategies; all are present. But he does develop a traditional strategy more obviously than is usual in realistic fiction, that of comparison and contrast. "Daughters of the Vicar" is far from pure fable, exemplum, or parable. But its "delight in design" also distinguishes it from the mode of straight realism.[44] Chekov, for example, would not give us a story so obviously patterned.

It is important to realize that Lawrence's first major reconceptualization of "Two Marriages" occurred during the summer just after he had written the extraordinary "Prussian Officer," a highly wrought visionary tale. In looking at that tale, I will discuss the new kinds of conventions it develops, but here let me simply note that the patterning in "Daughters of the Vicar" is related to those innovations and is an important factor in making the metaphysical language in this tale work. A designing author has made his presence felt from the tale's first words. When his language soars, using diction and rhythms the characters would not, one feels no break in narrative assumptions.

To turn to the Sleeping Beauty motif as it developed from "Two Marriages" to "Daughters of the Vicar" is to see how inevitably related the issues of craft and vision are. "Two Marriages," like "Daughters of the Vicar," gives us Mary, a proud, handsome young woman who towers body and mind over her pathetic mate. Unintentionally, "Two Marriages" gives a similar portrayal of Louisa. She is glad of Alfred, but glad as a mother may be in a dutiful son. Alfred is not meant to be pathetic; in both the 1911 and 1913 versions Lawrence inserts counternotes. But Louisa's superiority is clear. In revising the story in 1914, Lawrence does not undermine Louisa, who is still more active and insightful than Alfred, but he does rid Alfred of pathos and does alter the mother/son tone to their relationship. In a superb proposal scene, Louisa shows herself to be a true sister of Nell Wycherley in "A Prelude." She proposes to Alfred not once but time and again, insisting that they move beyond the shyness and fear of class that separate them. Her pain and embarrassment are evident; and at the same time the story's approbation of her victory is unequivocal. What we have here, as we had briefly in "A Prelude" and will have extensively in the fictions to come, is a sleeping prince, awakened by a courageous princess. Without backsliding or ambivalence, the Sleeping Beauty myth has been transformed.

The transformation has far-reaching consequences, for it releases Lawrence from the idea that a powerful female must be cast in the role of mother. With respect to this story, the motif gives the tale the direction and momentum it had lacked. All material now coheres around Louisa's quest. Alfred's Oedipal paralysis, so powerfully captured in the later versions, becomes, for example, one of the thorny bushes Louisa must cut through. The motif also gives Lawrence precisely the vehicle he needs to plumb the depth of his characters' beings, for Louisa, like so many female characters in Lawrence's fiction, is blessed with visionary powers. Through her and his implied narrator, Lawrence can deliver the insights he wanted to make, insights into what characters and human beings are, as sparks of life on this earth, beyond personal identity, individual intellect, and emotion. Thus, as rescuing princess, but not as mother, Louisa can recognize and celebrate Alfred's sexual richness and thwarted vitality. She can draw the connection between the miracle of his secret aliveness and the secret aliveness of the winter apple trees and bare current bushes that surround the Durant cottage. As she sees, this is a house, a man, shut up tight in death and winter but waiting for spring. Perhaps all of the advantages coalesce into this: developing this variation on the Sleeping Beauty motif significantly aids Lawrence in telling the love stories to come with the tension and freshness of vision so necessary to genuine art.

Thus far I have been tracing Lawrence's progress from his earliest Croydon story, which concentrates closely on familial relationships, through the stories that focus on frustrated young love, culminating in the one story to draw the two interests together,

"Two Marriages"/"Daughters of the Vicar." If one keeps the 1909–1911 material in mind, ignoring the 1914 revisions, one sees the young Lawrence responding to the *English Review*'s tone and support of his work, while keeping other irons in the fire of his imagination. At this time, a major part of Lawrence's appeal was his ability to create stories about a group of English people little known to readers in London, and to create those stories with art, sensitivity, and a lack of sentimentality. Judging from "Odour of Chrysanthemums," he grasped the techniques of realism all at once, though he was not able to exploit them consistently. As noted above, until he writes "The Old Adam" and "The Witch à la Mode," each of the Croydon tales and the revision of "Legend" show a blur, a major or minor lapse in coherence. Lawrence's attitude toward his characters—so closely related to himself and his circle of friends and lovers—had not been fully worked out. As the next chapter demonstrates, the ease and confidence of "The Old Adam" will carry Lawrence forward into the four strike tales written in early 1912. With the exception of "Strike Pay," these tales give us a master of the art of realistic short fiction.

However, even in the Croydon work, Lawrence's interest in modes of story-telling that challenge the assumptions of realism is evident. "The Witch à la Mode" shows Lawrence exploring different kinds of language. What speech brings true insight? The answer is not the language of pure, referential realism. In "Two Marriages," one sees Lawrence awkwardly striking out in another direction, a direction that, two years later will bring him to visionary fiction and eventually to fable and satire.

Master of the Art

3

A little less than a year after his mother's death, Lawrence himself collapsed and nearly died. Sick for a month with a severe case of pneumonia, he was nursed by his sister, Ada. By the middle of December 1911, he could sit up; by the end of the month he could walk. Heeding his doctor's warning against continuing to teach, he asked his headmaster for an extended sick leave. On January 6, 1912, he left Croydon for a boarding house in Bournemouth. There he made several important decisions. He would not marry Louie Burrows, not return to teaching, not stay in England. He would ask an uncle for help procuring a *Lektorstelle*—or lectureship—in a German university. On February 3, he returned to Eastwood where he stayed until leaving for Germany on May 3.

As readers familiar with Lawrence's biography know, he did not leave England alone. Frieda von Richthofen Weekley, the wife of one of Lawrence's professors at the University of Nottingham, went with him. They had met at the Weekleys' a month before. Through April, they saw each other often. As Frieda's father was going to celebrate his fiftieth anniversary in the German army in May, and as she was already intending to go, she and Lawrence planned to leave together. They counted on spending a week together at the very least.[1] In many ways, Lawrence's meeting Frieda and falling in love with her came as a grand finale to the severing of ties he had begun in January. When he met her, he was psychologically and practically ready to throw over his former life. That he and she were flying *to* something—a marriage and an existence outside England—became clear to both of them as their week abroad together grew into a year, then two. Talk of a German *Lektorstelle* disappeared as Lawrence settled into his life's work as a writer.

In introducing the Croydon stories, I suggested that the distance Lawrence put between himself and Eastwood helped him to write candidly about that country and its people for the first time. A similar situation pertains through the early months of 1912. Sitting in Eastwood, poised for flight, Lawrence writes a series of short pieces about his home country that are admirable in their balance, objectivity, and realistic detail. These are the strike tales of February 1912: "The Miner at Home," "Her Turn," "A Sick Collier," and "Strike Pay." Once he leaves England and begins to travel through geographical and emotional territory utterly new to him, an altogether different situation develops; but it is a situation that results in a temporary continuation of his work in realistic short fiction. In three of the four stories he wrote during his first summer with Frieda—"Love Among the Haystacks" (rewritten that summer), "Delilah and Mr. Bircumshaw," and "The Christening"—one watches him holding on to familiar themes, characters, settings, and techniques. Forays into the new land do occur, but they are brief and tentative. Only "Once," the fourth tale, switches from the familiar English locale and cast to a continental setting and couple. Yet, while it begins to explore issues crucial to the fiction of 1913, issues that will shatter the grace and ease of Lawrence's performances in the art of realistic short fiction and move him into something new, it too remains realistic in mode. For now, in 1912, the vision and the craft of realism hold, allowing Lawrence to turn out a masterful series of sketches and short stories, valuable in themselves and in their capacity to keep indicating the way to and beyond *Sons and Lovers,* which was revised for the last time in the fall of 1912.

"Strike Pay" aside, the tales Lawrence wrote from Eastwood in February and March convey an author who knows his material in all its nuances, has thoroughly mastered a form for conveying it, and has an audience waiting to receive it. Published in the *Nation*, *New Statesman*, and *Saturday Westminster Gazette*, they tend to be sketches rather than fully developed short stories; in fact, they are the first sketches Lawrence had tried. In all but "A Sick Collier," which does develop into a short story, the characters in these strike sketches are caught, for a brief moment, enacting the gestures and delivering the lines that capture the essence of their existence. Revealed by the drama, they are not changed by it. As Schorer explains, the moment of illumination in a sketch dawns for the reader alone.[2]

"The Miner at Home" opens early in the evening in a collier's home.[3] Sitting in his pit dirt, smoking "a solemn pipe," Bower has said little through dinner. His wife Gertie is busy with the three children and beginning to grow impatient with Bower's inertia. She would like to finish one more of her evening chores, his wash-up. He consents, and she prepares the pancheon. At last Bower rises, strips to the waist, and kneels at the hearth to wash. He scrubs his head and arms; balancing the baby on one arm, Gertie scrubs and begins to dry his back, ""Canna ter put the' childt down an' use both hands?'" says her husband. Yes, she replies, but it's bound to "'screet.'" She does put the child down, it does begin to cry, and she rubs Bower's back. The moment she is through Bower says, "'Shut that childt up'" (*Phoenix*, 776).

The detailed action is a well-designed prelude to the dialogue that follows. Bower shows her a slip of paper given to him by his union. It asks him to go out on strike in two weeks. Gertie is against the idea and gives her reasons. Bower counters with a prostrike argument. She rocks herself with vexation and weariness as he refuses to take the baby and goes out to the pub.

Dealing with material central to *Sons and Lovers*, "The Miner at Home" is a symmetrical, two-act sketch about labor, work, and power. What the first half of the tale dramatizes, the second half analyzes. Lawrence's structure illustrates the idea that the issues involved in the strike are acted out in other work places as well, including private homes. He is conveying a feminist position discussed and dramatized by Gissing and Schreiner, both of whom Lawrence had read and recommended to Louie Burrows.[4] On one level, Gertie is to her husband as he is to his boss. As she says, she waits on him hand and foot, and her reward is a lousy thirty shillings a week and a man who thinks he is the best in the almighty world. When he says, "'Shut thy mouth, woman. If every man worked as hard as I do . . . ,'" she interrupts, "'He wouldn't ha'e as much to do as me . . .'" (*Phoenix*, 779). But that simple equation does not encompass the reality. This is fiction not manifesto, and, as such, it can afford to include the contradictions of human experience.

Throughout the tale Lawrence urges us to see the Bowers' marriage and, by implication, the situation of the miners in terms that include but are not limited by labor-management vocabulary. For example, Bower waits on Gertie just as she waits on him. A hard worker, "a good husband," an "amiable" man, Bower is thinking about the strike as he sits after dinner covered with coal dust. He has not noticed that Gertie is tired. As he washes, he even has the kind of beauty Connie Chatterley will see in Mellors: "The red firelight shone on his cap of white soap, and on the muscles of his back, on the strange working of his red and white muscular arms, that flashed up and down like individual creatures" (*Phoenix*, 776). This miner is a far cry from the selfish, drunken, hymn-singing louts Gertrude Morel despises through the contemporary draft (and often enough in the final version) of *Sons and Lovers*. Bower is a sympathetic figure; within the terms of the tale, he is no simple, worthless, boss man. He does have economic power over Gertie, but obviously she has power over him — including economic power — which the tale presents as effective and legitimate. By the end of their argument, for example, it looks as though she has won; he stomps out of the house but apparently will not go on strike this time. Lawrence's suffragist friends as well as his own reading and experience at home would have shown him the ways in which Gertie *is* to her husband as he is to his boss. But the nature of fiction and his own powers of observation urge him to show as well the ways in which the equation fails to include domestic habit, affection, humor, and, in this case, Gertie's powers of argument.

In this tale, as in the three to follow, the narrator is wellnigh transparent. He focuses his camera on all participants, giving equal time and equally advantageous shots to each. Here, Bower is tired, so is Gertie. There are reasons to strike, reasons not to. The camera angle is judicious, the editing sure, the dialogues swift and full of color. Every line works to set before us this couple on this evening in this place.

"Her Turn" gives us another middle-aged colliery couple, though here plot competes with character in engaging the reader's interest.[5] A few years older than Bower, Radford is a good-hearted, prosperous miner. Healthy and hard working, he is fond of women and analyzes what he thinks of things by writing his ideas down in verse. His second wife is a sleek "dumpling," sly, satirical, and much in love with him. The sketch's center rests on her maneuver to get Radford to share his strike pay with her. On one level, it is a "trick" tale, but in its lack of character development it remains essentially a sketch.

In the previous strike, Radford had refused to share his strike pay, had spent it on himself and expected his wife to use her household savings to keep things going. For the current strike, he apparently has the same plan in mind. She has other ideas. The day after Radford reveals his intention, she goes to town and buys, from her savings, linoleum, a new wringer, a set of breakfast dishes, and a spring mattress. All are paid for, all are things they need, nothing is simply for her. Radford is struck dumb. She is now as poor as he. As in the other strike sketches, there is fine domestic comedy here. The sketch closes on the following week with him handing over his half sovereign.

Typical of these sketches, our glimpse into these people's lives is brief but rich in insight and detail. One senses in the young, convalescing Lawrence a delight in his ability to recreate for his new London readers a world so unfamiliar to them, so familiar to him. There is no large structure such as that in *Sons and Lovers* to wrestle with, no central character who needs defining or justifying. Because we have no Paul or Gertrude Morel, Lawrence can show us a miner who may often visit a pub and be a bit tight with his money, but who is also expansive and thoughtful. The few moments of humor that Mr. and Mrs. Morel enjoy become the dominant note here. Also, Lawrence's early tendency to see the mining community as having the same natural beauty as the farming community shows up in this tale as Radford putters in his garden among the daffodils, and finds and strokes a tortoise.

"Her Turn," like the other strike sketches, avoids sentimentality by the specificity of its details and by the complexity of the human relationships it manages to convey. Here, Radford's wife has crossed him. He has a moment of blind anger, feels like striking her, but walks out of the house. The wife, in turn, first feels smug about her trickery, then heavy of heart. Ultimately, however, she is satisfied. No particular judgment is rendered on their relationship or her act as Lawrence communicates their shifts of feeling with a wide scope of tolerance.

The third sketch in this cluster is longer but less sure in tone. "Strike Pay" is the first of the group to move us outside a colliery home as we follow a group of miners on a jaunt to Nottingham.[6] As in "Her Turn," Lawrence opens with a description of the Eastwood environs and, interestingly, gives us that description in present tense. The implication is that if his readers will drive up from London they will meet these people, see these places. Once the tale proper begins, Lawrence drops the tone of travel essay and moves into a traditional fictional past tense.[7] But the mood the present tense created reverberates through the rest of the tale.

The main scenes of "Strike Pay" parallel incidents in *Sons and Lovers*. The tale opens, for example, with a crowd of men receiving their strike money. In the novel, Paul Morel suffers as he stands in the crowded chapel waiting to pick up his father's wages. In the tale, the reader identifies with no one in particular and simply enjoys the kibitzing and elbowing that goes on as the miners push up to get paid by the union agent. The second scene also anticipates an incident from *Sons and Lovers*. Like Mr. Morel and his pals, Ephraim and his comrades head over the hills to Nottingham, drinking as they go, to watch a football match. They come upon a herd of pit ponies standing in the sunshine, a bit inert, unused to freedom. The ponies set the tone for Ephraim's day. He rides one, rolls off, loses his half sovereign. Though he keeps up with his friends, the day is spoiled. In the parallel scene from *Sons and Lovers*, Morel falls asleep on the damp ground, also loses his money, and returns home late in the foulest of humors. That evening he and Mrs. Morel have one of their bitterest fights.

In the novel, Lawrence does a better job capturing the ashy taste of spent frolic. In "Strike Pay," Ephraim's low spirits are credible and well dramatized until he leaves the football ground. Suddenly he comes upon a scene that feels awkwardly lifted from *Jude the Obscure* or *Tess of the D'Urbervilles*. A man is senselessly killed as he falls beneath his horse into a slough of mud. The tone Lawrence uses to convey the accident and Ephraim's response is flat; the tone on either side of the scene is bantering. The overall

flat; the tone on either side of the scene is bantering. The overall result is an unintegrated moment, leading nowhere.

Once Ephraim returns home, the parallels to *Sons and Lovers* reappear, though again with a difference. Like Morel, Ephraim fights a domestic battle, only here it is not a wronged wife who confronts him; it is a cold-eyed, domineering mother-in-law. The difference is significant, providing us with a reason to sympathize with Ephraim and, once again, evidence of the variety of ways Lawrence could interpret a scene. The battle never goes beyond shouting, but Ephraim fights back and wins. The mother-in-law sails out to her other daughters, leaving Ephraim alone with his young wife. She gives him tea, not because "she was really meek. But—he was her man, not her mother's" (CSS, 53). Tale turns to novel, offering a different view of things. Ephraim is no hero, no villain; his wife is neither martyr nor victor. Whereas in *Sons and Lovers* the same incidents protest the unfair lot of Mrs. Morel and the rationale for Paul's hatred of his father, in "Strike Pay" the actions and conflicts argue little or nothing. Instead, they present what Ford claimed English readers "enormously wanted": "authentic projections of that type of life which had hitherto gone unvoiced."[8]

"A Sick Collier," the last of the quartet, is the only one of this group we can fairly call a short story rather than sketch.[9] The main characters are newlyweds: Lucy is the fair, quiet, beautiful bride of Willy, a short, dark, warmly colored collier. Willy has some of the simplicity and lack of intelligence Lawrence gave the rivals in his Croydon stories, but here no intellectual enters, and Lucy is engaging and desirous. The tale's first developed scene shows Willy and Lucy sitting down to their first dinner at home together. Lucy is amazed at seeing Willy in his pit dirt. As do so many of the miners in these tales, he rises after dinner and washes himself with intent pleasure before the fire. He is "intensely himself," like a vigorous animal (CSS, 268). Lucy has some of Louisa's response in "Daughters of the Vicar." She is startled, afraid, even slightly sick at this open nakedness. But the implication is that she is also pleasurably intrigued. Lawrence briefly summarizes the next few years. Through general statements and several fine, brief glances at their daily routine, Lawrence makes clear Willy's sense of peace and pleasure in this marriage.

The second developed scene interrupts the genial mood of

the tale as Lawrence brings Willy home from the pit in great pain from an accident in the mine. He lies in bed for six weeks. The third scene is located at his window and in his bedroom where he remains laid up. The miners are out on strike; this afternoon they gather together in the street below to walk to Nottingham to see a match. Sitting in a chair by the window, scarcely able to walk, Willy cannot bear it. He shouts down, "'I'm goin'.'" When Lucy comes up to calm him, he turns on her. He tries to kill her, a neighbor comes running, and the half-crazed young husband collapses into a chair weeping. Thin and weary, Lucy begs the neighbor not to talk about Willy's state for fear the company will stop his compensation.

At first glance, Lawrence seems to have modelled "A Sick Collier" after the grim tales of domesticity that characterized the genre of realistic short fiction on the Continent and in England in the avant garde periodicals of the 1890s. But when one sets it alongside those tales, one sees Lawrence's different approach. The typical *Yellow Book* tale of this mode develops through an accumulation of dark detail, all done in the same tone. By contrast, our sense of tragedy in "A Sick Collier" comes from the familiar but effective tension between initial happiness and subsequent grief. The first third of the story gives readers very much what Crackanthorpe had asked for, a fine and vital vision of joy. The power of the remainder of the tale rests on the sense of loss prepared for by the opening.

The particular kind of loss Lawrence traces here raises a further point about his thinking at this time. Accidents do not happen in Lawrence's middle and late fiction. There, acts are based on choice, rewards are fitting. By contrast, in "A Sick Collier," there is no appropriateness to Willy's mishap and eventual madness, no fitting cause—neither personal nor cultural—for Lucy's misery. And yet the story has none of the fatalism that marks authors like Hardy or Zola: one feels no dour god, Hap, or labor boss lying in wait for Willy and Lucy. The lack of a sense of doom comes, I believe, from Lawrence's decision to keep a tight focus on the individual characters. Like Chekov in tales such as "Heartache" or "Vierochka," Lawrence is capturing the sights, sounds, emotions of particular people in particular places. Willy's accident is a tragedy for him and Lucy; but in this tale, that tragedy does not point to the mining industry, the twentieth century, or any habit of thought or emotion in Willy or Lucy. A year and a half later, in a tale such as "The Prussian Officer," the central incident will carry large cultural implications.

The strike sketches are the last stories Lawrence would write from Eastwood. And yet they are not the last tales he would write about Eastwood and its surrounding countryside. Lawrence's move to Germany and then Italy with Frieda was exciting, frightening, and painful for them both. As my next chapter indicates, Lawrence felt himself out on the sill of the great unknown. But through his first months with Frieda, he holds at bay the immense changes that are occurring in his life. "Delilah and Mr. Bircumshaw" and "The Christening" read as though they might have come across the channel with Lawrence in his satchel. They did not, but "Love among the Haystacks" did. In the same vein as the strike tales, the first two continue sensitively to dramatize the lives of the English working class from a perspective deeply embedded in that class and community. The third returns to the rich farmland and its inhabitants which Lawrence had written about in *The White Peacock*, and, briefly, in "Second Best" and "The Soiled Rose"/"The Shades of Spring." In all three, Lawrence works familiar territory, yet each tale also carries hints of his present life and the issues it had suddenly raised. In "Love among the Haystacks," Lawrence dramatizes for the first time his belief in the importance of touch—physical communion—as a primary basis for sexual relationship. "Delilah and Mr. Bircumshaw" glances at issues of authority and power; "The Christening" explores the same themes, relative to fatherhood, but ends up with an unsolved contradiction. And lightly, comically, "Once," the fourth tale, moves us toward the most important issue in Lawrence's middle fiction: the ways in which loss of self can lead either to enrichment of self or to the devastation of identity.

Lawrence speaks of "Love among the Haystacks" as early as January 7, 1912. Sagar suggests November of the preceding year as a likely date of composition. No manuscripts of that version exist, but David Garnett recalled Lawrence working on the tale during Garnett's visit to Frieda and Lawrence in Germany during their first summer.[10] Thus the version we have stands intriguingly poised between Lawrence's Croydon work from 1911 and the new directions his thinking had begun to take in 1912. Read in the context of the Croydon tales, one notes an interesting conversation going on between "Love among the Haystacks," "Two Marriages" (the 1911 version of "Daughters of the Vicar"), and "The

Old Adam." "Two Marriages" develops a quartet of relationships as it traces the differing fates of two sisters. "Love among the Haystacks" follows the same pattern through the lives of two brothers. As in "Two Marriages," point of view is given to the quiet, stubborn sibling, who watches, evaluates, and eventually wins for himself or herself an authentic love. This love is partly defined by contrast with the opposing sibling's choice. In each case, the successful match involves a crossing of class barriers, with the respective heroine and hero reaching "down" for love and vitality. Further, in each case, Lawrence has wrought changes on the Sleeping Beauty myth—giving us active heroines or sleeping princes— while he breaks with realism's proscription against stories that end with joy and success. At the same time, "Love among the Haystacks" also explores a side to the successful young lover that Lawrence had introduced in "The Old Adam." That side seeks to avoid adult, heterosexual commitment and finds security in the safe territory of homosexual friendship.[11] In "The Old Adam," Severn never ventures out of that safe land; in "Love among the Haystacks," Geoffrey outgrows the bond.

Each of these elements echoes interests and themes from Croydon; but if one reads "Love among the Haystacks" in the different context of the 1912 tales and the fiction they point toward, one discerns the tale's development beyond the Croydon stories. We have a glimpse of the first character in Lawrence's fiction to be modeled after Frieda, here a lively, provocative German governess; with her Lawrence introduces the possibility that shallow sensuality may be as real a barrier to warm-hearted loving as self-consciousness and repression are. This is a note he will develop further in "Once." In addition, the language in the tale is richer and its rhythms more pronounced than in the Croydon work. And most significant, the hero's major scenes show Lawrence developing a powerful vocabulary of images around which to structure the communion rites in the visionary stories he will soon be writing.

More than in the strike sketches, Lawrence chooses to tell "Love among the Haystacks" from one character's point of view. Youth, risk, and love unfold through the eyes and experience of Geoffrey, a young farmer. It is as though Lawrence had decided finally to give the "rival" from the Croydon tales—Smedley or Vickers—a story all to himself. Ambivalence disappears as the man of the land takes the center stage.

The reader first meets Geoffrey and his brother Maurice poised high on a stack of hay they are building with their father and the hired help. Geoffrey is as self-conscious, introverted, and unable to reach out and claim love for himself as any of the intellectual heroes we have encountered thus far. But unlike the Cyrils and Sysons, Geoffrey puts on no superior airs. He is hard working, nonverbal, sensitive. His young brother, by contrast, is confident of himself and his sexuality; he has just stolen from Geoffrey the German governess who is staying at the vicarage next door. The tale has a full plot and setting: we have a near-fatal quarrel between the brothers, a visit by a tramp and his wife, a night of rain and love-making for each brother, and, out of all this, a reversal of power from Maurice to Geoffrey. Setting is composed of brilliant, shimmering hayfields extending beyond hedges, horses, wild flowers, and trees; a vast pattern is created by the heat, sky, and fields.

In some ways, the story is a country idyl, too simple in its resolution. Certainly the appearance of the tramp and his wife and her subsequent return are fortuitous for Geoffrey. Her metamorphosis from a miserable vagabond into a lady, "honest and pretty with a sweet, womanly gravity" is explained but precipitous. The tone here echoes the pat conclusion of the original "Two Marriages." And her murmuring, as she curls up with Geoffrey in the shed, "'You *are* big,'" is a line out of pulp pornography.

But strengths balance the weaknesses. Among them is the language Lawrence develops for the setting. When Maurice goes across the fields at night to bathe in the spring, we have a setting that is detailed and rich in all three dimensions and takes on the shimmer of a fourth. One is reminded of Mrs. Morel's lily scene in *Sons and Lovers* as Maurice dusts himself with pollen and discovers not the wonder *of* himself but the wonder in himself—the wonder of the glistening, moonlit earth around him. Lawrence is no Elizabethan, but at times his pen can create a world fit for Titania or Oberon. Changing his mood greatly, Lawrence creates a variation on this scene several years later, in *Women in Love*, when Birkin casts himself naked into the ferns and pines to be healed by their blessedly nonhuman life. If this setting is excellent, the fact that Maurice goes pollen-decked to an unsuccessful tryst also helps to offset the tale's occasional sentimentality.

As important as setting in counterbalancing the tale's weaknesses are Geoffrey's two major scenes of human contact. Geoffrey lives easily with the earth; Lawrence's prose rhythms in the hay-loading sequence imply a strong, graceful relationship between the young man and the hay he loads. But he finds it difficult to approach another human being. The tale shows him breaking through that reserve twice. Both scenes have the dramatic weight to suggest a genuine "communion" scene.

In the first instance, one finds the same binding confrontation between two men that occurs in "The Old Adam." We are dealing with similar issues. In a moment of intense anger, Geoffrey and Maurice wrestle on top of the high load of hay; Maurice slips off and falls to the ground. Although for a moment it looks as though he has been killed, he has only had the wind knocked out of him. Through the rest of that day, there is a fondness between the two brothers that stems partly from relief that Maurice was not hurt and partly from the open, physical contact they have shared. The sequence of action here traces a pattern Lawrence's characters often follow. First, by accident, characters come into close physical touch with each other; out of that they try to establish a lasting bond. One often sees this in heterosexual relationships—in "Daughters of the Vicar," "The Horse Dealer's Daughter," or "You Touched Me," for example. Masculine relationships follow this same sequence of inadvertent, initial contact followed by lasting engagement, but with a difference. One man approaches another man in anger, they fight, and out of that comes engagement. In *Sons and Lovers*, "The Old Adam," and "Love among the Haystacks" for example, touch precedes camaraderie, though in this early work Lawrence seems unable to imagine the initial touch occurring other than in anger.

In looking at Geoffrey's love for Maurice and at the other early masculine relationships, I should emphasize that all these tales show the resulting friendship as healthy and satisfying. Severn and Mr. Thomas in "The Old Adam," Paul and Baxter in *Sons and Lovers*, Geoffrey and Maurice in "Love among the Haystacks" meet in anger but part in affection and peace. Unembarrassed and easy, the friendships also, as noted above, assume a taboo against homosexuality. Once the assumption is shattered and the tale admits the possibility of homosexual desires—as in "The Prussian Officer," *Women in Love*, *Aaron's Rod*—easy affection is destroyed. The relationship becomes tortured, unrequited, even tragic.

Geoffrey's second encounter is distinctly heterosexual and in it one sees a model for future tales as well as for the distant *Lady*

Chatterley's Lover. One of the most disturbing aspects of Lawrence's portrayal of Paul Morel's sexuality is his refusal or inability
to show Paul simply affectionate with Clara or Miriam or to write
a love scene that is not clogged with metaphors. Lawrence can
show Paul unaffectedly kissing his mother on the forehead or
brushing her hair back from her face, but he can never show Paul
reaching out so unselfconsciously to his lovers. With Miriam,
Paul is usually paralyzed with tension. With Clara, he apparently
makes fine love, but Lawrence describes it in traditional metaphors. There are swirling stars, tongues of flame, rivers surging. By
contrast, Lawrence uses direct diction to describe a direct act in
"Love among the Haystacks." Geoffrey reaches out and claims
Lydia with much the same open tenderness as Paul touches his
mother, as Pervin claims Bertie in "The Blind Man," or as Mellors
and Connie claim each other in *Lady Chatterley's Lover.* It is this
tenderness that is apparently missing in the encounter between
Maurice and the governess. Without self-consciousness, Geoffrey
grasps Lydia's cold, bare feet and rubs warmth into them. He
chafes them, breathes on the balls of her toes, clasps his large
hands over her instep. Out of his gesture comes their love-making
and subsequent bond. The importance of touch here prophesies
Lawrence's later presentations of physical communion as the first
step toward relationship. Further, "Love among the Haystacks"
works outside the Sleeping Beauty motif in that the lives of both
Geoffrey and Lydia have lacked direction. Now their future has a
quick and living basis. The drifting sleepwalkers have awakened
each other.

"Love among the Haystacks" and "Two Marriages"/"Daughters of the Vicar" are both long stories, almost novelettes. For that
reason and undoubtedly others—the narrative awkwardness of
"Two Marriages" and the sexual license of "Love among the Haystacks," for example—Lawrence found no magazine willing to
take either tale. His response in 1912 was similar to earlier responses. He complemented the long works with a series of much
shorter pieces, sending them off to Edward Garnett in hopes that
Garnett could find a publisher. "Delilah and Mr. Bircumshaw,"
"The Christening," and "Once" are three such short stories. It is
also important to recognize that Lawrence invested the three with
a "moral tone" unlikely to "agree with [his] countrymen", as he
put it (CL, 133). And, in fact, of these three only "The Christening" was published during his lifetime. This situation is typical of

Lawrence's work in short fiction. He may have written his stories partly to keep the pot boiling, but, in nearly every instance, the actual result—the tale itself—is no pot boiler, no easy fare for a magazine reader's entertainment. In contrast to the pat, formulaic tale, as common in short fiction then as now, Lawrence's stories consistently serve as vehicles for exploration, pushing his own thinking and English short fiction beyond formula. This is true even of a tale as clearly categorized as "Delilah and Mr. Bircumshaw."

A realistic story of domestic frustration and disappointment, "Delilah and Mr. Bircumshaw" harkens back in tone and technique to many of Lawrence's Croydon tales and to the realistic short fiction upon which they are modeled.[12] The key action of the story is the shearing of the hero, a sullen, bullying, young bank clerk named Harry Bircumshaw. Bircumshaw is a physically powerful, energetic man who is chained to an office job that turns his unspent energy sour.[13] He sulks, beats his wife and baby, and is continually torn between self-hatred and smarting pride. Gradually the wife comes to realize what a sorry husband she has landed.

To get at the heart of this tale and the ways it expertly performs the conventions of realism while it simultaneously hints at new directions, comparison with Joyce's "Counterparts" may be useful. In "Counterparts," Joyce also focuses on the miserable existence of a pathetic, vicious, powerful man, a similar victim of a society less in need of brawn than of the skills of clerks. Here, in shot after shot, Joyce gradually builds up the character and world of his antihero. The art is very much that of the highly skilled photographer. In Lawrence, we find photography every bit as apt. One of the finest scenes in all realistic short fiction comes at the end of this tale. Harry Bircumshaw has stomped upstairs in a fit of childish temper. Slowly tidying up downstairs, mulling over their recent quarrel, his wife makes him four large sandwiches and carries them up to him. He lies in bed feigning sleep. She sets the sandwiches and candle down on the floor beside him, blows out the light, and lies down on her side of the bed. Minutes pass. Once he assumes she is asleep, he relights the candle and wolfs down the sandwiches. Turned toward him in the dark, watching the movement of his powerful back, shoulders, arms, and jaw outlined in the flickering light, Mrs. Bircumshaw continues to think about him with a mixture of emotions—amusement, a moment of sexual desire, and finally weariness and disgust. It is an intimate moment and excellent summary image of this couple, this deteriorating marriage. So far, in these two tales Joyce and Lawrence may be said to be working in similar modes.

However, even in his realistic tales, even in a story as clearly focused on paralysis and defeat as "Delilah and Mr. Bircumshaw," Lawrence's work has an altogether different feel from that of Joyce's. Joyce's success in "Counterparts" rests with his ability to create an epiphany, to capture the quidditas—the whatness—of his scrivener's life and world. As far as possible, Joyce does that capturing through image, allusion, and dramatization. As Spilka has commented, there is a static quality to Joyce's epiphanies, his caught identities, in *Dubliners.*[14] Lawrence's intentions are more mixed and the result is more dynamic. He seeks to capture the essence of Bircumshaw's life, give us his wife's response, and to comment, albeit briefly, upon the social issues raised. As noted above, because the mode of realism allowed him little room for that commentary, in previous stories Lawrence often entered at the end, offering an unintegrated soliloquy or occasionally a bald sermon. Here, in "Delilah and Mr. Bircumshaw," he weaves a smooth narrative pattern of image, scene, and commentary. Mrs. Bircumshaw states the dreary facts; the tale's imagery brings them alive; and the omniscient narrator suggests causes and circumstances.

The blend is obviously not new to realistic short fiction, but in this tale one sees Lawrence growing more open and skilled in his commentary. That is new and a signal step toward visionary fiction for Lawrence. Further, it is the specific message of the commentary that reveals Lawrence's movement beyond one of the ideas in *Sons and Lovers* into an important aspect of *The Rainbow.* Delicate as this small tale is, the issue of male dominance and tyranny is central to "Delilah and Mr. Bircumshaw." In *Sons and Lovers,* Lawrence dramatizes Mr. Morel's occasional violence and tyranny but fails to dig very deeply into its causes. The focus is on the suffering of Mrs. Morel. By contrast, in *The Rainbow,* the character of Will Brangwen is a complex study of a would-be tyrant, fighting fiercely partly because he is fighting from a position of weakness. In several moving passages, he stands in contrast to Tom, his father-in-law, whose power lies very much in capacity. Harry Bircumshaw reads likes a pencil sketch for Will's portrait.

Further, both portraits are as interesting for what they skip over lightly as for what they concentrate on. Both draw a man who is ineffectual in the world and at home. Both indicate that the more each man realizes this bitter fact, the more each confuses "heroism and mastery with brute tyranny" ("Delilah and Mr. Bircumshaw," *Phoenix II*, 90). Another major element in each portrait is the presence and perspective of the wife. It is she, the brighter, more capable and vital, who registers, analyzes, and weighs the loss her husband's character implies. What is being skipped over is a genuine discussion of the idea that if the husband were stronger, he would be a proper master. Lawrence avoids dealing with that assumption—it comes into the tale only briefly in his commentary—because in a sense he is still on his honeymoon, literally and in terms of his thinking about himself and Frieda. The heart-wrenching quarrels to which the complex issue of mastery will lead—about identity, the right role for women, the fate of the Western world—are all to come. Here, in this tale from his first summer with Frieda, he in no way suggests that the wife is castrating the husband, in no way implies that Bircumshaw would do well to take over his household, violently or not, for good or for ill. Those ideas are years away, but the underlying issues they respond to are present, here, in one of the first fictions he wrote from his life with Frieda. It is a new note and an important one.

To turn to "The Christening" is to be impressed again at the conversation Lawrence's tales hold with each other. The story resembles "Delilah and Mr. Bircumshaw" in its realistic mode, English working-class setting, general tone of defeat, and continued tentative exploration of the issue of male dominance, here done in very different terms. Even more clearly than in the Bircumshaw story, in "The Christening" Lawrence also circles back to issues raised in *Sons and Lovers* while he looks ahead to later fiction.[15]

The tale has been read by one critic as "an extended jeer at conventional morality."[16] The jeer is indeed there, but I believe the central movement is less an attack on conventional morality and more an exploration of the relationship between fathers and children. To see the significance of Lawrence's insights into this relationship, we need briefly to review some of the earlier fathers in Lawrence's fiction.

For years Lawrence took the side of his mother in the battle between his parents. It is therefore not surprising to find *The White Peacock*, "Odour of Chrysanthemums," and an early draft of *Sons and Lovers* killing off the father early in the narrative or having him dead from the outset. In each of these fictions, the father is or was a drunk and a source of shame to his family. The "death" of

Walter Morel in Lawrence's final text of *Sons and Lovers* is less obvious but just as real. As Paul passes from childhood to adolescence, Mr. Morel passes out of the novel. The latter half of the novel generally ignores him. When we turn to Mr. Rowbotham, father in "The Christening," we encounter a strikingly different situation.

Like Mr. Morel, Mr. Rowbotham is socially and culturally a step below his children, especially his daughters. On the occasion of the tale, the christening of his youngest daughter's illegitimate baby, he is particularly annoying. There are preparations to be made; he is much in the way. His speech is slavering, his movements are clumsy. The children treat him like a bothersome child. However, in contrast to other early fathers, Mr. Rowbotham's disintegration is not caused by drinking but by a deterioration of motor nerves. Moreover, he fights against his condition. Throughout the tale, Lawrence shows this man to be fully alive. During supper, the collier is seen as an Old Testament patriarch beside whom the thin, otherworldly minister pales. The father celebrates life in a rich, religious strain and has managed to transmit some of his vitality to his children, in spite of their stiff-necked pride. Hilda is sensitive to the natural world and possesses a pent-up energy and dignity that make her something of a queen among the colliers. Emma, the unwed daughter whose child is being christened, also has clearly inherited some part of her father's passionate energy; Lawrence tells us she "hated the child when she looked at it and saw it as a symbol, but when she felt it, her love was like fire in her blood" (CSS, 277).

But the value of their paternal inheritance is limited, for they neither recognize nor understand it. Their sullenness is emphasized in *The Prussian Officer* text of the tale. In the last lines, the father stumbles into the kitchen and roars out a celebration of life, "'The daisies light up the earth, they clap their hands in multitudes, in praise of the morning'" (CSS, 282). The children shrink at the outburst, as silent and judgmental as the oppressive community in which they live. The narrator makes it clear that in dishonoring their father, they reduce themselves.

Running counter to this general appreciation of Mr. Rowbotham, however, is a note of distrust. At times he and the narrator state that he has suffocated his children, that in his very strength he has stunted their growth. If one sorts out the approval from the disapproval, one sees that the tale presents Mr. Row-

botham's vitality as distinctly admirable but takes contradictory attitudes toward his authority, admiring on the one hand, condemning on the other. The various stances show up well in the
christening scene and conclusion.

After the ceremony, in all versions, the father makes a general confession. He feels he has ruined his children. On his knees,
he prays, "'They've grown up twisted, because of me. Who is their
father, Lord, but thee? . . . Lord, if it hadn't been for me, they
might ha' been trees in the sunshine'" (CSS, 281). The omniscient narrator would seem to agree: "They had never lived; his
life, his will had always been upon them" (CSS, 282). Yet the
very form of the father's prayer, grounded in natural imagery and
heavy with rhythm, undercuts his confession. No one in the tale,
with the exception of the narrator, uses language as richly. The
narrator qualifies this confession still further by telling us that this
is "the special language of fatherhood" (CSS, 281). The prayer
and its effect upon Hilda, in particular, indicate that Mr. Rowbotham is an authoritarian but energizing presence in his children's lives. As such, he anticipates Tom Brangwen in *The Rainbow* as well as the wise father in the war tale, "England,
My England."

Nowhere in "The Christening" does Lawrence untangle his
conflicting attitudes toward right and wrong authority, but he has
allowed some of their intricacies to surface. Throughout the war
and postwar fictions, the issue will continue to interest him. Lawrence hated many kinds of authority, but other kinds he romanti-
cally admired. Interestingly, among the kinds he came to hate was
what he termed "maternal dominance"; in later fictions the hold
of a mother over her children is represented as cannibalism.
Among the kinds he grew to admire was something he saw as
quite different, something he called "paternal authority." The refusal of a father to maintain a powerful hold over his children is
often seen as a grave weakness. (Lawrence himself apparently experienced little paternal authority while growing up. Jessie Chambers tells of Mr. Lawrence often being out, rarely having a say in
the running of the home or his children's lives.)[17] Lawrence
never solved the ambivalence, but the seeds are clear in even the
1912 version of "The Christening." We find this mix in the coarse
but vital Mr. Rowbotham: the promise of Lawrence's eventual
sympathy for his own father, his admiration for patriarchal author-

ity, and his corresponding distrust of parental authority as it would eventually locate itself in domineering mothers.

Lawrence's capacity in "The Christening" to raise questions about legitimate authority recalls the issue of point of view. In *The White Peacock* and *Sons and Lovers*, we come to the shameful father by way of the condemning son. In "The Christening," the son's single, antagonistic point of view is dispersed among four nearly grown children. Moreover, in "The Christening," there is no suffering mother. We never encounter the wounded pride of Mrs. Beardsall or Mrs. Morel; we never witness the anxiety and anger of Mrs. Bates. Mrs. Rowbotham's point of view is absent, for in this tale it is she who is conveniently dead. Reading somewhat like a dream, the tale touches on hostilities and admirations of which the young Lawrence seems unaware. Ascribing this openness solely to point of view would oversimplify, but, judging from contemporaneous works, it does seem necessary at this time for Lawrence to rid himself of the point of view of the suffering mother and sensitive son in order to sympathize with a crude and powerful father.

With "Once," the last of the three tales from the summer of 1912, we remain in the mode of realism and find Lawrence turning still another face on the issue of identity and relationship.[18] "Delilah and Mr. Bircumshaw" touched on the links between tyranny and an empty sense of self; "The Christening" explored the ways parental energy and authority can both enrich and stifle the identity of the next generation. In "Once," Lawrence introduces a different idea: the possibility that an intimate relationship may be essential to the establishing of self and at the same time may deeply threaten self. The mood here is light and risqué. In fact, the journal *Smart Set* took "The Christening" but rejected "Once" as "too hot." (CL, 222, 229). In the fall of 1913, the story was considered for a volume of Prussian stories proposed by Austin Harrison, Ford's replacement as editor of the *English Review* (CL, 229). That volume was never realized, but the contents were to be "Once," "Vin Ordinaire"/"The Thorn in the Flesh," "The Prussian Officer," and perhaps "The Mortal Coil."[19] Read in the company of those tales, "Once" shows up for what it is, the first of Lawrence's continental short stories, bolder than the English tales that precede it yet cautious in tone and mood when compared to the other Prussian stories. "Once" treats lightly a theme that the other tales see as a matter of life and death: the need for an individual to discriminate between a creative and reductive loss of selfhood.

The first-person narrator of "Once" is a young, middle-class German who loves the aristocratic Anita. Anita married at eighteen, had two children, grew dissatisfied with her husband, and began to take on lovers. As the narrator sees it, he runs the risk of becoming just one more pleasant experience to her. The sexual innuendoes are clear as she confesses that she has put every man she has encountered into her pocket. Foreshadowing future tales, Lawrence has the narrator contemplate how easy and sensuous it would be to give over responsibility and conflict and let himself slip into her pocket, "'along with her purse and her perfume and the little sweets she loved'" (*Phoenix II*, 45). Preventing him, though, is his genuine love for her. He wants to give her more than pleasure.

Taking place one beautiful morning in a Tyrolese hotel, the tale divides neatly into two parts, a scene and an anecdote. The scene is introduced by the narrator's comment that he would like to be more to Anita than an amusement. There follows, significantly, a highly amusing scene; indeed, it is high-jinx comedy of a kind rare in Lawrence. Anita walks into their bedroom in a transparent chemise, boots, and immense hat. "'How,'" she asks innocently, "'do you like my hat?'" The narrator responds by taking off his dressing gown, donning gloves and his own hat. "'How do you like my hat?'" he says. (*Phoenix II*, 45–46). They laugh, talk, and he asks her how many times before she has played the same trick. She responds with an anecdote of a "'perfect'" encounter, a night she enjoyed years ago with a German officer at a hotel in Dresden. The narrator burns, not simply with jealousy but also with the awareness that what has pleased Anita most in her affairs has been sensation. He finally tells her so. And in that accusation, that true criticism of her, he enacts the refusal he had promised himself; he refuses simply to give her pleasure. The accusation is not meant to be a summation of Anita's character. The narrator continually has recognized and appreciated this woman's energy, her courage to live. But his abrasiveness—seen by her as legitimate—does sober her. When he attacks her shallowness by saying, "'up to now, you've missed nothing—you haven't felt the lack of anything—in love,'" she replies, "'Oh yes, I have.'" (*Phoenix II*, 52). The narrator quite rightly hears her admission as an invitation.

The ideas touched on here—that one can coolly preserve

oneself by avoiding commitment, alternatively that one can give up the self in a voluptuous abandonment to another, and that to abandon the self is in fact a betrayal of the other as well as the self—are central to Lawrence's middle fictions. Yet here, Lawrence's intention seems mainly to capture the specific characters of Anita and the narrator rather than to wrestle with questions of identity on a general plane. As in his other realistic tales, Lawrence gives precisely the line, physical attitude, costume, or lack of costume we need in order to see these two lovers. Their nakedness, the sun on the bed, the green dragons that writhe on Anita's black silk robe all take us directly to character and scene. They imply little beyond themselves, point toward no fundamental social malaise. Again, all this will soon change.

Lawrence's initial enthusiasm for "the new young school of realism" has carried him through four important years. If one looks back to the Eastwood stories of 1907–1908, to *The White Peacock*, or to the early drafts of *Sons and Lovers*, it becomes clear that the realistic short story offered Lawrence a means to learn his craft, discipline his romantic tendencies, and participate in a movement that English readers and critics considered innovative, fresh. The fact that Lawrence's work in realism coincided with his interest in and need to write autobiographical fiction meant that the writing he did during these four years also gave him the opportunity to sharpen his perceptions about himself, his family, his community. In moving on to visionary fiction—with its difficult task of yoking the physical and metaphysical, the individual and cultural dimensions of human experience—Lawrence's work in realism serves him well. It provides the basis for his flights into cultural anatomy and prophecy. It provides him with a saving toe in Liverpool.

If the stories Lawrence wrote during these years were central to his own development as a writer, they also influenced English short fiction in general. I have spoken of the new narrative tone in Lawrence's early short stories; that tone constitutes a break into communal language and point of view, a break out of the nineteenth century's tendency to frame its fictions with a literary voice and perspective. But Lawrence's early realistic stories were also influential in other ways. James and Conrad, more than Kipling and Stevenson, had forced English readers and critics to take short fiction seriously, to see the genre as capable of high and difficult art. Lawrence enters the field at a time when he can take advantage of their claim and extend it. It is the extending that is important here. Lawrence's realistic short stories, in the best sense, were imitable, more so than the stories of James and Conrad, more so than his own visionary stories to come. Granting Lawrence's individual voice and point of view, his realistic stories showed other English writers the ways they could participate in the movement Chekov had led in Russia and on the Continent. As Avrahm Yarmolinsky observes, well through the Second World War "most young writers of ambition" were still working in the mode of Chekov.[20] Lawrence, along with Mansfield and Joyce, set the high standard for this exciting movement in England. Yet what makes Lawrence stand out from his peers is his movement beyond realism. Writing a series of successes in the new mode of storytelling, he pushed himself beyond it.

Out on the Sill of All the Unknown 4

Readers who approach Lawrence from a psychoanalytic perspective generally agree that Lydia Lawrence and Frieda von Richthofen were among the most significant people in his life. Looking at the work Lawrence did after his mother's death, I have mentioned that he carried on through 1911, writing and living much as he had since moving to Croydon, not collapsing until nearly a year had passed. Frieda's entrance into his life in the spring of 1912 was an entirely different kind of event, but, as the previous chapter demonstrates, in his fiction it also took about a year for him to respond directly to the great changes she brought. In this chapter I trace the role the short stories of 1913 play in his growing ability to make fiction out of the terrible miracle of her presence.

The early years and eventual marriage of Lawrence and Frieda constitute a remarkable conjunction of contrasting backgrounds, personalities, classes, and nationalities. As one reads the entire canon of Lawrence's work, there is almost no way to measure the influence each had on the other. Frieda seems to have taken Lawrence out of England in many ways. If his artistic career gave her life a strong center of interest and intellectual activity, she seems to have helped banish the great loneliness and sense of despair Lawrence felt at the death of his mother. Frieda brought a lively continental perspective to Lawrence and rescued a capacity for joy, courage, and wonder which one feels he could have lost apart from her. Perhaps most important, with her he found himself out on the sill of the great unknown.[1] She was, perhaps for years, perhaps throughout their life together, his horizon.

At the same time, as the biographies and Lawrence's letters attest, the two fought bitterly. From the very first, this was no idyllic romance. Often the very lives of both of them seem poised on the battle lines they drew. There were troubles over Frieda's children, Lawrence's temper, Frieda's airs and arrogance, their different ways of viewing life. But in all the quarreling and material for quarreling, the knot Lawrence focused on most often in his middle fiction was this: men and women who live without an intimate relationship with another are men and women asleep, unborn, wrapped up in themselves. However, intimate relationships demand the sacrifice of self to realize self, the losing of one's life to gain it. The giving up constitutes a greak risk, for a close relationship can destroy the integrity of self. One can be swallowed up by the presence and character of the other. If the other is real, oneself may be a fabrication, without weight or substance. The nexus of issues forms itself along clear lines: there are ways to lose self which result in the birth of a new self; there are other ways that result in absolute loss. Identity is shattered and the self becomes a gap, shadow, piece of waste.[2] What Lawrence begins to do in the short fiction of 1913 is dramatize the difference in the two kinds of loss. Let me review and set the background.

Through 1912, Lawrence's letters, sketches, plays, and poems convey the joy and terror of his and Frieda's alliance, but his short stories and novels continue to draw on earlier material. With the exception of "Once," the tales he wrote during the summer of 1912 are realistic pieces set in the English Midlands. They sniff at new ideas, but cautiously. In November, Lawrence sent off his last revisions of *Sons and Lovers* and immediately moved on to the drafts of three novels, *Scargill Street*, *The Insurrection of Miss Houghton*, and a life of Robert Burns. *Scargill Street* and the Burns piece were soon laid aside, but *The Insurrection of Miss Houghton* (rewritten in 1920 as *The Lost Girl*) intrigued him until the end of March 1913. Only gradually did it get supplanted by *The Sisters*. Looking at Lawrence's letters to Edward Garnett as he worked on the latter two novels and at his short fiction from the summer of 1913, one sees an interesting pattern.

The Insurrection of Miss Houghton, a novel he insisted was *not* about Frieda and him, used material common to *Sons and Lovers* while it moved Lawrence away from the style of *Sons and Lovers*. As he explains, "it is all analytical . . . not a bit visualized"; it goes "a stratum deeper than I think that anybody has ever gone, in a novel" (*CL*, 194).[3] The novel which *is* avowedly about him and Frieda, but particularly about Frieda, is something else again. Written in first person, with Ella/Frieda as narrator, *The Sisters* began as a light piece, a pot boiler. Lawrence soon saw it as flippant, with too much "Ellaing" in it. It was only "the crude fermenting" of a book (*CL*, 208, 223). By June 1, Lawrence had completed this first draft of *The Sisters*. Before leaving Germany in mid-June, he had written "New Eve and Old Adam,"[4] "The Prussian Officer," and "Vin Ordinaire," eventually retitled "The Thorn in the Flesh"; in July, visiting England, he did important revisions on several earlier stories, among them "The Vicar's Garden," retitled "The Shadow in the Rose Garden."[5] Each of the tales named above powerfully examines the theme of lost and found self, finding a variety of styles in which to do that examining. In September, then, he returned to *The Sisters*, beginning it again in an altogether different mode.

To summarize this progress, early in 1913, in *The Insurrection of Miss Houghton*, Lawrence began to work toward the visionary style he would soon adopt. But he did that work only within the context of "old" material, which avoided the current central experience of his own life. To approach that experience in fiction, he needed to imagine himself at work on a lightweight novel, done off the cuff in a tone of flippancy. Bringing together the exploration of a new style and the content of his new, often frightening experiences is the breakthrough that the short fiction of 1913 represents. Two of the four tales—"New Eve and Old Adam" and "The Shadow in the Rose Garden"—figuratively follow the lovers of "Once" out of their affair, beyond their honeymoon, into a marriage filled with fear, pain, and love. In fascinating ways, "Vin Ordinaire"/"The Thorn in the Flesh" and "The Prussian Officer" expand the central concerns of the marriage tales to encompass

Lawrence's powerful impressions of prewar Germany. Again, crucial to each tale is an assessment of the ways self could be lost and then either enriched or impoverished. "New Eve and Old Adam" sets the issues of the quarrel in a style similar to Lawrence's description of the original draft of *The Insurrection of Miss Houghton*: it is analytical, discursive, reminding one of Lawrence's postwar thought adventures. By contrast, "The Prussian Officer" is Lawrence's first fully realized visionary fiction; made of powerful images and drama, it does nothing less than point the way to *The Rainbow* and *Women in Love*. In this chapter, I will concentrate on these two oddly related stories from 1913, "New Eve and Old Adam" and "The Prussian Officer," drawing on the other stories to help illustrate the exploration I see here.[6]

"New Eve and Old Adam" asks two questions, over and over: how does one realize a stable core of identity within the context of an intense, intimate relationship; and from where do our most profound understandings of ourselves, our relationships, and our world emanate?[7] The main characters, Paula and Peter Moest, are transparently Lawrence and Frieda. The plot is simple, in fact almost extraneous. The Moests receive a telegram: "'Meet me at Marble Arch 7.30—theatre—Richard.'" Having no idea who Richard might be, Peter assumes the invitation is for Paula. He lets it precipitate a quarrel and leaves the house to spend the night in a hotel. He decides he will leave Paula, at least temporarily, and go to Milan for a month. The next day the telegram is properly identified as intended for another Moest in the building. Peter returns and they approach reconciliation. That accord is brief, however, and the tale closes with an exchange of letters, written two months later. Peter is in Italy, Paula in London, each accusing the other of failure to love. Delavenay sees jealousy as a major theme in the story,[8] but Lawrence repeatedly tells us that Peter does not really believe the telegram was sent to Paula, does not really credit the importance of "Richard." The incident is a flimsy piece of dramatic action in a tale that is mainly a long conversation between Peter and Paula and within Peter himself. If one theme comes clear in these pain-filled dialogues, it is the immense danger to selfhood that both characters feel in loving *or* losing the other.

Although the contention is picked up, set down, turned back, and changed several times, a main bone emerges. Each character feels that complete abandonment to the other will destroy self. Conversely, each also feels that the other's refusal to give all—to relinquish self to other—implies a lack of trust, a coldness, the desire for a cheap and easy freedom. A key word in the long, tangled quarrel is "power." Each fears the other's power over him or her self; each fears his or her loss of power in relinquishing self to other. In later fictions, notably *Aaron's Rod*, Lawrence explicitly plays with the idea of power, seeing it as both control over something outside oneself and as *pouvoir*, something akin to energy, capacity, vitality. Although he does not specifically ring these changes on the word in "New Eve and Old Adam," nor in the other tales of this period, both senses of the word are at work. It is clear that Peter and Paula have destructive power over each other. It is also clear that each experiences a great loss of *pouvoir* when separated from the other. This is especially true of Peter, whose responses we monitor more closely than Paula's.

For example, on the night she asks him to leave, Peter checks into a hotel where he finds himself nearly suffocating in his sense of enclosure and entrapment. He showers, feeling himself "a piece of waste." He passes a night of horrors—after which, he believes, he achieves a selfhood apart from Paula. He sees himself as empty, a clean shell, a man of correct neutrality. In the tale's view, this would be a pyrrhic victory even if it were true. Its falseness becomes apparent when Peter returns to Paula the next day and feels himself restored by her. Their embrace reestablishes his self, his *pouvoir*, his capacity to live. Later that night, his love for her is so great that he feels himself going dim, again losing self but this time in a potentially positive way. The fear of her is still present, but she becomes a doorway to something beyond them both. The tale concludes with them losing this dangerous but potentially enriching connection once more.

For all the halts in Peter's development, certain facts stand out. To be without this relationship is either to be a clean, empty shell or to be a seething, trapped soul who feels itself a piece of waste. In neither case is Peter a creative self with energy or power. To be with Paula invites two different kinds of self-destruction, one an impoverishment, one a gain. Colin Clarke's theory in *River of Dissolution* may help here, partly for what it misses.

Clarke argues that Lawrence inherits from the English romantic tradition the tendency to equate dissolving with love, pleasure, ecstasy. He sees Lawrence as fascinated by the paradox that loss of self can lead to gain of self and as finally ambivalent about self-annihilation. It seems truer to say that Lawrence tried in his fiction, again and again, to discriminate between different kinds of dissolution, annihilation, pleasure. What Lawrence is analyzing in "New Eve and Old Adam" is the distinction between the dissolving of self in other, which leaves the self without energy or responsibility, and the dissolving of ego in other which leaves the self enriched and restored by its encounter with that which is not self. This distinction is at the heart of *The Rainbow* and *Women in Love*.

As Spilka has pointed out, Clarke neglects an important set of critical questions in his analysis of Lawrence's fiction.[9] Those questions relate to the dramatic progress of a novel or tale. To follow the progress of "New Eve and Old Adam" is to see Peter initially lose himself in an anguish that leaves him empty. In that experience we find no language or imagery connoting a pleasurable or positive loss. Later, in his reconciliation with Paula, his core, his grip on himself, again goes. But here is a loss of self that enriches being. Without it, Peter is "done," finished, sterile. By the tale's close, he has returned to the point he had reached in the hotel. More than examining a paradox, the tale charts a progress or, in this case, a frustrating circle.

Throughout Lawrence's fiction, the creative loss of self occurs by way of relationships. In *Women in Love*, he will develop the concept of star equilibrium to explain the idea of a dependence that nourishes independence. In "New Eve and Old Adam," we have only the first steps toward that resolution, only an introduction of the terms of the argument. But the terms are given fairly. Each terror—the terror of losing self in a relationship and the terror of losing self through the death of a relationship—is fully expressed by each partner; that balance is the tale's major strength and stands in distinct contrast to Lawrence's later leadership tales.[10]

To turn to the second question Lawrence asks in "New Eve and Old Adam," Lawrence begins to dramatize his belief in different modes and sources of human consciousness. Lying in his hotel room, superficially thinking of going to Milan, Peter registers deep within himself the real shock of his break with Paula. Peter's mind stays active, like a straw on a river, but beneath it a process crucial to his being is progressing. Supposedly, he is creating himself apart from Paula. This is an important scene to study in examining Lawrence's growing interest in dramatizations of the underself. But it is important partly for the way it is later qualified.

It is too easy to read this scene and others like it as simple enactments of a comment Lawrence made in 1913 to Ernest Collings: "My great religion is a belief in the blood, the flesh, as being wiser than the intellect" (*CL*, 180). If "New Eve and Old Adam" simply illustrated a belief in the blood, the tale could climax with Peter's night in the hotel. We would judge his blood's message as true; you are free of Paula. But the later reconciliation scenes indicate that he had not achieved an identity apart from Paula, nor should he. The initial blood message was false and will be qualified by subsequent blood messages that urge the powerful bond between them. Further, the various night or blood messages are being qualified throughout the tale by another kind of knowledge. As in most of Lawrence's fictions, the blood messages, again, are part of a progress. And among the forces in that progress is the activity of the intellect. Like Rupert Birkin, Peter literally sits through several scenes in this tale, energetically casting up solutions, possibilities, analyses, all clustering around the questions of what does she want, what do I want, who is right, who is wrong. He tries, in brief, to figure things out. And like Birkin, he does a fairly good job of it. These scenes remind us that Lawrence is, after all, part of a tradition that includes Henry James, a writer who believed that thinking was a dramatic activity. "New Eve and Old Adam" sets up a variety of ways by which Peter can understand his and Paula's dilemma, ways that are blood begot and mind begot, conscious and unconscious. That the two modes of knowing never come together into one sure insight makes this couple's failure to decide anything almost inevitable.

"New Eve and Old Adam" is not an accomplished short story, and Lawrence's failure to get it published is not surprising.[11] Yet, in terms of his own fiction, it succeeds in doing several things. It boldly sets forth themes that he will soon weave into far more subtle tales. It gives free rein to his analytical voice, which is only minimally dramatized by being located in Peter's mind. Once that voice has had its say, Lawrence can integrate it into scene, setting, and symbol as he does in the tales to follow, most skillfully in "The Prussian Officer."

The first successful wedding of Lawrence's realistic talents and tendency to write religious exempla, "The Prussian Officer" introduces Lawrence's great middle fiction as no previous story has. Exempla is readily definable; religious is more difficult. To the extent the visionary tales employ the approach of the exempla, they move from proposition to illustration. The logic is admittedly deductive, the illustration chosen for clarity rather than for the appearance of an objective randomness. Local plausibility can be attenuated; place and action are dictated by theme, and characters are largely terms in the proposition. Like comedy, with its latitude for distortion and fantasy, the exemplum distances itself from the reader, anesthesizing the heart. Our interest, at least on a conscious level, is "qualitative," to use Wayne Booth's term. We want to see the moral pattern elaborated, then completed.

Not all exempla are religious. A popular form of tale in the nineteenth century was the economic exemplum; most of us can remember some rather nasty-spirited exempla from childhood meant to inculcate proper manners. But Lawrence's are religious; like the stories of Flannery O'Connor or Graham Greene, they are aimed at mapping out the journey of the soul. Lawrence saw himself as a passionately religious man, adamantly not a humanist. For him, the measure of humankind was not humankind itself but all the vast cosmos, from Orion in the heavens to the foxes and poppies of the earth. To understand the true substance of a character's decision to move toward life or death, in Lawrence's view, demanded an understanding of that character's participation in the sacred, universal dance of life and death. He felt that humans are at once phenomena of things outside themselves—seasons, movements of the constellations, eruptions of godhead or mana, their nations' policies, and their grandmother's dreams—and at the same time self-responsible creatures of choice. How to convey that view of experience becomes Lawrence's heady enterprise. To accomplish it, he discovers a variety of strategies, the key to which is a dynamic balance between mimesis and exemplum.

As expressions in the mimetic mode, the visionary tales are convincing. Characters are psychologically believable and realistically motivated. They continue to have backgrounds, physical presence, individuality. A typical denouement in these tales— quite the opposite of the inflated, wrap-up closures in several of the earlier realistic stories—is a brief scene indicating the characters' return to normal, open, contingent living. Time and setting, like character, can be read as particular and local. We usually know, roughly, the chronological period and season in which the tale takes place. Lawrence's eye for the way the sun hits an object or a tree rises out of the earth is as exact as ever; the natural images are rich on the mimetic plane alone. Even plot, the element least sufficiently read mimetically, can support a realistic interpretation. In brief, we are not in the land of fable. No house whispers "more money" as in "The Rocking-Horse Winner"; islands do not shrink into nothingness nor characters burst out of fairy tale as in "The Man Who Loved Islands."

And yet, to read the visionary stories only through the lens of mimesis is to miss most of Lawrence's originality and intent. These stories take normal though highly selected human experience and present it in such a way as to read as an exemplary lesson. The lesson is not ethical. One feels that Lawrence has planted a road sign in the tale: this way lies death, this way lies life. The standard elements of short fiction are simplified and intensified. For example, characters are isolated from all normal social intercourse; they usually exist as clear pairs, trios, quartets, with few minor characters on stage to distract from the clear design of the cast. Gone are the Sysons, Cyrils, Miriams, and Winifreds, with their relatively normal range of feelings, their circle of friends, and their particularized interpersonal conflicts. Stripped down, the visionary characters engage in a different kind of intercourse, one that includes a few other humans but also the vast rhythms of life and death, convergence and dissolution around them. Both self-consciously apart and inevitably embedded in those rhythms, Lawrence's characters make a real break with realistic conventions in having dense, often relatively long, passages of semidramatized monologues in which they struggle with their state. These passages resemble more the fictional license implied by the soliloquies of Hamlet or Othello than the scrupulous insistence of James or Joyce that all characterization come through action and dialogue. In contrast to Lawrence's earlier soliloquies in the main character's mind, these passages in the visionary tales are well integrated into what is, throughout, a more fictional and also more analytical kind of story.

Further, when the visionary characters do speak—in either dialogue or monologue—one has the sense that, yes, they might say thus and so, but the words seem to come through them, not from them. If that makes them mouthpieces for Lawrence's dogma, then by his own standards these fictions are dead. But for most readers, the visionary characters do not read as puppets. What comes through has the ring of authentic vision. The characters express a view of the world that is larger, sometimes richer, sometimes more dire, than they might ordinarily see or voice, but we feel it is their vision.

The ring of authenticity comes partly from the language Lawrence begins to employ. The relatively transparent style of many of the realistic stories gives over to a denser, more complex style. We encounter long, intertwining sentences and paragraphs; we come upon puns, often consisting of words, especially the verbs of being, teased out of their normal usage.[12] Often Lawrence will use the definite rather than indefinite article: characters feel *the* joy or terror rather than *a* joy or terror. Biblical imagery and sentence rhythms are present throughout. In brief, when characters speak with heightened diction, their words register well with the tale's entire linguistic tone.

Setting and imagery also do much to realize the visionary nature of these tales. As in realistic fiction, place works partly to give action a world in which to exist, but here place works equally to state the powerful oppositions of life and death, creation and destruction, that rule these tales. Further, setting and the imagery it invokes strongly imply the characters' links to earth and cosmos, to all that they share with the beasts of field and apocalypse. Image patterns tend to be more pervasive, value laden, and complex than in previous tales. For example, in "Odour of Chrysanthemums," the flowers were realistically presented, served to indicate the tenor of Mrs. Bates's life, and created a sense of unity in the piece. Partly they existed to create narrative rhythm, to use E. M. Forster's words. By contrast, in "The Prussian Officer," the images associated with the mountains and valley are described in metaphysical language; throughout, their presence presses against the characters, forcing us to recognize the characters' ties to the earth they inhabit. At the same time, the image patterns are so arranged and developed as to indicate a series of starkly opposed values between which the characters must choose.

And each of these strategies—each of these approaches to character, language, setting, and imagery—is reinforced by the kinds of plots Lawrence devises. The plot of any great fiction will partake of the particular and universal, of time as chronology ("one damn thing after another," writes Kermode) and time as kairos (the continuous reenactment in the lives of individuals or communities of culturally crucial events—baptism, exile from God, crucifixion, descent into hell, ascent into heaven). So that

Lawrence's turning away, in the visionary plots, from individual histories toward central cultural rites is more a change of degree than kind. But the degree is important. Just as we cannot understand *Everyman* unless we perceive its allegorical level, so we cannot adequately read Lawrence's middle tales unless we recognize the rite, often of sacrament, that informs the plot. Also important to see here is that Lawrence takes the idea of sacrament—a religious act instituted by Jesus as a means of grace—and broadens its meaning to include acts born of dissolution and corruption which serve as means to death, paralysis, and damnation. As we will see in "The Prussian Officer" and other tales, Lawrence like Nathaniel Hawthorne occasionally organized his tales around a black mass.

The intention of the strategies is most persuasively realized in the fictions themselves. But Lawrence's letters, especially to Edward Garnett in June 1914 (CL, 281) and to Gordon Campbell in September of the same year (CL, 291), are also helpful in discerning the aim of his new techniques. When Garnett criticized the psychology of the characters in *The Wedding Ring* (a rewriting of *The Sisters*, leading to *The Rainbow*), Lawrence saw Garnett's comments as essentially incidental. He explained that he wanted to move beyond or beneath an individual's feelings, thoughts, or moral schemes. He wanted to express, for example, the part of a particular woman's nature that has to do with the underlying principles of resistence (as the molecules of steel may cohere and resist a bullet) and dissolution common to all matter, all existence. Her jealousy at a moment may be an expression of resistence or dissolution, but it is the energy beneath the emotion that is interesting. To Campbell he speaks of fiction's need—indeed humanity's need—to recognize what he believed the Egyptians and Assyrians had seen: that is, the nonhuman qualities of life, of which humans partake. In that letter he speaks of the need for males to allow their souls to be fertilized by the female stream of existence; as we have seen, in his fictions he repeatedly allows his female characters to carry out actions we associate with the male stream. In this theorizing, Lawrence is seeking out what he calls the "carbon" as opposed to the "diamond" or "coal" of human existence. The carbon is elemental, lying beneath even our specific form as human beings. It is again the part of us that inevitably participates in rhythms—cosmic or cultural—beyond our own body and mind.

Most of this is realized, vision and technique, in "The Prussian Officer." In his oft-quoted crow to Garnett of June 10, 1913,

Lawrence announced the tale: "I have written the best short story I have ever done—about a German officer in the army and his orderly" (CL, 209). Lawrence persistently called the tale "Honour and Arms" and was angry with Garnett for retitling it (CL, 296). As Cushman notes, Lawrence's title refers to an aria from Handel's oratorio "Samson."[13] In the aria, the giant of Gath tells the blinded Samson that he would not stoop to conquer so broken a foe. Whether we take Lawrence's officer or orderly as the giant, the tragedy comes of each one stooping to conquer the other. Lawrence often had difficulty finding good titles for his fictions, but "Honour and Arms" is an exception. Its levels of implication and irony are lost in Garnett's substitution.[14]

The central movement of the tale is comprised of an action and reaction. A Prussian captain by the name of Hauptmann becomes obsessed with his young orderly, Schöner. With sadistic pleasure, he demands the young man's constant presence, teases him, beats him. The orderly tries not to respond but eventually capitulates. Alone with the captain in a clearing in the woods, Schöner leaps on Hauptmann and murders him. The tale closes with the orderly's flight and death from "exposure."

In both structure and theme, "The Prussian Officer" is a transposed resurrection tale, reading like God's name spelled backwards. Many of the elements of Lawrence's tales of salvation are present: the coming together of two intense individuals; their growing awareness of each other on levels of perception beneath the conscious; their eventual embrace, filled as it is with joy and terror; and the culminating discovery—here by only one of the participants—of a new self and new world. But the wooing is bloody, the embrace murderous, and the discovery of a new self and world suicidal. Widmer sees the tale as an amoral fable, written to illustrate the perverse human quest for "ultimate beauty, purity, and innocence," a quest that denies life and yearns for annihilation.[15] Cushman reads it as a dualistic tale in which pure unconsciousness gets corrupted by consciousness.[16] Other critics have seen it as a confusing fable of split personality, a study of German hysteria, or an exploration of homosexuality.[17] While each of these interpretations has been ably argued, I would like to offer a different reading of this great tale, which redefines the image complex that stands at the center of the tale and speaks to the tale's links to "New Eve and Old Adam."

The story is set on a hot, fertile plain surrounded by distant mountains. Cushman provides a recent example of the way critics usually read the mountain/valley imagery. The valley, he writes, is associated with the orderly. It is the "warm valley of life," unconscious, fertile, sensual. The mountains are the captain's emblem. They represent the "icy eternity of death," conscious, sterile, hyperspiritual and mental. By association, Cushman's reading would have us further see the valley as feminine, the mountains as masculine. The tale's central movement traces the corruption of the orderly, a corruption that results in his loss of identification with the valley and his subsequent identification with the mountains.[18]

But the tale urges a different reading. One suspects, in fact, that critics who have seen the valley as "the life of the body . . . of the earth" and posed it against the mountains, "the heaven of the spirit," are reading the tale's images through the perspective of *Women in Love*. In the final chapters of that novel, the cold, snow-covered mountains can indeed be seen as a heaven of the mind, the will, the spirit. Ursula and Birkin escape their deadly cruelty by traveling down into the warm valley of the south. But in the tale, Lawrence tells us that the orderly's girl, primitive and independent, is from the mountains. The mountains themselves rise "out of the land," they are "half-earth, half-heaven" (CSS, 95). They are not the spirit of heaven, nor do they seem to divide heaven and earth: they range "all still and wonderful between earth and heaven" (CSS, 116). When the orderly dies, the mountains standing "in their beauty, so clean and cool, seem to have it, that which was lost in him" (CSS, 116). On the other hand, the valley is described as a confusing grid of glare and shadow. It is "wide and shallow," "a dull, hot diagram under a glistening sky" (CSS, 95). Its rye throws off "suffocating heat," its fruit trees are "scraggly" and "set regularly on either side of the high road." Its air is "deathly, sickly" (CSS, 106). Significantly, it is in the valley that the soldiers are compelled to act out their meaningless maneuvers. The questions one needs to ask are these. What has been lost in the orderly (which is not to say that he ever possessed it)? What is this flatland that contains both orderly and captain? What are the distant, earth-based, snow-capped mountains? Thinking of "New Eve and Old Adam," one also asks, what do these images have to do with different modes of knowing and how do they relate to the issue of identity and relationship?

No icy haven, the mountains represent an ideal of integration that points out what is missing in both of these trapped soldiers.[19] Imprisoned as they are in the valley, each lacks, surprisingly enough, consciousness. If any reference to *Women in Love* is germane, it would be to Birkin's quarrels with Hermione. Especially appropriate is his remark in "Schoolroom." She has said that people are constrained by having too much knowledge. No, says Birkin, people do not have enough knowledge. The burden of both novel and tale is to dramatize what kinds of consciousness, of awareness and knowledge, people need.

For all their differences, the captain and the orderly are a well-matched pair, especially in their ignorance. Lawrence's final paragraphs most clearly indicate the general bond between them, but he also establishes it repeatedly throughout the tale. Both are passionate men with very little understanding or awareness of passion.[20] The captain continually prevents his mind from contemplating his love/hate for his orderly. The orderly continually holds back his sight, holds it back from both his own and the captain's plight. He will not look, he will not see. Obviously, neither has any genuine sense of himself or the other. Both feel, as Paula and Peter do in "New Eve and Old Adam," that if the other's sense of reality is accurate, then their own must be a delusion. In both stories, key words are gap, shadow, insubstantial, restoration, regaining the self. The orderly and officer become obsessed with the other and with the terrifying possibility of nonexistence.

The tale's imagery suggests, then, that the orderly and the captain are in the same place in more than a geographical sense. Two trapped men, caught in a flatland of insufficient consciousness, they are unable to gain any integrating perspective on themselves or the other. If this were all there was to the tale, we would have a dramatic portrayal of a kind of human stupidity Lawrence felt to be all too common. But there is more to the tale, as Lawrence points to what he saw as a cause for this stupidity. As in "Once" and "New Eve and Old Adam," Lawrence again urges the link between intimate relationships and the establishment of self.

It is important to realize that both the captain and the orderly are virginal before their encounter. Admittedly, both have had relations with women. But the captain's have been brief, insignificant. No woman has ever moved him. After the beating scene, Lawrence identifies the captain's lack of self-knowledge with his "virginity," with his inability consciously to enter any intimate engagement with another. He will not think about the orderly and he will not think about himself. After the murder, Law-

96

rence makes the same point with respect to the orderly, but in an altogether different way.

One senses that, in murdering the captain, the orderly has made intense though horrible contact with someone else for the first time in his life. But he too represses the knowledge. His progress is worth pausing over.

Clearly the orderly was once integrated in his being. But, I suggest, he was integrated through default. The orderly has a girl, and, being from the mountains, she should be able to inspire consciousness in him. But she remains off-stage and seems more of a resting place than the kind of vivid partner whom Lawrence usually imagines as inspiring knowledge of self. Thus Schöner has moved through his days with a blank innocence, unconscious of himself and the complexity and richness of the world around him. He is rudely awakened by the captain, but Lawrence is far from condemning awakening. He dies, significantly, of "exposure"; but Lawrence is not arguing against exposure. Again, this is no simple tale of a primitive angel's fall into dreary consciousness. The orderly's wakening is a magnificent adventure. His ghastly embrace of the captain exemplifies the logic Lawrence has set up in his other tales: to confront and embrace other is to realize self. The tale's long third section continually echoes Lawrence's resurrection tales. After "embracing" the captain, the orderly suddenly opens his eyes. For the first time, he sees himself as an independent being, apart from the military, apart from the world. He has become conscious. His earlier state of unawareness appears as a sleep. Magnificently, however, the vision of a quick, multiple, shimmering self and world is here, a horrifying vision of self and world as discrete, isolated impulses and particles. Self and world are not multiple in any rich way; they are radically disintegrating. Lawrence is presenting here in highly dramatized, imagistic terms what he was analyzing in "New Eve and Old Adam": first, his belief that self is unrealized, asleep, or locked up when it exists apart from other; and second, his simultaneous awareness that an immense threat to self is inherent in any intimate relationship.

Critics who find Lawrence most interesting and honest when he is most annihilistic argue that in "The Prussian Officer" he is celebrating the ecstasy that can accompany the death of the self, the wondrous knowledge that can come of extreme experience. The orderly's "sense of arrival" is, then, the tale's main point (CSS, 114). But the obvious observation in this case is the accurate one: as in "New Eve and Old Adam," Lawrence traces the difference between a loss of self that finally leads to gain and a loss of self that finally leads nowhere. The difference is not found in the amount of ecstasy or beauty each experience offers. Western culture and Christianity in particular have always accepted the glittering and voluptuous possibilities inherent in giving away one's soul. But being aware of the attractiveness of damnation is not the same as urging its ultimate value or resting with the paradox that annihilation can be creative. The orderly dies. So does the captain. If the orderly's isolation, pain, and death throes bring him knowledge, the reverse is also true. The *kind* of knowledge the orderly gains—remarkable though it may be—brings him isolation, pain, and death. That is Lawrence's point. There are different kinds of knowledge, different ways of losing the self. Lawrence's images of annihilation or ecstasy are part of a dramatic progress within the particular fiction.

As I have stated above, "The Prussian Officer" shows the way to Lawrence's middle fiction. It introduces the visionary mode of *The Rainbow* and *Women in Love*, as well as the mode of stories such as "England, My England," "The Horse Dealer's Daughter," "The Blind Man," or "St. Mawr." Further, in its approach to character, scene, setting, image, and plot, it becomes important in Lawrence's revisions of his tales for *The Prussian Officer* volume, revisions he accomplished during the summer of 1914. Obviously in a writer as exploratory as Lawrence, no single piece of work stands alone as the forerunner of a new style and set of themes. Alongside successes, failures and things not done often inspire the imagination. But "The Prussian Officer," like certain of the successful realistic stories, stood as a highly accomplished, finished work within the sea of thought and paper represented by the successive drafts of Lawrence's novels. This is one of the special qualities of the short stories as they figure in Lawrence's fiction as a whole: by their brevity, they are highly contained successes or failures. They serve as beacons—avoid these rocks, steer this way—for Lawrence's long fiction.

In "The Prussian Officer," the orderly gives up his un-self-conscious, group-identified self to something that ultimately proves to constrict rather than to stretch the reach of his being. In the aptly titled "Vin Ordinaire," Lawrence relaxes back into a realistic style, returning to a question asked in "Once" and "New

Eve and Old Adam": what happens when the self will not risk the loss attendant in embracing the other?

As it was published in the *English Review* in June 1914 (no manuscripts exist), "Vin Ordinaire" takes a character somewhat like the orderly, engages him in another secret shame, and has him attack a superior officer and thereby sever his formerly easy identification with the masses represented by the military. Adrift, Bachmann seeks out the intense relationship with one other person which serves as the way to find self in loss of self. Only here, the would-be relationship never develops; the embrace never occurs. Timidity and a lack of courage stand in the way.

The beginning of the story sets up the character of Bachmann and the secret shame that leads to his fleeing the army. In "The Prussian Officer," the orderly is deeply ashamed of the intimacy implied in the officer's beating him. The formal, necessary distance between them has been violated. He is also, one senses, ashamed of the infantile position the beating has placed him in. He resents being "humble" and "obedient" to an individual he must now see as a person rather than a part of a structure that includes them both. In "Vin Ordinaire," the soldier's shame at being infantilized is especially emphasized (as is his need to redress that shame through an adult, manly embrace): Bachmann wets his pants. Terrified of heights and forced to scale the high stone walls of a rampart, he clings to the swaying ladder in sheer terror, reaching the far edge of panic and shame. Ignominiously hauled up just as he had begun to conquer his terror, he accidently strikes the sergeant who has "rescued" him. The sergeant tumbles over the rampart, and Bachmann flees to Emilie, a servant at the local baron's house.

In the late afternoon, hidden in her room, Emilie and Bachmann approach each other sexually for the first time. Lawrence characterizes her as proudly virginal, but as Bachmann kisses her and bares and caresses her breasts, she responds with yearning and desire. They do not consummate their love but each assumes they will be together that night. In the governess's room, she waits for him. In her room, he waits for her. Neither has the courage to seek out the other. Lawrence tells us that by the next morning Emilie is left feeling foiled, sullen, weak, mechanical. At one point during the night, she thinks of their afternoon embrace: "Why could he not set her free to be herself again?" (*English Re-*

view, June 1914, 312). Bachmann's sense of failure comes to define his entire being. Like Peter Moest and the orderly, he feels himself a void, a shadow, "without honor and without worth" (*English Review*, 312). When the soldiers come for him the next morning, he gives in. The point of the tale is clear: "If he and she were all right, the other thing [his earlier shame] would be all right. If she had done with him, then he was afraid—there was nothing for him to grasp, to keep himself together" (*English Review*, 313).

Though Lawrence will thoroughly revise the tale in 1914, part of the same tangle of needs and fears haunts this version as haunted "New Eve and Old Adam" and "The Prussian Officer," and will haunt "The Shadow in the Rose Garden." No longer can community, as it was celebrated in the realistic stories, nurture the self. One must break with community and establish self through an intimate relationship. Without that, one drifts, insubstantial, either a clean shell or a piece of waste, worth little. But within the relationship, one is far from safe. At any moment, the reality of the other—wonderful and terrible in its very otherness—may overwhelm one's own sense of being, making oneself again a shadow, a gap. In the last tale I will be looking at from this summer, Lawrence impresses us once again with the variety of ways he can stage a scene central to his imagination at any one moment. In revising "The Vicar's Garden" into "The Shadow in the Rose Garden," Lawrence combines the most provocative elements from the early tale, the powerful fear of obliteration that marks the fiction of 1913, and the fierce energy and release he is beginning to associate with marital conflict. Perhaps the most astonishing moment in the tale occurs when Peter Moest's dream of becoming an empty shell is imagined as literally coming true in the character of the vicar's mad son.[21]

In essence, "The Shadow in the Rose Garden" rests on a daring contrast. On the one hand we have the vicar's son, truly the shadow of a man as he stares vacantly, blankly, out at the world. On the other, we have a married man and woman, each of whom must struggle against the obliteration of self represented by the pathetic son. Throughout the tale Lawrence complements the basic contrast with an image pattern of eyes and windows, playing sight and blindness against each other. And here, blindness is used not only as a metaphor for the failure to perceive but more interestingly to make the point that realization of self often depends on our being recognized by the significant other, whether that be spouse, orderly, captain, or lover. In "The Shadow in the Rose Garden," the key characters have the potential to become mere shadows as they either fail to see or fail to be seen. Realistic in mode, "The Shadow in the Rose Garden" gains its power from Lawrence's ability to translate the argument of "New Eve and Old Adam" into imagery.

The tale opens with the visit of the couple to a seaside resort. Although they are young, the tenor of their relationship implies they have been married for some time. This is no honeymoon. From the outset, Lawrence introduces images of blindness. In the first scene, for example, the young husband gazes up at the windows of their suite. A woman appears whom he does not recognize. He is startled but then perceives that "it is only his wife" (*Smart Set*, March 1914, 72). The action takes only a moment but captures the problem the tale sets out to explore. He is turned toward her but does not recognize her; she, situated above him, looks out beyond him, oblivious of his presence. All this must be changed.

As the plot develops we learn that the wife has urged their coming to this resort although we do not know why. Their first morning she slips out and goes to the vicar's garden. There she cautiously enters the grounds. The one ominous note Lawrence strikes is in reference to the vicarage: its uncurtained windows "looked black and soulless," "the house had a sterile appearance as if it were still used but not inhabited" (*Smart Set*, 73). She encounters the caretaker, gains permission to stay, and then moves toward the roses. What took pages in the original version is now condensed to four strong paragraphs. There is no rhapsodizing over the roses. We infer from these paragraphs that she is revisiting a place and time laden with complex memories; she is both exhilarated and frightened.[22] She feels her own existence about to lapse; she feels "no more than a rose, a rose that was going to fall, slip its white petals" (*Smart Set*, 74). As a fly suddenly drops onto her knee, onto her white dress, one feels Lawrence's prose working for the same effect as his early poetry. If one breaks up the prose lines, one gets a taut imagistic poem, comprised of white roses, white dress, scarlet sunshade, black fly. Although the fly is too obvious a foreshadowing of impending blight, the overall effect is a fine, still moment before the appalling reversal begins. The woman is startled by the sudden appearance of a man in slippers. He sits down to talk to her and gradually she sees that he is mad. As one follows her reactions, one learns that he is her former lover and that he had left her. She had heard that he had died in Tripoli and had come back to this resort in order to relive her memories of their affair. Their conversation is a painful blend of shock on her part and failure of recognition on his. The remainder of the tale follows her back to her lodgings and a bitter quarrel with her husband.

Initially the quarrel pushes both characters toward a stunning awareness of the deep divisions between them. As the wife bitterly tells the husband about her love for the vicar's son, the husband is forced to realize that there are aspects of his wife's past and character about which he knows nothing. His assumption that he encompasses her—knows and possesses her—is destroyed. He is jealous, then enraged, at this attack on his sense of himself and his marriage. At that point he lets go of the entire situation for a moment; "He felt the suffering was greater than he was. It was queer to him to find himself submerged. . . . He was hurt into simplicity" (*Smart Set*, 77). She, who has just suffered her own obliteration under the blank stare of her uncomprehending lover, continues to strike out at the only object in reach. She tells her husband she is revolted by his lower-class origins, that she has never loved him, that she married him only on the rebound. But then she too lets go, "yielding herself up to pain" (*Smart Set*, 77). In brief, after mapping out the attacks and recriminations, Lawrence introduces language that forces us to see that each of these characters is in the process of shedding an old self. In each case, a momentary pause ensues. An instant of impersonal wonder—at the pain, the anger, and the otherness of the other—creates a space, a silence, time to breathe. A partial solution to the fear of losing self in intimate relations is being developed. As in later fictions—notably "Excurse" in *Women in Love*—the solution lies in maintaining a relationship with momentary hiatuses, hiatuses that allow each self to withdraw utterly from the relationship so the coming together again may be based on fresh perception and understanding.

In the 1913 version, the husband quietly announces, "'We can't stop here then'" (*Smart Set*, 77). The line may indicate that all is over between them, but judging from the slight revisions Lawrence worked on the tale's last paragraph in 1914, the line points to their need to move ahead. The collapse that has taken place in wife, husband, and marriage is defined partly by the entirely different collapse of consciousness represented by the vicar's son. In contrast to his blankness, the wife seems very much alive as she squats on the bed in her white dress. Nor is there anything sterile about the husband in his feelings of submergence in suffering. A triangle of blind characters has met in this tale; two of them have been shocked out of their blindness by having their sense of themselves and their world attacked. As many of Lawrence's middle fictions will, the story avoids neat closure. It is enough that eyes have been opened, that the stream of conscience has been undammed.

In the three new tales of June 1913—"New Eve and Old Adam," "The Prussian Officer," and "Vin Ordinaire"—Lawrence plunged into the great unknown represented by his elopement, his completion of *Sons and Lovers*, and his residence in Europe. In none can he imagine the unknown as a place where the self will find steady nurturance or joy. This, by the way, is in contrast to his poems and letters of the period. At the same time, in none can he imagine turning away from the unknown without an immense cost. In brief, these tales focus on dilemma. "New Eve and Old Adam" states the problems in highly personal, autobiographical terms. "The Prussian Officer" dramatizes them in a bold new voice, extending their significance to the entire Prussian culture and beyond. "Vin Ordinaire" pulls back from the intensity of "The Prussian Officer," reminding the reader in the language of realism that although the break into some relationships can be deadly, the refusal to break into any relationship at all is equally deadly.

In his 1913 revisions, Lawrence's sense of the unknown grows more positive. Perhaps, back in England, surrounded by familiar places and people, his terror of the unknown dims when compared to his certainty that people must venture out beyond the cozy confines of their known reality. "The Shadow in the Rose Garden" traces a break with the past that cautiously promises new life. As I will demonstrate in the next chapter, Lawrence's revisions of "The White Stocking," done over the years including 1913 but culminating in 1914, even more explicitly reward its adventuring souls. The same is true for his 1914 revision of "Vin Ordinaire" into "The Thorn in the Flesh."

For now, the important point is that, during the summer of 1913, Lawrence moved beyond the long fiction he was writing—*The Insurrection of Miss Houghton* and the initial draft of *The*

Sisters—and found a series of ways to approach the issues that lay at the center of his heart and mind. In particular, the visionary mode he discovered in "The Prussian Officer" would serve him for years to come; it would help him express his sense of the war and the ways individuals could combat it. Later it would allow him to reverse the understanding of "Vin Ordinaire," arguing that intimate sexual relationships bind the souls of men. What they must find is a masculine community, even a military one, to release their true identity. Later still, it would give him the fictional means to overturn that stance. More immediate to his needs, the writings of the summer led to renewed work on *The Sisters*, begun again, back in Italy, in September 1913. The fall of that year and the winter and spring of 1914 saw him completing a second and third version of the novel, now called *The Rainbow*. Occupied with that, Lawrence did not work on short fiction until he returned to England in late June 1914 and began a series of revisions aimed at creating his first volume of tales, *The Prussian Officer*.

War and the Comic Vision 5

When Lawrence and Frieda left Italy to return to England in June 1914, Lawrence's reputation and hopes were high. Published the year before, *Sons and Lovers* had won him an interesting circle of friends and admirers. A volume of tales again had been proposed and was in the works. As far as he knew, *The Rainbow* was finished; Methuen had agreed to publish it. Released from her marriage with Ernest Weekley, Frieda was finally free to remarry. Lawrence even had occasion to buy a set of tails that summer. Partly so that Frieda could see her children, the Lawrences planned to spend the summer in England and return to Italy in October. This was the same path they had traced in 1913: Italy in winter, Germany in the spring, and England in the summer. The war changed their plans, however, preventing them from leaving England again until November 1919. Far from fulfilling their initial summer mood of 1914, these years are commonly seen as one of the bitterest periods in Lawrence's life.

Doubtless, it was a dark time in nearly all respects. Between Lawrence and Frieda there were, as there always would be, long and painful fights. They moved from one borrowed house to the next, quarreled with friends, found themselves hounded and harassed by the War Office, and lived in severe poverty. In August 1914, Methuen backed out on publishing *The Rainbow*; and although Lawrence rewrote the novel and eventually persuaded the firm to publish it in 1915, it was immediately suppressed under Britain's Obscene Publication Act. *The Rainbow*—the novel that Lawrence believed would celebrate the end of the war and the beginning of a new day—was banned and the distributed copies were confiscated.[1] Needless to say, its publication marked no end of the war, no beginning of a new day in any discernible or immediate way. And the background to these personal woes was always the war. John Middleton Murry, living near Lawrence at the time, captures the tone of the times:

> One night, I remember, there was a knock on the door of the shed where I worked, and Lawrence came in. He said nothing, but sat in a chair by the stove, rocking himself to and fro, and moaning. I thought that there had been another quarrel with Frieda, and I felt it was futile to attempt to comfort him. Their struggle was beyond me; I was out of my depth. But on this night, it turned out, there had been no quarrel. Suddenly Lawrence had been overwhelmed by the horror of the war and had made his way across in the dark. That was all. I can see him now, in his brown corduroy jacket, buttoned tight up in the neck, and his head bowed, radiating desolation.[2]

That the years were bleak is undeniable.

But we misread this period of Lawrence's life if we stop with bleakness and desolation. Meticulously documenting the war years, Delavenay distorts them by seeing only despair.[3] In fact, the vision that characterizes much of the fiction and philosophy of the period is militantly antitragic, at times even comic. Northrop Frye's distinctions are helpful here.

Within Frye's paradigms of the modes of fiction in *Anatomy of Criticism* is a broad distinction between the comic and tragic modes based on the concept of choice. Tragedy draws on the related qualities of inevitability and incongruity to create its effect of pity and fear. Comedy, by contrast, assumes freedom of choice and a congruence of actions and rewards to create its vision of movement out of an old world into a new.[4] As one reads through the distinctions, one realizes how strongly during these years Lawrence argues against a tragic view of experience as Frye defines it. The reader who comes to Lawrence with the darker Dickens, Hardy, Kafka, or Camus in mind will hear in Lawrence a strange language: "And know that in the end, always you keep the ultimate choice of your destiny . . . the choice is yours, do not let it slide from you, keep it always secure, reserved" (*CL*, 381–82). Here are no Circumlocution Offices, no arbitrary gods or administrators, no penal colonies or plagues. One can control one's fate, Lawrence insists; one can "compel" one's destiny by the strength of one's desires (*CL*, 344).[5] Inevitability and incongruity are not adequate concepts for understanding human experience. There may be great pain in times of cultural breakdown but there is no overriding absurdity. Choice and justice reign.[6]

Further, within the tangle of Lawrence's responses to the ongoing war, a second assertion is repeated: it cannot be happening for nothing. Out of this cultural upheaval, this vast destruction, must come a new society with new visions of life, love, and purpose for its citizens. When Lawrence sought to formulate the rebirth of Western culture, he frequently resorted to talking and writing about Rananim, a new Jerusalem he hoped to establish one day with a few close friends. Virtually trapped in England, his imagination kept hoisting sails for that ideal community.

Both the specific location and the basic character of Rananim changed through the war years and after, but the vision of a new society born out of trouble stayed with Lawrence. The tales written during the war and afterward reflect many variations in the vision. With reversals and qualifications, Rananim gradually changed from a community founded upon the private, sexual relationship of men and women to one that emphasized the different roles men and women should play; still later, it became a society that legislated and celebrated male camaraderie, bonding, purposiveness.

But that constitution for Rananim was written years later. With the exceptions of "England, My England" and "The Mortal Coil," the tales in this chapter focus on the resurrecting relationship of individual men and women. Lawrence staunchly asserts that this relationship, entered into and maintained with courage and sexual warmth, can offset the massive coldness and carnage of the war, can show modern Western culture the way out of mechanized horror.

In the previous chapter I indicated that Lawrence's short fiction of 1913 offers its characters a dilemma: they are damned if they do not venture out of their old understandings and relationships, and damned if they do. The venture is terrifying, and in those tales, especially "The Prussian Officer," Lawrence finds the vocabulary of images, scenes, and analyses to convey it. In the short stories he wrote between 1914 and 1919, he continues drawing on the visionary mode, but the vision he now proffers is different. In the revisions he did in preparing *The Prussian Officer* volume and in most of the stories he wrote during the war, the emphasis on individual choice leads to a series of success stories. My phrase denies the pain, the fear, the qualifications these stories also encompass, but relative to other works and other periods, the short fiction of these years continually shows loss of self leading to resurrection of self. In a genre characterized first by its loyalty to realism, once realism was established, and second by its tendency to associate realism with a dour view of experience, the hard-won joy and victory Lawrence's visionary stories celebrate must be seen in all their originality. Finally, the emphasis on choice leads to a remarkable sexual balance in these stories. Again, with the exceptions named above, these tales and the revisions of 1914 contain some of Lawrence's most subtle reworkings of the Sleeping Beauty myth. That balance is especially worth noting since it will tilt drastically in the stories Lawrence wrote once the war was over and indeed shows signs of tilting in the essays written at this time.

In this chapter, then, I want to emphasize the comedic character of the war tales, underlining in particular their sexual balance and the belief in choice and resurrection they and the revisions of 1914 demonstrate. At the same time, I want the reader to hear distant thunder in the tales "England, My England" and "The Mortal Coil." While they do not generally deny comedy's insistence on the reality of human choice (both *partly* deny it), they do trace patterns of defeat and, in doing so, anticipate the extraordinary conservativism vis-à-vis male-female relationships that marks the postwar tales.

Because excellent work has been done on Lawrence's revisions of *The Prussian Officer* tales (see Cushman, Littlewood, Boulton, Sagar, Kalnins), I will not rehearse here the particulars of those revisions nor the way they relate to the work Lawrence was doing on *The Rainbow*. I do wish, however, to offer a few general comments and focus on two of the tales—"The White Stocking" and "Vin Ordinaire"/"The Thorn in the Flesh"—as a way of indicating Lawrence's development from the work of the previous summer toward the war tales to come.

A key phrase for understanding the development represented by these revisions is dynamic balance. As Lawrence gathered his tales for *The Prussian Officer*, he spotted, for example, discrepancies in the logic of certain pieces. Scenes and summaries did not always perfectly register. Images sometimes undercut argument. Often the warp gave an unfair advantage to figures representing himself or his mother, while denying fair treatment to figures representing his father and Jessie Chambers. "Odour of Chrysanthemums" and "The Shades of Spring" most clearly show Lawrence addressing himself to those disparities, "correcting" aspects of *Sons and Lovers*, and coming up with final versions of the tales that ring true throughout. Those particular revisions demonstrate a surprising humility on Lawrence's part. One has the sense that the security and success that marked this summer invited a thoughtful willingness to allow the ghosts of his past new opportunities to tell their stories.

Another kind of balance is achieved as Lawrence infuses his new visionary style into certain tales. "Daughters of the Vicar" is exemplary here. As Lawrence developed the tale in 1913 and 1914 from the awkward "Two Marriages," he found the means to draw the disparate energies and characters of the early story into a pattern of richly related comparisons and contrasts. Littlewood helpfully describes one example of that progress toward unity and balance when he notes that the early Louisa alternatively sees Alfred as a body, then as a soul. Her powers of perception "ricochet" from one understanding to the other, missing the point that Alfred, and she herself, are creatures of complex integrity. By 1914, Lawrence has found the language to convey the integrity. As Littlewood explains, the language and insights rest on a clear apprehension of the otherness of the other: the strangeness in the coal-covered Alfred "releases in [Louisa] the ability to attend to the other person with a deep, completely absorbed attention, and so to gain a new sense of life in herself, a sense of a new, real self displacing the old."[7] We read that "her soul" watches Alfred, "trying to see what he was" (CSS, 169). A dynamic balance is reached between awareness of other and self, between strangeness and complementarity, and between physical sight and spiritual insight.

Still a third kind of balance occurs in Lawrence's revisions, perhaps as cause, perhaps as effect of the previous two types of balance. This is sexual balance. Here he is not so much correcting an imbalance in the earlier versions as clarifying and strengthening the sexual dynamics of the tales. From "Odour of Chrysanthemums" to "The Thorn in the Flesh," a careful, complex assertion is dramatized, though it is not yet stated in such terms. Men and women alike must undergo crucifixion to find resurrection, and each must individually choose and actively pursue death and rebirth. In several tales, this translates into a decision to leave a safe, communal understanding of self for a daring venture into the risky intimacy of sexual relationship. The two tales I have chosen to examine for their 1914 revisions are especially interesting with respect to this kind of balance. "The White Stocking" presents an almost insurmountable challenge to sexual balance; "The Thorn in the Flesh," a clear example.

In working on "The White Stocking," Lawrence sat down to a text already much revised. From the initial "amusing" anecdote of 1907, the tale had undergone changes in 1910, 1911, and 1913. The 1913 version, published in *Smart Set* in October 1914 owes much, I would argue, to Lawrence's work that summer on "New Eve and Old Adam" and "The Prussian Officer," and is closely related to the revisions he had done in turning "The Vicar's Garden" into "The Shadow in the Rose Garden."[8] I am discussing it here because of two important changes Lawrence made in 1914, the first related to Elsie's dancing with Sam Osborne, the second to the tale's ending.

As published in *Smart Set*, the tale has shifted season from Christmas to Valentine's Day. Not surprisingly, the tale is now about love and its tokens. Silly Prissy has become a vivacious young wife named Elsie, who for two years has been married to George, now called Ted. Lawrence's scenic skills are at their finest as he sets this couple before us. In a three-part structure, we move from Valentine's Day morning, when Elsie secretly receives love tokens from her old boss Sam Adams, to the party two years earlier when she drew out her white stocking and began her flirtation with Sam, then back to Valentine's Day and George's discovery of Elsie's deception. In the 1913 version, extraneous material muddies the second section but the opening and closing sections are clear and powerful. Following the same pattern traced in "The Shadow in the Rose Garden," Lawrence pushes these young marrieds out of their initial sense of themselves and their relationship, plunges them into a bitter quarrel, and then, especially in "The White Stocking," rewards them for their adventures as he ends on a note of renewal. The challenge Lawrence presents us with in the 1914 version of "The White Stocking" is to accept renewal as the result of a beating. One of the finest aspects of Lawrence's 1914 revisions and war tales, I feel, is the balance of power and energy he realizes between his male and female characters. How can the image of Elsie, cowering beneath Ted's rage, be reconciled with that argument?

For me the answer lies in seeing the link between Elsie's dancing with Sam in part 2, Ted's blow in part 3, and Lawrence's repeated dramatizations during this period of the different ways self can be lost and found. In the 1913 version, Elsie dances with Sam only briefly. In 1914 she repeatedly dances with her boss, giving herself up to the music, his sexual allure, and her own delicious sense of irresponsibility. A crucial word here is "fusion." Dance by dance, Elsie moves from a "real" and separate being to one "fused" with another.[9] The peace she feels comes from a loss of self, but it is a loss that leads to no renewal. As Lawrence makes clear in *Women in Love*, the sexual ideal is not the fusion of two into one but a dynamic balance between two distinct, essentially different individuals. Ted is Elsie's obvious alternative to Sam, and we need to see that in no way does he offer her a substitute receptacle for her selfhood.

In part 3, Lawrence emphasizes that Elsie has refused to recognize the depth and power of her own adult, sexual selfhood. Teasing Ted with the stockings Sam has sent that morning, she delights in seeing herself as a bright child, engaging and innocent. Enraged, Ted yells at her, calling her trollop and bitch. In contrast to the earlier version, however, here Ted does not leave the house. Instead, he slaps Elsie, making her bleed.

Clearly Lawrence is gambling with high stakes. The language he uses to describe Ted's lust to see Elsie bleeding and broken is similar to the language he uses to describe other lusts, for example the Prussian officer's lust to break his orderly. "He hung before her, looking at her fixedly, as she stood crouched against the wall with open, bleeding mouth, and wide staring eyes, and two hands

111

clawing over her temples. And his lust to see her bleed, to break her and destroy her, rose from an old source against her. It carried him. He wanted satisfaction" (CSS, 264). In both tales, a link is made between violence and sex. In "The Prussian Officer," the link is intended to be seen as a perversion; in "The White Stocking" it is not. If there is a difference, and I feel that there is, it comes from seeing Ted's rage within its dramatic context.[10]

Among the views that context offers is a sense of Ted's feelings for Elsie. At the moment, they are an intense blend of love and fury. Ted has loved Elsie. She has given him a fine sense of himself and his place in the world. In learning of the deception she has carried on for two years and in observing her pride in that deception, he is threatened, literally furious. In using sexual language to describe Ted's desire to beat Elsie, Lawrence may intend us to see that Ted longs to hurt her, sexually, as she has hurt him. He may further intend us to see that Ted wants to insult, as she has, the sexual relationship they have had. The case is entirely different in "The Prussian Officer."

An equally important aspect of the dramatic context is Lawrence's timing of Ted's lust. The passage quoted above comes after his actual blow. His anger has begun to ebb, and his hunger for satisfaction is more a complaint than an intention. What one sees here is the resurgence of anger that comes after the climax of a fight has passed. Among other things, Lawrence is trying to take the pulse of emotional rhythms, here the rhythm of rage. Immediately, nausea and shame overcome Ted. Those feelings are succeeded by exhaustion, flickerings of anger, compassion, and eventually anguished love. By the tale's close, both characters realize that Ted is no harbor, Elsie no child. Each had misread him- and herself, as well as the other. They can never love each other as simply again.[11]

Finally, dramatic context urges us to contrast the two dance scenes, Elsie's blissful fusion with Sam set against her taunting performance and consequent violent dance with Ted. The result of that first was again loss of self in the movement of the dance and the personality of Sam. The result of the second is not a loss of self in the personality of Ted, but a blow to self struck by fury and by the need to outgrow a childish sense of self. My wish to discuss the 1914 revisions of the tale here comes again partly from the challenge it presents to my overall sense of sexual balance in these works. At the very least, the sexual violence Lawrence dramatizes here invites full analysis. To refuse to recognize the hatred and fury that may be a part of love, as nineteenth-century fiction so often did, is perhaps an even worse kind of violence. There may be, in the other words, something more sexually imbalanced in a classic Dickensian ending than in Ted's miserable blow.[12]

Lawrence's 1914 revision of "The White Stocking" shows him intensifying his exploration into sexual relationships, in particular breaking the lamentable silences of the estranged couples of earlier love stories (e.g., "Odour of Chrysanthemums," "A Modern Lover," "The Witch à la Mode," or "Delilah and Mr. Bircumshaw"). "The Thorn in the Flesh," revised from "Vin Ordinaire," shows similar intensification, this time into the territory of sexual joy. From the defeat traced in "Vin Ordinaire" in 1913, Lawrence reverses the outcome to a victory.

In revising the tale, Lawrence carried forward the identification of self through relationship central to the stories of 1913. But, for the first time since his elopement, he dramatizes an entirely fulfilling relationship. A less swaggering Bachmann flees to a less reserved Emilie. They consummate their love, and he greets his captors with a sure sense of his own worth. Lawrence reinforces the possibility of a happy ending by telling us that the officer Bachmann struck may not be seriously hurt and by sending the baron off after the soldiers to see what he can do to help his servant's beau.

In making this major change in plot, Lawrence develops the character of Emilie and thereby begins to tighten and enrich the dramatic structure of the tale.[13] "Vin Ordinaire" focused on Bachmann. In essence, Lawrence built upon a simple repetition: Bachmann fails to scale the walls of the town and the walls of Emilie. By contrast, "The Thorn in the Flesh" traces a progress and focuses on both Emilie and Bachmann. Lawrence dramatizes their mutual, developing conviction that self and relationship are poorly realized through mass movements and institutions. When their individual sense of themselves and each other is secured, Lawrence reintroduces social forces as a way of testing what the two characters have learned. They pass the test. This pattern will be a familiar one in the war tales. As he does there, here he traces the couple's development through a series of carefully constructed parallels.

In both versions of the tale, the first section introduces Bachmann's situation. In each case, those sections end with him escaping the military and debating where to go. With minor differences, the second sections take him to Emilie. In the third sections, the tales part ways. The brief third section in "Vin Ordinaire" shows Emilie and Bachmann embracing and her deep excitement. In part three of "The Thorn in the Flesh," Lawrence stays the tale's action and gives us a full sense of Emilie's background and character. In revising his conception of her, Lawrence increases her responsiveness and warmth. Equally important, he describes her as one who has found her identity in the role of servant. In adding this, Lawrence has not only filled out her particular character but established a parallel between her situation and Bachmann's. We have already learned that he has "something of a military consciousness, as if he believed in the discipline for himself, and found satisfaction in delivering himself to his duty" (CSS, 118). Lawrence is careful to give a positive tone to the lovers' definitions of themselves as members of large social institutions. As servant and soldier, the two are relatively content. But like the orderly in "The Prussian Officer," they are also relatively asleep. The progress Emilie and Bachmann make toward awakening is again structured along parallel lines.

Both first must break their ties to the institutions that have contained them. For both, the severance is frightening. Bachmann breaks with the military by shaming himself, attacking his superior, and fleeing. Away from the company, he feels an initial freedom. But the freedom soon palls, and he finds himself longing to return to the barracks: "He could not take the responsibility of himself. He must give himself up to someone" (CSS, 122). At this point, Emilie looks like a possible someone. Emilie makes her break by lying to the first group of soldiers who comes seeking Bachmann and by secreting him in her room. By those acts, she finds herself thrust out of the easy freedom she felt in identifying with the system she has served. She has the "insupportable feeling of being out of the order, self-responsible, bewildered" (CSS, 129). "Insupportable" resonates: she finds insupportable or unbearable the situation of being without support. Cut off from their former worlds—in the language of an initiation rite, cut off from their old groups—each is now seeking a new relationship. But Lawrence does not allow the new self and relationship to resemble the old. Emilie and Bachmann do not simply switch from giving themselves over to an institution to giving themselves over to a mate. Their relationship brings an access of self-awareness and responsibility. As he will throughout the war tales, Lawrence repeatedly plays variations on the notion that, through relationship, each has now realized his or her self.

Beginning in parallel situations, breaking out of them in parallel ways, Emilie and Bachmann establish an intimate relationship and new self in similarly parallel ways. It is important to see the mutuality of their communion partly because a careless reading of the tale can discover a Sleeping Beauty myth. She is "helpless," infinitely grateful to Bachmann, and finds in their love-making her own "static" and "eternal" reality. Bachmann wears a male cliché or two himself. Lying "proud" and "easy" beside Emilie, he feels himself at last "able to take command" (CSS, 132). As he did in "New Eve and Old Adam," here Lawrence employs the language of trite romance, while alerting the reader to look beyond cliché.

Lawrence alerts the reader in two ways, first by using the same language to describe both Bachmann and Emilie and second by reversing the standard staging of certain scenes. For example, he tells us that after their love-making, Emilie lies close to Bachmann "in her static reality" (CSS, 132). She is "soft," "eternal," "absorbed." In most fictions, these would be trigger words for female primitivism. But Bachmann, we read, also rests in "a curious silence, a blankness, like something eternal possessed him" (CSS, 134). Emilie stands before the baron with a "naked" and "exposed" soul. So does Bachmann. Perhaps the mutuality is best said in this passage: "They loved each other, and all was whole. She loved him, he had taken her, she was given to him. It was right. He was given to her, and they were one, complete" (CSS, 130). Later Lawrence says, "They knew each other. They were themselves" (CSS, 134). This language lacks the richness of Lawrence's later love language, but obviously it is meant to convey a relationship that is refreshingly unhierarchical.

The mutuality of their courtship is perhaps best shown in Lawrence's staging of their first scene in Emilie's bedroom. Bachmann has gone to Emilie. In this instance, he is the initiator. But once there, he must lie upstairs in her bedroom and wait. In fact, he is in the situation of a mistress: he is waiting in his lover's quarters until she can finish up her responsibilities and go to him. Emilie does slip away from her work for a moment and goes up to visit Bachmann. As she enters her room, he is sitting on the bed. Reversing the staging he had set up in his earlier version of this scene, Lawrence has Emilie cross over to Bachmann. Bachmann remains seated, burying his face against her. In this their first embrace she towers above him; in fact, as she holds his head, they create something of a mother-son tableau. But this image no more sums up the dispersal of power in their relationship than does her curtsy on leaving him. As the tale repeatedly shows, both have power, both have need. As throughout the 1914 revisions, a life-enhancing balance has been struck.

Reshaping a tale that had far less structural interest or complexity, Lawrence reorganizes this story into a series of parallel scenes, motivations, images. And those parallels of course help state the theme. One of his earliest salvation tales, "The Thorn in the Flesh" implies the need for equality in a quickening relationship, a theme that again characterizes the war tales to come. Here, in particular, he asks the reader to shake the dust off gender-typed terms such as "helpless" and "grateful," inviting us to discover the human sexual meaning within them.

Lawrence worked hard on his revisions throughout the month of July. On August 5, he learned that war between England and Germany had been declared. Days later he was informed that Methuen had cancelled its plans to publish *The Rainbow*. In sheer rage at the war, and, one suspects, at his setback with the *The Rainbow*, Lawrence began "The Study of Thomas Hardy," a wide-ranging piece of unfinished personal literary criticism giving Lawrence's views of men, women, tragedy, art, and of course Hardy's fiction as well as his own. From there he returned to *The Rainbow*, writing it for the last time. His next work in short fiction did not come until the spring of 1915, when he wrote "England, My England."[14]

As I read this first of Lawrence's fictions to be conceived after the onset of the war, this first to deal explicitly with the war, I discern a shocked response, one that Lawrence will quickly repress, at least in his fiction, to revive years later. Among other things, the tale demonstrates Lawrence's sense, articulated in his letters, that he must make direct proclamations about the war. One proclamation is the assertion that the English people have chosen this war, chosen to die. He will maintain this insistance on choice through the war tales, but a second item is his proposition that a close sexual relationship between individuals can finally cloy; indeed, such love can stultify the female and make the vast impersonality and sacrifice of warfare look attractive to the male. This is an extraordinary statement for Lawrence to make at this time, and, again, he quickly drops it, as well as the sexual imbalance it implies. Overall, I see "England, My England" in both its 1915 and 1921 versions as a curiously flawed performance, in which Lawrence's assertions about choice are eventually contradicted by the male-female relationships he has imagined.

The tale has a peculiar biographical background. In January of 1915, the Lawrences moved from Chesham to a country cottage in Sussex, loaned to them by a friend, Viola Meynell. The various members of the family become the major characters in "England, My England." Percy Lucas, in particular, is satirized as Evelyn Daughtry (Egbert in the 1921 text), a passive, ineffectual dilet-tante who in the middle of the tale is shipped to France and dies in action. The story came out in October 1915; the following July, Percy Lucas lived out the tale, dying of machine gun wounds in a base hospital in France.[15]

Lawrence originally structured the tale as a flashback. Pre-sumably, one is in Evelyn Daughtry's mind as he lies wounded in France. The tale opens with Evelyn dreaming that he is at home. But his wife, Winifred, quickly takes over and controls the first third of the narrative. In fact, after the first few sentences, all pre-tense that this is a flashback disappears; the tale progresses with Lawrence's usual blend of omniscient and third-person intimate points of view. As the reader learns through Winifred, Evelyn is purposeless. With an income of £150 a year, "he merely lived from day to day," working in his garden (*English Review*, October 1915, 239). His failure to commit himself to anything begins to gall his wife: "She wanted some result, some production, some new active output into the world of man, not only the hot, physical welter, and children" (*English Review*, 240). When their oldest child, Joyce, contracts blood poisoning from a cut on her knee, the quar-rel between Evelyn and Winifred deepens. Evelyn can do nothing to save the child's life; he simply suffers. As she has for years, Winifred turns to her father for emotional and financial help. The child lives but will be crippled for life. The tale's focus shifts here as war is declared; for the remaining two-thirds of the tale, we adopt Evelyn's point of view as we follow him through his induc-tion, occasional weekends at home, and death in France.

That Lawrence intended "England, My England" to capture timely truths about his compatriots is clear from his letters and the tale itself. He writes to Lady Cynthia Asquith in September 1915,

"The story is the story of most men and women who are married today—of most men at the war, and wives at home" (CL, 364). At the very outset, Lawrence's title asks the reader to think beyond the particular. As we meet his characters, he continues his generalizing tendency. Although Winifred, Joyce, Evelyn, and even Winifred's father are based on immediate acquaintances, through most of the tale Lawrence refuses them individual presence, mainly by refusing them any dramatic scenes. Remarkably, it is not until halfway through the tale, when Evelyn is shipped to France, that we get a developed scene. Before this, all is summary and analysis.

Further, in that very summary and analysis, Lawrence uses images, contrasts, and language that increase one's awareness of these characters as types.[16] Evelyn is the flower of an old, refined, south-of-England family. Lost in his love of the past, he sees his farm as separated from the world, changeless, full of peace. Winifred, by contrast, is a northerner, daughter of a practical, self-made man. Like the Brangwen women, Winifred insists that the peace of the farm is a nullity. It cripples the children, the future. In Evelyn's preciousness, Winifred sees "something evil" (*English Review*, 242). Having to turn to her father, she is forced into a kind of incestuous relationship that leaves both her and Evelyn bitter and sterile. The wedding—of old England and new, south and north, poetic and practical—has failed. Like Englishmen in general, Evelyn responds to that failure by joining the war, literally and psychologically. Like Englishwomen in general, Winifred responds to the failure and the war by denying herself all feeling, joy, and desire.

In its generalizing tendency and patterned characters, "England, My England" looks toward the visionary quality of other wartime fictions. In its specific judgment on Evelyn, it introduces those fictions in another way. Although Evelyn and English soldiers by the thousands lie shattered, bleeding their life's blood into the fields of France, the tale judges them not as tragic but as dying the death they have chosen and deserve. In both issues—the cultural generalizations and the refusal of the tragic vision—the tale introduces the work of the period. However, in its dramatization of Evelyn as ineffectual because he has no purposeful, masculine life outside his marriage, "England, My England" denies the controlling vision of the contemporaneous tales and anticipates Lawrence's postwar fiction. A brief look at Lawrence's thinking on masculine activity and camaraderie may clarify the foreshadowing "England, My England" represents.

As early as his 1911 drafts of *Paul Morel*, Lawrence writes that it is the male's duty to transform the energy he derives from the female into social or artistic products.[17] By nature, women live a full, earthy, present-centered life. They need men, who do not live that same life, to formulate their experiences and energies into lasting expressions, such as art, philosophy, social institutions. (It is characteristic of Lawrence's early work that here he studies male activity as it relates to women's fulfillment; the man's fulfillment does not yet especially concern him.) Among the other things one notices in *Paul Morel* and *Sons and Lovers* is that male activity and responsibility are not related to male camaraderie. Walter Morel and the other colliers enjoy male friendships, but their solidarity signals little purposive activity from them. In fact, it tends to signal the opposite: a lot of wasted time, drunken talk, and wandering.

In "The Prussian Officer," Lawrence comes at the issue from a different although related angle, arguing that unalloyed masculine closeness and "purpose" are claustrophobic and lead to perversion. This is roughly Ursula's contention in her arguments with Skrebensky in *The Rainbow*. Lawrence also announces this stand in an earlier letter: "Soldiers, being herded together, men without women, never being *satisfied* by a woman, as a man never is from a street affair, get their surplus sex and their frustration and dissatisfaction into the blood, and *love* cruelty. It is sex lust fermented makes atrocity" (CL, 156). In much milder terms, "The Thorn in the Flesh" also speaks to the need of a single man for a single woman. In that tale, the world of masculine activity is a dead end. If I am right about Lawrence's original version of "The Mortal Coil," it argued the same view. (See chapter 5.)

"England, My England" draws together many of these concerns, but takes them in a new direction. Like Walter Morel, Evelyn dams up his wife's energies. Like Mrs. Morel, Winifred suffers for that confinement. But in "England, My England," it is partly the man's close relationship with his wife, his vital marriage as it were, that is leading him to purposelessness. One feels that Mrs. Morel, furiously rocking away the lonely hours, would be surprised at this development. In that novel, the male's purposelessness is linked to his *distance* from wife and home. In "England, My England," Lawrence also poses a new question, one that will come to plague Rupert Birkin: what goals in the world are available, what purposes worthwhile? In the rejected "Prologue" of *Women in Love*, Rupert's answer is despairing: he hates his work with the schools because he does not believe in it. But "where should a man repair, what should he do?"[18] For awhile, Evelyn simply "dodged everything" (*English Review*, 242). The war then offers him a way to escape his major problems—his cloying dependence on his wife and his inability to find anything apart from or beyond her to which he can devote himself. A solution it is, but a deadly one.

The fact that Lawrence asks only Evelyn to wrestle with the problem of finding purposeful social activity in a time of cultural disintegration raises the issue of sexual balance and, I believe, points to the fundamental flaw in the tale's argument. That flaw is only made worse by Lawrence's revisions in 1921.

Consisting largely of additions, Lawrence's revisions doubled the length of the tale. Developing all of the characters, he adds long passages that trace the thinking of Evelyn (now called Egbert) and Winifred, explanations of Godfrey Marshall's character, and dramatic scenes of Joyce's accident, illness, and slow recovery. He also expanded the role of the narrator, an issue I will deal with below. The additions to Egbert's portrait cause no difficulties, underscoring as they do the hero's radical decision to die. The passages developing Winifred and Mr. Marshall, however, point up the tale's weakness.

In the *English Review* text, Winifred speaks only through the first third of the tale. Her primary statement is a declaration of frustration and disappointment in her husband. Once war is declared, she fades, leaving the stage to Evelyn. In the expanded text, her voice is heard until almost the end; and a dour voice it is. Now a bit of a tragedienne, Winifred becomes a "lump of seriousness," a "Mater Dolorata." She turns her back on the irresponsible Egbert and coldly devotes herself to whatever she sees as her duty. Gloomier than the earlier Winifred, this later Winifred is "explained." The explanation lies with her father, Godfrey Marshall, and, of course, with Egbert.

In the revised text, Marshall blossoms from a sketchy character into an idealized leadership figure. He is what all men should be, what all women long for, an irrepressible power, a glowing representative of masculine energy. (This characterization of Marshall reminds us that Lawrence was revising "England, My England" at the same time as he was writing *Aaron's Rod*.) A burly businessman, Marshall is "unscrupulous" as "a striving tree . . . pushing its single way in a jungle of others." He is, obviously, Egbert's foil. Having known real authority in her father, Winifred can only resent her husband's diffidence and neutrality.

The problem with the tale lies in the contradiction between Lawrence's antitragic stance toward Egbert and his vision of Winifred. As I have noted, Egbert prefers to do nothing, is the ultimate cause of his child's being crippled (a significant statement in this tale of the English nation), chooses to join the war, chooses to die. Choice—continuing choice—is the governing idea behind his character. The narrator may express occasional admiration for Egbert's honest anarchism, but he maintains that there is nothing tragic, nothing inevitable or incongruous, in Egbert's life or death. All is appropriate to his deepest desires and inclinations.

When one turns to Winifred, an altogether different view of human experience is presented. Unlike Lawrence's more spirited heroines, Winifred is defined mainly in reaction to Egbert. Saying little for herself or her own capacities, she assumes that his failures spell out her own. Lawrence's characterization of the second Winifred extends the fatalism. The narrator explains that all women for all time are like fragile vines. To live, they must have a male trellis. If the times are such that no males will assume this authority, the women must suffer, languish, die. Here it seems to me that Lawrence is employing the very view of experience that his tale is set up to disparage. The life of the pathetic Winifred, once so gay, so full of promise, is foiled "inevitably and incongruously." Through no fault of her own, she becomes as twisted as her crippled Joyce. For her, things should have been otherwise, Egbert should have been more, she has not deserved or chosen this fate. The notion that "our desires compel our destinies" is inappropriate to her life.

Winifred's relationship to her father emphasizes the difficulties. In a tale about radical choice, she—a strong and lively woman—craves an endless childhood, a perpetual escape from choice. Her father, although similarly strong and lively, encourages her desire. What we have here are classic, gender-based stereotypes. As Lawrence continually saw in other tales of the period, people are more complex, more interesting. The vision of Godfrey Marshall as an oak tree, of Winifred as a vine, denies Lawrence's usual sense of each human consciousness as a field of conflicting needs and desires, of human identity as a mixture of masculine and feminine traits, as our culture defines those traits. Winifred may speak to the longing in all of us to be ruled, but to rise above caricature she must also speak to our opposing longings to kill our fathers and mothers, to be free, self-responsible. Marshall may speak to our wish to rule, but he must also speak to our yearnings to submit.

Whether the tale's views of choice and responsibility are seen as contradictory in themselves or as oversimplified in reference to the world, the tale itself reacts in interesting ways to the problem. That reaction, especially clear in the 1921 version, shows up in the voice of the narrator. According to Lawrence, the worst thing about narrowing one's fiction, or thinking, toward any exclusive stance is the inevitable reaction that sets in.[19] His remark is appropriate to "England, My England." In presenting his contradictory or overly simplified views of Egbert, Winifred, and Mr. Marshall, in proclaiming his doctrines of absolute choice, submission, and authority, the narrator becomes a study in actions and reactions. At one point he is didactic, at another rhapsodic, now flippant, now jeering. At times, one feels Lawrence overworking his rhythms, even his punctuation marks, in hopes they will create the intensity that he usually captures through imagery or ritual action. The unaccountable shifts in tone—added to the inflated rhetoric, forests of exclamation points, question marks, and wearisome explanations—are, of course, irritating and confusing.[20] And yet, in a peculiar way, they ultimately argue for Lawrence's integrity as artist and thinker. As in *Aaron's Rod*, where similar weaknesses plague the performance of a prolix narrator, one suspects that Lawrence is not convinced by what he is writing. Could he argue cogently that the world needs absolute leaders, that men must choose to be those leaders, that women must simply and joyfully submit, we might put Lawrence aside without a qualm. As it is, in this strained tale—and in others—we are compelled to watch him track and backtrack, assert a position and then withdraw into flippancy, and protest too much. One could say that his "art speech" or true message comes through in the tale's flailing about.

I have analyzed "England, My England" at length partly because in its original version it stands at the threshold of Lawrence's war tales and in both versions typifies certain aspects and difficulties of the leadership tales. In closing I would em-

phasize that its weaknesses are not necessarily related to its rejecting the conventions of realism. The clear presence of the narrator
in the passages of explanation and analysis, for example, is no
problem in itself. It is the story-teller's tone that weakens the
tale. Similarly, the stylization of character—realized through
symbolic gestures, exaggerated contrasts, few developed scenes
—is no problem. Only when the stylization yields a type that
either contradicts one of the main points of the tale or leads
to an oversimplification of human experience do objections
seem appropriate.

After "England, My England," the flailing about abruptly
ceases and we encounter a series of beautifully worked, visionary
tales which assert the authority of private experience and its power
to resurrect cultures and individuals alike. The first of the avowed
resurrection tales is also the simplest and least ambitious. Written
several months after "England, My England," "The Thimble" is
soft in tone, simple in plot. The heroine is apparently a portrait of
Lady Cynthia Asquith. Lawrence writes to her in October 1915,
"Your showing me that detestable Selfridge sketch of yourself reminds me that I have done a rather good word sketch of you: in a
story. I think it is good" (*CL*, 372). According to Roberts, the
central incident is based on an event in the life of the Asquiths.[21]
Lawrence published the tale in *Seven Arts* in March 1917. He
then entirely rewrote it as "The Ladybird" in 1921.[22]

Lawrence told Lady Cynthia explicitly that the story is a tale
of resurrection. Arguing that England should give in to Germany,
he minimizes what would be lost: "One should give anything now,
give the Germans England and the whole empire, if they want it,
so we may save the hope of a resurrection from the dead, we English, all Europe. What is the whole empire and kingdom save the
thimble in my story? If we could but bring our souls through, to
life" (*CL*, 372–73).

The tale's center is a conversation. Married in the early days
of the war, the hero and heroine were once enthusiastic comrades,
enjoying their quick, intense honeymoon as "a sort of Bacchic
revel before death" (*Phoenix II*, 53). In their initial situation, they
remind the reader of Clifford and Connie Chatterley. Soon after
the honeymoon, the husband is sent to France and the wife, in
Mayfair, builds around herself a complete, separate world. Amid
all her war work and activity, she suddenly falls ill with pneumonia. That spell of sickness becomes for her a dark night, killing

her old self, leaving her adrift. While she is ill, her husband is badly wounded. The tale opens with her still somewhat convalescent, awaiting his return. As she sits nervously on the sofa, her hand digs down into the cushions and retrieves an old, tarnished thimble. Her husband comes, his jaw shattered, mouth badly sunken in. Hepburn's wound has its symbolic appropriateness: he cannot speak clearly, he can only mumble. By this point in the tale, Lawrence has moved each character through his and her respective journeys into death and brought each up to a moment of decision.

The Hepburns's conversation is initially awkward and painful. Through the first half, we see mainly through the wife's perspective. She feels the object of accident; but as we would expect in this antitragic fiction, the belief in accident is undercut by a belief in the possibility of self-creation. Hepburn at first wavers between his old, bright, superficial response to things—a false language, a mumble—and a new response that takes into account his near death, his present helplessness, his desire for life. The new response wins out, and he takes control of the conversation; as in "The Blind Man," in this tale the war wound takes on ironic significance. The war has made the blind see, the mute speak. Wooing her in strange language, Hepburn seeks to persuade his wife not to surrender to a belief in accident, but instead to believe in her capacity to love, grow, be born again. "'Resurrection?'" she asks, almost mockingly (*Phoenix II*, 62). For a moment she refuses, using a phrase that Lawrence will introduce in the tales to come: "'Touch me not, for I am not yet ascended unto the Father'" (*Phoenix II*, 62). Having commanded him not to touch, not to approach, she at once switches stance and asks to be approached, to be touched. In a gesture that constitutes a pact between them, Hepburn reaches out to her, "and the touch lay still, completed there" (*Phoenix II*, 63). With his first strong movement, he takes the old thimble and tosses it out into the street.

Thin as the tale is, it does chart a clear progress out of superficiality, into death, and toward resurrection. As such, it introduces subsequent tales such as "The Horse Dealer's Daughter" and "The Blind Man." Like them, this tale locates the leap of faith in a physical gesture of touch; it locates resurrection in the coming together of two individuals. Exemplifying the visionary quality of these war tales, plot in this story is a ritualized action, here a rite of passage focusing on the stage of transition. The characters have lost an old, secure identity. They are now in limbo. The tale dramatizes three possible futures: they may return to their old selves; they may remain untied and uncommitted; or they may attempt to create a new self, capable of self-direction and of forming new, life-bearing relationships. As in most of the other wartime tales, here Lawrence dramatizes the last choice.

The character of the heroine is interesting for several reasons, among which is the fact that she is the antithesis of Winifred in "England, My England." Like Elizabeth Bates, Louisa Lindley, Ursula Brangwen, Isabel Pervin, Lou Witt, Kate Leslie, and Connie Chatterley, the heroine of "The Thimble" is a woman eternally trying to understand her own life. Lawrence's description of her could almost fit Birkin: "For she was a woman who was always trying to grasp the whole of her context, always trying to make a complete thing of her own life" (*Phoenix II*, 54). As must Birkin, Ursula, Mellors, and Connie Chatterley, she must learn to see herself as neither the object of accident nor the agent of total control. She must learn to live somewhere between responding to the life around her and trying to change it.

If "The Thimble" intimates the direction Lawrence's resurrection tales would take, "The Horse Dealer's Daughter" exemplifies the genre.[23] It is perhaps Lawrence's best-known tale of resurrection. First called "The Miracle," it reminds one of a comment Lawrence made on Thomas Hardy's fiction. His characters, Lawrence observed, are always bursting into being. The *via media* for their struggle is usually love; the rhythm is explosive; nowhere "is there the slightest development of personal action in the character."[24] Mabel Pervin and Sam Fergusson similarly burst into flower, but Lawrence adds an important dimension. In both characters there is "development of personal action"; one character in particular must consciously, deliberately choose to flower.[25]

The dramatic action of "The Horse Dealer's Daughter" is another ritual progress out of superficiality into death and rebirth. Upon her father's death, the heroine Mabel Pervin, aged twenty-seven, has been struggling to run a household for her grown brothers. Her efforts are ineffectual, the family is in debt. The tale opens on the day that their house is being sold out from under them. The children convene for their last breakfast together. With what has become a characteristic narrative technique, Lawrence gives that opening scene in detail and then steps back and fills in background and motive. Mabel, we learn, has managed to tolerate the family's declining fortunes, her brothers' slumberous ineffectuality, and her own loneliness partly because she has felt that she held an ace in the hole. Whatever happens, she can join her mother—who has been dead thirteen years.

With this background established, the tale comes back to the present as Mabel goes for the last time to clip the grass and arrange the flowers on her mother's grave. She believes that she is invisible in the churchyard although she is in fact "exposed to the stare of everyone" (CSS, 447). The crucial watcher this day is Sam Fergusson, a young doctor in the town. As he stands gazing at her rapt devotions, she becomes aware of his presence. Their eyes meet briefly, each is startled, and Fergusson walks off feeling mesmerized by her. Later that afternoon as he is continuing his rounds, he sees Mabel, far in the distance, walk slowly into a deep pond and disappear. He runs to the pond, saves her, takes her home, undresses her, and wraps her in a blanket. As she returns to consciousness, she asks with the simplicity of desperation that he love her. His assent is halting, but assent he finally does. They make plans to marry.

In constructing this tale, Lawrence uses precisely the same principle he had employed in "The Thorn in the Flesh." We have a dual rescue here, a double vision of death and resurrection.[26] For example, Mabel finds joy and company in tending her mother's grave. Lawrence tells us that the life she followed in the world was less real than the death she inherited from her mother (CSS, 448). In her struggles, she has escaped humiliation only in her "subtle, intimate connection" with her mother. Sam Fergusson's experience is similar. Equally lonely and exhausted, he struggles along trying to treat an endless succession of illnesses in a community that he feels enslaves him. His escape is a similar subtle connection, in this case, with the working people he treats. Both compensatory connections are deathly. Lawrence implies that Fergusson's excitement in rubbing up against the lives of these "rough, strongly-feeling people" is voyeuristic. Like so many other characters in the middle tales, both Mabel and Sam physically exhibit their soul's malaise. Mabel's look is set, impassive, blank. Sam is pale, perpetually coughing, scarcely able to make his rounds.

The parallels continue as Lawrence moves into the tale's two crisis scenes, which one might call the pond and kitchen rescues.[27] The pond scene in particular illustrates Lawrence's superb ability to capture the apocalyptic in the colloquial. The scene opens with Fergusson standing on a rise, looking down into a hollow. He stares in fascination as he perceives Mabel, then runs to save her. His wading into the pond is horrible to him, as the cold, slimy water gradually rises up to his waist. In reaching for her, he loses his balance and goes under for a terrifying moment. She rises near him and he drags them both back to land. Like Mabel, Fergusson has descended from sickness to death. But in the descending, both have also initiated the first steps of an ancient rite of ascent, the rite of baptism by immersion. Fergusson goes under for what seems "an eternity," but he then "rose again, . . . gasped, and knew he was in the world" (CSS, 450). The key verb is of course "to rise," but as Lawrence often does in his visionary fiction, he also makes his verb of being resonate with meaning.[28] Fergusson knows that he *is* in the world, that he exists. Mabel rises alongside him.

The pond scene operates on both a ritual and literal level. But it works on another level as well. For both characters, Lawrence uses the scene to chart a psychological progress. Previously, Fergusson has kept his loving on an abstract, charitable, and voyeuristic plane. When he descends into the pond, he forces himself to participate in a loving that is first-hand and threatening, a loving that furthermore includes the horrible, the rank. In this descent, Fergusson is undergoing an act his near-contemporary, Rupert Birkin, highly recommends. He is becoming aware—here, physically aware—of corruption, rankness, the cold, muddy, processes of decay, the possibility of death. The sexual dimension of the issue is clear to Birkin and clear within the language of Fergusson's descent. Further, as one critic has persuasively argued, Mabel has symbolically acted out her need to return to maternal depths. Fergusson then "delivers" her, as she will soon deliver him.[29]

If Fergusson rescues Mabel in the pond scene, in the kitchen scene Mabel rescues Fergusson. Back up on land, in the world again, Mabel forces Sam to recognize what has happened. In a sense, she makes him go through the experience again, this time consciously. At the beginning of the pond scene he was literally above her, on a rise, distant. Now he is mentally and emotionally distant from her, feeling superior, aloof. He stands on his professional honor, with "no intention" of descending into genuine sexual contact. As Lawrence traces Fergusson's mental struggle, he shows Fergusson's reluctance and pride, his impulse to remain apart, battling with his desire to yield to the love and intimacy Mabel offers. Finally Fergusson loses his "professional balance," falls into love and desire, grasps Mabel, kisses her, and rises to a new life, a new self. As they each draw back, change their clothes, make plans, stifle misgivings, anticipate the future, the reader realizes that now they are truly on land again.[30]

In its insistence that these characters make conscious what their physical or primal selves have experienced, "The Horse Dealer's Daughter" exemplifies a point introduced above with respect to "New Eve and Old Adam." The underself is of deep interest to Lawrence, but he does not isolate it from other selves. To see this, especially in this tale, absolves the tale from a charge Graham Hough leveled years ago. Like many of Lawrence's tales, writes Hough, this one has "a disconcerting air of harshness and cruelty." Hough is speaking to what he sees as a lack of choice in the line of action the characters take. Too often, he argues, Lawrence's characters are driven to do "just what they do not want to do. . . . Lawrence feels the primacy of unconsciousness and unrecognized forces so strongly that he must show them harshly victorious over all opposition. A harmonious accommodation between conscious and unconscious would not serve his end, however frequently this occurs in normal experience."[31] But what "drives" Mabel and Sam together is mutual need. Keeping them apart is not a conscious disinclination toward each other as Hough suggests, but fear, reserve, shame, morbidity. Further, the scene in the kitchen would seem to provide very much what Hough finds lacking, that harmonious accommodation between consciousness and unconsciousness.

Nevertheless, Hough's charge of an air of harshness rings true up to a point. The air comes from several sources. For one, Lawrence's methods of dramatizing the underself create a mood of starkness. As in "The Prussian Officer," he thoroughly isolates his characters in "The Horse Dealer's Daughter." Also, Lawrence keeps particularizing detail to a minimum. Characters are, again, stripped down. Few "slight incidents" display the fine shades of these characters' lives. The reader knows less about Mabel Pervin's appearance, house, feelings, clothes, turns of speech, for example, than about Elizabeth Bates's. Further, Lawrence rarely gives the tale over to any character's point of view. To see a situation through a particular character's eyes is usually to comprehend his or her psychology and often to sympathize. Lacking that perspective, one may, again, register a feeling of starkness. But still another source of the feeling may come from the kind of hero and heroine Lawrence has given us here. In some ways, they resemble the unbeautiful characters that populate the novels of the Brontë sisters. Like those sisters, Lawrence avoids the conventional love match. In this tale of rescue and true love, Mabel is anything but a coy, fair princess, Sam anything but a stouthearted prince. When Mabel aggressively woos this man, their climactic love scene reads as unconventionally as their characterizations. Yet, much as these characterizations may further a sense of the tale's harshness, the fact that a staunch, unlovely woman can claim her mate as urgently as Mabel does—without earning the tale's opprobrium, rather earning its praise—may suggest something very different from harshness. The years during which Lawrence was writing "The Horse Dealer's Daughter" were bitter. During them he writes some of his strongest essays about the need for males to dominate, females to submit.[32] Yet this tale, like most of the others Lawrence wrote during the war, dramatizes its male and female characters with a fine tolerance for and recognition of their mutual human needs, powers, dreams.

In "The Blind Man," written in November 1918, just after the Armistice, the story-teller in Lawrence continues to hold out against the claims of the essayist. Again, dynamic balance more than dominance and submission marks the complex structure of this resurrection tale. Before turning to the tale, I want to review some of the arguments that inform one of his major essays of the period, "Education of the People," written during the same month as "The Blind Man."

The essay begins with the claim that men and women are different but equal. Men and women should greet each other as "magic foreigners." But, not surprisingly, men are the proper leaders. Men must go ahead as the scouts, the "outriders," at the tip of life (*Phoenix*, 665). To fit themselves for this activity they must be trained, as boys, in battle; as men, they must create bonds with each other as they travel out in the "womenless regions of fight, and pure thought and abstracted instrumentality . . . " (*Phoenix*, 665). My intention at this juncture, however, is less to point out these sentiments, and more to reinforce the idea that one of Lawrence's great strengths as a writer was his ability continually to see opposing possibilities in the issues he confronted. "The Blind

Man" explores the need in both a man and a woman to move beyond the closed circle of marital love. In doing so, it recognizes a complexity in sexual relations nowhere apparent in "Education of the People."

Using a structural principle that had worked well for him since *Sons and Lovers* and the Croydon stories, Lawrence builds this tale of men, women, and friendship around a triangle of characters: Bertie Reid, Isabel Pervin, and Maurice Pervin.[33] Keeping in mind Lawrence's sentiments in "Education of the People," one may initially wonder if Bertie Reid is one of those heroes who works in a region beyond women, a region of abstraction and grand, inhuman activity. Bertie does engage in "pure thought" and "abstracted instrumentality"; he is "a brilliant and successful barrister." But in the tale he is hardly a male wonder. Bertie is in fact pathetic. He is childish, afraid, sterile. In Bertie, Lawrence perceives that the desire to live in the "womanless regions of fight and pure thought and abstracted instrumentality" may be related to a man's withdrawal from sexual relations, to his negative sense of himself as a physical being. Bertie is kind, constant, but also "unable ever to enter into close contact of any sort" (CSS, 359). His kindness, womanlessness, and abstraction are part of a whole personality, which we, like Isabel, can admire, love, despise, and pity all at the same time. The essay eschews this kind of subtlety. In the tale Lawrence also denies the idea that being womanless will free a man to make close male contacts. It is the same inability to open himself up to the adventure of heterosexual love that makes Bertie wince and draw back from Maurice's invitation to male love and friendship.[34]

Lawrence develops in Maurice a similarly complex figure. Harkening back to the early Brangwen men, Maurice is a tower of darkness, quick in his perceptions, fine in emotion, and in touch with the earth he moves through; in one sense, his blindness, caused by a war wound, is ironic. But it is also appropriate. For again like the Brangwen men, Maurice is occasionally swamped by his sensuality. It is important to see that the closeness he feels toward his wife and farm are beginning to constrain him.[35] He needs to move out, establish contacts and centers of interest beyond them. At this point one may ask if Lawrence's tale is simply dramatizing the essay's point that "men who can only hark back to woman become automatic, static" (*Phoenix*, 665). Asked another way, is this tale a curious retelling of "England, My England"? The answer is no, for in the tale, as few critics have seen, Isabel also requires an expanding of her own boundaries.[36] And here Law-rence introduces a new note, a note of friendship.

Like Maurice, Isabel has begun to feel exhausted by the tight intimacy of their exclusive relationship. In arranging Bertie's visit, she is partly hoping that he and Maurice will establish some friendship, but, equally, she is yearning herself for a breath of fresh air. In analyzing this tale, too few critics have looked sufficiently at the relationship between Bertie and Isabel. Bertie is, quite simply, her friend. Lawrence tells us, "They had been brought up near to one another, and all her life, he had been her friend, like a brother but better than her own brothers. She loved him—though not in the marrying sense. There was a sort of kin-ship between them, an affinity" (CSS, 348–49). In fact, Isabel feels for Bertie almost precisely the kind of love—a love of likes, not of opposites, and therefore not a sexual, marrying love— that Lawrence wants men to share. This is important to see for several reasons.

For one, Isabel's love of Bertie recognizes the similarity within difference that has always been one of the cruxes of male-female relationships. In a wide-ranging study, "Untangling the Roots of Modern Sex Roles," Ruth Bloch states what most of us probably intuit: "The history of sex roles and sexual symbolism can be viewed as an interplay between two fundamentally different definitions of the social relations of the sexes, one of which stresses similarity, the other dissimilarity."[37] In "The Blind Man" and in much of his art, Lawrence dramatizes that very interplay beween similarity and difference. For example, Isabel and Bertie are not "magic foreigners"; their friendship is based in part on their similarity. Maurice and Isabel, however, are magic foreign-ers. (And surprisingly, she, the female, is the intellectual and works in the world; he, the male, is sensual and in close contact with the earth.) Out of their differences comes the adventure into the opposite that brings attraction and new life. But Lawrence does not rest the issues here either. Maurice and Isabel are not only foreigners to each other; they are also similar. Both, for ex-ample, need intimacy and friendship. Between them there is much sympathy, much of the ability to feel with another that Lawrence saw at this time as so vital an aspect of Walt Whit-man's vision.

Isabel's needing and having the friendship, which Lawrence

envisions in "Education of the People" as masculine, points then to his awareness on one level of the similarity in needs and gratifications that men and women share. But it also points to a different, more personal issue in Lawrence. That issue is Lawrence's tendency to imagine women as somehow holding the secret to the universe. In "The Blind Man," for example, Maurice reaches out to Bertie and as a result, grows, sends out a new shoot. But we cannot avoid the fact that Bertie turns him down. Isabel gets just what she wanted. Given room, she is able to fulfill her sexual and social, her intellectual and emotional needs. She and Bertie are friends, she and Maucie are lovers and friends. Of the three, she alone has everything. She is not pregnant for nothing.

In his study, *D. H. Lawrence and the New World*, Cavitch offers a clear analysis, first of the tendency in Lawrence to equate the female with the creative and capable, and second of the reaction the tendency caused. Arguing that, with his mother's death, Paul Morel embraces the positive values he perceived in her, Cavitch writes that "the feminine image is identified with his essential self."[38] What is true for Paul here is true for Lawrence; Cavitch goes on to state that Lawrence's "creative self was so closely bound to his image of women that he needed constantly to defend the genius of himself against the conscious shame of effeminacy." As a man in society he at times tried to deny what he saw as the feminine within him; as an artist, however, his very ambivalence about his male and female identities "led him into preternaturally sensitive examinations of all human relations and institutions. . . . "[39]

That Lawrence might have gone along with at least parts of this analysis is suggested by his own observation in "The Study of Thomas Hardy" that there is an imbalance of male and female energies in most artists. "A man who is well balanced between male and female, in his own nature is as a rule happy, easy to mate, easy to satisfy, and content to exist. It is only a disproportion, or a dissatisfaction, which makes the man struggle into articulation" (*Phoenix*, 460). Examining "The Blind Man" in relation to "Education of the People" demonstrates that the "disproportion" in Lawrence can but does not always produce highly sensitive, complex images of human relationships. In "The Blind Man," Lawrence dramatizes an understanding of human relations that includes love and friendship, accounts for similarities and differences, and asserts the inseparability of one's sexual self from one's other selves. In the essay, as in the postwar tales to come, his masculinity is much on the defensive as it orders and implores women to give up energy and responsibility.

In emphasizing sexual balance in "The Blind Man" I have neglected Lawrence's remarkable evocation of Maurice's particular mode of knowing and existing. In fact, as in any well-designed tale, the interests complement and imply each other. Just as the central threesome dramatizes multiple facets of quick relationships, so does it dramatize multiple ways of knowing. And just as the clue to Lawrence's understanding of males and females does not lie in simple antinomy, so the clue to his vision of right knowledge does not lie in dualism. If one sees Bertie as mental, Maurice as physical, and Isabel adjudicating the two, one misses the point. Bertie is partial; if anything, a dualistic view of experience characterizes him, not Lawrence.[40] Bertie says, for example, that he can have friends but not lovers. By contrast, from the outset, Maurice is highly sensitive on a multiplicity of levels. The sources of Maurice's consciousness lie in his emotions, mind, and "intelligent" hands, in the "curious tentative movement of his powerful muscular legs," and "the clever, careful, strong contact of his feet with the earth" (CSS, 354). Lawrence tells us that Maurice's mind is slow, yet we hear that he shares Isabel's literary activities and watch him quickly and accurately analyze his own confused resentment upon Bertie's arrival. He seems far more mentally alert than Bertie. In brief, Maurice is alive to the information he receives from all sources, blood, bone, mind, heart. As such, he has the potential to overcome his cancellation by the war, to become the strange colossus Isabel sees at the tale's end. Maurice is Bertie's opposite; Lawrence tells us so. But he is so as an embodiment of richness, multiple responses, and growth. To see the tale as structured about contrasts is useful only if we see beyond the simplified mind-body, male-female poles.

In "Hymns in a Man's Life," Lawrence tells of how the old nonconformist hymns resonate in his mind. And in praising the Congregational church in which he was reared, he tells us that it gave him "a direct knowledge of the Bible" (*Phoenix II*, 600). One senses that knowledge in reading almost any of his fictions. In "The Blind Man," dramatic and linguistic echoes from John can be heard as Lawrence first suggests that Maurice, like the disciple Thomas, must touch to believe. Roles are then reversed as Mau-

133

rice presses the hands of Bertie against his scars.[41] In John, Jesus reprimands Thomas, saying that those who believe without seeing and touching are truly blessed. Lawrence argues for touch.

"The Horse Dealer's Daughter" and "The Blind Man" are two of Lawrence's major tales. They are complex embodiments of the visionary mode first articulated in "The Prussian Officer." Underlying each is a grid of ancient, generalized religious acts: crucifixion, baptism, resurrection, communion, and laying on of hands. At times beneath those acts is an even deeper, more generalized grid of activities, one that links human rituals to all of the activities of matter, of existence, in particular the fundamental activities of cohering and dissolving, of attraction and repulsion. Yet each story is also sensitive in its perception of individual psychology and circumstances. The landscape of each tale pulses with symbolic significance while also giving us the exquisite earthly detail that makes us see our own landscape anew. In brief, the story Lawrence tells in each instance is one that captures his sense of human reality as always partaking of individualized circumstances and of vast repeated movements toward life or death. As suggested above, this work is inimitable. Other writers plumb the religious dimension with subtlety and consistency, writing marvelous allegorical tales. But generally—think again of Flannery O'Connor or Graham Greene—their religious sense is far narrower than Lawrence's, far more closely tied to one dogma, and they lack his apprehension of human experience as tied to basic material forces running deep beneath our race's ancient religious rituals.

Four tales round out this important cluster—again devoted to serious, visionary comedy, tracing patterns of resurrection, sexual balance, and individual choice. Three can be read as interludes, reenacting the key ideas of the major visionary tales. These three tend to present those ideas in either more realistic or more obviously ritualistic structures. The fourth comes forward as an antagonist, leading Lawrence's tales on to the darker works of the postwar period.

Two of the interludes, "Samson and Delilah" and "Fanny and Annie," strike up a particularly interesting local conversation. While both employ the myth of the revivifying stranger, both keep reference to that myth at a distance, focusing instead on particular characters. In "Samson and Delilah" the returning stranger is male; the focus is on his wife's reluctance to welcome him home. In "Fanny and Annie," the returning stranger is female; here the focus is on her reluctance to *be* home.

Almost entirely scene and dialogue, "Samson and Delilah" brings Willie Nankervis back to Cornwall after fifteen years in America.[42] During that time he has never written to his wife, never given her any indication of his whereabouts or continuing existence. In his absence she has built a life for herself running a pub. When he first enters the pub, she treats him as a stranger. When he asserts his husbandly claim on her, she has him bound in ropes and tossed into the street as an imposter. Lawrence will redo part of this tale in "The Fox" as he has Henry return home, claim March and the farm she has been running. In "Samson and Delilah," after the customers have left the pub and the wife sits alone in the kitchen, Willie enters by way of the door she has left unlatched. In a typical pattern of Lawrence from "Love among the Haystacks" on, accord and acceptance are established through touch. A thousand questions remain to be asked and answered, but, finally, he wants her, she wants him.

Postwar tales such as "You Touched Me" or "The Fox" set up their own conversation with this tale as Lawrence tilts what is delicately balanced here. The wife in this tale is large, handsome, capable, independent. She clearly is not languishing over the desertion of Willie. At the same time, Willie is warm and beautiful himself. It would seem that the point of the tale is not to show Willie's power over his wife but to demonstrate the power of desire. His caress and her response are beyond reason, politics, or our keen sense of fairness.

"Fanny and Annie," in an altogether different tone, tells much the same story.[43] Here the returnee is the beautiful, brilliant Fanny, come home to the deadly familiarity of her home town to marry Harry Goodall, her old sweetheart. Her first Sunday back, she is witness to the public denunciation of Harry in church. A Mrs. Nixon rises up from the congregation and shouts shame to Harry for making her daughter Annie pregnant. Fanny, Mrs. Nixon says, should know "'who she's dealing with. A scamp as won't take the consequences of what he's done'" (CSS, 467). Having pushed herself all along to accept the rather limited Harry, Fanny has a moment of fresh indecision. As she and Harry walk away from church, they literally come to a possible parting of the ways. To the extent the tale has a crisis, this is it. "Should she go on to her aunt's? Should she? It would mean leaving all this, for ever. Harry stood silent" (CSS, 470). She decides to go along with Harry. Lawrence does not suggest that they will be happy nor that their unhappiness will be either one's fault; more, he presents in muted form the same persistence and illogic of desire dramatized in "Samson and Delilah."

The tale's balance and choice of strong heroine also parallel "Samson and Delilah" and provide another contrast to the contemporary essay, "Education of the People." Indeed, the feminism in this tale goes beyond "Samson and Delilah." At the center is Fanny, a handsome, sensitive, critical woman, faced as so many of Lawrence's heroines are with a major decision about the shape her life is to take. The tale reminds one of Gissing's feminist fiction, for Lawrence sees Fanny's situation with a fine eye. Like Gissing in "The Foolish Virgin" or *The Odd Women*, Lawrence conveys the limited choices intelligent, middle-class women have had in Western society. In a culture that generally denied women access to careers commensurate with their energies and abilities, marriage was the one road to a measure of independence and dignity. But marriage often involved compromise. In this tale, Harry is the domestic force, home-centered and glad to have this wanderer back home. While ultimately desirable to Fanny, he is limited. Lawrence associates him with the Harvest Home Festival but makes it a bit disappointing this year. The season had been wet and the crops were in a poor way. Fanny is not the new woman; she is no Ursula Brangwen. Rather, for all her engaging individuality, she takes her place in a long line of intelligent English heroines faced with the problem of what to do with themselves when no perfect suitor shows up. Shall they open a school, take in sewing, become a governess? Like Gissing, Lawrence avoids the happy ending of *Jane Eyre* and the tragedy of *The Mill on the Floss*. Gissing finds his women jobs, though rather dull ones. Lawrence has Fanny marry Harry, choosing a life that may include moments of physical fulfillment but that is narrower than she deserves.[44]

In discussing "England, My England," I commented on the sardonic note in the narrator's voice and criticized it as one element in a pastiche of tones that finally add up to inflated rhetoric and incoherence. There the sarcasm is entirely the narrator's; Egbert and Winifred are about as wry as churchmen. In "Fanny and Annie," Lawrence employs the same sardonic tone, but uses it to extend rather than limit the tale's understanding. In this tale, the tone complements Fanny's character, implying a wit in her that will eschew self-pity and keep a hold on common sense. Organized only indirectly and ironically around the ritual of a harvest festival and the myth of the returning stranger, "Fanny and Annie," like "Samson and Delilah," asks us to read for the individual characters and situations. The style in both follows Lawrence's description of *Sons and Lovers*: it accumulates objects and people and illuminates them under the light of a strong emotion, creating a scene (CL, 263). Fanny may typify the plight of many women, but Lawrence develops her and her situation in terms of a particular personality caught in a particular time and place. If these two tales show Lawrence relaxing the dynamic tensions of the visionary mode by writing in a light, realistic mode, "Tickets, Please" shows him taking the opposite tack and explicitly organizing a tale around a myth.

When published in *Metropolitan* in August 1919, the tale was called "The Eleventh Commandment," a phrase Lawrence elsewhere elucidated as "Enjoy Yourselves" (*Phoenix*, 821).[45] Although "enjoy yourselves" is indeed the rule by which the hero lives, the title "Tickets, Please" succinctly conveys the ritual drama that lies at the heart of the tale. While the characters in "Tickets, Please" are well motivated on a realistic level, once the motivation has been established, the tale also begins to signify ancient acts of destruction wrecked upon Dionysus. Lawrence's contemporary dramatization of those acts draws not only on the myths of Dionysus, but also on Ursula Brangwen's scene of annihilation in *The Rainbow*.

Of the many Dionysian stories, Lawrence uses two, combining them to make his point. The first tells of Dionysus—then called Zagreus or "torn to pieces"—being annihilated by the Titans. Led by the jealous Here, the Titans tear the young god apart; he descends to the underworld but returns every third year. The second tells of the destruction of Dionysus at the hands of the religious Maenads or Bacchae. Originally comprising one of his cults, they turn on Dionysus when he is caught intruding as a disbeliever on their ceremonies.

In *The Rainbow*, Lawrence alludes to the second story. Ursula blasts her young, militaristic lover, Skrebensky, as Lawrence indirectly dramatizes the death of Dionysus at the hands of the Maenads. Lawrence has repeatedly shown that Skrebensky's sexuality has no religious dimension; it can lead Ursula into no unknown.

Having separated the human from the divine, Skrebensky intrudes as a disbeliever upon Ursula's sacred-sexual vision of herself being visited by the sons of God. He is destroyed for his violation. In the scene in the novel, Lawrence develops several issues, implying the parallels with the Dionysian myth only indirectly. In isolating that scene in "Tickets, Please," Lawrence draws upon both tales of Dionysian destruction, alludes to them more directly, and qualifies the approval that accrues to Ursula.

"Tickets, Please" presents the violent revenge of a group of tram girls upon, significantly, their "inspector," who is "always called John Thomas" (CSS, 336). John Thomas shares with Skrebensky the sin of Dionysian disbelief as he has quite coolly trifled with the hearts of the tram girls. Even more clearly than Skrebensky, John Thomas separates his sexuality from all other aspects of human relationship or communion. As he and Annie grow more intimate, Annie wishes to consider him "a person, a man," not "a mere nocturnal presence." John Thomas will have none of it: "John Thomas intended to remain a nocturnal presence. He had no idea of becoming an all-round individual to her" (CSS, 339). Further, his intrusion into sacred territory is more literally acted out than is Skrebensky's. On the evening of his punishment, the sabbath as it happens, John Thomas breaks in on the seven women who sit gathered around a communal fire sharing a pot of tea in their waiting room at the tram depot. "'Prayer meeting?'" he asks. "'Ay . . . ladies only,'" replies one of the girls (CSS, 340). Obviously he has no ticket, no right to be there. Impudent and condescending, he lingers, mocking them. This time, however, the women are ready for him. They are Titans, organized and well led by a reincarnated Here. Annie and her chums pounce upon John Thomas, tearing his clothes, his face, his arms. When they are finished, John Thomas is a "strange, dazed, ragged creature." With "his face closed, his head dropped," he disappears like Dionysus into the darkness (CSS, 345).

Lawrence's attitude toward this Titanic revenge is important to understanding the tale; given his essays of the period, one might expect Annie and her compatriots to be denounced. But here Lawrence refuses so simple a stance. John Thomas, playing the role of Dionysus, is a scoffer, a rebel to any system of belief, cohesion, stability. He is and plans to remain a creature of the night. But in this tale he is not romanticized. Neither good nor bad, he is the dangerous, attractive, Dionysiac principle of license. The tram girls too are neither good nor bad. They are not wearisome hags to be avoided or tricked, nor are they female devourers, emblems of a culture gone mad. Opposing John Thomas, they zealously embody the principle of commitment, responsibility, ultimately of marriage. Choose, they repeatedly say, choose whom you will marry. If attacked, they will destroy that which would destroy them. If Lawrence intended "Tickets, Please" simply to illustrate a war-torn society in which the women have taken the upper hand to the detriment of themselves and the men, the characterizations and myth work against the intention. More, the myth and characterizations present the male-female conflicts almost as psychomachia. They invite one to see the tale's central conflict as a clashing of equally valid psychological principles. By not rendering judgment and by alluding to the ancient tales of Dionysus, Lawrence presents a battle that organizes itself into a struggle between freedom and responsibility.[46]

I spoke above of an antagonist on the edges of the cluster we have been studying, pointing the direction of Lawrence's postwar stories. "The Mortal Coil" is clearly a transitional number, for it contains within itself and its history a dialogue between the vision of the earlier war tales and the vision Lawrence formulated after the Armistice. Piecing together references Lawrence makes in the fall of 1913 to a planned volume of four soldier stories, one can estimate the original date of composition as the fall of 1913 or perhaps winter of 1914. The Lawrences were then in Italy (CL, 229, 234–35). No manuscript of this version has surfaced. In 1916, after finishing *Women in Love*, Lawrence wrote the version we do have (CL, 480).[47] The tale consists of two movements, the first at night, the second the next day. Full of color, candle flames, flashing stars, and bright glances, the night poses the dramatic situation; delivered in tones of grey, with images of mud and frost predominating, the day traces out the results.

Initially, the tale's basic situation recalls "Vin Ordinaire"/"The Thorn in the Flesh." Lieutenant Friedeburg is another puppet dancing to the tune of the military. Friedeburg defines himself by its code of honor. Having failed that code by habitual gambling and debt, he feels himself nothing, "a cipher," a "rag of meaningless human life" (*Phoenix II*, 70). With fear and grief, he anticipates being discharged; this is very much the language we hear in other stories from 1913. Challenging his definition of himself and his life's meaning is his fiery mistress, Marta. In the tale's first major scene, she rails briefly against the gambling and then long and passionately against his equation of himself with his career and his apparently low estimation of their love. She prepares to leave.

Terrified by her threatened departure, Friedeburg suddenly changes his mood. He wants only her. This late-night battle ends with their making love but without their solving Friedeburg's problem. Leaving Marta still in bed, Friedeburg rises before dawn and joins his men for the day's maneuvers. Initially, he looks out at the world with the heightened perceptions of a doomed man, but as the day progresses, so does his despair. Lawrence repeatedly intones the word "dead" as the young Friedeburg chews on thoughts of suicide. Late that afternoon, he returns to his hotel to find the police in his room. Marta and their friend Teresa have been asphyxiated by fumes from the stove. The dead bury the dead.[48] Though most critics have disagreed, Lawrence felt it was "a first-class story, one of my purest creations" (CL, 480). He may overstate its virtues, but it is not as "pointless" as some critics have found.[49]

One cannot know what Lawrence's intentions were in the version of 1913 or 1914, but in reading the version we have, I believe one can discern the shadow of a prewar tale very like "The Thorn in the Flesh." The revision may have been done partly to question the optimism of that earlier tale.

Read in conjunction with "The Thorn in the Flesh," "The Mortal Coil" would seem to approve of Marta, to disapprove of the lieutenant. Friedeburg is a wicked fool if he defines himself as a soldier and throws away his life and love because he has failed in the army. He should listen to Marta, who resembles an articulate Emilie. His ecstatic perceptions during the predawn maneuvers should be read as similar to the orderly's in "The Prussian Officer." Neither ecstasy leads anywhere. Finally, one should see Marta's death as a result of his stupidity, his incapacity to live and love. Dead at the core, he kills the living things around him.

Read from the perspective of "England, My England" or the postwar stories to come, our view changes. As the war progressed, Lawrence's complicated hatred of the war was haunted by questions of masculine identity and worth. The resolution he offers in "Vin Ordinaire"/"The Thorn in the Flesh"—withdraw from the mass, realize the self in relation to one other—no longer consistently suffices as Lawrence begins arguing that a man must engage in the social and political work of the world. If he fails to do so, because of his nature or the lack of meaningful work, his private life will become stagnant, his sexual self hollow and decadent. He will bring nothing to his relationships with women, and his woman may respond by dominance, by seeing—with a mixture of fear and joy—that he is in fact nothing apart from her. Reading through this perspective, one notices Marta's insistence during their love-making that Friedeburg belong to no one but her, that he be nothing but her possession. Memories of Gerald and Gudrun, even Ursula and Rupert, should guide our reading of this scene. Gerald claims he is nothing without Gudrun. It is, alas, too true. Like Ursula on occasion, Marta would have Friedeburg be nothing apart from her. To an extent, Friedeburg rightly resists that reduction. Marta's death, according to this reading, is partly of her own making. She and Friedeburg are each blighted, she by trying to keep him bound in a personal relationship which is by definition too limited for his masculine nature, and he by failing to find a way to participate responsibly in his culture's work.[50]

As I see it, "The Mortal Coil" is a "problem" tale. It skillfully raises issues, most important the issue of masculine identity. Friedeburg's difficulty, like Egbert's in "England, My England" or Birkin's in the discarded "Prologue" to *Women in Love*, is that he must find genuine, creative work in a world that offers none. Rupert withdraws, resigns, and is resigned. He is presumably making the right choice. But Egbert and Friedeburg choose the only engaging, masculine activity they can see, the military. In both "England, My England" and "The Mortal Coil," it is a deadly choice; but in these two tales, the refusal to do anything is seen as equally deadly. In the postwar tales to come, Lawrence avoids this particular dilemma while he continues to think about the problems it raises. For one thing, he employs a cast of returned soldiers. They have fought their society's war and come back full of purpose and masculine energy. Once home, all they need to do is get their stubborn women to accept them as proper leaders.[51]

Leaving aside Lawrence's revisions during the summer of 1914, I have begun and ended this chapter with stories that point ahead to the sinister lullabies Lawrence is about to write. Clearly there is a current and an undercurrent in the short stories of the war years. The main current argues that courageous, warm-hearted, sexual relationships are the answer to public insanity,

141

cowardice, and mechanized destruction. This is the view taken by both novels of the period, *The Rainbow* and *Women in Love*, as well as by the great visionary stories of these years, "The Horse Dealer's Daughter" and "The Blind Man." A recurring double pattern is the descent of the individual (and culture by implication) into darkness, dissolution, and death, followed by a painful reassembling of self or culture. The ascent into light, coherence, and life carries with it important, continuing associations with the forces of darkness.

A different stream flows under this main current, however. If we want to see the forerunners of *Aaron's Rod* and *The Plumed Serpent*, we must look to "England, My England" and "The Mortal Coil." In them Lawrence hints at the regrettable simplification to come: women must learn the art of descent. They must relax, dissolve, lapse out—and remain so. Men must marshall their energies, move forward, ascend, and take up the challenge of civilization. This undercurrent avoids the complexities of human experience; it offers a view of men and women that does not convince Lawrence or us at the deepest levels of our understanding.

Sinister Lullabies

6

After the Armistice was signed in November 1918, Lawrence broke the almost two-year moratorium he had kept toward short fiction with a spate of stories, many about soldiers home from the war ready to continue the fight. Three of the stories from 1918–1919 have already been discussed: "The Blind Man," "Tickets, Please," and "Fanny and Annie." They, like the tales Lawrence wrote during the war, generally resist the omnipresent sexual stereotyping that wars encourage, maintaining a balanced, complex stance toward men and women, and toward their sexual, psychological, and social needs. In his short fiction, the war years were Lawrence's years of armistice. Once the world's war was over and the historical Armistice signed, Lawrence's stories take up arms. Who should lead, who should follow, who should dominate, who should submit are simplifications he avoids in the resurrection stories written in 1915 and 1916. After 1918, those questions become central.

At this time Lawrence's changing sense of social realities and of his responsibilities deeply altered his vision of Rananim. Increasingly during the war and after, he expresses his loneliness and awareness of being cut off, mainly by his inability to support the war. The vast masculine action and camaraderie of his time had taken place without him, albeit largely by his own choice. The difficulties he and John Middleton Murry had always experienced in their strained friendship only exacerbated the loneliness and frustration. Out of Lawrence's feelings of being on the margin comes, one feels, his steadily growing need to dramatize some kind of acceptable male leadership and bonding.

The title of this chapter suggests the actual nature of the fight engaged in by Lawrence's returning soldiers and the generation of men who follow them: Bohemian counts, American Indians, Mexicans, and a collier or two. Most often it is a fight between men and women, and the key issue is dominance. No longer can Lawrence imagine "star-equilibrium" as a fit metaphor for sexual relationships. In any private relationship, as in any culture, there must be rulers and ruled. Lawrence's insistence—at times almost his plea—is for women to recognize men as the proper rulers, themselves as the properly ruled. An image Lawrence frequently draws in these stories is of women perversely insisting on staying awake or occasionally, smilingly, drifting off to sleep. This is indeed a switch in the Sleeping Beauty tale. Because he cannot actually imagine what kind of leadership roles his assortment of heroes might convincingly take (a major exception here is *The Plumed Serpent*), he focuses on their struggle to win recognition and acquiescence from their women. It turned out to be a hard fight.

In July 1916, Lawrence had written to his agent Pinker, "When I have done the novel [*Women in Love*], I shall *only* write stories *to sell*" (*CL*, 469). Perhaps the original "Miracle" and "Samson and Delilah" were intended to be such saleable items. The general scheme does not seem to have inspired Lawrence, however. After these two tales and his revision of "The Mortal Coil," he put down that particular pen for nearly two years. Through the unsettled years of 1917 and most of 1918, Lawrence was reading and writing essays. In October of 1917, he and Frieda were accused of spying and forced to leave Cornwall. In a high rage, they went to London, then to Berkshire, and eventually, in April 1918, to a cottage in the Midlands which Lawrence's sister generously rented for them for a year. In February of 1918, Lawrence had begun *Aaron's Rod* but put it aside. His next sustained interest in fiction comes with the Armistice in November 1918. Frieda and Lawrence had been in London when the Armistice was signed. Judging from a stream of letters in the following weeks and months, Lawrence had had a good visit with Katherine Mansfield, who was ill there. His letters are warm and suggest conversations they may have had about projected tales. Over the next seven months he wrote "The Blind Man," "Fanny and Annie," "Tickets, Please," an early version of "The Fox," "Wintry Peacock," "You Touched Me," and "Monkey Nuts." Throughout this time he and Frieda were most anxious to get out of England. Permission finally came in the fall of 1919. Their five years of enforced residence in England would be matched by five subsequent years of traveling.

Frieda left England in October 1919, and went directly to Germany to be with her family. Lawrence left in November, meeting her in Florence in December. From there, they wandered all over the globe. Early in 1920, they were in Capri. For two years, March 1920 to February 1922, they lived in Sicily. Through the spring and summer of 1922, they visited Ceylon and stayed several months in Australia. Moving on in August, the two sailed for San Francisco and from there traveled to Taos, New Mexico, arriving in September 1922 at the ranch and art colony of Mabel Dodge Luhan.[1] Life under her patronage was far from easy, however. Moreover, Lawrence found the artiness of Taos irritating and confining. He and Frieda moved up to Del Monte Ranch, seventeen miles north of Taos, for the winter. Through the spring and summer of 1923, they were in Chapala, Mexico, planning to leave for New York and Europe in July. In New York, however, Lawrence found himself unable to return to England. His soul, he said, was like Balaam's ass. Quarreling bitterly, he and Frieda parted, she sailing for England, he returning to Mexico. Letters indicate that they felt the separation was permanent, but Lawrence joined Frieda in England five months later, in December 1923.

After three months in London, Paris, and Germany, the Lawrences returned to New Mexico and spent the next seven months on the ranch Mabel had given to Frieda. When winter approached, they traveled back down into Mexico, living in Oaxaca from November 1924 through February 1925. There Lawrence collapsed with what the doctors diagnosed as tuberculosis. Slowly he and Frieda got themselves back up to Taos. That spring and summer Lawrence rested; in September 1925, they sailed back to England, never to leave Europe again.

As many critics have remarked, this long trek was very much a pilgrimage for Lawrence. To assess the motive behind his years of wandering, one must keep in mind his hopefulness during much of the war. He had believed that he and others would help form a new England. When he saw that England would not commit herself to his programs—be they political, educational, sexual—he set himself the task of finding a land that would. That land, a very different Rananim from the one he had conceived of in 1914, would recognize above all the essential inequality of human beings. If there is one thread that runs through the fiction of these wander years, it is the theme of right power, of inspired leadership. Yet within that central theme, there is a range of enactments, of conflicts and resolutions. Many of the fictions, for example, associate leadership with a return to ancient cultures; others associate it with male fellowship; some avoid both issues and concentrate simply on dramatizing different kinds of power and resistance to power.

A consistent feature of the fiction of this period is the difference in vision between the long and short fiction. Earlier I argued that the stories that cluster around *The White Peacock* and *Sons and Lovers* often explore issues and techniques those novels avoid. The stories Lawrence wrote alongside *The Rainbow* and *Women in Love* tend first to anticipate then to highlight their style and vision. But the tales that surround *Aaron's Rod* and *The Plumed Serpent* often approach the issues of leadership and power from new and different perspectives.[2]

The short fiction of the leadership years comes in distinct groups. From 1918–1919 comes the series of tales named above. Through 1920 and much of 1921, Lawrence wrote no tales. Then, in the fall of 1921, in Sicily, he had a burst of activity on his short fiction as he gathered together magazine texts of earlier tales for his second volume, *England, My England*; wrote "The Captain's Doll"; and revised and expanded "The Fox" and "The Thimble," the latter becoming "The Ladybird." Covering the same issues but varying the terms, "The Captain's Doll" in particular helps illuminate *Aaron's Rod*, finished five months before, in June 1921. (Comparing the three novelettes of this period with Lawrence's revisions for *England, My England,* one discerns that the novelettes were receiving most of his creative attentions. Unlike his work on *The Prussian Officer* and contrary to his claim that most of the *England, My England* tales were rewritten [*CL*, 683], his genuine "re-seeings" of this time lie with "The Fox" and "The Thimble"/"The Ladybird." The exception to this tendency to leave the earlier tales relatively unchanged is "England, My England," as discussed in chapter 5. Within the volume, the one tale that had not been previously published was "The Primrose Path." Here too however, the collected text closely follows the earlier version, in this case the 1913 holograph.)[3]

Ceylon, Australia, and Lawrence's first stay in New Mexico and Mexico inspired *Kangaroo,* the initial version of *The Plumed Serpent,* several essays, but no tales. Not until he is back in Europe at the end of 1923 and beginning of 1924 does Lawrence return to short fiction. Written while the Lawrences were traveling in England, France, and Germany in January and February of 1924, "The Last Laugh," "Jimmy and the Desperate Woman," and "The Borderline" are clear attacks on John Middleton Murry and the old crowd Lawrence saw in London. Two months later, again in Taos, Lawrence added a fourth, rather different tale, to this bitter trio. "The Overtone," probably written in April 1924, continues to examine the failure of love which informs the Murry tales, but drops Murry and concentrates on a weary, battle-scarred couple.

Lawrence's decision to drop the rival and explore the death of desire on its own terms contributes to the last cluster of tales from this period, the fascinating trio of American tales, written during the summer and fall of 1924: "The Woman Who Rode Away," "St. Mawr," and "The Princess." Particularly interesting is the way they progressively alter the terms of the leadership vision, serve as a transition between Lawrence's first and second versions of *The Plumed Serpent,* and look toward his last novel, *Lady Chatterley's Lover.*[4]

In examining the leadership stories, extending as they do from 1919 through 1924, I want briefly to indicate Lawrence's transition from his wartime to postwar perspective by looking at the new face "Wintry Peacock" puts on "Tickets, Please" and by noting the shift in sentiment represented by "Samson and Delilah," "You Touched Me," and the 1918 version of "The Fox." From there I will examine the approaches he took over the next three years to the task he had set himself. One approach worked surprisingly well, some succeed in part, most fail. The chapter closes with what I see as a beautiful disaster, "The Woman Who Rode Away," a tale which literally puts the woman to sleep forever. It is the first of the American tales from 1924. The two that follow, "St. Mawr" and "The Princess," pick up on a note lightly sounded in "The Overtone" and begin the reveille that follows these sinister lullabies. They take Lawrence's short fiction into new territory and will be discussed in the succeeding chapter.

The setting of "Wintry Peacock" is a small farm in the Midlands just after the war.[5] The tale's tone is lightly sardonic; its sense of the wintry Midlands and the peacocks is Lawrence at his descriptive best. In the crispness and brilliance of the natural detail, one notices not only what Katherine Mansfield admired so greatly in Lawrence but one of her own strengths as a writer. For the second time since the early "A Fragment of Stained Glass," Lawrence uses a first-person narrator. But the convention does not limit or expand his usual voice because the tale is not about the narrator or anyone in particular. Like the collier tales, it is anecdotal, expressive of a time, place, mood. Like them, it is almost all scene and dialogue.

Neatly organized, the tale opens with a wide-angle view of the narrator, snow, and peacocks. Quickly Lawrence moves in to follow the narrator's conversation with his neighbor over a letter that has come for her absent husband. Written in French, the letter is from a Belgian girl whom the husband, or some other English soldier, has gotten pregnant. The narrator agrees to translate for the suspicious wife. Although he has never met the husband, the narrator purposefully misreads the contents, covering the husband's tracks as best he can. To the extent one feels any narrative suspense, one wonders whether the husband will manage to get away with his indiscretion. He does. The tale closes with him home from the war, in a conversation with the narrator, denying any particular responsibility, thoroughly amused. When they part, the narrator runs down the hill toward his place, "shouting with laughter" (CSS, 397).

Counterpointing this anecdote and giving clues as to how one is to read the tale are the pathetic peacocks. In the first paragraph they suggest the same spirit of wildness and independence represented by the fox in "The Fox" and the stallion in "St. Mawr." But this tale is about the ways in which humans—specifically, women—trap that wildness in a silken net of caresses. As the tale unfolds, the peacocks come to stand as emblems of defeated masculinity.[6] As Joey, the main bird, crouches at the feet of the cajoling wife, one sees him as the foil to the independent, undefeated husband. Joey is a wintry peacock, lacking the grandeur of his full, proud tail. The husband, by contrast, is going to allow no clinging Belgian girl, no devious wife, to clip his feathers.

In this image pattern, the tale approaches issues central to "Tickets, Please" from the perspective one finds in essays such as "Education of the People" or in *Aaron's Rod*. In essence, the tale upholds John Thomas's view of life: the female and the love she represents are to be avoided. She signifies an old cluster of demands and domestic responsibilities that must be shunned if one is to take flight. In fact, through its imagery, the tale answers the precise complaint that Lawrence makes in a later, peculiar essay, "Autobiographical Fragment": "the men of my generation are dumb: they have been got under and made good" (*Phoenix*, 818).[7] In the tale, that "good" male is Joey. The husband's hatred of his wife's peacocks expresses his revulsion at Joey's diminishment. He will do better by himself. His last scene, with the narrator, is a brief image of the masculine understanding, fellowship, and wildness that Lawrence had begun to pit against heterosexual ties.

Lawrence wisely keeps the Belgian girl contained by her flat—or flatly translated—letter. Clearly, sympathizing with her would conflict with the focus on masculine independence. Similarly, he makes the wife into a sly, wily soul; one suspects that she will always find ways to satisfy her needs. But the problems readers may experience in reading the tale are not so easily answered. The tale lacks that quality Lawrence names as essential to any work of art: the capacity to contain within itself its own criticism.[8] In "Wintry Peacock," Lawrence fails to examine or criticize the rather simplistic characterizations he has set up. Rather than on character, he focuses on the set of ideas he handles so well in "Tickets, Please": in our society women often represent domestic responsibility, a force in the culture against license. Having little overt power, they have traditionally used manipulation as one way to control masculine behavior. But here Lawrence simply condemns the wife's claims. The psychomachia of "Tickets, Please" is presented flatly, with no points going to responsibility and all points given to freedom.

The settings for the 1918 version of "The Fox" and "You Touched Me" are again soon after the war, the first on a farm in Berkshire, the second at a failing pottery in the Midlands. Each follows the basic plot of "Samson and Delilah" as it traces the return of an exile, the reluctance of the women at home to accept him, and the eventual acceptance—or inability to refuse—his presence. In "Samson and Delilah," however, the woman was a strong character. Her mate, playing fair in the war of the sexes, woos her with legitimate caresses. If she accepts his return and thereby limits her own future freedom, she does so out of capitulation to her own desires. By contrast, both "The Fox" and "You Touched Me" give us sadly broken females, no longer young, desperately in need of rescue.

The form "The Fox" took in 1918 traces the same initial situation as the 1921 novelette, which is the version we now read.[9] Lawrence opens with March and Banford, two thirty-year-old women trying to run a poultry farm during the war; one learns of their struggle to make the farm go and watches as March becomes captivated by the fox. Henry enters the tale, very much the fox in glimmer, glamor, liveliness, and cunning. At his coming, March is relieved. On a practical level, Henry is quite simply a help to March. He brings home rabbits, he saws wood. But clearly he also makes possible a new integrity in her. If one sees the fox as a vital wild creature which she has been compelled to fight off, then Henry allows her legitimately to cease that fight, to welcome this creature. March has her first dream: she hears the fox singing, it bites her wrist, burns her mouth with its fiery brilliance. Like Henry, the fox represents a highly attractive and dangerous alternative to life with Banford. In this text, Henry stands outside one evening in the early twilight and suddenly sees that he might have this farm by marrying March. He ponders for two days, fighting off the feeling that his wanting her is ridiculous. He overcomes his hesitancy however and proposes. By insinuating his voice into her, he makes her his creature. She surrenders in "deathly darkness." They go to tell Banford. The fact that Banford owns the farm and is not likely to give it up is avoided in this version. The tale closes with March and Henry married and Banford bitter. Always a bit "odd," March becomes even more so. To her the fox and the boy are "somehow indistinguishable." Henry must leave for ten days, but he will "come home by instinct."[10]

It may be difficult to limit one's sense of "The Fox" to this configuration. There is little suggestion of lesbian attraction between March and Banford. March accepts Henry's proposal with few qualms; her struggles against him and her feelings of divided loyalty scarcely exist. Most important, there is no murder. Henry does have great and subtle powers, but they are held in reserve. No one crosses him in any significant way. All this will be changed in the 1921 text. One way to see what is going on in the 1918 version of "The Fox" is to read it in conjunction with "You Touched Me." In dramatic shape and characterization, the two are close cousins.[11]

Like "The Fox," "You Touched Me" opens with two women in their thirties, Matilda and Emmie Rockley.[12] In a limited way, Emmie will play the role Banford does in "The Fox." She will stand guard over Matilda, trying to "protect" her from the intruding male. Much like Henry, Hadrian bursts in on the dreary but tolerable world the women have created and destroys it by carrying off one of the women. Hadrian too is a soldier back from the war, visiting his old home. In both tales, the intruder is presented as crude, young, dangerous, calculating, vibrant; he is very much the returning stranger.

In this tale, Lawrence portrays Matilda as a desiccated spinster much in need of Hadrian's youthful sap. Everything around her has turned to dust. Her father is ill. At thirty-three, she is thin, tired, frail. When Hadrian arrives, he has no designs either on Matilda or on their father's money. But an incident occurs that changes at least the first circumstance. Anxious about her father, Matilda enters what she believes is his room at midnight and, whispering to him, she gently, lovingly caresses his face. It is Hadrian who answers, Hadrian whom she has touched. The father has been moved downstairs. The touch, so unlooked for, so new to this loner's experience, goes deep. As he has in past tales, as he did in "Samson and Delilah," here again Lawrence focuses on a literal laying on of hands, a touch, to dramatize a contract or connection between people that extends fathoms below their daytime, conscious selves. The father countenances Hadrian's plan to have Matilda and writes a proviso into his will: if Matilda will marry Hadrian, she and Emmie will retain their inheritance. If Matilda refuses, all goes to Hadrian.

Graham Hough would have more reason to complain of an air of harshness, compulsion, and cruelty in this tale than in "The Horse Dealer's Daughter." There, compulsion came from within

151

and demanded at some point the acquiescence of consciousness. Here, although he never seems conscious of what he is doing, Hadrian's compulsion does come from within his own being. It is Matilda who is being compelled from outside. No one has "touched" her. Read purely as a fable, perhaps the tale works. It does act out the myth of the revivifying stranger; as a metaphor for the necessary fertilization of the genteel classes by the lower it may be palatable. Even as a Sleeping Beauty fable it might be seen as a fresh retelling, for here Matilda captures Hadrian—literally wakes him up—every bit as much as he captures her. But the problem is the tale cannot be read as only a fable. One cannot dismiss Matilda simply as dry land in need of water, an old princess locked in a tower. Draper is responding to this when he says Lawrence "has not done enough to counter the impression of brute will."[13] Lawrence has created Matilda as a critical woman, thirty-three, exhausted from nursing her father, facing destitution for herself and her sister if she refuses to marry a man for whom she feels no interest, no desire. Historically, it is not an unheard-of situation. As he did in revising "England, My England" two years later, Lawrence here gives his father figure an absolute, magic prestige that may sound good on some level—and may work within the conventions of fable—but raises the spectre of bullying within a realistic context. The same is true for Hadrian. On some level his inexorable demand works; but on another, more quotidian level, he has not awakened Matilda, he has forced her.

In looking at this cluster of tales from just after the Armistice, one sees Lawrence dramatizing two different kinds of answers to the question of who shall lead. In "The Fox" and "You Touched Me," he answers quite clearly: the male. But he sets up a singularly unlikely hero and heroine. The unlikeliness is not unusual for Lawrence: as early as "The Daughters of the Vicar" and as recently as "The Horse Dealer's Daughter," he had chosen curious casts for his love stories. But in "The Fox" and "You Touched Me," he repeatedly emphasizes the unlikeliness: March and Matilda each feel they could be this "boy's" mother; the men's youth, obtuseness, and lack of perception and tenderness are central to their characters; and the absence of any warmth, pleasure, or discernible passion between the two "lovers" is a given in the plots. One key to the tone and plot is Lawrence's attempt to undermine the conventions of traditional, romantic love stories. However, unlike the earlier stories where romantic cliché is attacked throughout, in these stories the other key to tone and plot is a wholesale capitulation to romantic convention. Most important, in "The Fox," "You Touched Me," and in many of the tales to follow, one sees Lawrence dramatizing the notion encoded through centuries of law and custom that there is a real gain for man and woman alike in the woman's giving up self-responsibility. The gain derives of course from the fact that each is following his and her "natural" bent, his to lead, hers to follow.

An odd hero is, then, one answer to the question of who shall lead. The other answer, formulated in "Wintry Peacock" and in the last tale of this 1918–1919 cluster, "Monkey Nuts," is related but different.[14] Men say to women, "Try as you might, you cannot make me follow. And one of the ways I will withstand you is by joining forces with another man." In "Wintry Peacock," the wife and Belgian girl cajoled to no effect. The husband ends up in jolly company with the narrator, laughing at all the wife and girl represent. In "Monkey Nuts," the tale's title is also the heroine's nickname. "Monkey nuts" is slang for coconuts, but "monkey" can mean woman; it can also mean mock, as in "monkey money." The implication here is that the woman has woman nuts, which is to say no real nuts at all, aggressive and demanding though she may be. Through the brief tale, she woos Joe, a young shy soldier. But he will neither fall nor follow. Like the husband in "Wintry Peacock," he bands together with a male comrade, here Alfred, and in that bond maintains his independence and dignity.

In reading the four stories, we hear a curious conversation going on. The first two demand absolute privilege and power for the male leader, who, we should note, is a loner. The women, with more and less reluctance, submit. In the second two, one hears the female in Lawrence making a bid for the same power and privilege. But her voice is shrill, her demand disparaged. The male will certainly not submit. However, to hold out against the female, he very much needs a comrade. The presence of that comrade lets us hear one more intricacy in this conversation. In all four of these stories, we have a triangle made up of a same gender couple set in opposition to a figure of the opposite gender. March and Banford, Emily and Matilda stand against Henry and Hadrian. Breaking up the women is one of the hero's projects. Conversely, the husband and narrator stand against the wife in "Wintry Peacock," while Joe and Alfred pair up against Miss Monkey Nuts Stokes. Here the heroes' project is, of course, not to allow their friendships to be broken up by the female. Lawrence's ideas on female friendship will be discussed below, but I want to emphasize here the feature so characteristic of Lawrence's imagination and so evident in the short stories, the feature implied in the metaphor that introduces this book. As one watches the overall progress of Lawrence's tales, one is continually struck by local dynamics. Here Lawrence focuses on the issue of leadership between the sexes and then formulates image upon image, plot upon plot, to explore different aspects of the issue.

Turning to the long stories of 1921, "The Captain's Doll," the revised "Fox," and "The Ladybird," we see Lawrence working on elaborations of his first answer to the leadership question. Three lone men—a captain, a count, and the foxlike Grenfel—woo three reluctant ladies. In the first case, the wooing is carried out with surprising wit and sympathy; in the latter two, it is marked by increasing stridency and confusion.

In these stories, a contrast continually insinuates itself into the dramatic conflict, the contrast between love and power. The words take on special meaning for Lawrence during this time. If we are to read the leadership tales with any sympathy, we need to understand the connotations those words assume.

Upon finishing *Women in Love* in November 1916, Lawrence had written to Catherine Carswell: "The book frightens me: it is so end-of-the-world. But it is, it must be, the beginning of a new world too" (*CL*, 482). By May 1920, his tone is much altered. "Nothing will happen to the world: Bloomsbury will go on enjoying itself in Paris and elsewhere, no bombs will fall, no plagues, Etna will not erupt and Taormina will not fall down in earthquakes" (*CL*, 628). As he traveled through Europe and America after the Armistice, he saw mocked his vision of a world judged, much less redeemed. The *Dies Irae* had come, gone, and left continuing chaos in their wake. In another writer, the disillusionment might signal surrender or cynicism. In Lawrence it foretells the opposite. Lawrence responded to the decadence he saw around him by seeking new sources of energy and order all the more fiercely. And, like others at the time, he sought order through power.[15] "The reign of love is passing, and the reign of power is coming again. . . . There *must be* rule. And only power can rule" (*Phoenix II*, 436, 440). In Lawrence's view at this time, "men are powerful or powerless" and "the communion of power will always be a communion in inequality" (*Phoenix II*, 440). Thus, the true follower at some point recognizes his fundamental inferiority and consents to follow his leader unquestioningly. The leader, in turn, recognizes his power and consents, however reluctantly, to lead absolutely.

Love stands in contrast to power. At his best Lawrence despised cliché, in human responses and in language. Thus, in some ways the weariness with the love mode seems partly a reaction against the centuries of use that word has borne in Western society. To respond freshly to love, joy, happiness, home, mother, father, husband, one needs to see those entities apart from the cloying connotations that carry over from the past, especially the Victorian past. Although he will change it later, Lawrence's view at this time equates love with a fatal desire to merge. In earlier periods of threat, such as his first years with Frieda, he had registered this same ontological insecurity, this same fear of the total loss of self in another. In those fictions, however, he continually poses the possible gain in a loss of selfhood against the danger. Each participant in the relationship faced a potential expansion and potential reduction in the loss of self. Increasingly through the leadership years, Lawrence tends to separate the expansions and reductions, alloting expansions to one participant, reductions to the other. Specifically, to the extent a relationship encourages a loss of self, it will nurture the female (or "follower") while it paralyzes or cripples the male (or "leader").

Other aspects of love are reductive to both partners. Love encourages possessiveness, charity, and a belief in human equality; it looks toward the salvation of the soul. Possessiveness reduces both participants, male and female, in the act of possessing and condition of being possessed. Charity forces us all to approach the other through a film of preordained platitudes. We cannot genuinely hate, respect, or struggle with each other—or revolutionize the culture—if we consistently greet each other with charity. Indeed, our charitable greeting is no real greeting at all but a means of avoiding contact and relationship. A belief in human equality goes against all experiential evidence and hamstrings our culture's potential leaders through their own unwarranted humility and their compatriots' envy. As for salvation of the soul, in his essay on Walt Whitman Lawrence says, "Saving? Saving for what?" The soul is a walker, to be realized in no goal, no heaven, no ideal, but simply in its own journeying forth.

Perhaps partly because it is a shocking word in some ways and partly because it connotes the warrior society Europe enjoyed before the Middle Ages, "power" is the word and concept Lawrence chose to replace "love." In developing his argument, in giving scenes, images, and explanations to help the reader see this "power mode" more clearly, Lawrence specifies that separateness must replace merging; freedom to come and go must replace possessiveness; sympathy must replace charity; and the unfolding of the self or soul as it lives adventurously out on the open road must replace the ideal of saving the soul for heaven. Within these specifications, another tends to enter, especially in the long fiction: male fellowship must replace sacred marriage.

In these various reorderings, Lawrence is continually concerned to keep an area clear for power to express itself. And theoretically power is not necessarily power over something outside it. Often Lawrence defines it as "capacity." As he says, "Power is *pouvoir*: to be able to. . . . Power is not the least like Will" (*Phoenix II*, 439, 437). Aware of the invitation to force and bullying inherent in any power vision, Lawrence emphasized this lack of will. Frequently in *Aaron's Rod*, as well as in the novelettes of 1921, Lawrence emphasizes the leader's refusal to force his followers' allegiance. The bond that should draw people together rests upon honoring each other's energies and abilities. Love and its assumption of equality degrades us all; true recognition of our own or another's superior capabilities enhances us all. With several admitted difficulties, at its best, much of this seems like a potentially viable vision. Other writers have written within these assumptions; a hierarchical, nondemocratic vision of humanity is one view of human reality and needs.

But in Lawrence, the several tenets of the vision contradict each other and mask deeply held, opposite beliefs. For example, his ideal of a relationship marked by a freedom to come and go masks his equally firm conviction that the new society will foster relationships marked by absolute commitment. Good men and women will pledge themselves to better men and in that pledging forego forever the right to criticize or withdraw. Too, the concept of the living soul as an unfolding process with its own unfolding as its goal masks his equally intense belief that any decent man today is a fighter, active in the world, literally reorganizing the present society according to the new set of ideals. As noted earlier, as early as *Paul Morel* in 1911, the vision of male effectiveness in the world—a goal so difficult to realize for himself—has flowed in and out of Lawrence's fiction. And again, it is at its strongest when he feels least effective in the world. In this leadership phase, in characters like Rawdon Lilly of *Aaron's Rod* or Don Cipriano and Don Ramon of *The Plumed Serpent*, the vision of close, male friendship, especially friendship between unequals, runs into trouble with his belief that any close friendship will include the participants' sexual selves. The problems here are, first, the difficulty Lawrence had creating credible dramatizations of homosexual relationships and, second, his equating sexual relationships with a vital and continuous combativeness. One of the flaws in *Aaron's Rod* is the strain that develops between Aaron's role as uncritical follower and his role as critical mate. Still another contradiction in these fictions is the heroes' poignant yearning for solitude set against their equally poignant yearing for secure community, for never-to-be-broken friendships and pacts.

Finally, underlying these unresolved oppositions is Lawrence's constant tendency to identify with women and his strong need at this time not to do so. Men and women, he argues, are essentially opposite in their needs and natures. Women are best when they move within the spell of a powerful male; men are best when they can take or leave the women, when their energies are powerful enough to carry them through to their goal regardless. To extend Cavitch's analysis, the woman in Lawrence is being told to sit back and be quiet. As suggested above, if she is truly cooperative, she will go to sleep. The command raises problems in the fiction, both because it oversimplifies human complexity, male and female, and because it rests on a transparently defensive posture. The men are willful because they have so little *pouvoir*. In contrast to his earlier, more capable males—Tom Brangwen, Rupert Birkin, Hepburn in "The Thimble," Sam Fergusson in "The Horse Dealer's Daughter," Maurice Pervin in "The Blind Man" —many heroes in the leadership fiction must draw on mystical rituals to bolster their claims to strength and capacity. When present at all, the women who honor them tend to appear thoroughly manipulated by the author.

If this is a fair overview of some of the opposing elements contained in Lawrence's power motif, then, one asks of the fictions, what is the basic given of the tale? Which of these contradictory beliefs and perceptions are being enacted? Where is complexity being admitted? Where avoided? The place to begin is "The Captain's Doll," the one assured success of this period.

Closely related to *Aaron's Rod*, "The Captain's Doll" alters one of the key givens of the novel. In a way, Lawrence retraces the argument of *Aaron's Rod* but invites Lilly's wife home and dismisses Lilly's comrade, Aaron. Dropping the male camaraderie and female avoidance that characterize the novel, he returns to the theme of right power but tests it not through the strained homosexual relationship of Aaron and Lilly but through a lively heterosexual relationship. The problem raised in the novel—how a loyal follower can also be a helpfully antagonistic mate—is one of the tale's key questions.[16] Perhaps because it faces rather than avoids the conflict, the tale possesses a far sounder narrative structure than the novel and explores the possibility of new human relationships with complexity, irony, and humor.[17] Hannele is a typical Lawrentian heroine. Like Louisa Lindley or the Brangwen women, she is skeptical and perceptive; inevitably the energy and wit she brings to the prospect of a leader-follower relationship tightens the motivation for both leader and follower and makes Lilly's antiseptic aloofness a simple impossibility.[18]

Lawrence introduces Hannele and Captain Hepburn by showing Hannele holding him upside down, sticking pins into him, dressing him.[19] It is, of course, Hannele's puppet, her "doll" of him. This is the image of Hepburn "loved" by his mistress Hannele, and in it Lawrence economically accomplishes two things. First he provides dramatic motivation for both the leader's and follower's eventual dissatisfaction with the reductive, romantic love relationships they have known in the past, and second he sets up a foil against which to define the tale's vision of a new mode of relationship.

Like Hepburn's other early scenes with Hannele and with his wife, this first scene demonstrates that he is at a closed end; he is sewn up and going nowhere. Like the doll, his expression is characteristically blank; according to the narrator, most of his actions are "staged" and directed by others. Loving Hepburn, Hannele has literally made a puppet of him; and his wife, in the same loving spirit, has implicitly done so. Never entirely clear about his feelings, he drifts between the two women, accepting with equal lack of response his wife's continual, often cruel manipulations and Hannele's occasional condescension. On one of the few occasions when he talks about himself, Hepburn tells Hannele that he considers life a cage and himself an altogether insignificant prisoner.

Hepburn's one means of temporary escape and our clearest

indication that there is something in him that is being stifled is his keen interest in astronomy. When he is perched like a cat out on the narrow ledge of the boarding house which he and Hannele tenant, carefully tracking the movement of the stars, he seems for the moment "real," in genuine contact with himself and his world. Embarrassed at her use of the word, Hannele feels that there is a "'magic'" in him at those moments, and that it is without limits. What is "real" about him is his magic.

Drawn together, these early scenes constitute one of the key elements missing from *Aaron's Rod*. Through them, Lawrence establishes a dramatic motive for his leader's conversion, for his decision to seek out some new basis for human relationships. The enemy is the trite, dehumanizing conventions of the romantic love tradition. And, as I shall argue, far from being identified with women, these conventions victimize women as well as men.

When his wife obligingly falls victim to vertigo, Hepburn is shocked out of his doll-like trance, leaves Hannele for several months, thinks through his situation. Using a variation of the love triangle, Lawrence poses Hepburn at the apex and indicates the alternatives that confront him. Hepburn can return to Hannele and acquiesce in a love relationship he feels is wrong, or he can risk losing her for a power ideal he can only gropingly describe. When he returns, he has chosen to risk their love relationship by attempting to persuade her to "honor and obey" him. Hepburn's decision is dramatically effective because it is well motivated and because he risks much. Unlike Lilly, who sacrifices little in renouncing his former love relationships, Hepburn would lose a great deal if Hannele were to turn him and his new vision down.[20]

Turning from Lawrence's motivation of the leader to his motivation of the follower, one finds him employing much the same dramatic strategy. When Aaron rejects the love mode for the power mode, he does so almost blindly, for he is unable to define what he wants or where he is going. By contrast, in the tale Lawrence gives a sharp picture of Hannele's options and a clear sense of her making a decision. Like Hepburn, Hannele stands at the apex of a triangle; like his, her alternatives are presented with sufficiently balanced sympathy so as to create dramatic tension in her choosing.

When Hepburn returns to Hannele, she is about to marry the Herr Regierungsrat. Planning to write a history of his district in

159

Austria, he represents to Hannele a remnant of the romantic European order she grew up with, knew, and loved before the war. Opposing his deadly invitation to move backward are Hepburn and his vague vision of something new. I might note here that Hannele's choice between these two gentlemen may seem narrow to a liberated mind. If we read metaphorically, however, we see that, like seekers before her, Hannele is faced with a choice between difficult salvation and easy perdition. She is the vulnerable soul and saves herself by choosing rightly. Significantly, by using a triangular structure in this tale, Lawrence implies that she, unlike her brother follower Aaron, is capable of choosing.

Lawrence further alters the follower's motivation in the tale by making Hannele recognize that she not only suffers by being loved, but also that she destroys by loving. Lawrence indicates that Hannele will suffocate beneath the solicitous love of Herr Regierungsrat, but his major point is that Hannele is violating Hepburn and herself with her oppressive love. Aaron rejects love largely out of a vague resentment and self-pity. In Hannele's rejection there is an awareness of guilt and a growth in self-understanding.

But what of the alternative? Hannele may finally be convinced that the courtly love tradition has become oppressive to everyone, man and woman alike. But what should be put in place of the honeymoon tableau of the male kneeling at the feet of his lady? One wonders if it was at this point that Lawrence wondered how to get his characters off the mountain and on to some plain resolution (CL, 670).

In chapter 4, I emphasized the need to study Lawrence's thematic cruxes within their dramatic context. Dissolution in one context is different, for example, from dissolution in another. This need is especially clear in reading the climax of "The Captain's Doll." Lawrence takes the captain and Hannele on a comic, holiday jaunt to visit one of Austria's awesome glaciers. In making their way up the trail to the glacier, the two characters are caught between two worlds. On one hand are the tiresome crowds, determined to have fun. On the other is the cold, insentient glacier, challenging, dangerous, sterile. It is in this context that the reader listens to their quarrel. Having bickered most of the day, the two break into one of Lawrence's classic battles. And as was true in the sexual battle scenes of his earlier fictions, here each side makes valid points against the other. Hannele accuses Hepburn's power vision of condescension, conceit, impudence. Hepburn accuses Hannele's love vision of the same. The dialogue itself urges us to see this quarrel as balanced, raising rather than settling issues; but the dramatic context even more effectively urges us to credit both sides. The contrasting worlds of crowd and glacier reflect dangerous qualities in the two modes of relationship available to Hannele and Hepburn. Both worlds, like both modes, can destroy life, energy, *pouvoir*.

Delaying closure of this battle as long as he possibly can— not only to increase dramatic tension but also to indicate the difficulty of the issues—Lawrence moves his fighting couple off the mountain and sets them down in a small boat. They are for the moment suspended, as they row slowly toward Hannele's house. Hepburn's proposal—marry, honor, and obey me—hangs in the air. Hannele must decide. But her decision is difficult and holds them both in limbo. As they continue arguing, they approach Hannele's dock. Her friends begin hallooing to her across the water. She yells back, continues her intense dialogue in *sotto voce* in the boat, yells again to the friendly voices, continues the dialogue. Hepburn says he will leave in the morning if all is over between them. She calls him a solemn ass. They draw nearer to the dock and the jolly friends. She is exquisitely poised between options as Lawrence keeps the issues afloat. At the very end, in the most qualified terms, Hannele consents. "'Do you want to go away tomorrow? Go if you do. But anyway, I won't say it *before* the marriage service. I needn't, need I?'"[21] This is yes with a great deal of no in it, and her ultimate gesture in the tale points less to her pledging herself to the new way of relationship and more to her rejecting the old. As she steps out of the boat, she asks Hepburn for the small oil painting he has in his backpack. It is a still life of him, based on his doll, and clearly parallels her earlier icon to love. She intends to burn it.[22]

Set against the background of their past relationship, Hepburn's insistence that he be honored and obeyed translates to an insistence that his capacities be duly recognized, that he not be treated like a doll. Hannele's reluctance, however, is as important as her consent, for it becomes the safeguard of their humor and humanity. Each time Hepburn assumes his leadership position, Hannele begins to play the role of the gargoyle laughing at the cathedral, warding off melodrama, criticizing this hero and his vision. In sum, to recall a problem in *Aaron's Rod*, Hannele begins to assume the difficult role of consenting, loyal follower and critical mate.

"The Captain's Doll" is a leader-follower tale one can at least partially understand. Much like Lawrence himself, Hepburn is presumably a person blessed with vision and a wealth of capacities. He has books he wants to write, places he wants to go. He will largely define the pattern of his and Hannele's life together. This is not equality. But one senses that his relationship with Hannele will be dynamic, for Hannele, although not a visionary herself, is the essential, influential dissenter. As the tale makes abundantly clear, she is capable as Aaron is not of loyal and effective opposition. This is no lullaby, sinister or otherwise.

Lawrence never again attained the same complexity or clarity in the leadership tales or novels that followed. "The Fox" comes closest, partly because of the vibrancy of the natural imagery, but, like the others, it falls into a sea of troubles. Briefly summarized, the troubles are as follows. Insisting that his heroes be immune from criticism, Lawrence sets up a gallery of flat, melodramatic icons to male supremacy.[23] Demanding that his women—his usual critics and frequent visionaries—be mum, he prevents himself from drawing upon the side of him that so frequently brought complexity and insight to his stories. When he himself resists the narrow limits he has imposed on his heroines, he creates a series of characters who show up as highly contradictory or obviously manipulated by the author's message. Trying to imagine scenes that could dramatize the legitimate obeisance of one person to another, he manufactures affected gestures and strained images. And finally, lacking fundamental belief in this power vision, he fails to find the delicate, flexible language and the range of imagery he needs to convey the vision. Frequently he resorts to some exotic ceremony or foreign hero, with both ceremony and hero employing a false diction. It may be a semi-Biblical language or a pastiche of pidgin and standard English, but in no case does it approach the magic of the diction in *The Rainbow*, "The Prussian Officer," "The Horse Dealer's Daughter," or "The Blind Man," to cite only a few works where Lawrence's diction soars. Another way to state the problems that plague the leadership tales following "The Captain's Doll" is to say that they are either coherent and flat or dynamically confused.

"The Fox" and "The Ladybird" are the latter. In revising "The Fox" in 1921, Lawrence mainly took his 1918 text, altered the last pages, and added what he saw as a fiery tail.[24] March becomes more combative than in the earlier versions, Banford a bit kinder and more querulous. Henry enters their life, is equated with the fox, and casts a spell of attraction over March. With occasional deletions and additions, Lawrence fleshes out Henry's initial character; Henry becomes both more human—conversational, friendly—and more foxlike—calculating, vibrant.[25] The long tail consists of Henry's extended, tortuous campaign to win the now reluctant March. In the campaign, Lawrence expands the metaphor of the hunt. Through added scenes and analyses, Henry increasingly develops into a silent, watchful hunter, willing his prey to come into view and fall beneath his gun. The fox, Banford, and March will all be brought down. More than any other single factor, that metaphor develops the power theme implicit in the first version and creates increasingly noticeable problems in the tale.

Ian Gregor was one of the first critics to raise questions about the accomplishment of the tale. In "'The Fox': A Caveat," Gregor argues against appreciators Murry, Leavis, and Hough by contending that Lawrence did not in fact realize his own intention of showing life triumphing over death. The problems reside largely in his not making Banford sufficiently evil to merit murder and in narrowing Henry to fit his symbol, making that hero finally more a brute animal than a "man alive."[26] Since Gregor, critics have lined up in both camps. In general, those who find the tale successful emphasize its mythic or fairy tale elements. Some see Henry as embodying the ruthlessness of life; Banford stands as either the devouring mother, or the exclusively feminine side of March, or the deathliness of modern England. March is seen as a Sleeping Beauty or Persephone figure. A few critics in this camp argue that Lawrence intends the ambivalence one finds at the tale's end.[27] Those critics who find flaws in the work tend to see the mythic elements clashing with the tale's realistic, psychological complexities. Some elaborate on Gregor's qualms about the characterizations, others analyze switches in narrative tone, particularly in the conclusion, or study Lawrence's conflicting attitudes towards the mythic content.[28]

I join those in the second camp. Banford's murder seems unprepared for and unjustified; rather than Henry's humanity being sparked by foxlikeness, his nature grows simply vulpine. At the tale's end, the victory of life over death is still a long way off. As one critic argues, the narrator seems to sense this but his awkward shifts of tone and perspective seem not to argue for intentional ambivalence or a conscientiously open ending. Inviting the reader to review some of the excellent work that has been done on the many aspects of "The Fox," I will concentrate on Lawrence's formulation of "new" relationships, on March's character, and on her relationship to Banford.

Certainly an important intention in the tale is to show life triumphing over death, even ruthlessly; the conflict between Henry and Banford seeks to realize that intention. Another intention, however, is to dramatize the new relationship Lawrence was exploring at the end of "The Captain's Doll." Toward that intention goes the long conflict between March and Henry. Given the metaphor of the hunt, Lawrence must create, in the second half of the story, a series of obstacles that postpone March's capitulation to Henry. Shall the obstacles lie in Henry's character? In March's? Shall they originate in Banford's hold on March? The nature of the obstacles and the eventual resolution of the conflict are important as they help formulate a working definition of "new" human relationships, relationships based on the power of one, the submission of the other.

In his postponement strategy, Lawrence decides that the obstacles shall not lie with Henry. Almost from the moment he first genuinely notices March, Henry is unswerving in intention and desire. He wants the farm, he wants March. This integrity of desire is true in all three versions. On the other hand, Lawrence decides that Banford will present an important obstacle. Increasingly, in the revised version, she preys on March, seeking to keep her friend through appeals to loyalty, compassion, female love. But Banford cannot be the sole obstacle to the new relationship because that would reduce March to a pawn. Lawrence therefore develops qualities in March herself that balk at Henry's proposal, that postpone his victory. Growing less docile through the three texts, the revised heroine shows greater independence and reluctance. To fulfill her role in the new drama, she must basically desire but temporarily reject Henry's advances. It is in developing this blend of qualities in March that Lawrence runs into additional problems with his tale.

Faced with the question of what kind of character the new March shall be, Lawrence comes up with several different answers. Through repeated, brief, still shots of her, Lawrence gives us the impression of a young woman who is continually falling asleep. In this drowsiness, the new March is similar to the earlier one. Working, walking around the farm, sitting with Banford in the parlor, she slides into muses, goes quite blank. To save her, a hero must arouse her. But this characterization runs counter to the idea that a true follower—the role March must eventually play— needs to learn to sleep. To be her true self, she does not need awakening; she needs lulling.

With a slight shift of emphasis, then, Lawrence creates a different image pattern around March. She is like a rabbit. Hypnotized by the light that issues from Henry, she is frozen in fascination, yearning to be dominated. Within this reading of her character, March wishes to be caught and withholds assent out of perverseness, coyness, skittishness. But if this is the case, then the hunt is a ruse. One thinks of the genuine, dynamic conflict between Captain Hepburn and Hannele in "The Captain's Doll" for contrast. Lawrence's problem in this section in "The Fox" is that he wants to create an analogy between Henry's capture of March and the natural capture of rabbits by foxes. But he hardly wants to give us the image of March as a terrified rabbit being run down, killed, and eaten. For the image of the hunt to work on a human level—for the vision of the new relationship to be acceptable—March must want to be captured and fulfilled, not killed, by Henry's pounce. Within the reader's sense of the "natural," it is rare that the rabbit wishes to be devoured or finds fulfillment in the feast. Lawrence seems to have sensed the strained analogy, for the tale's last section is a relatively long explanation of March's character seen from a whole new perspective. In the explanation, Lawrence tries out another image pattern.

Once Banford is dead and March and Henry married, Lawrence turns to the reader and attempts to explain the kind of future March can and should look forward to. It is, of course, based on her nature. She must become as seaweed. She must never come up out of the water, but must learn to sway with the vast currents that surround her. In context, the metaphor indicates that March must find herself in Henry. He is the elemental force that can sustain her and give meaning to her motion. This sense of her new identity and fulfillment is based on a contrast to what she had been. And what was that? Here one learns that March has always been an intense striver. Not a blank, musing young woman, not a masochistic rabbit, March had nearly worn herself to ribbons seeking an elusive happiness, perfection. If the first scenes of the tale implied that the vibrant Henry had come to arouse the somnolent, drifting March, the last paragraphs explain that he has come for the opposite reason, to teach her to sleep, to drift. Ultimately, one is left with a March who seems more like a collage of disparate qualities than an integrated character or unified configuration of concepts. Like other women in the leadership tales, she is all too obviously manipulated by the tale's argument.

Lawrence's tail to "The Fox" is, again, a delaying of closure. The capture of March will be postponed so that Lawrence may develop this trio and the ideas they embody. In that development Lawrence elaborates the metaphor of the hunt as an analogy to Henry's wooing of March. The analogy is strained, however, and Lawrence himself seems aware of the strain. Unwilling to drop the organizing metaphor, he keeps adding qualities to March to justify it. The tale is similar to the revised "England, My England," also written in 1921, in its lack of unity and argument for submerging the heroine. A paragraph of exposition here contradicts a scene there; an image pattern in one place is undercut by an analysis somewhere else. Not surprisingly, the last explanatory sections of "The Fox" parallel the more continuous explanations in "England, My England": in both, the reader listens to an anxious, often sardonic narrator who tries in vain to convince us through assertions that the tale we are reading is perfectly coherent.[29]

Turning to the third angle of the triangle, the relationship between March and Banford, two issues are important to our understanding of Lawrence's views of women. Although Lawrence never explicitly says that the relationship between March and Banford is lesbian, he heightens the implications in his revision of the tale. Banford begs March to go to bed with her; March wishes she were sleeping with Henry rather than with Banford. If one views the relationship between Banford and March within the context of the lesbian relationship between Ursula Brangwen and Winifred Inger in *The Rainbow*, one will assume an inherent repulsiveness in the partnership. Further, one may follow Kate Millett, Deborah Core, and other critics and generalize that friendship between women is an impossibility in Lawrence's fiction.[30] It is threatening and always explicitly or implicitly repellent. In fact, the argument is not true.

In "The Fox," Lawrence is mainly interested in showing March's need for Henry and Henry's need for March, with Banford as one obstacle. There are lesbian implications and this female friendship is preventing the "right" relationship, but in themselves those implications and that friendship are not seen as repulsive, threatening, ugly. Lawrence simply does not employ the images of corruption he uses in referring to the relationship between Winifred Inger and Ursula Brangwen. Branford's whining and March's martyred attitude could occur in other unhealthy relationships between men and men, or men and women. Our sense that there may be nothing inherently or particularly nasty in their situation is further supported by the many close female friendships we do in fact find in Lawrence.

In a letter to Mansfield, November 1918, Lawrence wrote,

> I do believe in friendship. I believe tremendously in friendship, between man and man, a pledging of men to each other inviolably. But I have not ever met or formed such friendship. Also I believe the same way in friendship between men and women and between women and women, sworn, pledged, eternal, as eternal as the marriage bond, and as deep. (CL, 565)

Lawrence's critics have often focused on the masculine references in this statement, rightly seeing them as the motive behind such works of the period as "The Blind Man," *Aaron's Rod*, and *The Plumed Serpent*. But if they have attended to it at all, readers have seen the reference to women as an isolated statement in Lawrence: perhaps he felt female friendship was good in theory but he could not dramatize it in fiction.

Looking at the fiction, one sees Lawrence's view of love between women varying. As one might expect, whether female love is healthy or not usually depends on the context. Millett is right in noting that by the end of their affair, Ursula's love for Winfred is presented as unnatural, oppressive, ugly. The love of Banford for March is not presented as repulsive, but it is claustrophobic, deadening. The sisterhood of Emmie and Matilda in "You Touched Me" is similarly negative, claustrophobic. But countering these sour views of female intimacy are other views. Because they fit comfortably into their narratives, more comfortably than male friendships often do, they go unnoticed.

There is the love between Ursula and Gudrun, a sisterhood made up of long arm-in-arm walks, talks, swims, gifts, nicknames.

167

In the end they part ways, but so do Gerald and Birkin. There is the ease, trust, touching, and sharing of experiences that Connie Chatterley and Ivy Bolton enjoy as they plant spring bulbs together in *Lady Chatterley's Lover*. Ivy is in fact the only person other than Mellors to share the outdoors with Connie. There is Hilda's courageous and determined rescue of Connie from Wragby in the same novel. One has the friendship of Nell and Blanche in "A Prelude," the fondness and tenderness between Louisa and Mrs. Durant in "Daughters of the Vicar," the coziness of Marta and her friend as they snuggle up in bed together in "The Mortal Coil." (One has only to try to think of a comparably affectionate scene between males to realize how natural the closeness between women can be in Lawrence's fiction.) Lou and Mrs. Witt have a wry, life-long loyalty toward each other in "St. Mawr." Hannele and Mitchka have long been work mates and close friends in "The Captain's Doll." Fanny's aunt feels great sympathy and tenderness for her beautiful niece in "Fanny and Annie." The idea that in Lawrence there is an automatic barrier to female closeness, that the closeness automatically implies a shadowy and distasteful relationship, is simply not borne out by the fiction.

Indeed, just as it has been easier in our culture for women to embrace women than for men to embrace men, in Lawrence's fiction it is, in fact, usually the masculine caress that calls attention to itself, often prefaced by violence and carried out through such rituals as wrestling, oil rubdowns, prayer séances. Realizing that there is much room in Lawrence's world for female friendships and love helps, I believe, to lay to rest another common and related misconception about Lawrence's view of women.

Millett was one of the first to argue that Lawrence, the self-proclaimed liberator of dirty secrets, does not show women's bodies in his fiction. His men are fully described, from loins to haunches to thighs, penises, chests. But, Millett argues, the female body is basically repulsive, unclean, threatening to him—as it has been to men and women in our culture since Hebraic times. Rarely does Lawrence let it enter his work.[31] As with the issue of female friendship, the truth is more various.

In his early work, neither male nor female bodies are explicitly or fully described. In later works such as *The Plumed Serpent* or the several versions of *Lady Chatterley's Lover*, descriptions are more open and the female body is sometimes seen as threatening, horrible. As a youth, Parkin, an early figure for Mellors, sees a girl's pubic hair and is so horrified that he never quite gets over it. The clitoris in both novels is equated with a white-hot, frictional, ultimately sterile excitation. It calls forth images of birds' beaks and implies castration. All this is to be found in Lawrence. But other images are also present.

Given the censorship taboos, it is surprising to find Clara Dawes crouching naked before the fire in *Sons and Lovers*; Paul trembles at her loveliness. In that same novel, there is the milder but memorable image of Miriam in her new dress, with her round, bare arms, white as new blanched almonds. In *The Rainbow*, one has little sense of Will Brangwen's body but sees Anna dance naked like a full ear of corn in defiance of black-browed Will and in celebration of her pregnancy. Of Hannele in "The Captain's Doll" one reads, "She swam slowly and easily up, caught the rail of the steps and stooping forward, climbed slowly out of the water. Her legs were large and flashing white and looked rich, the rich white thighs with the blue veins behind, and the full, rich softness of her sloping loins" (*Four Short Novels*, 236). There is March, sensitive about exposing her knees in a dress, who is likely, Henry feels, to have small, soft, white breasts. But the real test of course is *Lady Chatterley's Lover*, a novel whose central intention was to take the wraps off dirty secrets. And there we have Connie with her tipped up breasts, sloping buttocks, soft pubic hair, and folded openings that Mellors gently, rhythmically strokes. Lawrence describes Connie gazing at herself in the mirror, studying her breasts, her belly, the crinkle at her waist. He writes of her wetness and wavelike orgasms. If Lawrence follows anyone's sexual excitation and climax in the love-making scenes in that novel, it is Connie's experience he follows. It is true that Lawrence does not use visual imagery to describe Connie's sexual arousal. Mellor's penis he describes, erect and glowing. But surely there are anatomical justifications for the lack of visual description of Connie's genitals. Mellors does not peer. If anything, he is fighting against that kind of watching, voyeuristic, mental sexual activity. The lack of visual imagery does not necessarily warrant our seeing an overwhelming dislike in Lawrence for female genitals. Finally, if one follows Barbara Hardy's lead, one will also turn to the poetry, to "Gloire de Dijon" or "New Heaven and Earth" for example, to see Lawrence's view of the female body in sensitive and celebratory terms.[32]

To summarize the argument: many friendships do not constitute an approval of lesbianism, nor do many fine bodies make a resolution of ambivalence. Just as he found male homosexuality threatening, Lawrence found lesbianism threatening. He found femaleness threatening, partly because he identified strongly with it. In many of the leadership works and in the sizzling passages on Bertha Mellors in *Lady Chatterley's Lover*, one sees Lawrence spilling forth his distrust and dislike of the female. But continuing to read the fiction, one sees that the images of distrust, dislike, repulsion do not go deeper or ring fuller than the many alternative images of trust, love, or tender and passionate attraction. Recognizing that the leadership fiction presents many qualifications, I believe Cavitch's overview is accurate: the threat, the ambivalence, the insecurity Lawrence felt in his sexual identification far more often led him to "preternaturally sensitive examinations of all human relations and institutions" than to the opposite: a steady, covert attraction to males and an unexamined repulsion toward females, be they alone, in concert, clothed, or naked.[33]

Thus, while there is much wrong in the relationship between March and Banford, there is little suggestion within "The Fox" that the wrong is inherent in female friendships. Outside the tale there is much evidence that female friendships are a natural part of the social world Lawrence imagined and painted. In "The Ladybird" Lawrence returns to his more usual triangle, a man or woman choosing between two suitors. But if "The Fox" has redeeming qualities in its powerful (using the word advisedly) evocation of the fox, "The Ladybird," which replaces the fox with an ancient scarab, has not. The small tale, "The Thimble," which served as the skeleton for "The Ladybird," shows through its remake in a variety of ways, but most curiously in the reversal of attitude Lawrence takes toward old objects.[34] The thimble reenters not as a token of old England best discarded but of a much older Europe best revived.

With this tale, Lawrence began explicitly to associate right leadership with ancient ceremonies and cultures. In doing so, he gives his power theme a clear social dimension. In Mexico in 1923, Lawrence wrote to Murry that he believed that, of the three novelettes, "The Ladybird" had more "the quick of a new thing" (*CL*, 743).[35] As Lawrence was then in the midst of *The Plumed Serpent*, he may have been referring to the tale's linking of the new world with the old and to the social perspective this implied. In "The Ladybird," the link to the past is provided by a tiny spark of a man, the Bohemian count Dionys Psanek. As do Don Ramon and Don Cipriano, Count Dionys wishes to move beyond the Christian and romantic one-sidedness of the present and establish a new culture with new relationships. But, he insists, the new must come out of the old. To give them their due, these heroes are not urging reversion; they are drawing on alternative cultures, particularly ancient ones, and assuming those cultures to be not primitive but sophisticated and rich. More than Henry of "The Fox" or even Captain Hepburn of "The Captain's Doll," Count Dionys has a powerful motive for rebelling against the current culture: behind the count's hatred lies his near-death in the First World War.

Set between 1917 and 1918, "The Ladybird" is very much a war tale in subject. Yet unlike the resurrection tales Lawrence wrote during the war itself, "The Ladybird" expresses hope for salvation only surreptitiously, confusedly. Lawrence's tone calls to mind Connie Chatterley's comment that any great shock to a person's spirit or to a culture forms a wide bruise that only gradually begins to ache but then aches for years. In "The Ladybird," written three years after the war, one feels an ever-present sense of the horror of the war. In it Lawrence mocks his earlier belief that the conflict was a great sickness through which Europe would pass into new health. On one level, the tale is a howl of anger expressing a yearning for destruction and solitude. The humor is acid; the hero demands and receives immunity from all criticism.

Although its organizing conflicts are complex and finally confusing, the tale's plot line is simple. Lady Beveridge, an elderly English aristocrat, goes to visit the London hospital where the German prisoners are tended. There she sees a family friend, Count Dionys Psanek. She returns several days later with her daughter, Lady Daphne. In the tale, Lady Daphne is Lawrence's "vulnerable" woman. Like Hannele, she must choose between a relationship based on love or one based on power. A slow attraction between Lady Daphne and the count develops, providing among other things an opportunity for the count to explain his view that right human relations are based on power, obedience, faith—he gropes for the right word. In the middle of the story Lady Daphne's husband returns from the war. Arguing for love, democracy, equality, he provides the dramatic counter to Dionys. Lady Daphne finds the count's ideas to be the truer and pledges herself to him. Yet he must return to Germany; she remains with Basil. But the real bond is now between the count and the lady. On a mythic level, the creative-destructive energies of the Dionysian hero have won out over the pale Apollonian virtues of the husband.[36]

This summary would suggest that the tale's key conflict is a clear one between Apollo and Dionysus, translated here to a war between love and power. The underlying question is which kind of human contact provides the better basis for relationships and cultural renewal. Within this argument, the count would be articulating what Hepburn of "The Captain's Doll" and Henry of "The Fox" only manage to imply. Over a series of conversations, the count explains that people must learn to recognize the natural aristocrats among themselves. To these aristocrats goes absolute power: in the count's words, "'My chosen aristocrat would say to those who chose him: "If you chose me, you give up forever your right to judge me. If you have truly chosen to follow me, you have thereby rejected all your rights to criticize me."'"[37] When Daphne blurts out, "'They wouldn't be able to help criticizing, for all that,'" the count makes the remarkable equation so characteristic of the leadership fiction: to criticize is to betray, pure and simple. Basil counters with an argument Birkin used in *Women in Love*: in right human relationships there is no submission or obedience to the other person but only to the thing between them. But Basil is wrong.

However, the tale's organizing conflicts are not simply or clearly between power and love. Other issues enter. For example, the count says that more than anything else on earth he wants room for his anger to grow. That wish signals a major motif in the tale, one that cuts across the power-love conflict, one that harkens back to *Women in Love*. In that novel, Birkin argues that cultures have seasons, they wax and wane. Western culture is decomposing. The process is a rotting, a dissolving, a vast going-apart. The count argues much the same thing. Referring to the Egyptians' honoring of the dung beetle, he even believes that the decomposing, the falling apart, is the beginning of all motion, all progress. Pledging himself to the god of destruction, he sees his every heartbeat as a hammer stroke of destructive energy.

But a problem enters when the reader poses the count's belief in corruption, anger, and destruction against his leader-follower vision. Is the leader-follower vision an ideal for future human relations or is it the nadir of human relations out of which some other ideal—presumably its opposite—will rise anew? The distinction is major, but the tale offers no help.

Another problem enters. The argument between love and power assumes that human relations are important, whether they are based on one model or another. But even more explicitly than Lilly, the count expresses a deep desire to be alone, generalizing it into a broad belief in the unimportance of human relationships. Arguing that it is cathedrals and wars that give the real measure of eras, the count says that the quality of human contact is a by-product of something else. He does not say of what. But human relationships are insignificant anyway. When one adds the count's belief that all real leaders must be alone to his belief that human relationships are unimportant, one ends up seeing the whole question of which model—love or power—creates the finer human contact as moot. Relations do not deeply matter.

Important or not, through the tale's climax and denouement Lawrence continues to wrestle with the problem of dramatizing a positive, power-based relationship. He has argued that solitude is best for the leader; for the follower, subservience is best, followed by sleep. In the tale's climax, Lawrence tries to make this argument concrete.

The count has gone to the Beveridge's house for a two-week visit before returning to Germany. Drawing on the myth in which Dionysus pipes his followers into the underworld each third year, from whence they shall issue reborn, Lawrence has the restless Lady Daphne captivated by the count's lonely singing in his room. She responds to what she hears as his call and enters his dark bedroom. Their first real encounter is acted out very much as the power vision suggests it should be. The leader seeks no follower. He wishes to be alone. But the follower comes, even intrudes. Daphne sits in Dionys's room, under his spell, until finally she reaches out for him and then suddenly slides down to his feet, crouching in an ancient gesture of adoration. What was horrible for Basil to do to her—worship, bow down, give over self-responsibility—is right for her to do the count. Dionys feels that he is no longer mere man. He is like an ancient Egyptian statue. Reluctantly he accepts her worship and desire, but his reward is negligible since he is a loner. Solitude is, again, all he genuinely desires. Her reward is great, however: she can finally sleep. No more self-responsibility, no more thinking. She is the count's "wife in darkness." As such, "She would not have contradicted him, no, not for anything on earth . . . he was to her infallible" (*Four Short Novels*, 107). Her eyes are wide and vacant. "She felt she could sleep, sleep, sleep—for ever." She is finally well.

How does Daphne's blissful state relate to Lawrence's earlier statement that she is essentially angry, a wild cat, an adder, a part of the vast destruction of the culture? As elsewhere in the tale, the power vision with its groggy followers is not speaking clearly or coherently to the vision of Western culture as needing angry souls to get busy with the activity of pulling down. Eventually, one feels that Lawrence is again manipulating his heroine according to his idea of the moment.

Simply stated, "The Ladybird" rests on the assumption that men and women are essentially different: men are active leaders, workers; women are passive followers, sleepers. As in "Wintry Peacock," "You Touched Me," or "The Fox," Lawrence is compartmentalizing what he once saw, and will see again, as a unified field of human energies and potentials. He oversimplifies by giving to men and women respectively what he formerly gave to humans collectively.

If "The Ladybird" shares thematic weaknesses with "The Fox," it also shares tonal difficulties. The awkwardness of the closing sections of "The Fox" mars most of "The Ladybird." Throughout, one encounters passages of undigested explanation and assertion. Undermining them is an occasional shift into flippancy. Echoing a tone that Lawrence employs in *Aaron's Rod*, these shifts reveal a half-mocking narrator who jeers at the story he has set up. One hears this unease in phrases such as "What next? Well, what followed was entirely Basil's fault" (*Four Short Novels*, 92). There is a dear-reader chattiness in this story-teller's intrusions that undermines the seriousness of the tale. The same tone undermines *Aaron's Rod* and will overwhelm *Kangaroo*, written six months later.[38]

More telling than the narrator's flippant tone, however, is Lawrence's inability to find a complex, natural image to dramatize his vision of new life issuing from old, if that is indeed his vision. Relying on the count's haughty and embarrassed explanations of his family's secret society, ancient rites, and odd crest, Lawrence fails to locate a believable or vivid source of resurrection. Lawrence even shows the same tendency here as he does in *The Plumed Serpent* and "The Woman Who Rode Away," of presenting mystic ideas through the voice of a character who usually speaks correct English but occasionally slides into a foreigner's awkwardness. The effect is stiltedness and a muffling of Lawrence's own clear voice. As with the flippancy, he is imposing a screen between himself and the tale's message.

In "The Ladybird," Lawrence states quite simply what he is after: a society that freely recognizes its natural aristocrats and gives them full power.[39] In a different work, Hannele and her like would criticize this vision for what it is, naive. Anna Brangwen would laugh, and Ursula would say it is only a theory, there is no way to define the "best" individuals. But the Hanneles, Annas, and Ursulas are not allowed to speak up in most of these leadership tales. Lawrence's leaders—Lilly, Henry, Count Dionys—speak to no genuine opposition. They are in the position their theory posits as ideal: alone, not to be criticized. But they are reduced by their very success. In their immunity from contact and conflict, they resemble less the Egyptian statues they emulate and more the small doll Hannele made of Hepburn. As her love once captured and diminished Hepburn, so Lawrence's power theory has captured and diminished masculine energies and produced these small, flat, changeless heroes.

What to do with his heroes? That is a problem Lawrence responded to in the trio of leadership tales written in early 1924. In each, his decision, based in no small part on his fury with John Middleton Murry,[40] is to shift focus from the beleaguered leaders and attend to their opposites, males who refuse their proper role. He will define a powerful male by giving a clearer sense of a powerless one. In the two smaller tales, "The Last Laugh" and "Jimmy and the Desperate Woman," the result is a more coherent story, but also lacking in complexity. In the more ambitious "Borderline," we again encounter basic confusions in the tale, and again the confusions are especially damaging to the figure of the leader.

A major character in each tale is a flopping, shambling man, tagged by his inability to walk firmly on his legs. He cannot lead, cannot be alone. In "The Last Laugh," Lawrence continues drawing on ancient cultures as sources of rebellion and health by having a Pan spirit strike down the weak, failed male.[41] The characters are a deaf girl named James who is modeled after Dorothy Brett, a shambling Murry figure named Marchbanks, and a policeman.[42] Marchbanks and James have just left the house of their friend, Lorenzo. Walking through the winter night, Marchbanks is the first to hear Pan's laughter. He alerts James to the sound, she turns on her Marconi listening machine, and soon the policeman on the corner joins them in searching out the source of the whin-nying laughter. Marchbanks gets waylaid however by a "Jewish looking" woman. James and the policeman continue, James begin-ning to hear voices saying, " 'He's back,' " then Pan's laughter itself. The climax of their search occurs by a demolished church. The windows have been blown out, the altar cloth and books whirled away, and inside, the organ pipes have become Pan pipes trilling out wild, gay music. If one did not know it from *Studies in Classic American Literature*, one would guess from this scene that Law-rence had been recently reading Hawthorne's "My Kinsman, Ma-jor Molineux."[43]

Morning follows night in a carefully designed denouement. For hearing, smelling, seeing, and believing in Pan, James is sig-nificantly freed of her dependence upon machines. Both her literal deafness and figurative blindness are cured. She can now hear per-fectly and can see what a fool she has been in her cloying friend-ship with Marchbanks.[44] For accompanying her on the search but never hearing, seeing, or believing, the policeman awakes the next morning crippled by the power of Pan. But Marchbanks, who heard Pan's laughter but left the search and went down the garden path to indulge in a romantic Hebraic affair, is struck dead.[45]

It is the first but not the last time that the Murry character will be killed off in these tales, but within the dynamics of this tale, the death works and the tale has coherence. Earlier, in "The Fox," the murder of Banford does not carry out Lawrence's inten-tion to show life triumphing over death partly because Banford never becomes sufficiently stylized to represent death. By contrast, in "The Last Laugh," Marchbanks is sufficiently stylized. Symboli-cally, his reward for refusing life is death. As Cowan notes, like each of the characters, including the Christian church, March-banks figures neatly in Lawrence's argument about modern sterility and the need for "a revival of the natural mode of religious percep-tion embodied in the figure of Pan."[46] The tale is, in fact, a pre-monition of the fables Lawrence would write several years later. Like them, it is nice in its logic, its characters are projections of that logic, and plot and imagery illustrate the moral.[47] If the tale falls below those later parables, "The Rocking-Horse Winner" or "The Man Who Loved Islands" for example, it does so because of its slightness. Pan is captured in the imagery of the story: in the bright snow, the trilling midnight organ music, the winter/spring contrasts, the image of the sky cracking and shriveling like an old skin. As a spirit, he is a vast improvement over Count Dionys or Lilly Rawdon. But what exactly he stands for, apart from more laughter and less soulfulness, needs fuller dramatization.

"Jimmy and the Desperate Woman" drags poor Marchbanks back to life in the person of Jimmy.[48] Focusing on its antihero's inability to stand alone and his ability to fool himself, the tale moves between three dominant perspectives: one mimics Jimmy's point of view; one offers the reader a sardonic commentary on Jimmy; and the third, used in relation to the tale's real hero, is straightforward narration. Although the plot is based partly on a parody of Ulysses's journey, Lawrence does not employ his ancient gods motif. Its structure is the familiar triangle. The targets of the satire are several: the weak-kneed male who cannot stand alone, who must either nestle against some woman or find a woman who will nestle against him; the romantic and middle-class cliché that among the working class live all the real people, the "'real stuff'" as Jimmy says; and the presumed allure of someone else's mate.

Stated briefly, the plot follows Jimmy Frith, editor of a high-class, high-brow London magazine, to a dark mining town in the Midlands. He has gone in search of Emily Pinnegar, who has sent him several poems that have intrigued him. Seeking a Gretchen who will curl up at his feet and let him be the strong man he feels he really is, he finds instead a proud, powerful, and miserable woman. With little difficulty, he convinces her to leave her miner husband and their failed marriage. She must, she will, go to London to live with Jimmy, and perhaps sometime marry him. To him, the proposal is a magnificent, daring stroke of courage, and he is proud of himself for having made it. Lawrence's conclusion implies that he has made a fool of himself; for his having convinced this woman to go away with him is a very temporary victory. She will always belong to her own hard husband. As Cowan observes, Frith sounds like "froth"; Jimmy is the froth of Emily's experience as well as of society's real concerns.[49]

Unlike Lawrence's usual triangular tales, "Jimmy and the Desperate Woman" does not focus on the vulnerable character's choice. In her pride, disillusionment, and basic kindness, Emily is engaging and interesting. She is, in fact, one more of the many strong, intelligent, colliery wives who populate Lawrence's fiction from first to last. But the tale's main conflict is between the men.

Jimmy has caught on to the idea that in personal, sexual relations, he should be the leader. Thus he speaks in language not all that different from Lilly, Henry, Count Dionys, or the narrator of the next tale, "The Borderline." But, alas for him, Jimmy is no natural aristocrat. He could be a "Pan person," full of wit, intelligence, and sardonic beauty, but he has chosen to be a martyr to whatever cause comes along. Having no grandeur, he can lead only by finding someone inferior, "some simple uneducated girl; some Tess of the D'Urbervilles, some wistful Gretchen" (CSS, 605).

Jimmy's foil is Emily's husband, Mr. Pinnegar. In his name, one hears a blend of Pan and vinegar. Pinnegar is acrid, bitter, unmovable; he reads like a forerunner of Lawrence's initial, abrasive vision of Mellors in *The first Lady Chatterley*. A collier, he is quite simply a natural aristocrat, a proper leader. He enters the tale "like a blast of wind." His fierce blue eyes and his vigorous wash before the fire urge his suave beauty. When he demands a submissive wife, one is meant to sympathize and agree. He most definitely does not "love" his wife nor feels he should. He assumes her. She is part of his world. Because she has turned cold to him, he has begun to keep a mistress. And if the wife wishes to leave their home, he will miss her. But urge her to remain? Never.

Emily initially promises to rescue Pinnegar from his flat, macho, leadership position, but Lawrence soon muffles her. She goes to London, but she still "moved in [Pinnegar's] aura. She was hopelessly married to him" (CSS, 629). Pinnegar retains Emily, but that is not all. What has begun to intrigue Jimmy most in Emily is Pinnegar: "He could feel so strongly the presence of that other man about her, and this went to his head like neat spirits. That other man! In some subtle, inexplicable way, he was actually, bodily present, the husband" (CSS, 629). As Widmer notes, Jimmy's desire for Emily has become perverse. He wants to capture her as a means of getting at her husband.[50] By the end, as Lawrence intended, Jimmy is demolished. But in giving everything to Pinnegar, Lawrence has inadvertently demolished him as well. Pinnegar is one more small, male statue in Lawrence's growing gallery of leadership icons. With his followers at his feet, Pinnegar sits dominant, humorless, reserved, all right for a museum but not a living fiction.

In "The Borderline," Lawrence takes certain metaphors and figures of speech from "Jimmy and the Desperate Woman" and makes them literal. In a sense, he traces out Emily's marriage to

Jimmy and introduces Pinnegar as an actual bodily presence, a real ghost. In its setting—out of Paris and into postwar, winter-locked, defeated Germany—the tale follows the Lawrences' trip to Germany in February of 1924.[51] Again using his triangle, Lawrence imagines Katherine Farquhar, who clearly resembles Frieda, married to Philip Farquhar, obviously Murry. Lawrence himself is represented by Alan Anstruther, Katherine's first husband, killed years before in the war, but now, like Pan, about to return. As noted above, Lawrence's tales often set up romantic clichés and either mock them or defamiliarize them so they take on genuine meaning. In "The Borderline," he begins by skillfully exposing the dynamics of that complex code of behavior and cliché we call female helplessness. But, at a certain point in the tale, romantic clichés take over; Lawrence ends up writing a story one has heard all too many times before.

"The Borderline" opens well. Through the first third, Lawrence maintains a careful balance between the tale's vision of right power and a skeptic's view. The tension promotes fine, subtle insights into his characters. Katherine is first on stage. Traveling through France and Germany alone, on her way to join Philip in Oos, Katherine feels a voluptuous pleasure in the attention she receives from the French porters. She compliments their masculinity with her show of helplessness; they respond with a mixture of obsequiousness and manly generosity. This brief glimpse into her character and into the social conventions upon which it rests is an arrow forward, pointing to her relationship with Philip. As do the porters, he makes her feel a queen bee; she luxuriates in his masculine fawning. Lawrence sees the dynamics of the relationship clearly. Her behavior is a ruse which carries conveniently contradictory messages: I am helpless, you are superior; I am superior, you must serve me. Either message can be dominant in the view of either party, male or female, at any single moment. In Lawrence's words, Katherine is at once complimented, helpless, out of all frays, manipulated, and manipulating.

Through Katherine's thoughts of Alan, Lawrence introduces an opposite code. Alan exists through the first section of the tale as a memory in Katherine's mind. She remembers him with a mixture of anger, admiration, skepticism, and affection; he could be fooled and foolish, but he was a born fighter, speaking for honesty and straightforwardness. He despised false compliments. He was ceaselessly combative but aboveboard. With him she associates fresh air and the ability to breathe. In a brief and powerful sequence, she looks out of the train window at the Marne country passing by and sees it as flat, grey, wintry, and corpse-ridden, a place where two cultural impulses, the Latin and the Germanic, neutralize each other into ash. The landscape stands as an emblem for a world without Alan and what he stands for. It is a world where differences—sexual, political, trivial, or grand—are defused and deadened by cowardice, lies, manipulation. It is the world of Philip.

A transition in the story's major movements occurs as the train approaches Strasbourg. Katherine has a dream in which she sees the normal, daylight reality she shares with Philip as illusory. Like Dionys's vision in "The Ladybird," her dream gives us an image of sunlight as artificial. Dionys explains that the light we see is the refraction off dust and debris of the original and true fire. The real fire is dark and invisible. Katherine's dream only goes as far as to see ordinary daylight as artificial. She does not yet define for herself what the alternative fire is. But, in both cases, Lawrence is using this imagery to dramatize his belief in human realities and centers of awareness that are similarly invisible and dark. Codes of behavior such as Katherine's earlier feminine posturing are like yellow sunlight, not Katherine's essence but a refraction of her essence off the dust and debris of culture and time.

As night approaches, we encounter what the imagery has prepared us to expect. In Strasbourg, Katherine gets off the train that is carrying her to Philip. She walks through the darkness, seeking the town's cathedral. When she finally finds it, it looms above her, the embodiment of a dark light, a power and an understanding opposite to both artificial sunlight and the grey flatness of the Marne in twilight. Built of pink stone, the cathedral face glows in the darkness. With imagery close to that of Yeats, Lawrence imagines this edifice as a blood-dusky monster about to leap on hyperspiritual, hyperintellectual Christianity, about to destroy the very forces that built it. In its mysterious, fiery glow, the cathedral introduces the ghost of Alan. The two are equated. Both are ghostly, glimmering, ruddy, and ready to pull down weary Western culture, embodied in Katherine, toward a fuller and more complex understanding of reality—cosmic, cultural, and personal.

As a tale that reveals subtle psychological states in its characters and examines aspects of Western culture in general, "The Borderline" succeeds thus far. With the introduction of Alan's ghost, however, subtlety and complexity disappear.[52] Immediately Katherine, like other female seekers in the leadership fiction, is told to stop searching, to realize that searching by definition is an unnatural activity for her. Up until this juncture, she has been our source of awareness. We have watched her thinking and changing. Now awareness, thought, and change in her are seen to be wicked. With Alan she becomes what she must be in order to achieve "her perfection and highest attainment": content, submissive, silent, trembling, absolutely unquestioning, "humble, and beyond tears grateful"—totally absorbed in his aura (CSS, 598). She repents her former questioning deeply. In Katherine's total subjugation, cliché and muddle take over. As Lawrence sets up his conclusion, the difficulties increase.

Alan's ghost drifts off, leaving Katherine to contemplate her good fortune in his return and to continue her railway journey toward Philip. The next morning she leaves Strasbourg for the Rhine Valley and Black Forest. Philip meets her in Oos and together they travel to Baden-Baden where Katherine's sister, Marianne, awaits them.

In the original story, written in 1924, Lawrence used a different conclusion than the one we now read, written in 1928. (See n. 51.) Marianne is a stoic, taking pleasure in the pitiless Tree of Life. Alan becomes that tree, crushing Philip in particular who has grown ill and begun to cough blood. After killing Philip, Alan's ghost embraces Katherine, not "in the old procreative way" but first as a "cloud holds a shower" (*Hutchinson's Magazine*, September 1924, 237) and then as a tree may grow around an object embedded within its bark. We end with Katherine devoured, crushed, enveloped, and ecstatic in the pitiless Tree of Life.

In the 1928 version, Lawrence leaves out the Tree of Life image, deletes the specific illness of Philip—by then, Lawrence himself was coughing blood—and has Alan possess Katherine in the old, procreative way. The action is condensed; this ending is only half as long as the earlier one. Philip falls ill; Katherine puts him to bed. One day when she is out walking, Alan appears, leads her among the rocks in the forest, and makes love to her. It is a grand consummation for Katherine; never has she been so completely possessed. Katherine returns home to find Philip now very ill. A bit disgusted, she nevertheless stays with him and tries to comfort him in his death throes. As in the 1924 version, Alan appears; this time however he merely releases Philip's hold on Katherine.

Philip dies and Alan leads Katherine to the other bed "in the silent passion of a husband come back from a very long journey" (CSS, 604).

The endings are different yet much the same. Explicitly in the earlier version, implicitly in the later, Alan stands for the pitiless but natural assertion of life over sickness, weakness, death. He crushes Philip as roots crush rocks; he and Katherine make love as grass grows up among the bones of a carcass. There is a fine irony in Lawrence's using a ghost, a supernatural lightweight, to represent a natural, persistent energy. But if the logic in both endings has felicitous moments, it also raises difficulties.

In a tale that opens realistically, with complex characters, humor, and a subtle analysis of human motivation, the movement toward stark fable is disturbing. One feels Katherine shrinking from a multidimensional character to a single dimension. Similarly, as Philip's subtlety and strength leave him, one wonders how he could ever have influenced Katherine. Like Miriam years before in *Sons and Lovers*, Philip begins as antagonist but ends up as a straw man, small, whining, sick, and foolish. Flat on his back, Philip is a pathetic rival to Alan.

But, as in the other leadership fictions, the tale's vision most powerfully diminishes the leader figure himself. In this case, Alan is not only rendered flat and melodramatic by his immunity from conflict and criticism, he is also rendered incoherent. He is introduced as an honest fighter, one who despises equivocation. That aspect is lost in his having no opposition, no battle. Also incoherent is the progress he traces. First identified with the cathedral as menacing, he is later seen as strong, silent, and kind; eventually he is identified with the barbaric Black Forest, the pitiless Tree of Life. By itself, his initial menace is fully understandable. As a representative of an old/new culture, he comes as a threat to the established order. Yet as the strong, silent type, he is a very different kind of menace. He is the embodiment of established, romanticized paternalism. His touted kindness toward Katherine does not seem much different from Philip's false obsequiousness. Both attitudes blindfold the woman. Philip and Alan both force Katherine into an eternal posture of gratitude, with no possibility for any real contact.

When the tale then identifies Alan with the Black Forest—as a German pine in the first version, more generally in the second—confusions multiply. In "A Letter from Germany," a brief essay Lawrence wrote during this same visit, he prophesies Germany's recoil from western Europe and withdrawal into its own Germanic past. In the essay, Lawrence sees that recoil as a deathly reversion to primitivism and racial singularity.[53] In the tale, Katherine makes similar observations, using the Black Forest as an emblem of ancient, northern Germany. She feels the forest to be sullen, guarded, waiting; the Germans themselves she sees as resentful and impotent (CSS, 600). But, as we might expect in a leadership tale, Katherine also anticipates Germany's return to its ancient past with some positive emotions. Thus she sees the forest—or the location of that past—as strong, unsubdued, bristling. By itself, her dual response to the Black Forest can speak to the complexity of a return to the past; the difficulty enters when Alan is identified with the forest.[54] Suddenly Lawrence asks us to forget Katherine's former sense of the forest as sullen, deathly, impotent. Alan—oddly dressed in a kilt—is to be associated only with the powerful energies of the forest. He is a ghost but no figure of deathliness.

To summarize, "The Borderline" exemplifies a problem found in *Aaron's Rod*, "The Fox," "The Ladybird," and "Jimmy and the Desperate Woman." That is, a tendency for Lawrence's characterizations to become contradictory or flat, his imagery to grow muddled or disappear, and his language to fall into cliché as his leaders succeed in their mission to overwhelm all decent conflict and opposition. In this tale, as in others, Lawrence hands the leadership role to someone or something exotic—a Bohemian count, a Pan, a ghost—who can be forgiven for his inability to state clearly what his view of the future and of right human relationships is. The home-grown, human leaders are no greater help, being strong, silent types; recall Lilly, Henry Grenfel, Pinnegar. On a related issue, the association of leaders with ancient gods, Lawrence offers a variety of statements. In "The Ladybird," "The Last Laugh," and "The Borderline," he does associate the leaders' power with pre-Christian religions and deities. In "The Captain's Doll," "The Fox," and "Jimmy and the Desperate Woman" that link is only implied if present at all. The followers—all women after *Aaron's Rod*—are given no room or inclination to disagree, with the exception of Hannele. In this supposedly revolutionary fiction, they act out the most traditional of gestures. They lean on the everlasting arms, sleep in the bosom of their lords. Like good, old-fashioned girls, they rejoice in their husbands and their peaceful, protected status.

So far, each of the invitations to sleep has been metaphorical. In the last tale I will look at from this leadership group, the invitation is a sentence, the sleep is permanent. For me, as for other readers, "The Woman Who Rode Away" has great power. As in "The Fox," much of that power derives from Lawrence's magnificent passages on the natural world, the world the heroine must leave. However, in this tale, as in "The Fox" and "The Man Who Died," the poverty of the heroes' visions shows up partly in contrast to the splendid breadth of vision articulated by the omniscient narrator.

Like each of the American tales from the summer of 1924, "The Woman Who Rode Away" traces the journey of a modern white woman into territory—a new or ancient world—that challenges her former understanding of herself.[55] Seen as a trio of works, these tales provide an important conceptual bridge between Lawrence's two drafts of *The Plumed Serpent*. (See n. 5.) In "The Woman Who Rode Away," Lawrence's intention is to map out his heroine's emigration from her own culture into American Indian culture. She does this by giving up her life. In one respect, that journey represents the shifting of human power from the white races to the dark. In another respect, it dramatizes the shift in an individual's consciousness from a rational, scientific, industrial mind set to a more mystical, sensual understanding of reality.

As with "The Fox," critics tend to praise or disparage the piece on the basis of their evaluation of its mythic dimensions. Hough, Leavis, Draper, Cowan, Allen, Scholes, and MacNiven praise the work as a coherent fable.[56] Emphasis falls on the careful preparation Lawrence lays for the sacrifice, the ritual dimensions of that sacrifice, the archetypal qualities of the characters, and the impressive imagery, culminating in the dark cave about to be pierced by the winter sun's last red rays. Critics who see problems in the tale question the human implications that lie within or obtrude upon the mythic dimensions. With varying emphases, West, Moynahan, Widmer, Rossman, Hardy, and of course Millett, see the woman and Indians as human, the sacrifice as brutal and pointless, and the scenes as failing to support the analyses.[57] In my view, one meets here the same problem Gregor identified in "The Fox": Lawrence's accomplishment does not finally fulfill his intentions, whether we take those intentions to be mythic or social-realistic.

Like March in "The Fox," the woman begins in something of a daze. She has married an older, wiry Dutchman, lived in a deserted mining area in Mexico for over ten years, and had two children. She is now thirty-three, growing fat, and is just arousing "from her stupor of subjected amazement" (CSS, 547). Lawrence emphasizes that she has been something of a prisoner and piece of property to her husband. Her journey into the hills one day is her first step out on her own for years. Having given us this kind of background, Lawrence might be expected to show this woman moving toward an awakening and an understanding of herself as more than property, other than prisoner.

But he does not. Just as Lawrence is confusing at the end of "The Fox" when he writes that March had worn herself to ribbons with her nervous search for happiness, so he is confusing at the end of "The Woman Who Rode Away" in stating that "The sharpness and quivering nervous consciousness of the highly bred white woman was to be destroyed again . . . " (CSS, 569). As several critics have asked, what sharpness? What quivering nervousness? In this pathetic woman, one has seen the opposite. Nevertheless, according to the fable, the answer to her salvation lies in her giving up her "strong will" and eventually her life. Her husband had kept her a figurative prisoner; the Indians, the locus of salvation, keep her a literal one. This woman simply moves from one jail to the next.

The problem arises again when one tries to understand the woman's actions as movements in the history of the individual soul or of human culture. The Indians' argument has merit: ways of seeing do change; Anglo culture, with its emphasis on science and reason, may eventually wane and a more religious, sensual, emotional understanding take over. But as the tale occasionally argues, the voices of reason will have to join the opposition for change genuinely to occur. Within the tale's terms, the woman can help bring about the shift in power only by voluntary submission. But if this is the tale's view on how modes of consciousness do change, what does one do with the fact that the woman is locked up, drugged, lied to, and, when not being lied to, addressed in a "semi-barbaric" language she can barely understand? Like Kate Burns in the first *Plumed Serpent*, she takes part in a movement she minimally comprehends. The few choices the woman makes are rendered meaningless by the very lack of the consciousness and understanding she supposedly holds in overstock. When she agrees to her death, the point in her journey at which the reader might expect her to be ushering in the new world most keenly, she is apathetic: "'I am dead already. What difference does it make, the transition from the dead I am to the dead I shall be, very soon'" (CSS, 579).

A further problem occurs in the sexual dynamics of the tale. Lawrence emphasizes that in accepting the woman's sacrifice, the Indians see her as culture bearer not sexual being. Within their prophecies, it is important that the white person they sacrifice be a woman, but Lawrence tells the reader that they show no sexual interest in her. The Indian's behavior in itself is surprising, as it implies the very split between one's spirituality and sexuality that Lawrence usually sees as an Anglo error. But more surprising is Lawrence's repeated use of situations, shots, scenes, that borrow their vocabulary from pornography. One thinks of his observation about *The Scarlet Letter*, that Hawthorne's art speech says something very different from his moral intent. "The Woman Who Rode Away" is presumably a religious and cultural fable; in its art speech, however, it often reads as a dramatization of sadomasochism. When the woman is first captured, for example, she must crawl on her hands and knees between her erect captors as they traverse a narrow mountain ledge. When she is first brought into the gathering of the priesthood, she declines to undress. Several strong men take knives and slit her clothes, lifting them away, leaving her naked in their company. At different times in her stay, she will find herself in the same situation. In the tale's climactic scene, the sexual content of this "asexual" sacrifice culminates. Through various ceremonies, the woman is stripped, massaged by the priests, reclothed. She is carried high up to a cave. Up there she is again stripped and presented, front and back, to the whole population below. They give a "low, wild cry" (CSS, 580). She is then laid upon a flat stone table, with "four powerful men holding her by the outstretched arms and legs" (CSS, 580). The main priest stands waiting with a knife. He will plunge when the sun's rays, at their ruddiest, shine through the shaft of ice and penetrate to the innermost recess of the cave.

One can understand Lawrence associating sexuality and changes in consciousness; seeing the relationship between the two was his forte. One can understand the symbolic appropriateness of

186

the red culture penetrating the white and of that penetration being a death as well as a fecundating of the white. One cannot understand why Lawrence would deny on one level the sexual dynamics of the relationship, while he covertly dramatizes them on another. There are many ways that the woman's sexual relation to the tribe could be legitimately dramatized. As Lawrence defined it, pornography appeals to sexual energies trapped in the mind. In this tale, the pornography suggests sexual energies trapped in the spirit. In neither case—that is, typical pornography nor this tale—is there any real interchange between the various aspects of the self nor between the participants. There is no loss or gain of self in the mystery of the union.

A still further problem intrudes. I observed above that the woman's trek is meant to represent a racial or cultural journey, the passing of power from the light races to the dark. But, at times in the tale, the journey is also associated with the passing of power from female to male, as if to say that, in our corrupt culture, the female has been in charge and must be broken. This is bewildering in two ways. First, within her world, this woman has been in charge of nothing. Second, in this regard the Indians would seem already to have an ideal culture. Lawrence emphasizes the submissiveness of the Indian women. They do not need the change the woman's sacrifice presumably will bring.

In the leadership tales, small conversational circles abound as Lawrence imagines a cluster of men—soldiers and Indians, a count, an astronomer, a ghost, and a collier—all laboring to bring forth a new mode of living. Some urge a return to ancient cultures, others to nature. Some see the new world as a society, some simply as a new way for men and women to relate to each other. All assert that men must lead the way. The women in turn vary from poor, dry, English spinsters to highly placed ladies, from a German artist to a fat mother from California. Some readily capitulate, most drag their heels; all are being asked to surrender to the larger visions and capacities of their mates. But the men seem flat and the women manipulated. Behind the men are too many Lawrentian heroes with a capacity for self-criticism and yearning for genuinely healthy conflict. Behind the women are too many Lawrentian heroines who have no intention of falling asleep, of giving up the struggle into consciousness and understanding that makes them human. Finally, behind the tales are too many earlier stories that contain, above all, a vision of human experience that undercuts the vision presented here. These earlier stories present the stream of conscience which Friedman cites as a hallmark of modern fiction. The leadership tales set up dams. Do not question, do not disagree, trust me, they seem to say. The mode of the leadership tales is often visionary, employing many of the techniques described in chapter 4. But here the exempla are narrow, expressing views that confound such realistic aspects of the tale as characterization.

A key problem at the heart of the leadership tales is one Lawrence began to discern as he moved from "The Woman Who Rode Away" to "St. Mawr," "The Princess," and "Sun." The problem locates itself in finding a fitting object to worship. Neither a Bohemian count nor a tribe of American Indians will do.

7

Waking to Worship

E. M. Forster once said that it takes a person of real character not to need religious faith as he moves into the middle years of his life. Though he would not have applied the sentence to Lawrence, by Forster's criterion Lawrence never had much character, and certainly lost what he had as he turned forty. In previous work, his religious impulse led him to see the world as alive with godhead. At any moment, the natural earth, other people, a situation could separate itself from the welter of normal living and stand revealed for a moment as the location of mana or theos. His earlier visionary tales capture these revelations of power, of crucial signs pointing toward life or death. In the period we are now looking at, something different occurs.

In *The Plumed Serpent*, Kate Leslie issues the call that resounds through much of Lawrence's fiction during the mid-1920s: give me something to worship, she cries, something vast, terrible, and beautiful. For her a world rich with godhead is much harder to

189

discern than it was for Anna Brangwen or her daughter, Ursula. Moreover, for her, discrete experiences of awe—whether rare or frequent—are not enough; she wants the power of god to be present in a continuous, coherent, even organized form. With many reservations, Kate decides that the religion of Quetzalcoatl will almost do. But in Lawrence's short stories, the heroines—and during this period it is heroines not heroes who cry out—are given another solution.

Through the leadership tales, they had been asked to worship male leaders. As Lawrence apparently saw, when the heroines acquiesced they robbed the leaders of all decent opposition, rendering them flat and affected in their aloof dignity. There was no way the heroes could deserve genuine worship. The reward for the woman was thus not the keen joy that comes of celebrating something truly larger than the self, but, when she would accept it, an ability to sleep and thereby avoid disillusionment and the desire to criticize. In Lawrence's late fiction, written after he had returned to Europe in 1925, he ridicules his leadership vision and generally avoids the issue of worship altogether. We do not think of *Lady Chatterley's Lover*, "The Man Who Died," "The Man Who Loved Islands," "The Rocking-Horse Winner," or "The Lovely Lady" as stories that focus on the need to worship. This chapter argues that four of Lawrence's stories from 1924–1925—done during his last summer in America and in one case upon first arriving in Europe—provided him with the bridge that moved him out of his leadership vision toward the accomplishment of the late fiction.

In these four stories, Lawrence continues to try to find something to which a person can honestly submit. But he turns from a vision of secularized, human hierarchy to a more cosmic vision. Awe, the refusal to measure all things by oneself, the joy and terror implied in recognizing any vast power are no longer seen as the attitudes women must feel toward men, or inferior men toward superior men. These are the attitudes any person must have toward magnificence of any kind. In "St. Mawr," for example, Lou Witt feels awe in response to a stallion and a landscape, and her response saves her. It is the inability of the princess ever to recognize or touch a world greater than her own small imaginings that damns her.

But buried within the theme of right worship is a yearning that will become a central issue in the tales to come, the yearning to be alone. It is indeed wise to give over the desire to worship another human being, but to worship a landscape or the sun may be a covert withdrawal from all human intercourse. Only a few of these issues are raised in "The Overtone." They become central in "St. Mawr," "The Princess," and "Sun."

In each of these tales, the formerly disparaged figure of the searching woman returns justified to the center of the stage. She may not conduct a successful search (the princess is a signal failure) but her activity of seeking is seen once again as potentially honorable. Surprisingly, the secondary role Lawrence had urged upon his females in the leadership work falls here to the males. Having insisted for much of the last five years that their inherent superiority be recognized, they now seem exhausted or distracted by petty concerns. Romero, in "The Princess," is an exception. In their stead Lawrence gives us women who crave something in this world worthy of belief and commitment, and thereby become leaders in their stories by example rather than rhetoric.

"The Overtone," written in the spring of 1924, soon after "The Last Laugh," "Jimmy and the Desperate Woman," and "The Borderline," reads like a quiet reconsideration of the issues that inform those bitter tales.[1] The tale opens in the living room of an older, married couple, Edith and Will Renshaw. It is a soft, warm night; Mrs. Renshaw is talking to two women friends about state aid to mothers while Mr. Renshaw dozes on the sofa. One of the friends, a young woman named Elsa Laskell, eventually becomes our window on the tale. As Elsa sits vaguely attending to Mrs. Renshaw, to the sounds and smells of the night, she begins to assume the role of a judge presiding over the older couple's deep quarrel. First, she figuratively hears each partner's brief against the other, then she responds.

Through a silent reverie, Mr. Renshaw opens the hearing, presenting his view of the death of his marriage. Once, years before, he had asked his wife to make love with him high on a hill beneath the full moon. Lawrence's prose conveys the young husband's longing, his belief that he could rid himself of all embarrassment and shame if he could come naked to her, here, just this once. His desire is as clean and bright as the moon. But she will not, cannot, respond. At this point, we feel sympathy for the husband. But in a move distinctly different from the leadership tales, Lawrence then gives Mrs. Renshaw the floor. In a lyrical voice— also interior monologue—she presents her view of the death of their marriage. Because she had denied him once, six months after

191

their wedding, he could never approach her again without fear or mistrust. With a mixture of cordial deference and cold disapproval, he has remained aloof through the years. Both have grown old in spirit, poor in hope and belief. Our sympathies have broadened.

After both speak their piece, Elsa Laskell takes over, adding, as Merivale comments, her tone to the series of overtones.[2] Mr. Renshaw has gone outside; Elsa joins him. He jokingly assures her not to be afraid of him, for "'Pan is dead'" (CSS, 755). He refers to himself, but she leads the conversation to cultural implications. Mrs. Renshaw comes out and enters the conversation. All begin with the assumption one hears in "The Last Laugh," that Christ has killed Pan, that shame and law kill passion and freedom. The reader understands that the Renshaws are still sadly accusing each other, although Mr. Renshaw has begun to assume the greater portion of blame. But Elsa turns the conversation; in another significant departure from the tales of this time, she asserts that Pan is not dead and that only Christ and Pan together can create a complete world, a full self, a living relationship. Christ is day, ethical procedure, and marriage; Pan is night, amoral ecstasy, freedom. Not only does Elsa insist that both spirits are still alive, but she asserts that she partakes of both. She is no fragment or half-thing but a bright blend of light and dark, "'a black bird with a white breast and underwings'" (CSS, 759). With relief and gladness, she leaves the Renshaws. The implication, only touched on here, is that she has something to believe in, a Pan-Christ spirit that is alive in the world. The Renshaws's quarrel over who has hurt or betrayed whom need not detain her any longer.

After the Murry tales of a few months earlier, with their adulation of the Pan spirits—Pan, Pinnegar, and Alan Anstruther—and disparagement of the martyred Christ figures—Marchbanks, Jimmy, and Philip—the balance Lawrence maintains in "The Overtone" marks a clear switch in his thinking. Here is no simple celebration of the whinnying Pan.[3] On a related level, here is no sinful woman who has ignominiously criticized and betrayed her husband. And, here is no one-dimensional man, cool, reserved, superior. As if to comment on the previous tales, Lawrence calls our attention to the tones and overtones of the characters he has created, the issues he has raised. Even more surprising than the balances Lawrence builds into the tale, however, is his finally returning to the figure so compromised in his previous leadership tales, the figure of the searching woman. Brief as her role is, Elsa Laskell revives and reinvigorates the female seeker of earlier fictions, anticipating most directly Lou Witt, heroine of "St. Mawr," discoverer of the god of two ways.

"St. Mawr" returns to issues raised in the leadership fiction, especially in "The Woman Who Rode Away," but addresses them from a different stance.[4] For example, in their human, political manifestations, the leadership characters fade. They default. But the need that stands behind them is carried forward. Further, the split described in the previous chapter between the masculine gain in asserting self and the feminine gain in losing self disappears as Lou's search helps her recognize her *human* need to find *and* lose self. But most important, in "St. Mawr" Lawrence removes the dams he had constructed in the leadership tales. Lou Witt has a voice, a mind, and the freedom to use them. With her mother and the stallion, Lou Witt joins the woman who rode away in a journey out of her old culture and toward a new one. Like the woman, she finds something to worship, something to give herself to; but one of the tale's great strengths is that she continually questions herself and the objects she worships. The tale's key images, of St. Mawr and Las Chivas, reinforce Lou's healthy skepticism.

Presaging Kate Leslie of *The Plumed Serpent* and echoing Hannele of "The Captain's Doll," Lou Witt and her mother are critical and intelligent characters. Like Kate, Lou struggles in passage after passage to know where she is going and where she has been. A world traveler, she finally decides to leave Rico and England, her husband and most recent home, and try America. The impetus for leaving is the claustrophobia she feels in England and the danger St. Mawr is in. He is about to be shot or gelded. A richly ambivalent embodiment of alien life and consciousness, St. Mawr is one of Lawrence's laudable solutions to finding imagery to capture what "the Aeon of the little Logos," or the time before "the white man stole the sun," or the ladybug sought to convey. The stallion helps us visualize a concept of life and vitality as mysterious and amoral, beyond rational comprehension or ethics. For example, in the image of the terrified and infuriated Rico holding down the struggling, upside-down stallion, Lawrence dramatically captures *The Plumed Serpent*'s allusion to fallen Adam's denial of the body. At the same time, there is a basic stupidity to St. Mawr; sometimes he is even equated with Rico.[5] In himself he is not the miraculous presence Lou should worship. But the miraculous presence is in him; Lou succeeds in rescuing him. Once in Texas, St. Mawr saunters out of the tale, but Lou is left still questioning. She finds herself torn between judging Texas as nothing more than a garish backdrop for a Zane Grey novel or seeing it as a place with "energy, courage, and a stoical grit"; blank with wonder, she asks "What under heaven [is] real." (*St. Mawr and The Man Who Died*, 131).

Lawrence's description of Las Chivas, Lou's lonely, wild, New Mexican ranch, carries on the magnificence and ambivalence. In part it represents what characters like Dionys or the Indians or the ghostly Alan have presumably represented in previous tales, that is, a powerful alternative to safe, sterile, modern experience. Las Chivas is alive with color; the Michaelmas daisies are a purple mist upon the hillside, spangled with clumps of bright yellow flowers. There are dark pines and mariposa lilies. Few places could stand in more vivid contrast to Lou's claustrophobic English home. "It was the place Lou wanted. In an instant, her heart sprang to it. . . . 'This is the place,' she said to herself" (*St. Mawr and The Man Who Died*, 141). Yet Lawrence's marvelous description of the experience of the previous owner's periodic revulsion from her ranch also makes clear the difficulties, the horror, and the squalor of the uncivilized place. He speaks of the rat dirt, the bones of dead cattle and goats, the swarming of lower life. With its recognition of the beauty and the horror of Lou's ranch, Lawrence again gives the seeker something to worship that is vaster than any man, yet at the same time he insists that she recognize the duality of the god she has chosen. It is a god of creation and destruction, of Michaelmas daisies and of strewn bones and rats. In "The Ladybird," Count Dionys tried to represent this same vision of god to Daphne, but here Lawrence associates cosmic, awesome energy with something vaster than the count's militantly masculine heart beat.

Through Lou's consciousness, "St. Mawr" also begins to face an issue that has been hovering in the background of Lawrence's fiction since *Women in Love*, the desire to be alone. Ursula laughs at one of Birkin's visions of the future, saying that all he really believes in or wants is grass: plain, lonely, unpopulated, and unengaging grass. Lilly continually yearns to be alone in *Aaron's Rod*. In many of the leadership tales of 1921–1923, the leaders covertly succeed. They like the human conquests they make, they believe in their new relationships, but they come, go, and, with a distant smile on their faces, remain essentially apart. By contrast, Lou admits and stands by her desire. As she explains to her mother: "'I want to be alone. . . . I want to be by myself really'" (*St. Mawr and The Man Who Died*, 156).

Lou's mother initially pretends not to understand or agree with Lou's desire, but eventually she capitulates. By the last pages, she respects Lou's marriage to a landscape, a spirit of place. In this tale, the issue is at least temporarily closed, as Lou is allowed to end up worshipful, but also where nearly all of Lawrence's male leaders have longed to be, alone, untouched. However, as one sees in "The Princess" and in Lawrence's last satires, once he imagines a character succeeding in this hermit's quest, he sees the sterility it invites.

In "The Princess," Lawrence keeps his woman in search and yet undercuts the very movement toward consciousness and ambivalence that he had honored in "St. Mawr."[6] Reversing the argument, he exaggerates the critical aspects of Lou's character to an extreme. Lou's awareness of the horror of the vast, untamed, natural world is the princess's exclusive attitude. The princess feels none of Lou's simultaneous awe, as Lou's withdrawal from human touch becomes a hysterical purity in the princess. One more journey tale, "The Princess" follows Dollie Urquhart (one hears Irkheart) into the center of the Rockies. Once there, she destroys the character who is identified with those Rockies and goes mad. Through Romero's murder, Lawrence seems to be reminding his reader, himself perhaps as well, that if the return to more primitive religions and beliefs entails danger, the refusal to stand in awe of anything invites death and insanity.

There is a curious analogue to the tale in Lawrence's correspondence with Catherine Carswell. Visiting her in London in early 1924, he had been intrigued with an idea she had for a novel. Lawrence hoped they might collaborate, and to that end he gave her a synopsis. The idea went no further.[7] While interesting in itself, the analogue is significant in showing Lawrence's ongoing ambivalence to his project of dramatizing a modern character's return to an ancient form of belief. For in the analogue, the Princess's Druidic, demonic, fairylike nature is delivered in respectful tones. In "The Princess," it is satirized.[8]

Dollie Urquhart and her father are consummately delicate, conscious individuals. She can see only squalor in anything more corporeal than her fairylike father.[9] The perfect lotus, she sees her frail, beautiful self as "the only reality" (CSS, 477). The princess and her father eventually come to the United States for part of each year. She grows older, twenty-five, then thirty. When she is thirty-eight, her father, who is slightly mad and occasionally violent, dies, leaving her with a companion, Miss Cummins. Dollie remains exactly as she has always been, a princess, a child, a delicate fairy. She and Miss Cummins decide to travel, ending up in New Mexico. There she meets Domingo Romero. And suddenly, appropriately, the tale's tone changes. Up until now, the narrator's tone has mimicked Dollie and her father. Now the narrator becomes essentially transparent as Romero takes over responsibility for communicating the tale's values.

Romero is the man with the demon between his eyes, the character we might have seen in earlier tales as a leadership figure. Like nearly all of them—Henry Grenfel, Count Dionys, Pan, Pinnegar, Alan Anstruther, the Chilchui Indians—he has been dispossessed of his rights in the present order. Like them, he is a stranger, exotic, quiet, somewhat sinister in the view of the tourists he serves, guides, and cooks for. Unlike them, however, he has little desire to dominate and no aversion to contact. For all the racial mystery and allure Lawrence gives him, he seems refreshingly open and human.[10] Dollie wants him.

Obstinately, she urges him to take her on an overnight ride deep into the Rockies. Her desire has much the same tone as that of the woman who rode away; it is based on curiosity, the desire to be titillated by wilderness. She quite lacks Lou's capacity for awe. Once there, freezing in the cold autumn night, she invites Romero into her bed to make love to her. She is immediately repelled, however, and makes her disgust clear. Feeling used, Romero is humiliated, bitter, and understandably afraid that he will be charged with raping her. For three days, he keeps her trapped in the cabin. He is eventually shot in the back by a forest ranger. The rangers escort the princess down to the dude ranch and the narrator resumes his former, ironic tone. Mad, Dollie represses all knowledge of what occurred in the mountains.

As we might expect of the last American tale before Lawrence's return to *The Plumed Serpent*, the imagery here is powerful. Through natural imagery especially, Lawrence conveys his sense of a god of creation and destruction, his understanding of the beauty and horror, the elegance and cruelty, in any return to older faiths.

Most vivid are the quaking aspen and cottonwoods posed shimmering and yellow against the cold, blue-black spruce of the Rocky Mountain forest. The princess of course continually seeks out and identifies herself with the idyllic, sunny places. Refusing to recognize the god of darkness and light, the princess wants only the delicate, fairy beauty of the virgin forest; the granite rocks, dark shadows, and "dense, black, bristling spruce" are anathema to her. She will not see that real virginity or newness of being can come only through accepting the same qualities of light and dark, of delicacy and oppressiveness, that mark the forest.

Also vivid is Lawrence's image of the princess's need. Freezing in the cabin on her first night in the mountains, she dreams that she is being covered by snow. It is a fine image of her consciousness. As no previous women have been in Lawrence's power-leadership fiction, the princess is entirely consistent in her hypersensitivity and overdeveloped individuality and intellectuality. In contrast to our response to the woman who rode away, we fully appreciate—both emotionally and mentally—the gain that would accrue to the princess could she give herself to someone, something. Further, for all their differences, Romero reminds us of Captain Hepburn in "The Captain's Doll" in that he is a hero who is complex and interesting. The difference between Romero's character and that of the Chilchui Indians may be seen in the way Lawrence has Romero respond to the princess's insult. Balked, hurt, and violent, he throws her clothes into the lake and forces her to have intercourse with him. But his acts are seen for what they are, vengeful and born of misery. Even she perceives that. There are no vivid, pornographic images associated with Romero's rape. Romero soon leaves her alone. Between the two all is dreary deadness. Finally, in the image of the princess's greying hair and blank, mad gaze at the end of the tale, Lawrence concisely and aptly measures her loss. There are no explanatory paragraphs, no switches of intention. What is now wrong with her has always been wrong, only more so. Looking ahead to the final version of *The Plumed Serpent*, Lawrence makes the princess very much the shattered old grimalkin that Kate Leslie imagines herself becoming should she refuse to believe in Don Cipriano and the Quetzalcoatl movement.

"Sun," written in late 1925 after Lawrence and Frieda had returned to Europe, is the last tale to study the issue of worship in the terms I have been employing here. As Spilka first noted, this is not a tale about sunbathing nor is Lawrence tracing an action meant to symbolize the need for humans to regain awareness of their links with the natural world.[11] Juliet literally turns to the sun as to a god. Infinitely grander than she or anything the modern world has to offer, the sun is awesome to her in the same way St. Mawr and Las Chivas were wonderful to Lou Witt. In this tale Lawrence drops his emphasis on the god of two ways and his interest in exploring ambivalence. A healthy critique of Juliet's devotionals is nevertheless a part of the story.

Although it explicitly rehearses ancient sun-worshiping rites, "Sun" is not a fable but a visionary tale, done in terms typical of Lawrence. There is an exemplum at the heart of the tale, but its terms are dramatized realistically. Lawrence uses a transparent, omniscient narrator, a specific and natural locale, clearly motivated characters, and complex, psychological conflicts. As he did in earlier visionary tales such as "The Horse Dealer's Daughter," Lawrence starts with a ceremonial rite—here, sun worship—and makes it contemporary, believable. This is the opposite strategy from the fables and ghost stories to come, in which he begins with the contemporary and naturalistic and renders them timeless and mythic.

There are two versions of "Sun," the first written by December 1925, the second in 1928. Although there has been controversy over the dating of the texts, Sagar's view is most convincing: the shorter, less sexually explicit text is from 1925. Lawrence expanded it in 1928, sending it to Harry and Caresse Crosby for their Black Sun edition of the tale (October 1928).[12]

Through the opening movements, both versions of "Sun" read much the same. Each begins with the heroine, Juliet, and her child sailing down the dark Hudson River, across the Atlantic, away from New York, her husband, and her own neuroses and despair. Settling in a beautiful villa along the Italian coast, during the early winter months she gradually learns to relax and give herself fully to the sun. Her little boy begins to accompany her, growing agile and rosy himself. For all its grand circularity, the sun is very much a cosmic phallus, rising each dawn, penetrating the woman's willing self, declining each night. At this point in the tale, the woman's experiences parallel Lou Witt's in "St. Mawr." Yearning to give themselves, to relax within the power of something possessing genuine grandeur, both women turn away from the counts, farmers, even the ghosts that their earlier sisters have submitted to, and offer themselves instead to sun, mountains, cosmos. They are managing to fulfill their need to worship.[13] But in both versions of "Sun" Lawrence goes beyond Lou Witt's love of her Las Chivas Ranch as he follows Juliet's progress out of her love affair with the sun. And it is in the next step, back into the world, that Lawrence indirectly critiques Juliet's sun worship; further, it is in that critique that the two versions of "Sun" importantly part ways.

In the first version, the journey back is relatively straightforward, its gains and losses balanced. In the second version, the return from solitude is hesitating, grudging. In comparing the two versions, Michael L. Ross judges the second to be superior. He sees Lawrence improving the tale's language, symbolic suggestiveness, and narrative structure. In my view, Lawrence's revision intensifies the tale's solipsism to such an extent as to mar whatever gains he makes in enriching the tale's language. Also, I find the narrative structure in the second version awkward.[14]

In both versions, Lawrence has Juliet's husband, Maurice, eventually visit her in Italy. Although Maurice is a different kind of failure, it is as though Lawrence had invited Rico to visit Lou Witt at Las Chivas. In the first text, his visit and her thoughts form a relatively brief conclusion to both the tale and her period of withdrawal. As they sip coffee on the hillside patio, Juliet looks down and sees an Italian peasant and his wife. It is the first we have heard of the peasant. In a single page, Lawrence explains that Juliet and the peasant have been aware of each other through the past months. We learn a bit about him, but mainly we follow Juliet's thinking as she faces her desire for the peasant and accepts Maurice's desire for herself.

Structured like Lawrence's other triangles, the last passages of the tale consist of a weighing of alternatives. With fine dramatic skill, Lawrence sets up the last scene to dramatize Juliet's situation and the paradoxes within it. She has repeatedly descended from her villa to lie open to the ascendant sun; if she so chooses she can now descend to the peasant and open herself to his ascendant power. The peasant is equated with the sun: "he would have been a procreative sun bath to her" (CSS, 545). But set against the momentary contact he offers—"Why not meet him for an hour, as long as the desire lasts, and no more?" (CSS, 544)—is the continuity represented by Maurice. There is a sureness to him that carries its own more mundane connotations with the sun. While it is

clear that Maurice oppresses Juliet, making her feel trapped in circumstances, in this first version of the tale he is not an entirely undesirable mate. Juliet's wise servant woman sees him as "good"; Lawrence tells us that he is kind and shows us that he is generous. But, more explicitly, Lawrence explains that "There was a gleam in his eyes, a desperate kind of courage of his desire, and a glance at the alert lifting up of her breasts in her wrapper. In this way, he was a man too, he faced the world and was not entirely quenched in his male courage. He would dare to walk in the sun, even ridiculously" (CSS, 544). He watches Juliet with "growing admiration and lessening confusion" (CSS, 541). That Juliet decides she will remain with him and bear him another child is both a credible and relatively complex decision. In contrast to her alternative—that is, choosing the peasant—it is also the decision that ushers her back into the world of human relations. She will continue her sun rites but bear another child by Maurice.

In rewriting the tale, Lawrence alters the progress of Juliet's return from solitude. In the Black Sun version of 1928, he develops two important lines of motivation that push Juliet out of her hermitage. The first relates to the state of Juliet's general sexual desire; the second, to her specific desire for the peasant.

Using an Eastern image, Lawrence says that Juliet's intercourse with the sun has opened her womb like a lotus flower; this in spite of herself, in spite of her wish simply to be peaceful. At times Lawrence's language is stilted and awkward, especially in phrases such as "the trouble of the open lotus blossom" or Juliet's desire for "man dew." But his metaphor for female arousal as a radiant series of outwardly moving waves, as "the purple spread of a daisy anemone, dark at the core" is good; compared to other contemporaneous attempts to describe female arousal it is very good. When Blazes Boylan penetrates Molly Bloom, for example, Molly feels hoisted and stuffed; when Molly gives honey cake and says yes to Leopold, we read more of Leopold's joy than of Molly's. But when Juliet, and Connie Chatterley, lie open to consummation, we read for one of the first times in English literature of the particular joy of female arousal and orgasm. Within this particular tale, the language Lawrence uses to describe Juliet's state of sexual excitement also complements and balances the phallicism of the sun. His potency is matched by hers, his ruddiness, streaming blue brilliance, and radiant, pulsing roundness are answered by her own. She may regret her renewed desire, but in her body's yearning she becomes as active a sexual being as he.

If this first added line of motivation and the language it employs are gains, however, the second line of motivation is a loss. Just before Maurice arrives, Lawrence gives us a long expository passage on the peasant. In much greater detail than before, we learn about him, his older, possessive wife, his awareness of Juliet. We learn that Juliet had sat on her patio one evening while he worked below in the fields. They had watched each other, aware of one another's desire.

As in the first text, Juliet must make a choice between husband and peasant. She ends up making the same decision, for the tale has committed itself to tracing this would-be hermit out of her hermitage, to making her worship of the sun lead to something beyond itself. But Lawrence alters the terms of her thinking, intensifying her bitterness toward Maurice. With a loss of economy and impact, Lawrence now has Juliet's contemplations extend through two somewhat repetitive sequences, the first occasioned by her initial watching of the peasant, the second by her having to decide what to do about the arrival of Maurice. In both passages, Lawrence amplifies the idea that one of the pleasures of being with the peasant would be the lack of complicated engagement. Juliet's longing now seems based on the presumption that the peasant would never exist for her in any personal way. The real loveliness would lie in their never talking to each other. In these passages, Juliet sounds like the tired and touchy leaders we encountered earlier. She wants no real relationship, no conflict, no ties. "She was so tired of personal contacts, and having to talk to a man afterwards. With that healthy creature, one would just go satisfied away, afterwards."[15] Neither the tale nor she admits it, but her longing for the peasant seems simply a fancy version of the old human longing for the perfect brief affair.

In the early text of "Sun," Lawrence dramatized the understanding that he had implied in "St. Mawr" and "The Princess." He indicated that prolonged solitude can lead to sterility and preciousness, that one-night stands are an unrealistic answer to human longings for relationship, that seeking out "wild ones" inevitably denies the "wild ones" their humanity. The peasant, like Romero, is a human being. In his later text, Lawrence seems to have temporarily lost these understandings. The Black Sun edition of "Sun" was written during approximately the same period—the first half of 1928—Lawrence added a new conclusion to "The Borderline" and wrote part 2 of "The Escaped Cock" / "The Man Who Died." In discussing "The Borderline," I noted the tale's insistence that Katherine Farquhar leave her dying husband Philip and embrace the will-o'-the-wisp ghost of her former husband, Alan. In part 2 of "The Escaped Cock" / "The Man Who Died," Lawrence concludes his dramatization of Christ's reentry into the world with a marriage that envisions the most intermittent of contacts, the most fleeting of encounters. The 1928 text of "Sun" carries the same message: *noli me tangere*, unless briefly.

The journey out of the leadership fiction has been accomplished. No one is asking anyone else to choose a leader and kneel in awe. Awe and wonder remain human feelings crucial to the modern individual's ability to lose self in a way that will nourish and sustain self. But in choosing sun and earth as fitting objects for his newly awakened heroines to worship, Lawrence has imagined a reveille that carries within it the potential for solipsism. In the fictions to come, Lawrence continually recognizes that temptation, as he mocks preciousness and withdrawal in a wonderful variety of guises. Only occasionally does he, a sick and dying man, fall prey to it.

8

Furnishing the Ship of Death

Lawrence's late short stories show a division of energies. The dynamic blend of realism and exemplum that created the visionary tales separates into two voices, the realist and the fabulist, with the latter taking on the accents of satirist and fable maker. For some critics, the dividing constitutes a loss.[1] In comparison to earlier stories, the last stories are thin fare, the weary performances of a dying man. Other critics counter that judgment with analyses of particular tales. In their view, the superb formal complexity of "The Man Who Loved Islands" or the many layers of meaning in "The Rocking-Horse Winner" argue for an imagination still vibrant with energy. The question before us is, what does Lawrence's late short fiction in general show?

In the preface to this book I observed that an adequate reading of Lawrence's short fiction cannot fix on variety alone as the theme, regardless of how varied the stories are. Nevertheless, variety is the theme in this last period, at least to a certain extent. And it is worth emphasizing for several reasons.

In Lawrence's famous late poem, "The Ship of Death," he imagines the soul of the person who has died as a small "arc of faith," adrift on the black seas of oblivion. But the soul comes through to a new dawn of consciousness, and crucial to its passage is a collection of needful objects, things required for living: small dishes of food, a change of clothes, wine. Rescuing him from oblivion, Lawrence's late short stories are furnishings for his ship of death. Alongside *Lady Chatterley's Lover* and his late poems and paintings, they work against his own obliviousness to the world as his death impends and, with his other works, against our obliviousness to him once he has died. As a body of work, the late short stories in particular comprise a wonderfully various assembly of verbal artifacts—sharply observant realistic tales, brief coherent satires, complex fables—that show Lawrence still very much alive in the world between 1925 and 1930; they keep him alive still.

The virtue of the variety may be clearer if we contrast the late tales with the previous leadership stories. Speaking of Lawrence's long fiction, Raymond Williams states that *Lady Chatterley's Lover* marks a return to realism, openness, and contingency after the moral schematics and rigidity of the leadership novels. I remarked in my introductory overview and argued in chapter 6 that Lawrence's leadership work is more often confused than tightly schematic. With "The Captain's Doll" as the exception, premise fights premise and realism fights exemplum through both the novels and the tales of that period. By the summer of 1924 and in the late work, the conflict between voices stops, but, Williams notwithstanding, not because one voice has taken over. When Lawrence dropped what was for him the untenable leadership vision, he began to exercise a series of complementary voices. The prophet speaks through fables and satires, summing up his views of life and death; but the straightforward realist also has his different say.

Not surprisingly, as Lawrence's voice takes on a variety of tones, his tales themselves celebrate variety rather than founder in unresolved contradiction. When Lawrence is successful—and he is not always—he creates vivid tales to illustrate his prohibition against fiction that tilts the balance toward only one value or perspective. Many of the best stories of this period—"The Rocking-Horse Winner," "The Lovely Lady," "The Man Who Loved Islands," and smaller pieces such as "Smile," "Two Blue Birds," and "Things"—make the point for life's variety through negative examples. They offer superb images of life leveled to a deadly flat-ness. Significantly, the major positive example, "The Man Who Died," runs into serious difficulties.

Finally, the variety of this late work and its virtue show up in the range of topics Lawrence handles. Several of the stories are about death: how people avoid it, how to kill, how and how not to be resurrected in the flesh. Other stories are more clearly about single, rigid values as suggested above, or about silly modern sexu-ality, or willfulness. The variety of topics suggests, quite rightly, that one cannot survive oblivion with only wine or only a change of clothes. Staying alive demands many things. In the range of tales and voices that compose Lawrence's late short fiction, one hears a sick and frail human being giving extraordinary voice to life.

The chronology of this peripatetic period is complicated. I will trace it briefly, then move to the realistic tales, and close with the truly distinctive work of the period, the fables and satires.

Although the distance between resting places was smaller, the last four and a half years of Lawrence's life were nearly as no-madic as the previous five. In America he had been seeking Ran-anim.[2] Back on the Continent he more simply sought the sun. Moving between Italy, Switzerland, and southern France, he and Frieda followed the temperate seasons whenever they could. The first two years, from late 1925 through February of 1928, they spent mainly in Italy, first briefly at the Villa Bernarda near Monte Carlo, then at the Villa Mirenda near Florence.[3] In the summer of 1926, they revisited the Midlands, Lawrence and William Hop-kin strolling through areas Lawrence had known since childhood. The countryside was full of painful memories, the sight of the miners thoroughly depressing.[4] Lawrence eventually records his mood of desolation in Connie Chatterley's despair over Wragby and the ugly town of Tevershall. It was to be Lawrence's last visit to England.

As Lawrence's tuberculosis grew worse—he had a constant cough and occasionally hemorrhaged—his doctors recommended the clear air and altitude of Switzerland. With Earl and Achsah Brewster, he and Frieda spent part of the spring and summer of 1928 in Les Diablerets. In the winter they moved down to Bandol, France. April 1929 saw them briefly in Majorca, but as the hot summer moved in they returned to Italy, traveling from there to the mountains near Baden-Baden. In September they returned to

Bandol and the bright Mediterranean for the winter of 1929–1930. Growing weaker, Lawrence was persuaded to try a sanatorium in Vence, five hours from Bandol, in February 1930. Being there only aggravated his condition, though. As he longed to be in a private home, he was moved on March 1 to a villa close by where he died the following day, March 2, 1930.

Through these last years, Lawrence speaks in letters of his pleasure in not writing; he rejoices at one point that he need never, will never write another novel. And yet, almost from the moment he unpacked his bags at Villa Bernarda in December 1925, he began to write again. In the four months he was there, Lawrence wrote a draft of a novel—*The Virgin and the Gipsy*—and four tales: "Sun," "Smile," "Glad Ghosts," and "The Rocking-Horse Winner." The two years at Villa Mirenda brought three versions of *Lady Chatterley's Lover* as well as a cluster of tales; from 1926 come "Two Blue Birds," "The Man Who Loved Islands," and "In Love"; from 1927 come "The Lovely Lady," the first part of "The Escaped Cock" (later expanded and eventually retitled "The Man Who Died"), "None of That," "Things," and "Rawdon's Roof." The last year Lawrence wrote short fiction was 1928. In January he gathered together the stories that were to be collected in *The Woman Who Rode Away*.[5] During the summer, he wrote "Mother and Daughter," added a "phallic second half" to "The Escaped Cock" / "The Man Who Died," and wrote his last story, "The Blue Moccasins."

Compared to the fables, the realistic tales do not show Lawrence moving in new directions. Witty and generally well realized ("Rawdon's Roof" is an exception and "Mother and Daughter" has an occasional lapse in logic and complexity[6]), they are Lawrence's small cooking pans, his practical, down-to-earth objects, his ballast for the journeying ship. "Two Blue Birds" is one of the best of these late realistic stories.[7]

Underscoring Lawrence's dramatic gifts, "Two Blue Birds" would play well on stage. Lawrence opens with an exposition on the marriage and life style of Cameron Gee and his wife. The initial tone has the fairy tale quality one finds in many of the late tales: "There was a woman who loved her husband, but she could not live with him. The husband, on his side, was sincerely attached to his wife, yet he could not live with her" (CSS, 513). The simplified opening prepares us to meet naive Miss Wrexall (Wrecks-all?),

Gee's secretary. Lawrence quickly drops that tone, however, as he moves into the tale's second movement.

The prevailing voice of the second movement is Mrs. Gee's, and her style is anything but naive. Like many Lawrentian heroines, she is well traveled, cynical, and an honest critic of her mate. Introduced as fatuous, she soon shows herself to be a shrewd observer of Cameron Gee. As she sees it, Gee has contrived to create around himself a harem of Wrexalls. Miss Wrexall is his adoring secretary, and her mother and sister are his valet, cook, housekeeper, laundress, table maid, and literary fans. The wife is revolted by the ways Gee uses these three women, by the pleasure they get out of being used, and by the complacency that has crept into his writing. Her credo on human relationships is worth quoting: "His comfortableness didn't consist so much in good food or a soft bed, as in having nobody, absolutely nobody and nothing to contradict him. 'I do like to think he's got nothing to aggravate him,' the secretary said to the wife. 'Nothing to aggravate him!' What a position for a man! Fostered by women who would let nothing aggravate him" (CSS, 518). One thinks back to lines from the leadership fiction, lines that equate criticism with betrayal, and realizes that for the first time in five years Lawrence is reintroducing the important concept of loyal opposition.

In contrast to the opening expository movement and second analytical movement, the third movement of the tale is purely dramatic. Comprising nearly half of the story, the last section drops all sense of a narrator and develops the tale's two extended scenes, one setting up and one carrying out the defeat of Miss Wrexall. The staging is excellent. It is a beautiful spring day; Cameron and Miss Wrexall are working outside. He lies dictating; she sits scribbling down his remarks on the future of the novel. Mrs. Gee stalks along, wolflike, behind the hedge and hears with disgust the drivel her husband is speaking. Suddenly she sees a blue titmouse at the secretary's feet. It is "the blue bird of happiness." Appropriately for this tale it is immediately joined by a second titmouse. A fight ensues, feathers flying. With her head in her notebook, the secretary misses the intense small scene. Cameron finds the birds disturbing. But the wife is delighted, and the tale has provided a miniature tableau of what is missing in Cameron's thinking and living. Lolling in his hammock with his secretary at his feet, he never wrestles, makes no feathers fly, has no bright blues or yellows on the pallet of his mind. His wife is determined to change things.

Mrs. Gee invites Miss Wrexall to join her and Cameron later for tea in the garden. By coincidence, each woman comes out dressed in blue; the tussle commences. Mrs. Gee covertly insults Miss Wrexall, mainly for being too self-sacrificing. Carefully, she prepares to deliver her major shot, and a good one it is. In dulcet tones, she asks Miss Wrexall to tell her more about Cameron's next novel, for, she states, she has believed for some time now that Miss Wrexall has been writing most of his books. Within the limits of the one-liner, it is a fine thrust. Miss Wrexall is horrified and embarrassed. She cannot be flattered since the implication is that the books are so weak Cameron could not have done them. Not only has she been insulted but the possibility of her hero being a dullard has been suggested. The thrust to Cameron is equally nice. Mrs. Gee has conveyed that his work has sadly deteriorated. More devastating, she reveals his real contempt for his secretary. He responds: if Miss Wrexall might have written them, they must be utterly without merit. Mrs. Gee walks off, victorious.

Nor does her winning appear malicious. She has broken up a relationship that has been bleeding her husband of whatever literary abilities he might have and his secretary of any sense of her own value as a woman and an independent human being. The tale is not simply a caricature of Compton Mackenzie, though it may be that.[8] It is also a coherent satire on fawning, on using people, on laziness. If Lawrence's biography is to be used in reading it, it might better be used in reference to his having left Spotorno for his visit with the Mackenzies while in a fury with Frieda. The recognition that fury, aggravation, and a continual bumping up against the otherness of the other were basically good calls to mind a letter he had written years before to Catherine Carswell: "Frieda's letter is quite right, about the *difference* between us being the true adventure and the true relationship established between different things, different spirits, this is creative life" (CL, 468). One senses that if Lawrence had not returned to this love of difference and respect for the opposite, in even so small a work as "Two Blue Birds," he would have written a very different *Lady Chatterley's Lover.*

"In Love" is a slighter piece, but it points to the continuing need for any reader to take into account the medium of Lawrence's messages. Among Lawrence's literary activities during the last years of his life was the writing of topical articles for various London newspapers. The work paid fairly well, was not taxing, and allowed him to formulate his views on a range of social issues. Rossman observes that these late topical articles show that Lawrence had not changed his basic thinking on men's and women's roles, that he is as determined as in his leadership years that men must live in the world, women at home, that men are leaders, women followers. His tone changes, becoming more sympathetic, but not his ideas.[9] Recalling discrepancies between his thinking in the nonfiction and fiction of 1918–1919, I would say that the articles offer evidence that Lawrence's ideas could and did vary depending on the medium of expression. As "In Love" and "Two Blue Birds" show, Lawrence has no difficulty in these late fictions imagining men in domestic roles or women leading. Written in October 1926, after Lawrence's last visit to England, "In Love" is a well-conceived domestic comedy. Pointing up the insult and foolishness inherent in romantic love conventions, the story delivers a clear critique of a social ritual—premarital spooning—that stifles rather than stimulates authentic response.[10]

Like the best fiction of manners, "In Love" turns upon a change in behavior that implies a change of character. It analyzes and dramatizes mannerisms while implying the values that lie beneath. Hester, the fiancée of Joe, has stopped by the small farm they will live on to see the bungalow Joe has built. She is duly impressed. They have lunch, then supper, then do the chores. Ahead of them lies the long evening. A bit smug, Joe begins awkwardly to cuddle. Hester hates the falseness of their petting, and, getting him to play the piano, slips out into the yard. Her task, like Mrs. Gee's in "Two Blue Birds," is to set things on a healthier footing. A scene familiar in Lawrence since his earliest tales follows. Hester walks along the fields in the darkness, passing by some horses, longing for something beyond that small bungalow, that soupy man, that mawkish sex play.[11] Miserable, she is about to return when his playing stops. She cannot face him at the moment and quickly climbs into a tree. Crouching there invisible, she watches Joe, ineffectual and embarrassed, as he calls out to her and gropes along in the darkness. Hester sees him as dense, hypocritical, "tiresomely manly" (CSS, 651). For the moment, she is right. But when she is forced to get down, literally and figuratively, and confront him, he shows other colors.

Eventually a proper quarrel ensues, the outcome of which is

Hester's confession that she despises Joe's love-making and Joe's infuriated response that he does as well. The plea on both sides is for more honesty, genuine tenderness, and passion. Once Joe repents of the game he has been playing, Hester suddenly notices a "quiet, patient, central desire" in him that she has never seen before (CSS, 659). Their mutual recognition of the other celebrates the contrast that has been implied between being "in love" and loving.

Like Lawrence's early Croydon tales of modern love, "In Love" is largely social comedy. But unlike the earlier tales, "In Love" imagines this critical, sharp-witted, young woman and rather slow, young farmer loving each other. The posturing young hero who used to dim the light of the rival has long since disappeared. Throughout, the tale reveals a sensitivity and complexity in both the man and the woman that allow for tenderness, a key value in *Lady Chatterly's Lover*.[12]

If desire and tenderness are central in the human relations Lawrence imagines at this time, then, as we would expect, he conveys that value through both positive and negative approaches. "None of That," apparently written between drafts of *Lady Chatterley's Lover*, reads like a sharp knife among the furnishings of Lawrence's ship.[13] One of the few tales Lawrence wrote in which he gives the narration to a voice distinctly not his own, "None of That" is told to the narrator by a Mexican exile, Luis Colmenares, in Venice. As Luis and the narrator chat about the people they knew in Mexico, Luis takes over and tells about Cuesta, a famous toreador and friend of Luis. Luis, I should note, is not the inarticulate foreigner one meets in the leadership tales. In giving the anecdote to him, Lawrence maintains a natural, un-self-conscious tone. Luis tells the tale with fine psychological insight.

In brief, he tells of Cuesta's brutal affair with a wealthy, willful, American woman, Ethel Cane. First one hears about Cuesta, and in these passages Lawrence is giving a different view of bull fighting than that in *The Plumed Serpent*. In the novel, the bull fight is a cruel, dreary business. In "None of That," Luis admiringly describes Cuesta's skill and insouciance in the ring. Luis then brings in Ethel Cane. She has come to Mexico, fallen for Cuesta, and begun to see him as a challenge to her whole philosophy of life. She has believed that one's imagination can control one's experience, especially one's physical experience. If a person can enter an experience but remain in complete control of it, by seeing it only in the images one chooses, that person is free. In his unrelenting refusal to be defined as an alluring or even interesting hero, toreador, or lover, Cuesta nearly drives Ethel mad. She is used to defining her world and having her world dance to her tune. Cuesta simply sits.

The tale's climax comes when she agrees to go to Cuesta's house. Both are open about the sexual implications. For her, it is the supreme challenge. As she tells Luis, she will see whether she can mold her encounter with this obdurate man into some controllable image. If she cannot, her life will not be worth living, and she will kill herself. A good story-teller, Luis maintains suspense as long as possible. Ethel goes to Cuesta's house and then is not seen for several days. She is discovered dead. Luis's companion nods and believes he understands; Ethel found her body's desires enslaved by Cuesta. Because she could not imaginatively control her relationship with him, she killed herself. Luis shakes his head. Yes, she killed herself but not because of her desire for Cuesta. Cuesta had met her at his house with a gang rape. He had organized the extreme challenge to her belief. Not only did he refuse to be her hero or lover, he also attacked her belief that anyone can control all that happens to one's body through a trick of the imagination.

In some ways, "None of That" reads as a sister tale to "The Princess." Both focus on heroines who are types of cold intellectuality, on individuals who will control what happens to them as long as they possibly can. Of course, Dollie succeeds in imagining her encounter with Romero out of existence; Ethel fails and kills herself. But the tales may be seen as sisters in another way as well.

"None of That" and "The Princess" are violent tales, with a rape at the center. One must ask, is the art speech in these works expressing covert approval of these rapes? To answer yes would be to ignore Lawrence's dramatic context and imagery. The rapes of Dollie Urquhart and Ethel Cane are ugly acts. In "None of That," the rape—in its physicality and total victimization—is the extreme counter to Ethel's vision of experience as perfectly controllable by the imagination. The tale does not imply that Ethel "deserves" to be raped. In fact Cuesta, once beautiful, is now fat and yellow; the tale indicates that he stopped bullfighting after the affair with Ethel. The concept of "desert" avoids the issue. The rape is the extreme foil to an extreme attitude. Both extremes are deadly and brutal. In contrast to "The Woman Who Rode Away," a work truly split between its overt and covert intentions, there is no lingering intrigue with Ethel's rape. It is conveyed in one brief sentence, with no details, no images given. When one finishes reading "None of That" one carries away two powerful images. The first is of a brutal but magnificently agile bull-fighter; the second is of a driven mind, a hysterical will.

After reading "The Princess," I believe one is left with a similar sense of the work. Romero's rape of the princess also serves as the extreme response to an extreme attitude. The princess's will to be titillated but never touched or moved is answered by her losing all control over her body and mind. Both the attitude and the response are brutal. Lawrence describes Romero's lust as a "sombre, violent excess" (CSS, 509). Within the terms of the tale, his forcing of Dollie dramatizes the fact that between the two of them there is nothing. The rape, then, is significantly judged; it is also, again, not a dominant scene in the tale. In a tale rich with imagery, Romero's rape is described in a short, general paragraph. There is no heightened intensity to the prose, no memorable image, no detail.

The last two realistic tales continue to present the sense of Lawrence as an energetic craftsman, creating a goodly store of objects for living. Both "The Blue Moccasins" and "Mother and Daughter" return to the relationship between parent and child which Lawrence had been exploring from his earliest work. "Mother and Daughter" parallels "St. Mawr" in tracing the relationship between a domineering mother and her stubborn daughter. In the earlier story, the two women join together in a final sympathy, apart from men, apart from sexual entanglements. In "Mother and Daughter," Lawrence looks again at that exclusive sympathy for its potential to sterilize. The tale draws on a motif present throughout Lawrence's fiction: the literal or figurative murder of parent by child in the child's quest for adult sexual fulfillment.[14]

The tale opens with Lawrence's favorite dramatic structure, the triangle. Rachel Bodoin and Henry Lubbock are competing for the affections of Rachel's daughter, Virginia.[15] The competition, however, is lax. Within the tale's first two pages, Henry "backs out," and Lawrence settles in on his key interest, creating the characters of Rachel and Virginia. Like a pair of dissatisfied lovers, this odd couple has been living together, breaking up, rejoining, going apart for years. There will be a final break, but it is preceded by a fairly long period of cohabitation. Mrs. Bodoin furnishes for Virginia and herself a beautiful set of apartments and gives them to Virginia. Here they will live and here they will part. And here Lawrence paints their portraits.

Rachel Bodoin is a wonderful, comic creation. Like older women in Lawrence from Gertrude Morel on, she has been blessed with extraordinary energy and cursed with having no adequate channel to release it. Realizing "the bad taste in her energetic coevals," Mrs. Bodoin intensely "cultivates repose" (CSS, 808). As she sits with folded hands in the parlors and tea rooms of her allotted domain, she betrays her suppressed energy in her gift for mimicry, her perfect appearance, and, within her own rooms, her handsome, "positive" furnishings. Loving her daughter, she would pass all this on to her—the energy, the style, the wit, the discrimination. But Virginia, alas, is not an accommodating heiress.

Early in the tale, Virginia is entranced by her mother. But as Virginia persistently tries to draw a male lover into her life, only to watch him curl up beneath the devastating wit of her mother, she begins to hear a cackle in her and her mother's laughter. To her mother's surprise and dismay, Virginia manifests traits of her father, a gentleman long ago dismissed by Rachel. Most horrible, Virginia develops a proclivity for work. In her mother's eyes, Virginia becomes that ugliest and dreariest of all creatures, "a young woman out of an office" (CSS, 815). In fact, Virginia has a good job. A translator for the British government, she is that rare thing in Lawrence, a career woman. But Mrs. Bodoin is all too right about the dreariness. Virginia returns from work each evening looking tense, haggard, wrung out. Assiduously avoiding her mother, Virginia either locks herself up in her own room or lies on the sofa and listens, over and over, to a humorous record. Always able to capture the feel of keen irritation, to take the pulse of petty domestic rage, Lawrence beautifully draws out the daily battle between mother and daughter. Finally the mother can stand no more. The *ménage à deux* not working, Rachel suggests that they break camp. Startled out of her blankness, Virginia asks for a little time. Using the interval well, she procures for herself her own ticket out—not out of the lovely apartments but out of her mother's exhausting embrace.

To counter her mother's dryness and her own ever increasing emotional and physical emaciation, Virginia brings into their home a mound of Turkish delight. His name is Monsieur Arnault. An Armenian with whom Virginia has worked closely in her job, he is sixty years old, fat, quiet, shrewd. He wants Virginia for her need of love and protection, her cleverness, and her apartments. With Arnault, Lawrence breaks the deadlock that has developed between mother and daughter and reintroduces the triangle with which he began. This time, however, the pattern is reversed. Aghast at Virginia's choice and at her own obvious inability to define her daughter in her own image, Mrs. Bodoin backs out. Virginia is left with a future—a home and a mate. Mrs. Bodoin retreats to Paris.

Seen from within this configuration, the tale has clarity and complexity. The central movement is the child's breaking away from the parent. We see Lawrence tracing out in mother and daughter what he has so often in the past traced out in mother and son. An essentially realistic drama, the tale gives both Mrs. Bodoin and Virginia credibility and depth. Virginia's total exhaustion within her job even makes sense within Lawrence's general view of the necessary complementarity of work and love. In fact, in Virginia, Lawrence almost gives us for the first time a female character with the potential both to work in the world and to love at home. Arnault indicates that he anticipates them working together; he assumes that Virginia, with her sharp business sense and remarkable facility with languages, will help him with his trade transactions. We might expect that, once married, she will balance her private and public life, allowing each to nourish the other.

But there is more to the tale. The dramatic configuration I have described is accurate, but within it are motivations and occasional asides by the narrator that both muddy and simplify. Working against Virginia's progress toward adult sexual fulfillment is Arnault's paternalism. Arnault appreciates her for other reasons as well, but her childlikeness is primary. In turn, and even more damaging to the tale's clarity, Virginia seeks him out as a sweet release from all effort. She who has battled her mother's oppressive dominance now luxuriates in the thought of total irresponsibility. What she fought in her mother she looks forward to in a father.[16]

Yet, at one point in the tale, the narrator states that the bond between Rachel and Virginia is in fact female, not filial. This is not really a tale about a child; Virginia is escaping a sterile relationship with a female who dominates her for a fertile relationship with a male who protects her. Shades of "The Fox," we are back to the leadership fiction. If we could believe the narrator, the incoherence that arises from seeing Virginia as rebellious daughter would disappear. But working against his comment is the whole weight of the tale, the many scenes and analyses that establish the dynamics of the relationship between Rachel and Virginia as mother and daughter. Lawrence has caught too well the feelings of a daughter who admires and resents her mother. He captures too clearly the selfish disappointment of the mother who finds herself trying to promote an unpromotable child. Of course, the bond is female. But no aside from the narrator can dismiss all the ways the tale has dramatized the bond as essentially one between mother and daughter.

If the tale's coherence is weakened by the narrator's comment on the relationship between Rachel and Virginia, its power to speak complexly to human experience is weakened by the narrator's comments on women and work. In describing the work-weary Virginia, the narrator suddenly shifts from a past-tense analysis of Virginia to a present-tense analysis of all women. Arguing in clichés that have been heard for centuries, the narrator serves up all the standard stereotypes. Women do all right if they work for someone else. They are in fact remarkably facile in giving quick, shallow responses to the task at hand. Like clever parrots, they can pick up information, languages for example, with wonderful ease. But give them real work—work that takes concentration, persistence, responsibility—and they simply fold. In facing Lawrence's views here, it helps to recall that with the exception of farmers, no men in Lawrence's fiction work with any sense of fulfillment, persistence, or pleasure either. No men manage the balance between work and love that his theory upholds as ideal. Within this issue of balance, the only difference between a work-driven man such as Gerald Crich or Clifford Chatterley and a work-driven woman such as Virginia Bodoin lies in Lawrence's belief that Gerald and Clifford could throw themselves into their labors and be fulfilled were they able to find decent labor and combine it with love. For Virginia no such balance is even theoretically possible.

Perhaps Lawrence's views on women and work are especially disturbing here because the clichés contrast so sharply with other areas of the tale. In moving from his portrait of Mrs. Bodoin at five o'clock—fresh, anxious for good talk and company—to his explanation of women's work, he lays down his fine brushes and subtle colors and picks up a roller that is dripping with institutional grey.

By contrast, "The Blue Moccasins" has none of this unevenness.[17] On its primary level, the tale reads like a realistic anecdote. The three characters Lina M'Leod, Percy Barlow, and Alice Howells form a contemporary, postwar triangle. Just before going off to the war, Percy marries Miss M'Leod, the grande dame of the small English town he lives in. She is forty-seven, he is twenty-four. He returns three years later and they settle down in her family's small mansion to a quiet married life. She paints; he sits watching her. The years go by and she gradually withdraws herself from all contact with him. She often thinks "that the highest bliss a human being can experience is perhaps the bliss of being quite alone, quite alone" (CSS, 830). As with the princess and with Cathcart in "The Man Who Loved Islands," Lawrence gratifies Lina M'Leod's desire. Percy vaguely feels that her withdrawal is his rightful due from so fine a lady, but he also begins to develop a life of his own outside her walls. Among his town friends is Alice Howells, whose husband was killed in the war.

With easy dramatic skill, Lawrence lays in the background of his three characters and then moves into the tale's central incident, a church play, performed on Christmas Eve, a key prop for which are the bright, blue, beaded moccasins of Miss M'Leod. Vivid in its humor, physical detail, and psychological acuity, the scene dramatizes the seduction of Percy by Alice and the shift of his allegiance away from his wife.

We have indications throughout the tale that in telling his story of Percy, Lina, and Alice, Lawrence is employing one more reversal of the Sleeping Beauty myth. Percy is, quite simply, "not wakened up." Under a spell, imprisoned in an old castle, he walks around in a dream of fair old ladies. His prince, Alice, is quite clear as to her duty and desire: "The rector's daughter took it upon herself to wake him up" (CSS, 830). Given these references as background, the full intention of Lawrence's play within a play grows clear. The church play is another triangle, but one that employs more recognizable male and female roles. A young Turkish girl, Leila, is married to an old, grey-bearded Caliph. She has captured the love of the gallant Ali, and, in Lawrence's words, "the whole business was the attempt of these two to evade Caliph and negro-eunuchs and ancient crones, and get into each other's arms"

(CSS, 835). The blue moccasins are "shoes of bondage, shoes of sorrow": Leila wears them when there is danger and Ali must stay away. She kicks them off when he may come near. The story acts out, of course, the very plight of Alice and Percy. In real life, Percy is the trapped Turkish girl, who has captured the love of the gallant Ali/Alice. The old caliph is Miss M'Leod; the blue moccasins, her gift to Percy, are a symbol of bondage and sorrow.

The beauty of Lawrence's dramatic structure here is that he wakes up the polite, conventional Percy in the one way Percy could be awakened, through indirection. The Turkish tale is close enough to Percy's plight to bear application, far enough away to be participated in without feelings of disloyalty or threat. Miss M'Leod may be branded as tryant, Alice may frankly seduce, Percy may unabashedly succumb—all within the nonsense and fun of the occasion. Outside the play, Percy is in awe of his wife, but on stage he enters a separate world. When Miss M'Leod interrupts the play, he is roused as out of a dream and gazes down in "sheer horrified wonder at the little white haired woman standing below" (CSS, 837).

Lawrence's play functions as does Shakespeare's forest scene in "A Midsummer-Night's Dream." Away from legal relationships, daytime reality, and sexual conventions, the characters act out fears and desires. And, as in Shakespeare's play, the retreat has lasting benefits; the insight the characters gain through their dreams accompanies them back into civilization. Lawrence had always held that one's body and emotions may understand something before one's conscious mind does; off-stage, during intermission—both terms are significant—Percy's mind grows gradually aware of what his body and emotions felt on-stage during the play. In this sequence of action and consciousness, Lawrence finds a fine dramatic illustration of his belief.

Adding to the rich interrelationships between Percy's actual situation, the plot of the play, and the revolutionary power of "play" are the details Lawrence builds into the scene's setting. This play is set in a school, a place where children—Percy is often called "a boy"—learn. The time is Christmas Eve, an occasion that anticipates rebirth in the darkest, dreariest season of the year. And it is a church play; Alice's last word is "goodness."

Many pages back I referred to Mark Kinkead-Weekes's warning that one must mainly try to account for moments in studying Lawrence's highly exploratory ideas about sex and sexuality. I stated that one of the goals of this book was similarly to account for moments, for the local dynamics, in Lawrence's short fiction, while simultaneously tracing his general progress from realistic to visionary to fabulistic short fiction. His work is moving toward its close, but his stories are still full of local variety and cross currents. The material we have just seen developed in realistic terms was reworked fabulistically by Lawrence. He will explore in depth the witty attractions and repulsions of "In Love" or "The Blue Moccasins" as he alternates in his fables between expressions of solipsism and strong attacks upon it. As we move toward those fables, I want to raise two issues, both related to the link between Lawrence's leadership novels and the late fabulistic tales.

As stated above, Lawrence's leadership figures from the early 1920s often express a desire not to compel or bully anyone, but the desire is usually linked to unconscious or half-expressed yearnings to avoid contact of any kind. Lawrence examined those yearnings in "St. Mawr," "The Princess," and "Sun." But the issue continued to engage him. The leadership ideal became a cold egg but not the desire to withdraw which is an unadmitted part of the ideal. To perceive the manner in which Lawrence continues examining that matter, and other matters as well, I must return to another feature of the leadership fiction.

The worlds depicted in *Aaron's Rod*, *Kangaroo*, and *The Plumed Serpent* tend to emphasize public rather than private concerns. None of these novels closely traces the development of a private relationship; each focuses on the relationship between leaders and followers within a social context. This is most evident in *Aaron's Rod* where Lawrence removes all female characters and the private relationships they represent.

Now, when describing Lawrence's late long fiction, most critics contend that once back in Europe he dropped the social emphasis of the leadership fiction and returned to the intricacies of private experience.[18] Simultaneously, he dropped his interest in abstract visionary fiction and returned to the conventions of realism. The key example is *Lady Chatterley's Lover*. I suggest that in his late work—in several of his short stories and to an extent in *Lady Chatterley's Lover*—Lawrence does return to realism and private experience but in his fables and satires he continues to explore social issues directly, and does so through the only mode short fiction offers, fabulation. Frank O'Connor's observations in

The Lonely Voice help clarify the links between fabulation, short fiction, and the focus on society.

O'Connor observes that, as a genre, the short story does not have the scope to develop the relationship between society and the individual in any complex or realistic way.[19] The typical short story responds to this generic limitation by focusing on characters who have only a marginal relationship with society; it looks at "a submerged population group," at "outlawed figures wandering about the fringes of society"; it records "lonely voices."[20] In concentrating on the isolated Akakii Akakiievitch, a tale such as Gogol's "The Overcoat" illustrates O'Connor's point well. But O'Connor does not consider the possibility that a short story may respond to its generic limitations in another way. It may focus on characters well embedded in a social context but decline to develop those characters and that context realistically. It may explore characters enmeshed in broad social issues through the stylizing conventions of fabulation. And it is this exploration that characterizes Lawrence's late fables and satires. If the realistic tales are the pots, pans, and change of clothes he needed in his Ship of Death, the fables and satires are flags and banners, the bold pronouncements of a man about to leave the earth, eager to make closing assessments. In place of particular complexity and detail, these works offer ethically controlled fantasies, giving the reader schematic plots, stylized characters, landscapes that are mind-scapes, active story-tellers; in brief the conventions of fabulation.

Behind the full-fledged fables stands a series of explorations in the mode, some trial balloons, some false starts. "The Last Laugh" from 1924 was a trial balloon, fabulistic in its miraculous plot and highly patterned structure, but a slight work. The ghostly "Border-line" was more fully developed but failed to resolve the confusion that resulted from its mixture of realism and fable. In "Smile" and "Glad Ghosts," Lawrence continues trying out approaches to this new mode; the first is as slight as "The Last Laugh" but similarly neat in its logic and brilliant in its imagery. Also, it shows Lawrence developing a mocking stance toward the clichéd conventions of the fables and ghost stories he is about to write. The second story shows Lawrence flailing about, trying a bit of spiritualism here, ghostly presence there, and ancient lore somewhere else. Like "The Borderline," "Glad Ghosts" is pulled apart by its inclinations toward realism and fabulation.

The occasion but not necessarily the subject of "Smile" is the death of Katherine Mansfield in January 1923. Suffering as did Lawrence from tuberculosis, Mansfield had left John Middleton Murry to stay at the Gurdjieff Institute at Fontainebleau. Written three years after Mansfield's death but in the midst of one of Lawrence's many quarrels with Murry, the tale is too easily dismissed as "one of the mean little anti-Murry stories."[21] Murry felt them all to be "a very shabby sort of revenge," coming out of "the most *dishonest*" aspects of Lawrence's character.[22] But Lawrence's tales "about" Murry are various, often make a point beyond capturing some trait of Murry's, and succeed or fail for intrinsic reasons. For all its brevity, "Smile" succeeds, and, Murry aside, partly because of its honesty.[23]

The tale develops as a series of fine, brief images, portraying the continual peeking out of life in the face of death, the continual eruption of honesty in the face of hypocrisy. The tale's predominant colors are black and white. With sharp skill, Lawrence sets flashes of white against a dark background and thereby establishes the contrast that carries the main theme. Like the Colonel Hale episode in "Glad Ghosts," it dramatizes the psychology of a character by showing us what possesses, what haunts him.

Reminiscent of Philip Farquhar in "The Borderline," the central character, Matthew, is a gloomy man who courts his losses. Like Gerald Crich, who was also partly inspired by Murry, Matthew has a tendency to invite his own murder. Working against his gloom and providing the tale's central conflict is something akin to the laughter in "The Last Laugh." Sensual, sexual, unconventional, and essential, here that anarchic energy takes the form of a catching, uncontrollable smile. Faced with the corpse of Ophelia and intending to concentrate deeply on his own imperfections, Matthew has set himself up to avoid the truth of their difficult relationship. He will assume all the blame in a sentimental penance. But some momentary spirit of honesty in Matthew will not let him avoid Ophelia's character by wallowing in his own. The smile that dances about his lips and spreads to the attendant nuns is like the gargoyles that capture Anna Brangwen's loyalty in the cathedral in *The Rainbow*. The smile does not mock Ophelia (indeed, the title reads as her command), nor anything genuine in Matthew. Instead, the smile mocks Matthew's preoccupation with his own gloom and his intention to paint a sentimental whitewash over his memory of willful, changeable, ironic Ophelia. The tale's small moment of miracle occurs when the nuns turn to Ophelia's corpse and catch it smiling.

Neatly complementing this image of Matthew's smile and further working against his wallowing in his martyrdom are the repeated images of the nuns' fluttering hands and voluminous black skirts. The nuns sail through the corridors like dark swans. Set against the swirl of their habits are their white hands. Lawrence compares these to small, creamy birds nesting in the nuns' skirts, fluttering out occasionally, settling in again. From the beginning, Matthew is voluptuously aware of the nuns and of their soft hands. He longs in particular to hold the hands of one of them. Unfortunately, Matthew's longing receives the same treatment as his smile. He squelches both, ducking out of the convent and running away. In the end he avoids facing Ophelia, himself, and his own capacity for joy, wit, irony, and desire. The tale concludes on a dark, desperate, and "utterly smileless" note.[24]

In writing "Smile," Lawrence satirized the ghost story conventions of a convent at night and the unveiling of a corpse. Their implied Gothic gloom is part of what the story is smiling about. In writing "Glad Ghosts," he seems trapped by similar conventions, unable either to employ them as givens in the tale or to use them ironically. The tale was planned for Lady Cynthia Asquith's collection of ghost stories but was considered unsuitable.[25] Lawrence Clark Powell states that the main characters are Lady Cynthia and her husband Herbert; Moore suggests that the resemblance may have been the reason for the tale's exclusion from *The Ghost Book*.[26] Powell and Moore may be right, but another reason for its exclusion may have been its affected tone and the incoherence of its plot and character.

The general intention of "Glad Ghosts" would seem to be to take a cast of realistic characters and dramatize their conflicts and situation through ghost tale conventions. The tale is told by Mark Morier, one of Lawrence's infrequent first-person narrators. As is usual on the rare occasions when he assumes this point of view, Lawrence gives the narrator a role peripheral to the main action. We assume that Morier is reliable, that we are meant to look through him, not at him. The story is his reminiscence of a woman he has known for years, Carlotta Fell. "Glad Ghosts" has a large cast for a short story. Through Carlotta, Morier meets her husband Lord Lathkill, Lathkill's mother, and his mother's friends, Dorothy and Colonel Hale. There are also two ghosts, both female: Colonel Hale's former wife Lucy, now dead and haunting the colonel, and the beneficent but elusive family ghost of the ancient Lathkill house.

The tale has two major movements, neither necessarily tied to the other. Colonel Hale is being paralyzed by the ghost of Lucy. She bangs around the house and comes between him and his new wife. As the tale develops, the colonel learns that Lucy refuses to release him to his new wife because he did not love her warmly and physically when she was alive. His cure is to embrace her ghost. On a psychological level, he must recognize his guilt and neglect; he must learn to love rather than fear or abhor the memory of Lucy. He does so and is cured. The second movement works in somewhat the opposite direction and makes less sense.

Unlike the colonel's obstreperous ghost, the Lathkill family ghost has avoided the family for many years, leaving it struggling beneath a pall of ill luck. All three of Carlotta's children have died, and between her and Lord Lathkill there is nothing but ashy memories. Mother Lathkill rules the house according to the wisdom she garners from her readings in spiritualism. Her grotesqueness will be developed later in the mother of "The Lovely Lady" while the gloom she casts over this old English house will spread through Wragby Hall in *Lady Chatterley's Lover*. The key action of this part of the tale is Morier's breaking the spell of bad luck by wooing the ghost. Unfortunately, both the wooing and the results it brings are confusing.

On one hand, Morier is established as the challenger of the spell. He is invited to Riddings to do what the spellbound Lord Lathkill cannot, that is, take the sleeping princess Carlotta and sexually love her, awaken her. To do so will be to reawaken the family ghost and thus the family fortunes. Morier consents, gaily referring to himself as a sans-culotte who will be king only when britches are off. But, once at Riddings, he seems as paralyzed as anyone. If we can make out the conclusion through the haze of innuendo that envelops it, we see that even his eventual embrace of Carlotta is on her initiative. In fact, Lord Lathkill becomes the real challenger, the real wooer. He releases the colonel and explains to him his plight, he stands up to his mother, he chants out the call to the family ghost. By itself, Lathkill's success is hard to accept, for he began as all too much a ghost himself. One could argue that somehow he fundamentally changes; but, then, why is he still without the power to awaken Carlotta in the tale's last movement? She and he see each other anew, the theme of resurrection is sounded, the smell of the plum-scented ghost is in the air, but it is to the ineffectual Morier that Carlotta goes. For no understandable reason, Lord Lathkill ends up with the colonel's gloomy new wife.

If the overall plot fails the criterion of unity and the second movement of the plot seems incoherent, the tale's language and the dynamics of the concluding love scene raise still other problems. The difficulties that the tale's visionary diction create are ones I have spoken of before; in the visionary passages, one hears echoes of the esoteric language that weakens much of the leadership fiction. This time it is not Chilchui pidgin English or Count Dionys's foreign phrases that we hear. Rather it is a passage from the diary of Lord Lathkill's great grandfather. The diary describes the family ghost: "'For she is of the feet and the hands, the thighs and breast, the face and the all-concealing belly, and her name is silent, but her odour is of spring, and her contact is the all-in-all'" (CSS, 695). As Lathkill recites, we read how "he rose curiously on his toes, and spread his fingers, bringing his hands together till the finger tips touched" (CSS, 696). The posture and the language are equally affected; one senses that here, as before, Lawrence has turned to the exotic because he is not sufficiently convinced of his vision to find the natural image or language to express it. He is again drawing a curtain between himself and his idea. Although by 1926 most of the leadership motifs have died, this tale uses the same stilted language and shows the same tendency to protect the tale's fragile vision from any laughing, skeptical women. Only the sons in the Lathkill family are permitted to read the grandfather's diary; once lively and independent, Carlotta grows progressively silent as the tale develops.

The concluding love scene points to a related problem. Carlotta goes to Morier in the depth of night. Not only is there no talking, there is no conscious contact. Morier never knows whether he experienced a dream, the family ghost, or Carlotta. (A child is born to Carlotta nine months later looking much like Morier and giving us a clue as the the nature of his midnight encounter.) But whatever it was, the encounter was wonderful. In Carlotta's words, "'At last it was perfect'" (CSS, 699). This is the same ideal nonrelationship one encounters in most of the leadership fiction and in the expanded version of "Sun"; it is a fantasy fulfillment of the most obvious quality. Solipsistic in itself, it is also incoherent within the terms of the tale. Morier, for example, does not need the family ghost to visit him. More important, one key point in the tale is the necessity for people to embrace physically, to touch each other. In its insistent incorporeality, the embrace of Morier and Carlotta celebrates the opposite.

Many of the tale's problems lie in its hesitancy to be a genuine ghost tale.[27] On one level, Lawrence introduces Morier as a recognizable character of the genre, a skeptic who is persuaded to sleep in a haunted house and arouse the house spirits. On this level, Morier is the prince who enters the haunted castle to free the denizens. The love, children, and prosperity that result from his visit are appropriate. But on other levels, Lawrence hedges on the issues, undercutting a fabulistic reading. For example, Morier is hesitant, realistic, an observer rather than challenger. Lathkill is not spellbound, indeed, quite the opposite. Belief in the uncanny is debunked partly by the fundamentalist Christian tone of the spiritualism and partly by the fact that the key spiritualist is the dowager Lady Lathkill. This debunking results in our seeing Lucy's ghost as being all in the mind of the colonel and Lady Lathkill, the family spirit as simply Carlotta in Morier's room for the ideal affair, and Lord Lathkill as a superstitious fool. Yet throw out the fabulistic possibilities, and the tale becomes a tawdry incident, a night of wife swapping in plum-scented rhetoric. For whatever reason it was excluded from Asquith's *Ghost Book*, the exclusion seems justified. The tale falls between stools, working neither fabulistically nor realistically.

By contrast, Lawrence's substitute submission for Lady Cynthia's book amply has the courage of its own fable. The first of Lawrence's genuine late fables, it is one of the most frequently anthologized of all his stories.[28] At its center is the implacable, devouring mother who haunts several of these late works. In brief, the story traces the efforts of the young hero, Paul, to supply his mother with the money she needs to see herself as "lucky." Carefully kept as a secret from his mother, Paul's strategy for gaining the money is to ride himself into a trance on his hobbyhorse. With astounding frequency his riding brings him the name of the winning horse in whatever race is about to be run. Anonymously, he portions out the money to his mother; his fortune mounts but so do her needs. The tale ends with him knowing the name of the winner of the Derby but killing himself in the process.

In contrast to the tone of personal reminiscence Lawrence

uses in "Glad Ghosts," "The Rocking-Horse Winner" opens with the distant, singsong voice of a fairy tale: "There was a woman who was beautiful, who started with all the advantages, yet she had no luck" (CSS, 790). So begins an ancient tale. A brave young boy is challenged by his true love. He rides off into a dreamland where he struggles and succeeds at attaining secret knowledge. He brings the secret knowledge back and with it wins treasure houses of gold, giving all to his love. Undercutting this fairy tale, however, is another, which forms a grotesque shadow, a nightmare counter to the wish fulfillment narrative. The "true love" of the brave young boy is his cold-hearted mother. The quest he has embarked on is hopeless, for every success brings a new and greater trial. Like the exhausted and terrified daughter in Rumplestiltskin, this son is perpetually set the task of spinning more gold. In this tale, no magical dwarf comes to the child's aid; the boy finally spins himself out, dropping dead on his journey, his eyes turned to stone.[29] Like all good fairy tales, this one has several complementary levels of reference: social, familial, psychological.[30]

On the social level, the tale reads as a satire on the equation of money, love, luck, and happiness. The target of the satire, the mother, cannot be happy without an unending flow of cold, sure cash. As she sees it, luck and lucre are the same thing. Yearning for some response and real affection from her, Paul adds the term "love," making a solid, tragic construction. Quite simply, the tale concludes that these equations are deadly. The mother, representing a society run on a money ethic, has given the younger generation a murderous education.

On a familial level, the tale dramatizes an idea implied as early as *Sons and Lovers* but overtly stated only in a late autobiographical fragment and these last tales.[31] The idea is that mothers shape their sons into the desirable opposite of their husbands. Whatever they are powerless to prevent or alter in their mates, mothers will seek to prevent or alter in their sons. In "The Rocking-Horse Winner," the woman cannot alter her husband's ineffectuality. She herself tries to be effective in the world of commerce and money, but she fails, partly because of the lack of opportunities available to her. So she turns unconsciously to her son. In this reading, Paul's death owes less to the specific character of his mother's demands and more to the strength of those demands. He dies—cannot live, cannot grow and flourish—partly

225

because he is too good a son, and she is a woman with unbounded desires and no way to work directly toward their gratification. In *Sons and Lovers*, the young son kills, literally and figuratively, the paralyzed and paralyzing mother. The alternative pattern, which Lawrence felt to be common among the men of his generation, is played out in "The Rocking-Horse Winner."

But the tale acts out still another nexus of meaning, one implied in both the satire on a society governed by a money ethic and in the dramatization of a mother devourer. On this level, the hobbyhorse comes more to the fore. As Snodgrass and others have observed, this lonely, preadolescent boy continually retreats to his own room where, in great secrecy, he mounts his play horse and rides himself into a trancelike ecstasy. His action and the result it brings powerfully echo Lawrence's description of masturbation, physical and psychic, in his essay "Pornography and Obscenity." Discussing censorship, Lawrence praises art that inspires genuine sexual arousal, that invites union with the other, whether the "other" is another person, an idea, a landscape, the sun. Obscene art is essentially solipsistic; it arouses the desire to turn inward, to chafe, to ride the self in an endless and futile circle of self-stimulation, analysis, gratification. In masturbation, there is no reciprocity, no exchange between self and other. Applying Lawrence's indictment of masturbation to Paul's situation, we see that Paul has been taught to ride himself, that is, his hobbyhorse or obsessions, obsessions he inherited from his mother. The obvious contrast to his dead horse is a startlingly live one such as St. Mawr; the obvious alternative to his self-enclosed mode of "knowing" horses is Lou Witt's insight into the radically alien mode of consciousness in her stallion. Lou's revelation leads to an awareness of the other that nourishes and expands the self; Paul's revelations lead to no consciousness of other and reduce his field of intercourse to a vanishing point.

If one takes these three levels of reference and seeks out their complementarity, one sees the rich logic of the tale. The money ethic, the devouring of sons by mothers, and the preference for masturbation are parallel in cause and result. All develop and respect only the kind of knowledge that will increase one's capacity to control. For example, like any money-maker, Paul learns about the horses only to manipulate his earnings—money and love. Paul's mother, in a variation on the theme, does not bother to learn anything about her son because she does not perceive him as useful to her. Further, Paul mounts his hobbyhorse, his surrogate sexual partner, only as a way of fulfilling his own narrowly defined program for success and happiness. In no case is the object that is to be known—horse, son, sexual partner—seen to have a life of its own, an otherness to be appreciated rather than manipulated, a furtherness that can give the knower a glimpse into all that is beyond him or her. In addition, the resolution of each nexus of meaning carries the same ironic denouement: the quest for absolute control leads to the loss of control. The mother's house, which she wants to be luxurious and proper, is haunted by crass whispers. She and her son, striving to control love and fortune, are compulsive, obsessed; Paul dies and thereby loses all chance for the very human love and contact he sought. The mother loses the very means by which her fortune was assured.

Lady Cynthia Asquith was apparently pleased with Lawrence's submission for she soon asked him if he would contribute to her second collection, this one to be called *The Black Cap: New Stories of Murder and Mystery*. Writing a fuller tale than was eventually published, Lawrence agreed, returning in "The Lovely Lady" to his interest in the "uncanny." Lawrence had sent the manuscript off by March 11, 1927. As Brian H. Finney notes, letters exchanged between him and Nancy Pearn at Curtis Brown make it clear that Lady Cynthia asked for cuts and changes. Lawrence responded with a shorter version in May. Although now too brief for Lady Cynthia, this is the version she accepted and printed in the collected tales. As when she turned down "Glad Ghosts," Lady Cynthia's response here was helpful, for Lawrence's cuts greatly improve the story.[32]

In Lawrence's opening paragraph we met Pauline Attenborough, an exquisitely preserved, seventy-two-year-old woman. Praising in particular her frame—skeleton and skull—he gives us a *memento mori* and nicely intimates things to come: her character as a death's head, her death at the end of the story, and his own playful satirizing of the typical atmosphere of a murder story. As the story develops we come to see that this will be a murder story to mock the mechanics of the genre, to discriminate above all between mystification and real mystery. As Lawrence himself explained, he was no Poe.[33]

The story presents two murders and one foiled attempt: Pauline's smothering her first son Henry with her own will and personality; her attempt to do the same to her younger son Robert, now thirty-two and much under his mother's spell; and the retaliation by Pauline's niece Ciss, which results in the death of Pauline, the release of Robert, and the gratification of Ciss. (In its fabulistic mode, the tale sets up intriguing parallels with "Daughters of the Vicar," written sixteen years before.) The structure of "The Lovely Lady" consists of a rhythmic motion back and forth between outdoor sun-bathing scenes, evening dialogues, and unifying explanations by the omniscient narrator. After a long exposition, the first scene gives us Pauline and Ciss sun-bathing in proximate areas of the estate.[34] Ciss, on the roof-top patio, hears a voice defending itself against the guilt of murdering Henry. Lawrence nicely spoofs the conventions of the genre as he has Ciss initially horrified at this visitation by the uncanny. Just as she is about to scream in terror, she discovers that Pauline is unintentionally speaking into a hidden drainpipe connecting her garden retreat with Ciss's rooftop. That evening, a dialogue in the parlor ensues as Ciss urges Robert to love her a little, to see his life's futility. Though it has taken courage for Ciss to speak, Robert remains caught up in his shyness and his mother's spell. The relationship is at a temporary impasse.

In the second sun scene, Ciss lies stunned and angry at Robert's passivity. Pauline again lapses into her guilty reveries, revealing that Robert's father was a Jesuit, and again defending herself from responsibility in the death of Henry. This time Ciss responds. Hissing down the pipe, she assumes the voice of Henry and accuses Pauline of murder. She warns her to leave Robert alone. Pauline is devastated at this voice from the dead. As she totters off to her room, a storm gathers.

The second evening scene is again set up to capitalize on the breakthrough accomplished by the previous sun scene. Outside the rain pours down. Robert and Ciss wait in the parlor for Pauline to appear. Just as she enters, Ciss turns on a bright electric light. Pauline shows up as the little old witch she is. Robert realizes for the first time that his mother really is an old woman. He is finally free to care for Ciss.

Throughout the tale Lawrence spoofs murder and mystery tales while drawing richly from fairy tale motifs. The spoof is founded on a distinction between mystification and mystery. Pauline is the author of a series of mystifications and as such she weakens, traps, kills others. Mystification is related to the uncanny and thereby to evil. The uncanny here, as in "The Rock-

ing-Horse Winner," represents modes of intelligence or relationship cut off from opposition, mutability, the natural powers that
are located in the changing earth—the mud and ooze as Birkin
would say. By contrast, mystery enters in the sun's caress and in
the love of Ciss and Robert. Mystery resides in the natural, above
all, in youthful desire. Mystery strengthens, releases, impowers
life. It accepts death. Lawrence bolsters the distinction by setting up a curious dialectic among fairy tales, and between them
and reality.[35]

Working against the wicked witch is the courageous and successful challenger, the rescuing "prince." And as Lawrence is wont
to show, the rescuer is female, the prisoner male. In fact, when
Ciss defeats Pauline, the language and imagery closely resemble
another fable about a feminine challenger, *The Wizard of Oz*.
Dorothy pours water on the wicked witch of the North and
watches her curl up, shrivel, and melt away. Ciss pours light, literal and figurative, on Pauline and watches while she, in much
the same way, crumples up. Finney objects that Pauline's decline
is too rapid; he asks that we contrast her defeat with the "similar"
situation of Walter Morel.[36] But surely this misses the fairy tale
tone of the story and the unusual dialectic Lawrence has set up. It
is a curious dialectic because reality is represented by those fairy
tales allied with mystery (the defeat of the witch, release of the
prisoner, victory of the challenger). Falsification is represented by
the fairy tale that is allied with mystification—that is, Pauline's
attempt to maintain eternal youth.

The lovely lady is the most obvious of Lawrence's maternal devourers. Thinking back over his fiction and noting his definition
of murder as the destruction of another in order to possess his or
her essence,[37] one asks if devouring is primarily a female act, and,
within that, a maternal act? Remarkably, in Lawrence, fathers almost never devour, although "The Christening" is a possible exception. Fathers sin by their absence, their weakness. The specter
of paternal tyranny that haunts many nineteenth-century authors
does not haunt Lawrence. But other males do devour, do murder
to possess, and their motives, methods, and relative success resemble those of their wicked sisters and mothers. Usually they devour
to fill the vacuum within. Will bleeds Anna Brangwen, Gerald
puts a sucker into the soul of Gudrun, Clifford attaches himself
like a leech to Connie and to Mrs. Bolton. The list could be extended. Results vary. At times the victim shakes off the devourer,

at times he or she is sucked dry. At still other times, an outside agency steps in to the rescue. In general, the murderous acts seem well understood by Lawrence, betraying neither uncontrollable terror nor desire. Mothers devour to be sure, but so do husbands, wives, lovers.

Within the context of family, "The Rocking-Horse Winner" and "The Lovely Lady" give fierce critiques of the difference between love and power, with those terms now carrying their usual connotations. Both show mothers in the process of killing sons; both set nightmares against wish fulfillment fantasies to create a rich interweaving of fairy tale motifs. In each case, Lawrence's story takes the conventions of the genre—ghost tale or murder mystery—discovers the human depth within them, and then plays the conventions off against a series of classic fairy tale motifs.

If these two tales may be said to work in parallel ways to explore parallel themes, Lawrence's last two major fables, "The Man Who Loved Islands" and "The Man Who Died," are an interesting blend of parallels and contrasts. Both stories examine the element buried in the power issue named above: the covert desire of the person who seeks perfect power to be essentially alone. In "The Man Who Loved Islands," Lawrence continues to use roughly the same strategy as in "The Rocking-Horse Winner" and "The Lovely Lady"; but in "The Man Who Died" he sets up a different dialectic. As a consequence, in "The Man Who Loved Islands" Lawrence judges the desire to be alone; in "The Man Who Died" he unintentionally celebrates it.

One way to see how these two tales speak to each other is to invite in a third and fourth party, both very much their contemporaries: the small satire "Things" and *Lady Chatterley's Lover*. Within Lawrence's canon, the conversation between "The Man Who Died" and *Lady Chatterley's Lover* is typical. "'I am risen'" says one character. "'Rubbish,'" says another. The inner quarrel continues up until the end, and so do the poetry and rhetoric it produces.

In discussing "Two Blue Birds," I commented on Lawrence's renewed respect for the spirit of combativeness. "The Man Who Loved Islands," written close to the same time, demonstrates the same renewal. Like Conrad Aiken's memorable tale, "Silent Snow, Secret Snow," Lawrence's story moves from a world that is engaging, stimulating, and irritating in all its infinite variety to

a world that is perfectly univalent: white, still, peaceful, and utterly suicidal.[38]

As do the other late fables and satires, "The Man Who Loved
Islands" opens simply: "There was a man who loved islands." En-
countering these words immediately after reading the title, one is
struck with the obvious repetition. After speaking briefly about islands in general, the narrator introduces the reader to "our islander." With respect to plot, all follows rhythmically in patterns
of three from there. I will first look at the several overlying and
complementary plot structures Lawrence has built into his fable
and then at its controlling ideas.

Like the world of many fairy tales, Cathcart's is a study in
threes. Most obvious, Cathcart moves successfully to three islands, each smaller than the last. And, as in most fairy tales, the
neatness of the plot belies the fiction's complexity. In Cathcart's
geographical progression, one reads a variety of movements. For
example, on his first island Cathcart begins with the ambitious intention of creating a perfect society. By the second, his optimism
and scope have shrunk to the extent that he is only trying to create a manageable relationship with one other person. By the
third, he works only at managing his own narrow needs for food,
shelter, and a quiet consciousness.[39]

But working against this pattern of progressively shrinking
ambitions is an opposite movement, an expanding pattern. Cathcart begins hoping he can control a farm and a community of
workers. He will remain a bit distant. When that benign plan
fails, he takes up a more intense challenge. He will control an intimacy. First feeling distant pity for Flora, he goes through a bat-
tery of responses—aversion, guilt, lust, self-contempt, humiliation—each emotion more intense and shattering than his
previous vague trust and disappointment in his workers. When
that relationship slides beyond his control, he is faced with the
most rigorous challenge of all. He must control himself; and this
elemental challenge appropriately implies controlling the elements; as winter descends on his third island, he grows ill and
cold. He cannot stop the wind and snow, he cannot call the sun.
Realizing his cosmic impotence, he loses heart and finds himself
without the will to control himself. He profligately spends his energy, does not eat, does not stay warm. As have the challenges,
the stakes have increased. On the first island he lost only money

and distant acquaintances. On the second he loses a portion of self-respect and the possibility of a relationship with wife and daughter. On the third, he loses his life.

The progress from island to island works in other ways, too: Cathcart moves from a fatuous enthusiasm to a fragile neutrality to a fatuous nihilism. The basic pattern here is a dramatization of Lawrence's belief that any action, response, or attitude contains within it its own reaction or contrary. Thus, insistence that one will control one's island is likely to result in one's island gaining control. Related to the action-reaction tension, the first and third islands respond to the terrors that first motivate Cathcart's quest for control, his terror that time will lose its proper mooring in the present, and his terror that space will become fluid, unknowable, unchartable. To his genuine surprise, Cathcart finds that he can control neither time nor space.[40]

Apart from the patterns of threes, Lawrence has built in other movements as well. There is a progress from opening spring to closing winter. Like "The Rocking-Horse Winner," the tale also sets wish fulfillment against nightmare. The wish fulfillment stream gives us a man with the longing to create a world of his own. Thrice he is challenged, and on the third island wins. Looking out at his snow-locked island, the islander recreates it: "'It is summer,' he said to himself, 'and the time of leaves'" (CSS, 746). The nightmare stream shows us that his original wish, like that of King Midas, is foolish and wicked. Granted in a way that the wisher had not foreseen, fulfillment brings insanity, misery, and death.

A further structural pattern lies in the tension Lawrence has set up between the tale's several voices. David Willbern sees two main voices that create an ultimate ambivalence in the tale. I see three—an ironic narrator; Cathcart; and a transparent, omniscient narrator—which together make an ultimate judgment.[41] The ironic narrator is opaque, sardonic, familiar. He tells us at the outset that Cathcart is a fool, giving us the moral of the story within the second paragraph: Cathcart will die of egoism and vanity. It only remains to see how he will do it. But as the narrator begins to illustrate Cathcart's thinking by mimicking him, Cathcart's voice takes over. With the islander, the reader walks about the fields admiring the flowers; we suffer his occasional nightmares. The ironic narrator interrupts, reassumes control, then Cathcart takes over again. This alternating point of view characterizes much of the first two sections. But, by the third island, both voices fade. By now, Cathcart is noticing little and thinking less. He is no longer capable of presenting himself or his realm. By now, he is pathetic, defeated. Only a sardonic narrator could club a dying man. Thus, it is ultimately an omniscient, neutral narrator who follows Cathcart through his last days, recording his actions, his occasional responses, the weather. The relationship between the voices helps to provide the tale's judgment.

The texture of the language—its rhythms, syntax, diction, vocabulary—varies with the voices. The ironic narrator's voice is full of rhetorical questions, asides to the reader, and the kind of simplistic sentence patterns that direct us to see the simplistic quality of Cathcart's hopes. Cathcart's voice changes within itself. At the outset, he is something of a poet, his voice lush and captivating. By the end, he refuses to have anything to do with language. The language of the omniscient narrator in part 3 is spare. Appropriate to the defeated Cathcart's minimal, stark designs and demands, it gives only necessary information. Inevitably, the contrasts force the reader to evaluate Cathcart's initial elaborate, magnificent, soaring voice. It is all cathedral, no gargoyles. The reactions it invites are predictable: the initial narrator's irony and Cathcart's own eventual aversion to all language. On his third island, the once-eloquent Cathcart pries the brass label from his stove and obliterates all print and lettering in his cabin. The omniscient voice of the closing section may be seen as a compromise between Cathcart's initial flights of rhetoric and his ultimate grim silence. It neither inflates nor deflates, but seeks accurately to report responses and events. Lawrence's voice, or the voice of the tale, of course combines all three voices—ironic, lush, spare— indicating that full expression resides in no one voice but in the relationship between them all.

The tale's controlling ideas may be inferred from the above discussion of its rich overlying structures and progressive shifts of tone, but two points need emphasis. Both can be made by looking at Widmer's and Willbern's discussions of the tale.

According to Widmer, an attack on idealism is only the ostensible intent of the tale. On a deeper level, Lawrence has written an amoral fable dramatizing "the yearning for the extremity of experience."[42] The tale's images do not criticize Cathcart, they convey Lawrence's disgust with the physically human, his nausea toward sexuality, his view of knowledge as an esoteric hobby, and his wish to withdraw from living. According to Widmer, Cathcart's shaking his fist at the heavens is not illustrating Cathcart's vanity but "his heroic defiance." His gesture is "Lawrentian."[43] Willbern would agree that the tale is amoral, but in emphasizing Lawrence's ambivalence toward Cathcart and his psychological battles, he finds no support for Widmer's contention that Lawrence argues "for" Cathcart's view.[44]

I would contend first that an attack on idealism is not even the ostensible intent. In his foreword to *Fantasia of the Unconscious*, Lawrence sees something very like idealism as important and inevitable in human consciousness. He writes: "And finally it seems to me that even art is utterly dependent on philosophy: or if you prefer it, on a metaphysic. . . . Men live and see according to some gradually developing and gradually withering vision. This vision exists also as a dynamic idea or metaphysic—exists first as such. Then it is unfolded into life and art."[45] That Lawrence sees the ideal as waxing and waning may separate him from traditional idealists; but here as elsewhere, to see him as an antiidealist, as finally a sensationalist, is to ignore much of what he writes. It is Cathcart's "islanding," his foolish attempt to immunize himself and his thinking against all opposing energies, that is his sin and stupidity.[46] Recalling the other late fables, "The Rocking-Horse Winner" or "The Lovely Lady," convinces me that the target of satire in "The Man Who Loved Islands" is any mode of knowing that attempts to separate knowledge and inquiry from opposition and change.

Widmer's second point, that beneath Lawrence's conscious satire lie hidden longings, seems equally to distort parts of the tale. As Willbern observes, in "The Man Who Loves Islands" Lawrence openly admits the allure of extreme monasticism; he sympathizes with the temptation of total withdrawal. This is not a repressed longing; the longing is one of the main subjects of the tale.

But the terror of relationship and the longing for isolation are not simply dramatized, they are, again, convincingly judged. Widmer writes that negation is Cathcart's "final ecstasy."[47] But Cathcart grows not wild, not fiery, not urgent; the words Lawrence uses are "uneasy," "sullen," "helpless," "sickened," "overcome," "dumb," "stupid," and "in a stupor." Cathcart's final gesture of defiance—when he digs his boat out of drifted snow, insisting that he will be imprisoned by his own choice but not by the "mechanical power of the elements" (CSS, 745)—is given in four short paragraphs. And within them, little of the text is devoted to Cathcart's frantic efforts; most records his exhaustion and the physical surroundings of snow, rock, water. Had Lawrence seen Cathcart's defiance as "heroic," surely he would have made more of it. Further, Cathcart's complaint against the elements is set within the opposite of a heroic context. Lying in bed "in a stupor," Cathcart "dumbly" repeats to himself, "'The elements! The elements! You can't win against the elements'" (CSS, 746). This whimper is hardly an "ecstasy of denial." Finally, Lawrence brings the curtain down with images and language that point to Cathcart's undiminished desire to fool himself. Standing on a hill, he "pretended to imagine he saw the wink of a sail. Because he knew too well there would never again be a sail on that stark sea" (CSS, 746); looking "stupidly" over the snow, he believes it is summer.

In "The Man Who Loved Islands," Lawrence vividly dramatizes and judges human longings for simplicity, perfection, control, isolation. He states its governing spirit in his review of Dr. Trigant Burrow's book, *The Social Basis of Consciousness*: "Men must get back into *touch*. And to do so they must forfeit the vanity and the *noli me tangere* of their own absoluteness. . . ."[48] To refuse is to court insanity, to commit suicide.[49]

In this last cluster of Lawrence's tales, "The Man Who Loved Islands" speaks briefly to "Things," and eloquently and intricately to "The Man Who Died" and *Lady Chatterley's Lover*.[50] When "Things" was published in *Bookman* in August 1928, Lawrence assured his friends the Brewsters that it did not satirize them. Moore finds Lawrence's disclaimer a diplomatic lie.[51] But here, as with the Murry and Mackenzie tales, the story's possible origin is less important than its execution. If the Melvilles find their origin partly in the Brewsters, they also more interestingly find it in the man who loved islands and the man who died. In setting themselves "to eliminate from their own souls greed, pain, and sorrow," the Melvilles envision the same perfect existence as that sought by islander and resurrected man. Like Cathcart, the Melvilles are mocked.

A carefully controlled satire, "Things" flaunts the unities of time and place as it follows its hero and heroine, Valerie and Erasmus Melville, through thirteen years of constant movement.[52] We travel from New England to Paris, Italy, New York, the Rocky Mountains, California, Massachusetts, Europe, and

eventually Cleveland, Ohio. One recalls Frank O'Connor's stric-
ture that no short story can realistically dramatize characters
deeply enmeshed in a social context; as in his fables, Lawrence's
response in this satire is to forego realism. Within the tale's sprawl
of years and locales, Lawrence creates his social types and establishes his artful design. He introduces design and critique with the
image of a vine. The Melvilles are enthusiastic idealists from New
England. Through their thirteen years of wandering, they are like
vines, continually trying to find something strong to hold on to,
to lift themselves up. They try Paris, then Buddhistic thought,
then Europe in general. But always running counter to their vertical attempts to climb off the mundane surface of the earth is their
horizontal, materialistic craving for things. The reaction to their
love of the ideal lies in their love of chairs, curtains, tables, desks.
The elusive *via media* would be, of course, to find the mode of
thinking and living that would honor both the ideal and material,
timeless and decaying, vertical and horizontal.

As the vertical and horizontal image pattern suggests, this
tale, like "The Man Who Loved Islands," is only ostensibly about
idealism. More, it is about a failure to recognize oppositions, that
is, actions and reactions. The idealism the Melvilles felt in their
youth grows into "pure skepticism" and unabashed materialism in
their middle age. The central movement of the tale, the swing
from one extreme to the other, from vertical to horizontal, is
clearly seen in the opening and closing paragraphs. The key words
of the opening are "idealism," "freedom," "beauty." The key words
of the closing are "skepticism," "caged," and "lobster and mayon-
naise." In reference to the last phrase, Europe has descended from
"the fountainhead of tradition" and beauty to the supplier of may-
onnaise for American lobster.

Throughout the tale, the narrator moves between mimicking
the Melvilles and offering sardonic commentary on their delu-
sions. Never do these characters take over the tale and give a
sense of their lives from within. Their child, for example, is simply a prop, no different in presence than the couple's dusty belong-
ings. Lawrence includes little dialogue and no dramatic scenes.
Combined with his clear structural pattern of opposition, this narrative strategy reinforces the tale's integrity as a satire. In contrast
to "The Man Who Died," to which I now turn, the settings, characters, and plot in "Things" remain flat throughout; each fictional
element exists as a term in the tale's argument.

The two parts of "The Man Who Died" reflect Lawrence's two separate writings of the tale. Part 1 was composed in April and May of 1927 and published as "The Escaped Cock" in the February 1928 issue of *Forum*. Lawrence revised that text and wrote part 2 in the summer of 1928.[53] Writing to Brewster in May 1927, Lawrence names what he originally intended to be the tale's focus: "I wrote a story of the Resurrection, where Jesus gets up and feels very sick about everything, and can't stand the old crowd anymore—so cuts out—and as he heals up, he begins to find what an astonishing place the phenomenal world is, far more marvelous than any salvation or heaven—and thanks his stars he needn't have a mission any more" (*CL*, 975).[54] If this were, in fact, the tale's single action, "The Escaped Cock" would read as a fortunate reversal in the adventures of Cathcart, the man who loved islands. We would be studying, in essence, the resurrection of the islander. But the awakening of Lawrence's new Christ to the marvel of the phenomenal world and his resulting disgust at his former mission are not the single action of either "The Escaped Cock" or "The Man Who Died."[55]

Much of the *Forum* text can be read within the first section of the later two-part story. Lawrence opens with a description of the resplendent game cock, the poverty of its owners, the cock's tethering, and its escape. Following the principle of sequence implying simile, Lawrence moves at once to the awakening of Christ. A potentially resplendent figure himself, Christ also belonged to the peasants. He too has been tied up; he too has just escaped. In combination with the subject, this neat parallelism suggests that we have a fable before us. Although usually read that way, the *Forum* version is, in fact, less fabulistic in style than other tales of this period. After the opening parallelism, the tale shifts into a relatively realistic plot structure as it traces the gradual revival in spirit and body of the man who died. In contrast to "The Rocking-Horse Winner," "The Escaped Cock" realistically explains the uncanny, here the return of the man from the grave. The soldiers simply took him down too soon. One is to see Christ demystified and transformed into an understandable, changing man within the phenomenal world of the here and now. As in "The Lovely Lady," Lawrence draws attention to the distinction between mystification and real mystery. In some ways, the tale is set up to criticize the very qualities of timelessness and placelessness that characterize fables and fairy tales.

Like the later version, the early text shows the Christ figure helping to catch the cock and going to stay with the peasants until he is strong and well. The rhythm of the tale is double as we watch the resurrected man loosening his ties with his former apostles and being wooed back into life, desire, and a capacity for wonder by the brilliant gamecock. The *Forum* text ends with the man donning the garb of a physician, acquiring, then giving away the cock. Faced with the "'vast complexity of wonders'" that is the "'phenomenal world,'" he asks a closing question: "'From what, and to what, could this infinite whirl be saved?'" (*The Escaped Cock*, ed. Lacy, 120). One thinks of Lawrence's famous statement in *Apocalypse*: "For man, the vast marvel is to be alive."

Summarized this way, "The Escaped Cock" sounds identical to part 1 of the eventual story and seems to be a fine realization of Lawrence's stated intention to show Jesus awakening to the miracle of this world. But there is an important image pattern in the *Forum* version that muddies the intention he stated to Brewster. We encounter the image in several contexts and forms, but the following is typical. The Christ figure looks out at the surging life around him and feels both wonder and revulsion at the incessant clamor of life. Coming back to life himself, he wants to experience joyous desire, but not assertiveness and insistence. Of the latter, he feels, he has had enough. He expresses his need through the image of an iris. An iris, he believes, unfurls its beautiful nakedness "'alone.'" It "'touches nothing.'" It lives within its own isolate sphere. He would be like the iris, surrounded and protected by his own delicate "'inner air,'" naked and procreant in his essential singleness. Perhaps he will meet others who move within the same ambience, perhaps not: "'if not, it is no matter . . .'" (*The Escaped Cock*, ed. Lacy, 117).

The problems are several. In this image Lawrence supports the desire to be alone and untroubled that he mocked in "The Man Who Loved Islands." The Christ figure would be a moving island, or, to approach more closely the man's own image, a man within a bubble. Intending to lead no more, he strangely reminds us of Lawrence's earlier leadership figures: he sees himself as alone, distant, silent, desirable, potent. Like those earlier figures, he speaks with a vaguely exotic accent, when he deigns to speak at all. Wishing to show a Christ awed by earthly beauty and desire, Lawrence was honest and perceptive to include the possibility of revulsion within awe. But revulsion comes to dominate. One of the last passages of the *Forum* version begins with the man's awareness that life is dirty and clean together, but, as the passage builds, the man repeats his disgust at the stinking atmosphere most men create and wishes for their death.

The image of the iris—desireless, isolated, still—also undermines rather than complements the image of the cock—desiring, mating, vibrant. Within the tale's dramatic development, the two images indicate a hero who intends to come alive in this world but who still has his eyes on heaven. In his iris world, he is envisioning the mating of angels.

Apart from its puristic connotations and tendency to undermine the image of the cock, the image of the iris points to related problems in the early "Escaped Cock." One is the contempt that the Christ figure feels for the peasants who shelter him. We have only to think of the sharply realized, fully human, collier families in Lawrence's earlier stories to be amazed at the characterizations we find here.[56] Widmer says Lawrence is being unsentimental.[57] The man who died says that the peasants are only different from himself. But one reads that they are of a class of humanity that is essentially dirty, greedy, and kind only out of fear. They are "clods of the earth," incapable of salvation or resurrection. The following observation is typical. The man who died has just left the peasants who have sheltered him. In recompense for their care, he has paid them a small fee. "The peasant woman shed a few tears, but then went indoors, being a peasant, to look again at the pieces of money" (*The Escaped Cock*, ed. Lacy, 118). To terms like "dirty" and "greedy" one must add "incapable of real affection." In fact, the man who died has his own greed, cunning, incapacity for affection, and tendency to manipulate. If the peasants are kind out of fear, so apparently is he: "And the stranger had compassion on them again, for he knew that they would respond best to gentleness, giving back a clumsy gentleness again" (*The Escaped Cock*, ed. Lacy, 108).

The condescension and aversion he feels toward the peasants together, he feels especially toward the woman. His attitude toward her includes contempt because of her class but goes beyond it to gender, for it parallels his attitude toward the other woman in the tale, Madeleine. Both women ache to give themselves to the man who died: Madeleine wants to fall at his feet, devote herself utterly to him; the peasant woman, in behavior presumably appropriate to her class, simply serves him silently, "her soft, humble, crouching body" wishing for his touch. But, like Lawrence's earlier leadership figures, he responds only with a weary preference not to. It is here especially that we hear him repeat, "'Touch me not.'" If this virgin is ever to make love, he will make love as the iris does, without the messy contact these adoring women offer.

The image of the pure, still, untouched iris relates also to the tale's denunciation of language. To the Christ figure, words are like midges and gnats. They only swarm about experience and cake it with mud. Silence is best. In "The Man Who Loved Islands," Lawrence sets Cathcart's revulsion at the printed word within the context of his earlier soaring language and his ultimate suicide. But the man who died is not an ironic figure; presumably he traces a progress into life, health, and even healing. Nor does he denounce language at a low point in that progress. On our own we may see irony in the contrast between Christ's distrust of language and Lawrence's own superb descriptions of the cock or green, flaming tips of the sprouting fig tree. But we do so without directions from Lawrence.[58]

Lawrence's 1928 tale slightly alters the first "Escaped Cock," but the problems remain and, indeed, deepen. In revising the first section, Lawrence dropped the image of the iris. Condensing the man's contemplative passages in general, Lawrence tends to have the man express the iris's qualities by the phrases "the greater day," and/or "the greater life of the body." In contrast to both is "the little day" and "the little, narrow personal life" (*The Escaped Cock*, ed. Lacy, 28). The phrases are carried over from the fragment of a novel Lawrence wrote at the end of 1925, "The Flying Fish."[59] In general, they express the idea that there is a way of living and relating to others that escapes entanglements, compulsion, fret, conflict. But the language creates the same problem as the iris image. It tends toward preciousness and exclusivity, accompanied by the same contempt for the peasants, futile yearning for insouciance, weariness with female adulation, and revulsion with language. The man's program is still the same: "'I will wander the earth, and say nothing. For nothing is so marvelous as to be alone in the phenomenal world, which is raging and yet apart'" (*The Escaped Cock*, ed. Lacy, 30).[60]

The tale's second part is intended to reverse the man's earlier need not to be touched as well as fulfill his hope of meeting someone one day as irislike as himself. Structurally, the story follows the same basic pattern as many of Lawrence's late tales. The first half provides background and states situation and conflicts. The second half develops a dramatic incident to illustrate the main points and resolve the conflicts. Here, the flowering iris becomes the priestess of Isis, the human embodiment of "the greater day." The man's longing to be in touch and yet still alone is answered by their brief, silent affair.

In action the affair is simple enough. The man who died goes to the priestess's villa, asks for shelter, and stays through the spring and summer. She sees him as Osiris, the god who has been killed and scattered and who awaits reintegration and re-creation at the hands of Isis.[61] As often happens in Lawrence's tales, the woman invites the man to make love to her. At first he is reluctant but eventually gives in to their mutual desire. Through the months of the man's stay, they meet often and make love in the temple she has built to Isis. She becomes pregnant. Feeling threatened by her mother, the Roman overseer, and the slaves, the man leaves, promising to return, "'sure as spring'" (*The Escaped Cock*, ed. Lacy, 60).

Their affair is intended to objectify the man's resurrection. Throughout his writing, Lawrence sought ways to imagine a return from death that would celebrate rather than deny the physical self. In the admittedly awkward pun, "'I am risen,'" Lawrence seeks to establish the same switch in direction we saw in "Sun": what is usually seen as a descent into physical desire is seen here as an ascent. The man who died has presumably conquered his earlier terror of contact, his wincing need not to be touched. He has ascended to the Father, which is the world of desire, and can now enjoy the closest touch of all.

The affair also presumably objectifies the fulfillment of the priestess's search. Before she encounters the man, we are given some sense of her background and the nature of her seeking. To identify with Isis, in this tale, is to identify with subtle shade flowers blooming in filtered sunlight. Without the sun, the woman's flower—her womb, her desire—remains cold, unopened. At times the language is much the same as in "Sun," especially in some of the rejected passages, which Lacy prints (*The Escaped Cock*, ed. Lacy, 131–133). But in contrast to Juliet, the priestess would wither in full light. She needs to be met with a delicate rather than a hot or brassy desire; that need is obviously in tune with the need of the man. In her yellow and white tunic and mantle, she is associated with both the narcissus and the moon.

241

The man who died becomes the sun—his wounds, specifically—but again, the light, warmth, and energy he offers are quiet and filtered.

But obtruding into this ideal of delicate fulfillment are all the energies, circumstances, and needs this fulfillment denies. The material Lawrence leaves out cuts across the intended meaning at two major points in particular.

One of the most disturbing scenes in the tale occurs in the opening of part 2. Standing at a distance from each other and from the two slaves working below them, the priestess and man watch the naked young people dressing pigeons. At the escape of one of the pigeons, the boy falls on the girl and, in "an access of rage," begins to beat her with his fist, which is covered with pigeon's blood. She goes limp. He stops, turns her over, and, pushing her thighs apart, covers her for the frenzied moment of his first sexual intercourse. Her response we never get.[62] The association Lawrence casually makes here between anger, brutality, and sexual arousal of course is one we find throughout our culture. But Lawrence is not examining or questioning it. A pathetic, cruel scene in itself, its cruelty is matched by the response of the man who died and the priestess. Appropriately stationed above and distant, they merely watch. And when the scene is over and the boy has "scuttled" away, the priestless responds with disgust: "Slaves! Let the overseer watch them. She was not interested" (The Escaped Cock, ed. Lacy, 37). The pattern continues. The contempt the man expressed earlier toward the peasants, he and the priestess now express toward the slaves. She finds her slaves "invariably repellent, a little repulsive. They were so embedded in the lesser life, and their appetites and their small consciousness were a little disgusting" (The Escaped Cock, ed. Lacy, 43). He listens to their "babble" as they work, seeing them as "common" and "hostile." When he leaves, he takes a boat from one of the slaves and finds the oars "yet warm with the unpleasant warmth of the hands of the slaves" (The Escaped Cock, ed. Lacy, 61). The priestess would seem to be the princess all over again. Like the man who died, she sees anything less delicate than herself as repulsive, as not quite human. Sterile in itself, this preciousness contradicts aspects of the tale's characterization and narration.

This proud and rigid priestess, for example, is praised for serving "'a kindly goddess, and full of tenderness.'" Her goddess mates only with "'warmhearted'" gods (The Escaped Cock, ed.

Lacy, 58). Earlier, the man who died said to himself, "'Life . . . bubbles variously. Why should I ever have wanted it to bubble all alike?'" (*The Escaped Cock*, ed. Lacy, 31). Yet faced with these common slaves, he sighs over their all-too-little day: "It was the life of the little day, the life of the little people. And the man who died said to himself: 'Unless we encompass it in the greater day, and set the little life in the circle of the great life, all is disaster'" (*The Escaped Cock*, ed. Lacy, 50). What has happened to his joy in the variety of expressions life takes? But most damaging to the tale's coherence, the contempt of this ostensible hero and heroine works in opposition to the discerning eye of the narrator. With what one may call loving detail, the narrator draws for us the many sights and sounds of the everyday world that go on below the priestess and man. He shows us the smooth, rounded shape of an old, fat slave cleaning fish as the last rays of the sun touch him, twinkle, and fade. At one point, the old slave takes on personality and individuality as he obstinately ignores the domineering mother of the priestess. Following the direction of the narrator's eye, one sees women "dusky and alive" piling wet linen in flat baskets. The images we get of this ancient working community are vivid, specific, and memorable, making the blindness of the hero and heroine all the more disturbing.[63] That blindness is especially unsettling, because one of Lawrence's intended goals was to show the hero awakening to the wonder of the world of phenomena.

Creating the second major warp in the tale's intended design is the relationship of the man and priestess. In this engagement, which presumably marks their simultaneous birth into love, touch, and relationship, there seems to be little love, little touch, little relationship. In fact, haunting the tale is Lawrence's description of masturbation in "Pornography and Obscenity" and his image of it in "The Rocking-Horse Winner." In both "The Escaped Cock" and "The Man Who Died," procreation implies no real contact with otherness. In part 2, the priestess comes, goes, and eventually conceives wrapped in her own dream. Except in Lawrence's attitude toward her, she is, in fact, not fundamentally different from Ethel Cane in "None of That," Paul in "The Rocking-Horse Winner," or Cathcart in "The Man Who Loved Islands." Like Ethel, she can deal with the world only to the extent it fits her dream: the man who died must be Osiris. Like Paul, the priestess is naive and childish, a captive of her own secrets, a rider of her own hobbyhorse. Like Cathcart, she sees herself above and beyond the world that surrounds her. Ethel, Paul, and Cathcart are damned for their self-enclosure and inability to let any real impulse from the outside break in on their isolation. The priestess is praised.

The Christ figure does not try to fit the priestess into as elaborately prefabricated a dream as she does him. But he circumvents her in another way. The whole point of their coming together against the vulgar crowd would seem to be their essential similarity. Yet, in the man's view, the opposite is true. They are utterly different. In the greater day—where, different as they are, both live—each is and must be a total unknown to the other. To exchange names, histories, hopes, indeed to talk much is pointless or threatening. She makes him into Osiris, he makes her into the incomprehensible. And both avoid any resistence to their dreams, any disturbance of their fantasies.[64]

It may be asked, is the tenor of their relationship understandable within the conventions of fabulation? Might the lack of personal engagement between the priestess and man be attributed to the general stylization and flatness of character in fable? I believe fabulistic conventions could help us to formulate Lawrence's intentions in this tale were the tale more consistently a fable. A key difficulty here is the characterization of the hero. He is not sufficiently flat nor stylized. We know his history, his thoughts, his plans. He is developed in too much psychological detail for us to see him simply as a figure of sun or returning spring. The priestess is more stylized. But because she must interact with a realistically developed partner, she ends up appearing stilted, affected. The same is true of their relationship. Because the man is too round a character, their stylized intercourse seems posturing. Nor can their attitude toward the slaves be understood as permissible within fabulistic conventions. If anything, those conventions—as they govern plot and theme—would lead us toward seeing the priestess as a haughty queen, likely to be punished for her highhandedness.

The two warps—the characters' contempt for the slaves and their ultimate indifference to the identity of each other—are, of course, connected. The slaves live "the little day," "the personal life," "the little life of the body." Personal history and identity similarly partake of the mundane. The hero and heroine are above that aspect of existence. Logical in itself, this pattern is not logical within the larger intention of the tale to dramatize a man awakening to the wonder of the whole natural world and a woman seeking to mate with a complete—not fragmented, not partial—man. Pledged to delicate fulfillment, the man and the priestess cut themselves off from the world of striving, talking, sharing, copulating, quarreling, and growing old. From the outset it seems Lawrence set himself a task that was self-contradictory. He wished to dramatize a man awakening to the full wonder and variety of the world and to dramatize the same man's need to avoid everything common.

Lawrence's failure to create a coherent tale in "The Man Who Died" is especially interesting when one considers the tale in relation to *Lady Chatterley's Lover* and "The Man Who Loved Islands." Read as precursor to *Lady Chatterley's Lover*, "The Man Who Loved Islands" is a concise enactment in fairy tale rhetoric of several issues that are developed in the novel. With its fine exploration of Cathcart's willfulness, yearning to be alone, and eventual suicide, the short story examines issues through one character that the novel examines through two, Clifford and Mellors. On his first island, Cathcart acts out Clifford's dream of being the benevolent overseer of a perfectly run enterprise. Clifford would run the mines, Cathcart a farm; but both see themselves as the guiding spirit of all social and technological progress. What each leaves out of account is quite simply the independent existence of everyone around him. And what each fails to see in other humans, each also fails to discern in the natural world. In Clifford's view, the world is to be conquered or poeticized. When Cathcart's islands press against him, asserting histories and cycles quite beyond him, he responds with the same desire to conquer or turn nature into literature. Both men derive energy and motivation almost entirely from their will. The end of Cathcart is a literal and localized portrayal of Clifford's continuous suicide. Both trace a progress out of adult human complexity, liveliness, and curiosity into infantilism, an icy rigidity, and an ever-narrowing scope of interest.

But in Cathcart Lawrence had also woven qualities of Mellors. Like Mellors, Cathcart has a strong wish to be alone.[65] We are given to understand that both have had experiences with women that have left them shattered and miserable. On his second island, Cathcart anticipates Mellors in wishing to exist in "a new stillness of desirelessness." Beyond it, perhaps, there may be "a new fresh delicacy of desire" (CSS, 737). Mellors fortunately meets Connie, who fulfills his best hopes and cures him of his worst. Cathcart lives out one of the futures Mellors escaped.

In turning to Lawrence's retelling of Christ's resurrection in "The Man Who Died," one might expect to find an even closer correspondence to the Chatterley story than that offered by "The Man Who Loved Islands."[66] Both fictions open with a man who has almost died—Clifford and Christ—and both close with a pregnant woman—Connie Chatterley and the priestess. Given these opening and closing elements, it is not surprising that both works ask, what is resurrection and what is immortality? Having almost died himself, Lawrence asks, what can it mean in human experience to die and come back to life? What kind of immortality is available or desirable to humanity?

Ostensibly, Lady Chatterley and the man who died come to similar understandings: the traditional answers, which rest on a division between body and spirit, are wrong, inadequate. Both characters fight against the assumption that death resides in the body while resurrection resides in the spirit; for ultimately that assumption argues that one can only know immortality—defined in the novel as perfect, eternal beauty—in a bodiless state, in the hereafter. On a different tack, both characters also dismiss the idea that immortality is available through children. A child is conceived in each work, but it is the by-product of the characters' belief in immortality, not the means to immortality. Both the man who died and Connie look at themselves and out at the world and eventually decide that real immortality resides in the changing, glimmering beauty of the earthly, fleshly, desiring life in them and around them. Connie first sees that perfect beauty when she comes upon Mellors behind his cottage washing himself. The man who died first sees it in the cock and fig tree. For both characters, the vision is momentous; the beauty revealed is eternal. In both tale and novel, resurrection and immortality presumably consist of dying to one's former blindness to this perfect, earthly, bodily beauty and being reborn into awareness and the desire to participate in it. Clifford's return from the dead stands as a sharp foil to Lawrence's definition of resurrection, because Clifford's resurrection fosters in him blindness and greed. He tries to clutch and hoard his life and the lives of others, while he simultaneously denies the ultimate importance or value of life.

But the resemblances traced here are false. In *Lady Chatter-*

ley's Lover, Lawrence does dramatize the concepts of immortality and resurrection outlined above. In "The Man Who Died" he dramatizes the opposite. Both the priestess and the man who died have aspects of Clifford within them. Both are as classbound as that English gentleman, both as incapable of noticing or caring about the very real lives supporting them. One can imagine their likely response to broad-talking Mellors. Both man and woman have Clifford's habit of seeing the world through a haze of metaphor. Among the key points in *Lady Chatterley's Lover* is the need to call things, such as flowers, intercourse, genitals, people, by their right names. In spite of powerful passages of natural imagery in "The Man Who Died," the tale presents human relationships through a veil of indirection and poeticizing. The priestess sees the man as Osiris. She is "My Lady." (Connie Chatterley is also "My Lady," and the difference in tone is instructive.) The man wishes to be an iris; he sees the priestess as a narcissus. In "Pornography and Obscenity," Lawrence attacks the sentimentality of comparing a woman to a flower, especially to a lily. The comparison, he states, leads to pornography, implying as it does that any real sexuality in the woman must be dirty, secret, denied. Certainly any frank sexuality in the priestess is denied. The problem in this tale is precisely what Lawrence understood it to be in English culture in general. The thin man and crouching priestess are humanity seen through veils of disguise, avoidance, allusion. By contrast, Mellors has the courage of his own sexual lust when he waylays Connie on her walk home from Marehay. Connie has her own courage when she demands a key to Mellors's hut and then waits in the persistence of her desire for him. Each intrudes on the other and insists that the other be aware of all that is between them, the delicate and the powerful, the intrusive and the respectful. And out of intrusion and respect come recognition—of self, other, world. In "The Man Who Died," there are no demands, no intrusions, no insistence, no real respect, and no recognition.

A second apparent parallel between the novel and story would seem to exist in the roles of Lady Chatterley and the priestess. Both are cast as women in search. Both despise automatic, careless sexual activity because for both such activity implies only a partial engagement. The priestess of Isis is seeking a whole man and a whole relationship. Connie imagines herself going into the streets and byways of Jerusalem, seeking, like Isis, a whole man, an integrated mate. This parallel is again false, but it introduces the primary plot of *Lady Chatterley's Lover*. At the center of the novel's symbolic action is not the Sleeping Beauty myth many critics see; it is the myth of Isis in search. Connie is not asleep. Were she, she would be passive, content, innocent of desire. Instead, long before she encounters Mellors, she is restless, active, longing. If anything, it is Mellors who is lying low, desireless, quiescent. In designing the novel's action, Lawrence gives us the repeated image of this lone-walking woman, trekking across fields and through woods, from castle to cottage, seeking resurrection and immortality—that is, seeking a relationship with her entire self, with an entire man, with the entire world of living, growing things.

Helpful as it may be in revealing the key action of *Lady Chatterley's Lover*, however, the Isis myth provides no more accurate a basis for comparing novel and story than did the issues of immortality and resurrection. The parallels between priestess and lady quickly break down. For all the specific associations Lawrence draws between the priestess and Isis, the priestess is neither searching for nor interested in a whole relationship with her self, a man, or the world around her. In contrast to the key dramatic images in *Lady Chatterley's Lover*, a repeated image in the second half of "The Man Who Died" is of the silent priestess withdrawing from the world of growing things and living people into the temple she has built and the dreams she spins. Here, indeed, is a Sleeping Beauty. A prince lies with her; but neither arouses the other, except within each one's respective dream.

One last apparent parallel bears brief discussion. In "The Man Who Died" and *Lady Chatterley's Lover*, Lawrence calls particular attention to his characters' diction. How people talk is important in each work. This is particularly true of his two heroes, Mellors and the man who died.

Usually Mellors speaks on a level identical with the rest of the novel. Generally, his particular syntax, accent, vocabulary call little attention to themselves. But occasionally he slips into dialect. Connie notices, questions, resents, mocks, enjoys the shifts. Her several responses are justified, for one set of pronunciations implies derision; another, affection and tenderness; still another, neutrality. The effect of Mellors's separate styles supports several of the large intentions of the novel. Lawrence uses Mellors's working-class dialect to emphasize the difference between Connie and the gamekeeper, and Mellors's change of style to help convey a range of sensitivity and response in him. Connie is seeking a whole relationship; she is seeking the kind of marriage Lawrence describes in "A Propos of *Lady Chatterley's Lover*" as capable of reflecting natural cycles—spring, summer, fall, winter. Mellors's levels of diction are one indication that he possesses the breadth of response to live out that kind of marriage.

In "The Man Who Died," Lawrence employs a relatively poetic level of diction throughout. The effect is not one of lushness. This is not the style of the opening chapter of *The Rainbow*, for example. At their best, these passages combine a delicate music with a clarity of atmosphere that leaves the reader with a vibrant and precise image. But this style, which works well for the omniscient narrator, does not work well for the tale's characters. In them, one senses a tendency toward circumlocution, narrow response, and an insistence on their aristocratic nature. In contrast to Mellors's diction, theirs has no range and seems intended to limit communication and avoid personal response. The vague conversations of the man and priestess continually justify the man's earlier disparagement of language as a concealer.

What can it mean to come back from the dead? The theater of Lawrence's imagination enacts a variety of responses. Given that he, himself, had "returned" to life after his collapse in Mexico in 1925, Lawrence seems keenly aware of the temptation to isolate and purify the soul, to stand above the physical passion and decay of human life. Recent biographical scholarship suggests that Lawrence was impotent after 1925. The probability has led critics to see his last novel, in particular, as a vast wish fulfillment. But equally, I think, one can see in his late work, especially in his stories, a courageous insistence that spiritual hermitage is tempting and deadly. In other words, responding to his own impotence and solipsistic longings, he generally deplores the kind of precious spirituality inherent in a withdrawal from ordinary, physical, and social life. As we have seen, the temptation to isolate the self is usually presented in exaggerated terms and then ridiculed. The telling images and figures—of both temptation and ridicule—are an infectious smile, a willful woman, a series of islands, a hobbyhorse, a posturing writer, a pair of moccasins, a couple of feisty blue birds, a piazza of fancy furniture, and an ancient crone. The hero in "The Man Who Died" says, "'Life bubbles variously'"; these latter tales, through realistic conventions or the complex use and parody of fabulistic conventions, celebrate that bubbling variety. To come back from the dead is to respect the countless forms life takes. When Lawrence does fall prey to the temptation, his characters do not openly say, "'Touch Me Not'" but they suffer contact under only highly circumscribed conditions. Here the telling figures are a distant Italian peasant, a plum-scented ghost, an iris, a priestess, and a reluctant Lazarus.

In important ways, Lawrence's tales of withdrawal, whether they mock or honor the wish, complement the curious interest he (and Lady Cynthia Asquith) evince during these years in the "uncanny." In every case, Lawrence creates a significant set of associations. Where the truly uncanny exists, as in "The Rocking-Horse Winner," it is linked with death. Knowledge and experience that separate themselves from natural, physical reality lead to damnation. In each of the other stories that explores the uncanny, Lawrence exposes it as mystification and then poses mystification against genuine mystery. Even in "Glad Ghosts," the arid spiritualism of Lady Lathkill is meant to be contrasted with the mystery and fruitfulness of the midnight love-making. Mystification is always caused by or causes a withdrawal from living; mystery always leads back to natural life.

A different but related temptation facing the resurrected individual is the desire to hoard life. Clifford Chatterley is the obvious example, but the lovely lady is an equally vivid figure of avarice. Carefully sipping the sun's energy and storing it away for her immortality, she stands as an implicit warning to Juliet of "Sun." In less direct ways, the well-preserved women in "Mother and Daughter" and "The Blue Moccasins" have the same tendency to create around themselves an exquisite and highly controlled world which keeps death and old age at bay but equally prevents life from entering. Alternatively, a key to the intention of "The Man Who Died" is Lawrence's emphasis on the man's lack of avarice toward life, his insouciance.

To identify several of the late stories as a series of imaginative responses to Lawrence's interest in the nature of human resurrection is to recognize a dominant theme in the late work and to see the dynamic process through which Lawrence explored that interest. But my emphasis may create a misleading atmosphere around these last stories. They do wrestle with the issue of how one comes back from the dead, but so do many of Lawrence's earlier stories. In Lawrence, death and destruction are necessary corollaries to life and creation. In his stories, as in his life, there is a re-

curring rhythm of death and rebirth. One hears it in his letters, one reads it in his stories, poems, essays, and novels from
first to last. He was always building his Ship of Death and fur-
nishing it with the stories that would carry him through
oblivion to new consciousness.

I began this book with questions. What is the shape of Lawrence's short fiction? How does it relate to the modern short story
in general? If Lawrence is the greatest short story writer in English, what is the nature of his accomplishment? In thinking about
his late stories, I have sought to assess their value in relation to
the rich body of tales that precedes them. In closing, let me return
to my original questions.

My description of Lawrence's short fiction as a movement out
of traditional, nineteenth-century conventions, into realism, visionary fiction, and fabulation gives a good assessment of his progress if one holds in mind two provisions. As we have seen, in
moving toward a new mode, Lawrence continued to practice previous modes. We find realistic stories throughout his writing; in
his late fables and satires, he uses many of the techniques of his
earlier realistic and visionary tales. It is a matter of emphasis, of
tendencies. If one stands the mother in "Odour of Chrysanthemums" beside the mother in "The Rocking-Horse Winner," one
will quickly sense the striking differences in conceptualization.
Both young, British, dissatisfied, they nevertheless come out of
different worlds. They speak a different language. One is not necessarily better or more interesting than the other; the two are simply born out of Lawrence's distinct visions of the stories he was
writing. Seek through the early or middle tales for a figure who
resembles Cathcart or a setting similar to his shrinking islands
and, again, Lawrence's genuine development in the mode becomes clear.

The second provision recalls the image of the dance used in
the introduction to this book. Lawrence's general movement from
realism to fable occurs by way of intense dialogues between stories
and between stories and novels. Time and again one sees him imaginatively return to a work he has completed, review its possibilities, and write a new tale that explores an alternative stance or
develops a new technique. To glimpse at least one of the ways
Lawrence's imagination worked, one must think of Louisa Lindley
in "Daughters of the Vicar" speaking to Ciss in "The Lovely
Lady"; one must sense Cathcart on his islands calling back to Lou

Witt on her lonely ranch. It will help to think of Mellors and
Lady Chatterley in dialogue with the man who died and the priestess of Isis. Far more than the novels, the stories exist as vital clusters, dynamically related to each other and to their contemporaneous novels. There is a shape to the *oeuvre*, but it is a moving
shape. And crucial to its movement are the complex interrelationships that develop along the way.

In thinking of how Lawrence's work relates to the modern
short story in general, one must consider the field as he found it in
England at the turn of the century. In particular, one must listen
to Ford's call for realism sounded in the early issues of the *English
Review*. In his view, America was following her own program
based on the different work of Melville, Hawthorne, and Poe, but
the Continent was clearly pointing the way for stodgy England. As
did Joyce, Mansfield, Bennett, Galsworthy, Maugham, and others, Lawrence responded to Ford's call, giving voice to the particu-
larities of daily living that realism demanded. As in Joyce and
Mansfield, the overt focus on the mundane in Lawrence hides
more general levels of meaning, levels rich with allusions to history and myth. But unlike his colleagues in realism, Lawrence
quickly began to expose those buried levels of meaning in his short
stories, turning away from realism and taking the English short
story in directions quite new.

As suggested above, his visionary stories were and are inimitable. Whereas his realistic stories still provide a model of craft
and seriousness for contemporary writers, such as the early Doris
Lessing or Alan Sillitoe, his visionary stories were so deeply a
product of his individual sense of life that they created no school.
For all the obvious differences, Joseph Conrad, who was certainly
not imitating Lawrence, may come closer than anyone else to
writing the kind of visionary tale one finds in Lawrence. What
Lawrence's visionary stories do toward influencing the genre is to
demand recognition for the diverse possibilities inherent in the
short story. The fables, by contrast, were imitable. Lawrence
might find Barth, Barthelme, Gardener, Gass, Hawkes, Landolfi,
Cortázar, Vonnegut, Rosenfeld, García Márquez, or Borges to be
very strange bedfellows; he might cry out, "That isn't what I
meant at all." Nevertheless his fables and satires clearly constitute
one of the breaks with realism that leads to contemporary antific-
tion and surfiction.

His accomplishments include, then, imbuing a recognized,

continental form—the realistic short story—with English content as well as with extraordinary depth and sharpness; carving out a new kind of story in the visionary tales by blending realism and exemplum; and pointing the way out of realism toward fabulation. Looking specifically at his own fiction, one can assess the value of his short stories in different terms. Time and again, they stand as the discrete, finished artifacts that paradoxically inspire his continued exploration of themes and techniques. Unlike the early drafts of a novel, the completed short story—sent off to an agent, published in a magazine—exists out in the world, an accomplished thing. It becomes something to react to; judging from the interrelationships that exist between the stories, for Lawrence the finished tale served admirably as a goad. A completed novel could and did play that role, but he wrote seven novels as opposed to over sixty stories. The individual tales, from 1907 to 1928, constitute a steady program of imaginative acts, each story having the potential to inspire Lawrence toward new projects or warn him of likely dead ends.

A still different way of assessing Lawrence's accomplishment leaves aside both his contributions to the genre of short fiction and his tales' contributions to his own art and thought. The focus in this last assessment is on the reader, novice or devotee, who picks up a volume of Lawrence's short stories and enters their world. What does that reader encounter?

At a conference on fiction several years ago, Julian Moynahan commented that, finally, we go to fiction to learn how to live our lives. The lessons come from the quality of both the art and the vision, the pattern and the life captured by the writer. Inevitably the two, the art and the vision, are linked. When one considers Lawrence's most wrongheaded tales—tales that deny human complexity, that offer stereotypes of men and women, that set up a posturing, defensive hero—one finds they are often incoherent. Image patterns do not complement each other; analysis works against scene; characters seem pastiches of traits rather than integrated personalities or concepts; language is uneven—strained, exotic, flippant. I have suggested that the incoherence may ultimately be to Lawrence's credit; it registers his inability to create a full and convincing dramatization of an inadequate idea.

Most of the tales are far from being wrongheaded. In response to Moynahan's comment, they urge the reader to question cliché —be it religious, sexual, political, psychoanalytic—to observe oneself and others with wit, critical intelligence, and courage; to commit oneself to one's beliefs while remaining aware of one's capacity to err; and perhaps, above all, to stay keenly alive during one's brief span of years on this whirling planet. To persuade the reader of these grand generalities, Lawrence works as all great fiction writers do; with complex craft, he draws together the seized particular and the dramatic action, the epiphany and the narrative explanation, creating a combination that captures significance in specific instance.

Like Shakespeare, Tennyson, or Hardy, Lawrence had an imagination that could leap from the domestic to the cosmic and back again. One sees his characters as sons and daughters, husbands and wives, Englishmen and Englishwomen. But Lawrence also urges the reader to see his characters as phenomena of and participants in vast systems and cycles. How human character reflects the general state of the culture, how it can identity itself with fox or scarab, how it can realize itself through quickened relationships with other humans, with sun, moon, stars, shaggy spruce and balsam pine are Lawrence's issues. More than any other writer of his time, he told the kinds of stories—and here I use the term broadly—that challenge narrow definitions of human nature, that insist on humanity's close ties with all life and all forms of consciousness on this earth. He felt that he lived in a tragic age; we feel that we live in a dangerous one. Faced with the devastation of World War I, he believed that life could begin anew only if people broadened and enriched their understanding of themselves, their nature, their place on this planet. Faced with the possibility of global destruction, the reader who enters the world of Lawrence's stories may be persuaded similarly that life will continue only if people recognize the literal truth in Lawrence's vision of the inevitable and intimate relatedness of human and horse, human and poppy, human and cloud, rain, sun. Leslie Silko, a contemporary story-teller with rich ties to Lawrence, states it simply: a people's survival deeply depends on the stories they tell themselves, the stories they cherish.

Notes

Preface

1. Leavis's series in *Scrutiny*, "The Novel as Dramatic Poem," examined "St. Mawr," *The Rainbow*, and *Women in Love*.

2. Moynahan, *Deed of Life*, 175.

3. Spilka makes the point in "Lawrence Up-Tight" (252–67), a review of Clarke's *River of Dissolution*.

4. Sagar's recent work, *Lawrence: A Calendar*, answers the need.

5. As Cambridge University Press continues its project of publishing the complete works of Lawrence, readers will have ready access to the manuscript material now located mainly at the universities in Austin, Tex., Berkeley, Calif., Tulsa, Okla., and Nottingham, England. Sagar's *Lawrence: A Calendar* and my notes give the present location of the known manuscripts.

6. Gullason notes the general deprecation of short fiction in comparison to long. While his observation, made in the late 1960s, remains partly true, important work on short fiction has been done over the last twenty years. Some of it comes out of the studies on narrative done by Russian formalists; some of it responds to the important journal, *Studies in Short Fiction*, begun in 1963 ("The Short Story: An Underrated Art," 13–31).

7. See the series published on the history of English short fiction in *Studies in Short Fiction*. It begins in the summer issue of 1966 with Schlauch's essay on fifteenth and sixteenth century short fiction.

8. In Cowley, *Writers at Work*, 123.

9. Shklovski, "La Construction de la nouvelle et du roman"; Ejxenbaum, "O. Henry and the Theory of the Short Story" (1925); Todorov, *Poetics of Prose*, especially the chapters "Language and Literature," "The Grammar of Narrative" and "Narrative Transformations." Ejxenbaum's emphasis on the presence of the story-teller in the *skaz* (or sketch) calls to mind an aspect of Scholes's

255

description of fabulation in *The Fabulators*. I will also be citing from Schorer's distinctions between sketch and short story as they are delineated in *The Story*, 61–62.

Introduction

1. I use "fabulation" here in the sense Scholes employs it in *The Fabulators*, to speak of fiction that calls attention to itself as verbal performance, as fiction.

2. Schorer, "*Women in Love* and Death," 50–60; Fadiman, "Poet as Choreographer," 60–67.

3. In writing about Lawrence's sexual imagination and his various pronouncements on the right relationship between men and women, Kinkead-Weekes makes this important observation: "One cannot generalize about 'Lawrence's treatment of sexual relationship' at any stage without both superficiality and distortion. One has to try to account intensively for moments, and simultaneously for the fact that they are momentary, partial arrestings of a flowing exploration . . ." ("Eros and Metaphor," 101–21). My view of Lawrence's short fiction, and also his understanding of sexuality, emphasizes the same "flowing exploration" if one adds to that image the sense of a general progress.

4. In America the situation was somewhat different. Stephen Crane was one of the great turn-of-the-century realists, but, in the latter half of the nineteenth century, America's short fiction had been stamped by the altogether different approaches of Melville, Hawthorne, Poe, and Twain.

5. This description follows a general critical tendency to equate the modern short story, as it thrived in the latter part of the nineteenth century and first three decades of the twentieth, with realistic narrative techniques. Certainly Lawrence made that connection. However, a different description is given by Baedeshwiter in "Lyric Short Story," 443–53.

6. Lawrence uses the phrase in a letter to Louie Burrows. See *Lawrence in Love*, ed. Boulton, 44.

7. In Nehls, *Lawrence: A Composite Biography*, vol. 1, 109–10.

8. Williams, *The English Novel*, 140.

9. Lawrence, "Mortality and the Novel," 110–11.

10. Williams, *The English Novel*, 180–84.

11. Friedman, *Turn of the Novel*, chap. 1.

12. See Schorer's introduction to the Grove Press edition of *Lady*

Chatterley's Lover for an interpretation of the novel that emphasizes its fable qualities.

13. The distinction between fiction that primarily presents reality and fiction that primarily assesses it is developed, with all its difficulties, by Watt in "Serious Reflections," 213.

14. O'Connor, *The Lonely Voice*, 17–21.

Chapter 1

1. Lawrence, "Autobiographical Sketch," in *Phoenix II*, 592.

2. My main source of biographical information throughout this study is Moore's *Priest of Love*. I supplement his book with Nehls's *Lawrence: A Composite Biography*, Chambers's *Lawrence: A Personal Record*, Sagar's *Life of D. H. Lawrence*, and the several collections of Lawrence's letters as indicated below.

3. In chapter 2, I discuss the criticisms voiced by Ford and his colleagues at the *English Review*, begun in 1908.

4. Wendell V. Harris, "English Short Fiction," 1–93. In his recent survey of English short stories, Allen concurs with Harris's description of the typical traditional tale. He observes that the traditional short story was a "manifestation of the romance. Its province was the extraordinary; its aim, if not to astonish, was at least to surprise; its purpose, to entertain" (*Short Story in English*, 5). Allen further agrees with Harris in observing that realism came late to English short stories, at least in comparison to the United States, France, and Russia (10).

5. Chambers, *Lawrence: A Personal Record*, 114.

6. The first version of "The White Stocking" is in a private collection. Cushman kindly let me see a copy. Other important versions are the 1913 revision published by *Smart Set* and the collected text published in *The Prussian Officer*.

7. The Humanities Research Center in Austin, Texas, owns a seven-page holograph entitled "The Vicar's Garden." The University of California at Berkeley owns two six-page carbon typescripts which follow the holograph. Chambers identified the setting of the tale as Robin Hood's Bay, a place she and Lawrence had visited (Delavenay, *Lawrence: The Man and His Work*, 193). As companion to his book, Delavenay published the documents upon which much of his study rests: *Lawrence: L'homme et la genese*. Chambers' reference to Robin Hood's Bay is on page 694.

8. Humanities Research Center holograph, 7.

9. The Humanities Research Center owns an eight-page holograph of "Legend." A six-page, incomplete holograph is in a private collection. The University of Nottingham owns a twenty-six-page holograph, which is the 1911 revision published in the *English Review*. Carbon typescripts of the original "Legend" are at the University of California at Berkeley and at the University of New Mexico. I will be citing from the holograph at Texas.

10. The Humanities Research Center owns a thirteen-page typescript of "A Prelude," entitled "An Enjoyable Christmas: A Prelude." It constitutes the version published by the *Nottinghamshire Guardian* and available in *Phoenix II*, 3–12.

11. Humanities Research Center holograph, 4.

12. See introduction, n. 3.

13. The Sleeping Beauty motif is frequently cited by Lawrence's critics. In *Priest of Love*, Moore sees it as an element in Lawrence's fiction from beginning to end (393). Gurko sees it as one of the binding elements in Lawrence's collection entitled *The Ladybird* ("Lawrence's Greatest Collection," 173–82). And Millett, in her criticism of Lawrence in *Sexual Politics*, sees it as everpresent evidence of male domination. In an interesting chapter on Lawrence's use of Gothic elements, Wilt offers an important qualification in suggesting that Lawrence's typical heroine is a "Waiting Beauty," a Penelope. While her archetype more closely describes many of Lawrence's heroines, it still obscures their frequently courageous activity (*Ghosts of the Gothic*, 251). That courageous activity and the way it relates to an altogether different myth in Western culture is the subject of a fascinating essay by Hinz and Teunissen, "*Women in Love* and the Myth of Eros and Psyche," 207–20.

14. There are clear exceptions to this wakefulness, especially within the leadership fiction. March, in "The Fox," is a highly contradictory character, but in several respects she does act out the role of Sleeping Beauty. Matilda, in "You Touched Me," initiates Hadrian's interest—she literally awakens him—but once awakened, he becomes sole pursuer. The wrinkle within the Sleeping Beauty myth that one does encounter in the leadership fiction lies in the curious invitation to sleep; the beauties are first awakened, then urged to doze off.

15. In his description of the "flourishing regional culture" that nourished the minds and hearts of Lawrence and his friends, Kermode is representative in overlooking the suffrage movement. He writes that Lawrence's culture "was founded on the chapel, the free library, and a flow of visits from great speakers, often exponents of English socialism" (*D. H. Lawrence*, 5). See also Cushman, *Lawrence at Work*, 11. With his

background on Alice Dax and her circle, Moore is a helpful guide to this aspect of Lawrence's youth.

16. In *Priest of Love*, Moore describes Lawrence's relationship to Alice Dax and quotes from a lively letter sent to Moore by Enid Hopkin Hilton. Her parents were longtime friends of Lawrence; her mother was a strong feminist and good friend of Alice Dax (118). Hilton gives a detailed picture of Dax and of the times.

17. See *Lawrence in Love*, ed. Boulton, 33, 52, 120–21.

18. A key passage in *The White Peacock* recognizes the fear that self-responsibility can inspire in a woman when contrasted to the relative security of defining herself as a "servant of God, of some man, of . . . children, . . . of some cause" (323–24). Lawrence will later explore this issue more fully in "The Thorn in the Flesh." The issue of self-responsibility, of course, is central and complex in *Sons and Lovers*; Lawrence relates the issue to women in general when he writes of Mrs. Morel's engagement in the Women's Guild, an arm of the local labor party (*Sons and Lovers*, chap. 3). Further citations from *The White Peacock* and *Sons and Lovers* will be indicated in the text.

19. A central issue in Lawrence criticism since the late 1960s, however, is the very quality of Lawrence's images of female and male experience. Millett's chapter on Lawrence in *Sexual Politics* (214–24) recalls many of Simone de Beauvoir's radical criticisms in *The Second Sex*. Beauvoir and Millett hit the truth often enough to have inspired a chorus of critics to look more closely into Lawrence's attitudes toward women. Perhaps the best sources to begin with are Smith's collection of essays, *Lawrence and Women*, and Simpson's *Lawrence and Feminism*. I regret not having had access to Simpson's book in time to use it in writing my own study. Among other important essays, see Blanchard, "Love and Power," 431–43; Rossman, "'You Are the Call and I Am the Answer,'" 255–328; Hardy, "Women in D. H. Lawrence's Works," 90–122; Wilt, *Ghosts of the Gothic*, especially 249–76; Janice H. Harris, "D. H. Lawrence and Kate Millett," 522–29. Other essays on specific topics dealing with Lawrence and women are cited below.

20. Cushman speaks of "A Prelude" as "the only innocuous story among the three submitted" and suggests that we see here a prophecy of Lawrence's "lifetime of difficulties with the reading public" (*Lawrence at Work*, 28). Similarly, Sagar considers "A Prelude" to be "the worst of the three" ("Notes from a Calendar," 32). My sense of the tale is that, given the times, it is more consistently innovative than the others, in spite of its admitted sentimentality.

21. Allen, *Short Story in English*, 5.

Chapter 2

1. For a fine description of Lawrence's three years at Davidson Road School see the reminiscences of A. W. McLeod and Philip F. T. Smith in Moore, *Priest of Love*, 89–96. See also Lawrence's two autobiographical sketches of the time, "Lessford's Rabbits" and "A Lesson on the Tortoise" in *Phoenix II*.

2. *Letters of D. H. Lawrence*, vol. 1, ed. Boulton, 139.

3. *English Review* (December 1908), 159. In a collection of the best stories from the *Review*, published in 1932, Ford Madox Ford makes the different point that good writers in the first decade of the century had no outlets for their work. "The cheaper periodicals published short stories so badly constructed, so oleaginous, and so ill-written that if ever by accident I came across them I always used to think that I was ready publicity for somebody's hair oil. So the short story writer had absolutely nowhere to go." *English Review Book of Short Stories*, viii.

4. *English Review*, 176.

5. *English Review*, 162.

6. Often in 1909, Louie sent Lawrence tales which he criticized or rewrote. "Goose Fair" was undeniably a shared effort, but neither Lawrence's letters nor the holograph at the University of Nottingham library reveal what his contributions were. (See *Lawrence in Love*, ed. Boulton, 44, 46, 50). The story was published under Lawrence's name in the *English Review* of February 1910. In the tale's attempt to evoke a historical atmosphere (the economic crisis of 1871) its reliance on a plot reversal, its lack of sustained interest in character development or confrontation, its emphasis on the heroine's superior manners and culture, and its distance from Lawrence's own experience, "Goose Fair" is unlike anything Lawrence wrote after he had moved to Croydon. In Will and Lois for example, we get nothing approaching the psychological complexity of Elizabeth Bates in "Odour of Chrysanthemums." One senses Lawrence's touch most clearly in the tale's images, as of the goose girl and her lamentable flock or of the Selby's lace factory in lurid flames.

7. In general, two contrasting ways to deal with Lawrence's revisions present themselves: revisions can be discussed alongside the original; or, with equal logic, they can be discussed within the period they were composed, often two or three years after the original. At different times, it has seemed to me that one or the other approach has advantages over the alternative. In chapter 1, aiming for a clear description of Lawrence's beginnings, I chose to discuss only the original

versions of the tales. Moreover, the changes Lawrence made in his Eastwood stories were so thorough that separating the original from the revision does not create a misleading breach in the analysis of the tale. By contrast, in examining the Croydon stories, I have followed the opposite method, looking at each tale and its revisions within one discussion. Here, the revisions are closely tied to the original; they may give it a whole new reading—as in "Odour of Chrysanthemums"—but the interrelationships among the texts are dynamic and intimate. In later chapters, I continue to alternate between the approaches, depending on the context. Readers interested in pursuing the nature of Lawrence's early revisions should consult Cushman's *Lawrence at Work*. The detailed work done by him as well as by Boulton, Kalnins, Sagar, Littlewood, and others has not only influenced my understanding of the early work but also shaped my focus in the first four chapters of this book. Not wanting to repeat their work, I do not discuss Lawrence's revisions per se but analyze aspects of them appropriate to my argument. See n. 1 below.

8. Schorer has made the early drafts of Lawrence's novel accessible in *Sons and Lovers: A Facsimile.*

9. Williams, *The English Novel,* 140.

10. The Humanities Research Center owns a six-page holograph of an early version of "Odour of Chrysanthemums" and a thirty-nine-page holograph, the latter being Louie Burrows's fair copy, done in 1911. The University of Nottingham owns the thirty-five pages of corrected proof sheets from the *English Review.* With the proofs are eight pages of corrections and additions too extensive for Lawrence to have included on the sheets. Readers interested in the story should also compare the tale with Lawrence's play on the same subject, "The Widowing of Mrs. Holroyd," written in 1914.

11. Boulton, "Lawrence's 'Odour of Chrysanthemums,'" 4–48; Cushman, *Lawrence at Work,* 47–76; Littlewood, "Lawrence's Early Tales," 107–24; Kalnins, "The Three Endings," 471–79; Moynahan, *Deed of Life,* 181–85. Kalnins argues persuasively against Boulton's view of the revisions as leading to a powerful image of mother love. Kalnins, Cushman, and Littlewood all emphasize the links between the 1914 text and *The Rainbow.* Cushman makes the point that none of *The Prussian Officer* tales is a "child" of the novel, since all were revised *before* the novel took final form. Neither are they "parents"; rather, they and the novel are aspects of a remarkable period of growth in Lawrence's life.

12. Moynahan, *Deed of Life,* 182.

13. Boulton, "Lawrence's 'Odour of Chrysanthemums,'" 44.

14. Ibid., 43.

15. Hudspeth offers a careful reading of the way in which the details of the first half of the tale foreshadow the theme of isolation and longing in the second half. His analysis is sound but understates, I feel, the victory that lies within the defeat of Elizabeth Bates. See "Isolation and Paradox," 630–36.

16. *Sons and Lovers: A Facsimile*, ed. Schorer, intro., 2.

17. Indeed, Jessie explained that the story was a direct transcript of an event in her and Lawrence's relationship. Delavenay, *Lawrence: L'homme et la genese*, 702. No manuscripts of the 1909 version are known to exist. The New York Public Library owns a fifty-six-page holograph of "A Modern Lover." Identical to the published text, it is probably Lawrence's 1912 revision. That it is not Lawrence's original 1909 story is clear from Jessie Chambers's remarks: "'A Modern Lover' D. H. L. showed me in December 1909. That was the first and quite different version; I'm sure he never intended it to be published" (Ibid., 694). Lawrence does not mention the tale in gathering and revising his tales in 1913 and 1914.

18. Sagar, "'The Best I Have Known,'" 146.

19. Lawrence inserts a note of irony through the names of each of his intellectual heroes in this trio. In "Second Best" he calls his hero Jimmy Barrass; in "The Soiled Rose" he is John Addington Syson, whose name echoes John Addington Symonds, a nineteenth-century scholar known for his homosexuality. Lawrence may see the ironic possibilities in his intellectual heroes but he does not approach a fully sustained, coherent, ironic portrayal of these heroes until he switches locale and basic situation, as he does in "The Old Adam" and "The Witch à la Mode," or until he writes the final version of "The Soiled Rose"/"The Shades of Spring."

20. Daleski in *The Forked Flame* (42–48) does an excellent job of analyzing the warp between scene and analysis in *Sons and Lovers*.

21. Spilka, *Love Ethic*, 43.

22. "Second Best" was probably written in April 1911; the *English Review* published it in February 1912, and Lawrence collected it in *The Prussian Officer*. There are few changes between the original holograph, the *English Review*, and *Prussian Officer* texts. Most come between the magazine and collected versions, occur in the tale's last lines, and emphasize Tom's passion for Frances and her awareness of what she will win and lose in tying her fortunes to his. The University of Nottingham owns the fourteen-page holograph of the original "Second Best."

23. Lawrence, *John Thomas and Lady Jane*, 233.

24. Lawrence may have written the tale as early as June 1911.

In that month, he tells Louie Burrows that he has just written a thirty-two-page short story (*Lawrence in Love*, ed. Boulton, 113). Sagar believes this may refer to "Two Marriages" (*Lawrence: A Calendar*, 20). Sagar may be right but Lawrence refers directly to writing "Two Marriages" on July 16 (*Lawrence in Love*, ed. Boulton, 121). The only other likely possibility for the June reference is "The Soiled Rose." We know from his letters that he either wrote or rewrote the story in December 1911 while convalescing from pneumonia (*CL*, 206). No holograph has been found, though. A corrected typescript also titled "The Right Thing to Do: The Only Thing to be Done," is at the New York Public Library. On it, Lawrence made several, minor, interlinear revisions before having it set up in proofs for *Forum*. At the Nottinghamshire County Libraries are corrected page proofs entitled "The Dead Rose." These I have not seen but comparison of typescript and published text suggest that the corrections were minor. *Forum* accepted the tale in March 1912, and published it with minor revisions in March 1913. The *Blue Review* published the same version in May 1913. During the fall of 1914, Lawrence revised it in significant ways for *The Prussian Officer*, retitling it "The Shades of Spring." The key versions are those published in *Forum* and *The Prussian Officer*.

25. Further references to the *Forum* edition will be indicated in the text.

26. See Cushman's discussion of Lawrence's copying Maurice Greiffenhagen's painting, "The Idyll." Showing a powerful man in animal skins embracing a Victorian maiden, it visually depicts the main action of the tale's last scene. Lawrence made two copies of the painting and commented on its power several times (*Lawrence at Work*, 132–34).

27. Cushman notes the parallels between this scene and a similar scene in Hardy's *Under the Greenwood Tree*. He adds that Lawrence characteristically alters the scene to make his heroine something of a vampire; yet here, it would seem, Hilda is putting off the gamekeeper ("Lawrence's Use of Hardy," 402–04).

28. For a good analysis of Lawrence's ambivalence toward the rival gamekeeper, see Sagar, "'The Best I Have Known,'" 148–49.

29. As I read the revisions, the tale gains in coherence and insight. For a different view, see Littlewood, "Lawrence's Early Tales," 124.

30. At least two recent critics judge "A Fragment of Stained Glass" more positively. Analyzing the 1914 version, Baim sees Lawrence contrasting "cautious modern society" with the more passionate society of the fifteenth century and judges it an "excellent gothic tale" ("Past and Present," 323–26). Baker, presenting a convincing case for

Lawrence's echoing Pater's "Denys L'Auxerrois" in *Imaginary Portraits*, terms the narrative strategy "ingenious" ("By the Help of Certain Notes," 317–26). Lawrence himself judged the tale more critically as "a bit of tour de force, which I don't care for" (*Lawrence in Love*, ed. Boulton, 126).

31. In a provocative overview of Lawrence's wide-ranging use of myth throughout his fiction, Vickery sees the bloodstone in "A Fragment of Stained Glass" as a talisman or amulet. He notes the power of the stone to protect the serf but also its function as "a place of self-keeping for [the] soul" (*Literary Impact of "The Golden Bough,"* 308). He does not comment on the odd conjunction between the serf's apparent loss and subsequent power. Vickery's chapter on Lawrence is an expansion of his essay, "Myth and Ritual," 65–82.

32. One of the best discussions of Lawrence's sexual ambivalence is Spilka's analysis in "Lessing and Lawrence," 218–40. Among many affinities he points out, Spilka sees Doris Lessing and Lawrence as extremely sensitive to the ways in which love can both jeopardize and nourish the self (239).

33. Widmer's *Art of Perversity* first mapped out this road to Lawrence. More recent studies include Kermode's *D. H. Lawrence* and his essay "Lawrence and the Apocalyptic Types," 14–38. See also Clarke's *River of Dissolution*. Spilka responds to Clarke in "Lawrence Up-Tight," 252–67. Clarke, Kermode, and George Ford answer in "Critical Exchange," 54–70. Lerner addresses the issue from the perspective of the irrationality of fascism in his chapter on Lawrence in *The Truthtellers*, esp. 230–33. Also recommended are Friedman's "The Other Lawrence," 239–53, and George Ford's chapter on *Women in Love* in *Double Measure*, 163–207.

34. A twenty-seven-page holograph of "The Old Adam" is currently in a private collection. I was not able to see it; according to Sagar, no other versions exist. For "The Witch à la Mode," two holographs exist, one titled "Intimacy," the other "The White Woman." These as well as a corrected typescript are owned by Bucknell University. A carbon typescript entitled "The Witch à la Mode" is owned by the University of California at Berkeley. This last item constitutes the published text. The revisions one sees between the two holographs and between the holographs and the published text are many but do not significantly alter the tale. See n. 37 below.

35. The maid's dismissal forms the subject of the tale's first and last lines; it is clear that she is being sent away because the Thomases consider her too bold, too free. Constituting a frame around the tale's

main action, her dismissal implies that the Thomases are the repressive forces that keep the Old Adam locked up or locked out. But to declare they hold overly civilized codes does not exempt Severn from a similar charge.

36. Reading Lawrence's fiction through the lenses of Freudian analysis, Weiss interprets Severn's attack on Mr. Thomas (like Paul's on Baxter Dawes) as the son's attack upon the father, followed in each case by voluntary castration or submission. The son will give up the older man's wife (*Oedipus in Nottingham*, 91). Weiss emphasizes the homoerotic attachment Severn feels for Thomas; I am underscoring the saving taboo and pointing out the parallels in the tale's three semisexual encounters.

37. "Intimacy," from 1911, is the first version of "The Witch à la Mode." It gives us a heroine named Margaret, who is not much different from the eventual Winifred. In "The White Woman," done in the summer of 1913, Lawrence gives some background to the heroine, now called Winifred. Her father was a Wesleyan clergyman, her mother a stiff-necked soul. In conjunction with this background, Lawrence "sums up" Winifred's cool sexlessness. Lawrence excised this biographical background and character summary from the holograph, leaving a version substantially the same as the one we now read. See n. 34 above.

38. Wendell V. Harris, "English Short Fiction," 62.

39. Ibid.

40. Sagar suggests that Lawrence may have begun the tale in June 1911 and returned to it in July (*Lawrence: A Calendar*, 21). Lawrence's letters to Louie Burrows on July 15 and 16 argue for July as the beginning date; his letter to her on June 14 suggests June (*Lawrence in Love*, ed. Boulton, 121, 113). Two holographs are in a private collection: an incomplete, early one of twenty-three pages that is untitled, and a complete one of forty-five pages, titled "Two Marriages," which Sagar describes as "a second draft," close to the version published by *Time and Tide* on March 24, 1934. The University of California at Berkeley owns two identical carbon typescripts of forty-four pages each. These constitute a revision of the second version and comprise the incomplete text published by *Time and Tide*. A third holograph and corrected typescript of fifty-eight pages, also in private collection, make up a complete third version.

41. Cushman, *Lawrence at Work*, chap. 4; Kalnins, "Lawrence's 'Two Marriages' and 'Daughters of the Vicar,'" 32–49.

42. Lawrence, *The First Lady Chatterley*, xiii.

43. Tentative conclusions become, in fact, a hallmark of

Lawrence's work from 1912 on. Whereas the Eastwood and Croydon tales often close with some definitive statement or image prophesying the future, the later tales often end with a question. For good analyses of the openness of Lawrence's fiction, see Friedman, *Turn of the Novel*; Lodge, *Novelist at the Crossroads*; and Engleberg, "Escape from the Circles of Experience," 103–13.

44. The phrase is Scholes's. In *The Fabulators* he sees this as one of the elements of the new, antirealistic mode of fiction (10). Vivas makes a strong argument against the highly designed structure of "Daughters of the Vicar." Emphasizing the ease with which Louisa condemns Mr. Massy, Vivas finds this tale like much of Lawrence's art, propagandistic (*Lawrence: The Failure and the Triumph of Art*, 165–67).

Chapter 3

1. From the beginning, Frieda was more tentative about their affair than Lawrence, but he too had to grow into the conviction that she was his mate for life. Thus he writes to Garnett, "Mrs. Weekley is going to Germany on the 4th of May. I want to go then, because we could have at least one week together" (*Letters of D. H. Lawrence*, ed. Boulton, vol. 1, 386).

2. Schorer, *The Story*, 61–62.

3. No manuscripts of "The Miner at Home" have survived. The story was published in *Nation*, March 6, 1912, and is reprinted in *Phoenix*.

4. See *Lawrence in Love*, ed. Boulton, 52, 120–21. Gissing's *The Odd Women* and Schreiner's *Women and Labour* are radical analyses of women and work, each emphasizing the need for equal pay and equal opportunity. Both recognize the shrinking of an authentic social need for large families and basic domestic labor, and both see the diminishing social status that kind of work commanded. Important to "The Miner at Home," each author names and eloquently describes the danger of female parasitism that results from women losing their former fields of labor. It is a condition Gertie fully recognizes as she accuses Bower of assuming she does no work, of believing that the money he gives her each week to run the house is somehow a gift. In "Her Turn," one sees some of the same issues raised. Clearly the specific issue of women's work interested Lawrence, but in general the issue is complicated by his response to the subject of paid work in general. Few

of the characters in his major fictions work in the world without becoming corrupted. His true heroes and heroines tend to get by on small, independent incomes. Thus Millett's point that in none of Lawrence's fictions do we see women work is more complex than she recognizes. Men also do not "work." The one exception to Lawrence's nonsexist discomfort with careers and professions comes in "Mother and Daughter." There he does trot out a lamentable list of clichés about women's native incapacity to work.

5. Sagar reports an unlocated ten-page holograph of "Her Turn" in his *Lawrence: A Calendar*, 216. Originally titled "Strike Pay I," "Her Turn" came out as a companion piece to "Strike Pay" (titled "Ephraim's Half-Sovereign") in the *Saturday Westminster Gazette*, September 6 and 13, 1913, respectively. At one point the stories were called "Strike Pay I" and "Strike Pay II." Both were collected in *A Modern Lover* in 1933.

6. See n. 5 above. A fifteen-page holograph of "Strike Pay" is in a private collection.

7. For a good discussion of the use of present tense in fiction, see Pascal, "Tense and Novel," 1–11.

8. Nehls, *Lawrence: A Composite Biography*, vol. 1, 109–10.

9. In a private collection are an eleven-page holograph and two-page corrected galley proof of "A Sick Collier." The story was published in *New Statesman*, September 13, 1913; it is the only one of the strike stories to have been included in *The Prussian Officer*. Lawrence did not revise the magazine text for the collection.

10. *Letters of D. H. Lawrence*, ed. Boulton, vol. 1, 345; Sagar, *Lawrence: A Calendar*, 23; Garnett's foreword to Lawrence, *Love among the Haystacks*. The only manuscript material that exists for "Love among the Haystacks" is a sixty-page carbon typescript owned by the University of California at Berkeley. This typescript was apparently done by Douglas Clayton in 1930 from the 1912 manuscript. See Tedlock, *Lawrence Manuscripts*, 42–43.

11. For further general discussions of Lawrence's homosexuality, see Meyers, "Lawrence and Homosexuality," 68–69; and Weiss, *Oedipus in Nottingham*. Other specific analyses are noted below.

12. The University of California at Berkeley owns an eleven-page holograph of "Delilah and Mr. Bircumshaw." It is incomplete, comprising pages 9 to 19, beginning in the middle of the tale and running through the conclusion. The Humanities Research Center owns a complete typescript of the published version. Lawrence's agent, Curtis Brown, had circulated this typescript after Lawrence's death, returning it

to Frieda in January 1939. In April 1940, the *Virginia Quarterly Review* finally published the story. Roberts and Moore include it in *Phoenix II*. Comparison of holograph and typescript indicates that Lawrence revised the story in the summer of 1913 or 1914, though not in major ways.

13. The plight of the physically strong and energetic man in modern society, which demands increasingly less physical labor to produce its necessities, is another issue Lawrence would have met in Schreiner's *Women and Labour*.

14. Spilka emphasizes, by contrast, the kinetic quality of Lawrence's vision, drawing on Ernst Cassirer's distinction between the infinite and the indefinite, the former being the upper limit of language and pointing to a static absolute, the latter being a lower limit, pointing to a kinetic mana concept. Spilka's point is that when Lawrence pushes his language to the limits of verbal experience, he is approaching the "indefinite," the quick and shifting energy of mana or theos (*Love Ethic*, 12–15).

15. The 1912, nine-page holograph of "The Christening," the only manuscript in existence, is at the Humanities Research Center. In a letter to Garnett on July 16, 1913, Lawrence says that he has just had the tale typed up and has revised the ending. In fact the holograph with its several crossed-out titles—"Pat a Cake, Pat a Cake," "Baker's Man," "A Bag of Cakes"—ends the same as the *Smart Set* version, published in February 1914. With minor revisions, especially toward the end, Lawrence included the tale in *The Prussian Officer*. The story is based on the indiscretions of one of Lawrence's friends, George Neville. Lawrence may have first written about the situation as a comic drama, "The Married Man" (*Letters of D. H. Lawrence*, ed. Boulton, vol. 1, 386).

16. Cushman, *Lawrence at Work*, 216.

17. Chambers, *Lawrence: A Personal Record*, 35.

18. A thirteen-page holograph of "Once" is at the Humanities Research Center. A carbon typescript of fourteen pages is at the University of California at Berkeley. The texts show no revisions. In the holograph one does see several sentences bracketed, presumably for their "hot" content. Published in *Love among the Haystacks* and reprinted in *Phoenix II*, the printed versions ignore the brackets, giving an unexpurgated text.

19. In October 1916, Lawrence entirely rewrote "The Mortal Coil." Because the 1912–1913 manuscript has been lost, I will discuss the tale in chapter 5.

20. Yarmolinsky, *The Portable Chekhov*, 27.

Chapter 4

1. Lawrence uses the phrase in his "Study of Thomas Hardy," *Phoenix*, 406. Sagar's *Lawrence Handbook* provides a miscellany of helpful background information on Lawrence and includes a thematic index to *Phoenix* and *Phoenix II* by Damian Grant. Readers interested in Frieda's biography should consult Robert Lucas, *Frieda Lawrence*; Green, *The von Richthofen Sisters*; Frieda Lawrence, *Memoirs and Correspondence*, ed. Tedlock; and Frieda Lawrence, "*Not I, but the Wind. . . .*"

2. For at least one critic, the terrors of threatened identity are Lawrence's main subject. See Marguerite Beede Howe, *Art of the Self*. Howe argues that, in each of his novels, Lawrence sets up an image of the self that tries, unsuccessfully, to wrestle with the demands of alien reality. I would agree with her emphasis on this issue in Lawrence, but not with her view that Lawrence never succeeded in establishing an adequate self nor that reality in Lawrence is generally alien. In the stories of 1913, the failure to establish a secure identity is indeed the outcome, but in the stories Lawrence wrote during the war the very opposite is the case.

3. These comments are often read as referring to *The Sisters*. As Sagar makes clear, the sequence of Lawrence's remarks indicates that he is speaking about *The Insurrection of Miss Houghton* (*Lawrence: A Calendar*, 37).

4. In his *Lawrence: A Calendar*, Sagar places the writing of "New Eve and Old Adam" in July 1913, after Lawrence and Frieda had arrived in England (41). My placing its composition in June is based on Lawrence's letter to Garnett, June 10, 1913. In it Lawrence mentions having written three tales, two of which are "The Prussian Officer" and "Vin Ordinaire"/"The Thorn in the Flesh." Referred to as a "good, autobiographical story," the third seems more likely to be "New Eve and Old Adam" than "The Dead Rose" (one of the names Lawrence used for "The Soiled Rose"/"The Shades of Spring"), as Sagar speculates. Garnett and Lawrence had discussed "The Soiled Rose" several months before (*CL*, 182). Lawrence would not speak of it as new in July. Further, there is ample internal evidence to infer the autobiographical dimension to "New Eve and Old Adam."

5. See Cushman for an analysis of Lawrence's other 1913 revisions, the most important of which are those he did on "Two Marriages"/"Daughters of the Vicar" (*Lawrence at Work*). Lawrence also may have written "The Primrose Path" during this visit to England in

1913. It is clear that he wrote the tale after he had met Frieda, because running along the margin of one of the holograph sheets, beneath Lawrence's penned-in words, is Frieda's signature, once in cursive, once in Gothic characters. In "The Mortal Coil," a contemporary tale, Marta Hohenest similarly doodles. Sagar's date of July 1913, is a likely supposition. A curiously flat tale, "The Primrose Path" is apparently a character sketch of Lawrence's maternal uncle. A young man meets up with his uncle, a cabby in London. Together they drive out to see the boy's aunt, who is dying of throat cancer and living apart from the uncle. Upon returning to the uncle's dreary home, the boy meets his uncle's young mistress and her mother. As the young woman and uncle disappear into a bedroom, leaving the boy and the mother awkwardly standing there, we feel ourselves equally left awkwardly. It seems to be a story about shallow sensuality and a guilt-ridden marriage, but its overall intention or point is unclear. The story found no magazine publisher but was eventually included in Lawrence's second volume of stories, *England, My England*. A holograph of twenty-one pages is at the University of Nottingham. At the Humanities Research Center are a twenty-one-page corrected typescript and a twenty-five-page corrected typescript and carbon copy.

    6. Cushman urges us to see Lawrence's 1914 revisions on *The Prussian Officer* stories as one of the key artistic activities leading to his maturity. My emphasis here on the breakthrough represented by the stories of 1913 is not intended to deny the significance of the 1914 work but, partly by looking at material that never got into *The Prussian Officer*, to fortify the argument for Lawrence's continual exploration in his short fiction.

    7. The University of Tulsa owns a fourteen-page holograph of "New Eve and Old Adam." The University of California at Berkeley owns two carbon typescripts. Comparison of holograph, typescripts, and published version shows no revisions.

    8. Delavenay, *The Man and his Work*, 191.

    9. Spilka, "Lawrence Up-Tight," 252–67.

    10. In her biographical introduction to *Lawrence and Women*, Smith discusses Lawrence's lifelong difficulties with his own sexual identity and corresponding difficulties relating to women. Her analysis of the problems is often sound, but missing from it is any sense that Lawrence was usually aware of those difficulties, that he himself continually provided us with moving analyses. For example, to quote passages from "New Eve and Old Adam" and not give Lawrence credit for setting forth the very problem under discussion is unfair ("'A New

Adam and a New Eve,'" 9–48). As Blanchard writes, "either through ridicule or through a serious examination of the opposite point of view . . . Lawrence was his own best critic" ("Portrait,") 277–85. In connection with the tale's title, Lawrence's letter to John Middleton Murry strengthens the sense of Paula having much right on her side: "Frieda and I have finished the long and bloody fight at last, and are at one. It is a fight one has to fight—the Old Adam to be killed in me, the Old Eve in her—then a New Adam and a New Eve" (*CL*, 479).

11. "New Eve and Old Adam" was published posthumously in *A Modern Lover*.

12. See n. 28 in chapter 5.

13. Cushman, *Lawrence at Work*, 209.

14. As the holograph of "The Prussian Officer" (at the Humanities Research Center) indicates, Lawrence's first version of the tale is essentially the same as that collected a year later for *The Prussian Officer*. The *English Review* text of August 1914 comprises an intervening version and shows a fair number of editorial cuts. These cuts were not done by Lawrence nor with his knowledge. (See Lawrence's letter to Pinker from September 15, 1914, in *Letters of D. H. Lawrence*, ed. Boulton, vol. 2, 216.) The deletions usually consist of dropping whole paragraphs or the latter halves of long ones. Often the excised passages are analytical, stating what Lawrence has already shown. At other times they contain brief dramatic scenes; in one instance, a necessary stage direction is lost. In general, however, the magazine version reads coherently and has a strong impact. It simply lacks fullness of development.

15. Widmer, *Art of Perversity*, 10. Through his book, Widmer emphasizes Lawrence's yearning for extremity, for a culmination of experience that will end experience. Friedman argues for our seeing this issue differently. The damned in Lawrence do yearn for finality; the saved refuse it (*Turn of the Novel*, chap. 6). Friedman's view is particularly appropriate to "The Prussian Officer."

16. Cushman, *Lawrence at Work*, 170–71. His reading of the tale as a study in oppositions is the most widely accepted view. See, for example, Amon, "Lawrence and the Short Story," 229–31; Kaplan, *The Passive Voice*, 163–67; Adelman, "Beyond the Pleasure Principle," 8–15.

17. Englander agrees with the "opposition" approach but then judges the tale as incoherent ("The Self Divided," 605–19). For West, the tale is about "a particularly German kind of hysterical violence" ("The Short Stories," 215). Scott does a more subtle analysis of the tale

as a reflection of Lawrence's thinking about Germany in "Lawrence's Germania," 142–64. Weiss sees the tale as an important plateau in Lawrence's dramatization of the Oedipal conflict and homoeroticism as it clearly expresses the attraction and terrors that hover in the background of earlier works (*Oedipus in Nottingham*, 91–95). Following up on Weiss's work, Sale draws interesting parallels between the Paul Morel-Baxter Dawes relationship and the officer and orderly. For him, the officer represents the conscious Lawrence who is shocked by his homosexual passions and seeks to obliterate them—within the story, that is—in "sleep, drink, and ultimately in death" (*Modern Heroism*, 46).

18. Cushman, *Lawrence at Work*, 170–71.

19. In *Ghosts of the Gothic*, Wilt offers a discussion of place in Lawrence in which she describes the mountains of "The Prussian Officer" in terms similar to mine (282). Her analysis of the tale also draws attention to the sun and shadow imagery and the way it dramatizes the two men's battle for being.

20. Allen and Draper call attention to the captain's inability to understand what is happening to himself and his consequent helplessness. See Allen, *Short Story in English*, 99–100; and Draper, *D. H. Lawrence*, 124.

21. The story was published in *Smart Set*, March 1914. The existing manuscripts are of the first version, "The Vicar's Garden." See n. 7 in chapter 1.

22. In *Poem of the Mind*, Martz praises the way Lawrence develops the garden image in this tale. In his view, the garden stands for a beautiful, irretrievable past (111–13). I would agree but would emphasize the sense of foreboding Lawrence evokes in the garden and its burden of memories: this way lies madness. T. S. Eliot uses the story in his discussion of heresy as a prime example of Lawrence's tendency to create characters totally lacking "any moral or social sense" (*After Strange Gods*, 38–40). As Lawrence himself declared, he was not interested in developing characters according to established moral schemes; for Eliot, no other kind of morality is worthy of the name.

Chapter 5

1. Delavenay presents evidence to suggest that *The Rainbow* was banned more for its antimilitarism than for its sexual passages (*The Man and His Work*, 235–42). Delany questions that evidence in his book on Lawrence's life in England during the war. He returns to the original

argument that the sexual material, especially the lesbianism, was the main cause of the suppression. Delany believes that Lawrence was too minor a figure in the anti-war movement to have had his book attacked on the grounds of military security (*Lawrence's Nightmare*, 158).

2. Nehls, *Lawrence: A Composite Biography*, vol. 1, 225.

3. Delavenay, *The Man and His Work*, 207. Delaney's study gives a fuller account of Lawrence's thinking during the war.

4. Frye, *Anatomy of Criticism*, 208–10.

5. See Schorer for a clear analysis of the link between character, choice, and destiny in "*Women in Love* and Death," 51.

6. In emphasizing the war fiction as a "kick at tragedy" rather than an expression of despair, I am going against accepted readings of these 1914–1916 works. Tedlock, for example, sees "England, My England" as expressing, in part, Lawrence's "agony of hopelessness," his "temptation to despair" (*Lawrence: Artist and Rebel*, 107–9).

7. Littlewood, "Lawrence's Early Tales," 111. See also Kalnins, "Lawrence's 'Two Marriages' and 'Daughters of the Vicar,'" (39); and Cushman, "'I Am Going through a Transition Stage'" (176–97) for further analyses of this changing focus in Lawrence and the subsequent stylistic changes.

8. Cushman indicates that the *Smart Set* version was written in 1911 (*Lawrence at Work*, 149). I believe that this is unlikely for two reasons. Sagar records Lawrence having "The White Stocking" typed up afresh and sent to James Pinker, his agent, in August 1913. Pinker apparently placed it at *Smart Set* where it came out in October 1914. Since Lawrence was revising many of his tales that summer, it is probable that he also revised this one. (*Lawrence: A Calendar*, 43). Arguing with equal persuasiveness that the *Smart Set* version is based on a 1913 text is the quality of the marital quarrel that forms the tale's climax. The same fury, jealousy, and love that characterize the autobiographical love poems in *Look! We Have Come Through!* characterize the climax of "The White Stocking." One feels that Lawrence could not have written the scene before he had met and lived with Frieda from March 1912 on.

9. Cushman interprets Lawrence's intentions in the dance scene differently. He sees Elsie as similar to the child, Anna, in *The Rainbow* when she finally stops crying and "flows with" her father's tenderness. Cushman is referring to Tom and Anna's scene in the barn the night of Lydia's long labor. But Lawrence never indicates that Anna has become "fused" with her father, that she has lost all independence and sense of her own reality. One of the major images in *The Rainbow* is the arch

created by Tom and Lydia's love, which protects Anna's growing up but allows her independence and freedom to grow. There is an important difference between Anna's relinquishing her grief and terror to accept her step-father's love and Elsie's relinquishing all sense of her own being in response to the advances of her cold and cynical boss. See Cushman's *Lawrence at Work*, 21; or his "The Making of D. H. Lawrence's 'The White Stocking,'" 51–65. ! 973 P 309

10. Delavenay argues that there is no difference. In both "The Prussian Officer" and "The White Stocking," he sees Lawrence as expressing rather than analyzing the link between violence and sex (*The Man and His Work*, 196). An interesting examination of the various kinds of violence in Lawrence's work may be found in Rose, "Physical Trauma," 73–83. Arguing against readers who see pain and brutality as steps toward love and wisdom in Lawrence, Rose cites from the many stories Lawrence wrote that argue the opposite: pain narrows, suffering limits, brutality numbs and animalizes. In general Rose is right; there are instances however—"The White Stocking" is one—when Lawrence does show his characters moving toward fulfillment through pain and physical violence.

11. Whether one admires the last scene or not, it powerfully complements the earlier emblems of redness and whiteness planted throughout "The White Stocking." This is, again, a Valentine's tale. The stockings and pearls that Elsie has received from Sam are emphatically white, but through them Sam is extending a very red valentine, an invitation that is complicitous, adult, and sexual. There is a tone to Valentine's Day that is both playful and sexual, white and red. Similarly, the whiteness of the stocking suggests girlishness, while the stocking itself connotes an intimate scene, even a risqué one. In both versions, the tension between the connotative meanings of redness and whiteness is carefully maintained. In *The Prussian Officer* version, however, Lawrence adds one more powerful image to the general pattern. As Elsie wipes the red blood from her mouth, Lawrence constructs a symbolic gesture that reminds the reader that she is a woman, a wife and not a bride, capable of bearing children, no longer a child herself.

12. In "Love and Power," Blanchard makes a similar point in noting that nowhere in his fiction does Lawrence hold up as admirable that mutilation of humanity, the Angel in the House. Nowhere does he give us an Esther Summerson. It may be shoddy criticism to take advantage of coincidence, but the value of what Lawrence has included in "The White Stocking" is partly indicated by what is left out in the

love poem that follows the tale in *Smart Set*. "The Little Inn at Dromehaire" by Clinton Scollard is a perfect reminder of the sentimentality Lawrence abhorred.

13. In Cushman's reading of the tale, the development of Bachmann is the primary gain of the revisions. Emilie, he argues, is both more developed and, owing to the emphasis on her need to serve, more confusing. I argue that she outgrows her need to serve just as Bachmann outgrows his dependence on the military (Cushman, *Lawrence at Work*, 173–89). Cushman concentrates on the magazine and *Prussian Officer* texts and includes brief comments on the stylistic revisions Lawrence made in October on the *Prussian Officer* proofs, referred to as the Hopkin proofs. See Scott, "Lawrence's Germania" for a brief reading of the tale which highlights its cultural setting (152).

14. "England, My England," was published in the *English Review*, October 1915. With revisions in 1921, it became the title story for Lawrence's second collection of tales. The only manuscript material is five pages of corrected galley proofs, owned by the Nottinghamshire County Libraries.

15. There has been some disagreement about the extent of Lawrence's acquaintance with the Meynell and Lucas families. Moore argues for close acquaintance (*Priest of Love*, 269–70), while Barbara Lucas argues for minimal ("Apropos of 'England, My England,'" 288–93).

16. Vickery urges the "typical" quality of the characters in "England, My England" by looking beyond the specific period of the war years and focusing on Egbert as an archetype of the scapegoat. He sees Lawrence as enacting the myth of the dying god, but satirically ("Myth and Ritual," 71–77). Vickery's analysis, characteristically, alerts us to the ways Lawrence continually adapted his studies in anthropology to his views on contemporary experience.

17. See *Sons and Lovers: A Facsimile*, ed. Schorer especially frag. 2, 32.

18. Lawrence, "'Prologue' to *Women in Love*," 99.

19. Lawrence, "Morality and the Novel," 110.

20. I find myself in disagreement here with a formidable critic of style, David Lodge. In *Modes of Modern Writing*, Lodge selects "England, My England" for an analysis of the way Lawrence skillfully uses imagery, metaphor, and repetition (164–76).

21. Roberts, *Bibliography*, 254.

22. Sagar reports a 244-page holograph of "The Thimble" at Stanford University (*Lawrence: A Calendar*, 261). This is a typographical

error. Stanford owns a twenty-four-page holograph that constitutes the same text printed in *Seven Arts* and *Phoenix II*. The Humanities Research Center owns a fourteen-page typescript that follows the holograph.

23. Although no manuscripts have survived, Lawrence's letters indicate that he revised the tale several times. Beginning it in January 1916, he sent the first part to Pinker that month. The following fall, he returned to it, again sending manuscripts to Pinker, first in November and then in January 1917. Over four years later, on October 26, 1921, he says he has written it once more and is mailing it to Mrs. Carmichael to be typed; this typescript he sends to Curtis Brown in December. (See Roberts's *Bibliography*, 342; and Sagar's *Lawrence: A Calendar*, 115). The tale was published by the *English Review* in April 1922, and collected virtually unchanged in *England, My England*.

24. Lawrence, "Study of Thomas Hardy," in *Phoenix*, 410.

25. Gullason uses the clear evolution of the hero and heroine in "The Horse Dealer's Daughter" to argue in general against Schorer's well-known statement that in novels characters evolve, in short stories, they are revealed. Gullason's point is well taken; a short story must imply rather than fully dramatize the evolving of a character, but, undeniably, that changing—that growing and evolving—frequently occurs ("Revelation and Evolution," 347–56).

26. By reading the tale as another expression of the Sleeping Beauty myth, Junkins misses the many parallels Lawrence develops throughout the story between Mabel and Fergusson's experience. He sees Mabel as a "frog princess," Fergusson as the prince, ignoring the fact that each character has been asleep, that each rescues the other ("Lawrence's 'The Horse Dealer's Daughter,'" 210–13). Cushman speaks of the parallels and sees the work mainly as a subversion of the Cinderella and Sleeping Beauty fairy tales ("Achievement of *England, My England*," 32). His sense of subversion corresponds with my own.

27. Phillips offers a perceptive analysis of the parallels Lawrence draws between the pond and kitchen scenes ("The Double Pattern," 94–97). A difference in our readings is his view that the paired scenes mainly repeat and confirm the fragile union between Mabel and Fergusson. I emphasize that Fergusson is the savior in the pond rescue; Mabel the savior in the kitchen rescue.

28. See Stewart, "Lawrence and the Allotropic Style," for an excellent analysis of the changes Lawrence rings on the verbs of being (217–42).

29. Ryals, "Lawrence's 'The Horse Dealer's Daughter': An Interpretation," 39–43. Among several insights Ryals's reading offers is

also the observation that the tale's light-dark imagery creates a frame of darkness around the central, flame-lit scene in the kitchen.

30. My view of Mabel and Fergusson's progress should not imply a finished quality to the conclusion of the tale. A fine discussion of the openness—the constantly shifting rhythms—in "The Horse Dealer's Daughter" is McCabe's "Rhythm as Form," 64–68. Cushman emphasizes the closing ambiguity or openness in seeing Sam as a man who commits himself without understanding what he is doing ("Achievement of *England, My England*," 32). I read the kitchen rescue as the scene that makes Sam conscious of what he feels.

31. Hough, *The Dark Sun*, 174.

32. The sentiment of those essays is neatly caught in a letter to Katherine Mansfield, November 21, 1918: "Frieda says I am antediluvian in my positive attitude. I do think a woman must yield some sort of precedence to a man, and he must take this precedence. I do think men must go ahead absolutely in front of their women, without turning round to ask for permission or approval from their women. Consequently the women must follow as it were unquestioningly. I can't help it. I believe this. Frieda doesn't. Hence our fight" (CL, 565). I argue that Lawrence does and does not believe it. Hence their continuing marriage, and hence, in part, the complexity of his fiction.

33. "The Blind Man" is set in the vicarage Catherine Carswell owned and loaned to the Lawrences in the summer of 1918. Details in the character of the heroine, Isabel Pervin, are apparently drawn from Mrs. Carswell, a longtime and loyal friend. The tale was first published in the *English Review* in July 1920, and collected with only two minor word changes in *England, My England*. No manuscripts have survived.

34. Ross offers a carefully documented, thoughtful description of the ways Bertie Reid can be taken as a portrait of Bertrand Russell. Arguing that Lawrence's failed friendship with Russell provided "an irritant" to Lawrence's imagination, Ross also shows how Lawrence identified with Pervin. The parallels are interesting and convincing, as is Ross's statement that the tale rises above personal vindictiveness and creates genuine images of sight and blindness ("Mythology of Friendship," 285–315). Ross's emphasis precludes much interest in Isabel; she is simply not a part of his argument. But Meyers, also concentrating on the relationship between Maurice and Bertie, makes a confusing statement about Isabel. "The Blind Man," he feels, is a step toward later works where the woman is excluded. If Meyers's comment is true at all, the tale is a very qualified step. Isabel's presence and actions are central to the tale. Bertie is clearly sought out to complement rather

than supplant Maurice's close relationship with his wife ("Lawrence and Homosexuality," 68).

35. This negative quality to Maurice's blindness cannot be overlooked without entertaining the oversimplification I discussed in looking at "New Eve and Old Adam." Lawrence is not an advocate of any one way of knowing, blood prescience included. When Fadiman, for example, helpfully analyzes Isabel's role in the tale and relates setting, character, and symbol, she misses an important aspect of the tale by judging Maurice as simply positive ("Poet as Choreographer," 60–67). Kaplan sees Maurice as "natural" man; his blindness is simply a blessing as it relieves him from "a cerebral or visual sensibility" (*The Passive Voice*, 161). Fadiman's essay takes off from Spilka's study of ritual form in "The Blind Man." Spilka argues that here, as in much of Lawrence, action is organized around rites of communion, moving the characters toward death or fuller life. Given Spilka's characteristic emphasis on dramatic progress—as opposed to Kaplan's view of Lawrence's fiction as "episodic" and/or "cyclic" (167)—he readily perceives Maurice's starting point, his genuine need to expand his consciousness and to avoid the swamp of pure blood prescience ("Ritual Form," 112–16). Cushman sees the story in more ambiguous terms than Spilka; he argues that the ending is sardonic, that Lawrence is mocking his own beliefs in the value of touch ("Achievement of *England, My England*," 34, 36).

36. In a provocative, Freudian study of "The Blind Man," Wheeler shows how similar Maurice and Bertie's needs are, but he ignores Isabel's needs and dissatisfactions. Tracing an unconscious, Oedipal drama beneath the surface of the tale, Wheeler indicates ways Bertie and Maurice alternately play the roles of father and son as they compete for a fearful and desirable reunification with the mother ("Intimacy and Irony," 236–53). As does Meyers (n. 34 above), Wheeler sees the tale as leading toward later fictions (*Aaron's Rod, Kangaroo*, and *The Plumed Serpent*) which simply exclude the mother and focus on the battles and reconciliations of the father and son. I would argue that even in those fictions and here in "The Blind Man," the woman is a major force.

37. Bloch, "Untangling the Roots," 237.

38. Cavitch, *Lawrence and the New World*, 29.

39. Ibid., 29–30.

40. The view that dualism is a key to Lawrence's thinking is shared by many critics; Travis offers a clear example of that view in "Lawrence: The Blood-Conscious Artist," 163–90. Although there are many passages, especially in Lawrence's letters and essays, which argue for a dichotomous view of consciousness, in his fictions, time and again, it is

multiplicity that is dramatized. As Van Ghent writes, "Both Emily Brontë's and Hardy's worlds are dual, and there is no way of bringing the oppositions of the dualism together. . . . But Lawrence's world is multiple rather than dual. Everything in it is a separate and individual 'other,' every person, every creature, every object . . . and there is a creative relationship between people and between people and things so long as 'otherness' is acknowledged" (*The English Novel*, 252).

41. Not only in actions but also in language, Lawrence echoes John: "Then saith [Jesus] to Thomas, Reach hither thy finger, and behold my hands; and reach hither thy hand, and thrust it into my side: and be not faithless, but believing. And Thomas answered and said unto him, My Lord and my God." John 20:27–28.

42. Lawrence wrote "Samson and Delilah" in Cornwall in the fall of 1916. The thirty-four-page holograph, missing several paragraphs, is at the Humanities Research Center, titled "The Prodigal Husband." The *English Review* published it in March 1917, the *Lantern* in San Francisco in June 1917. With few changes, it was collected in *England, My England*. Revisions done for the volume in 1921 consist of minor word changes which humanize the hero.

43. "Fanny and Annie" was written in the spring of 1919. No manuscript materials have survived. The tale was published by *Hutchinson's Magazine* in November 1921 and collected with minor revisions in *England, My England*. The revisions come midway through the tale. Rewriting parts of the hero's scene as church soloist, Lawrence shifts emphasis from Fanny's shame at Harry's mispronunciations to her emotional fluctuations between desire for Henry and repugnance. The changes work mainly to justify Fanny's eventual decision to stick by this clumsy hero.

44. Mainly arguing for Lawrence's lack of class consciousness, Leavis briefly analyzes "Fanny and Annie" as one more tale in which Lawrence finely dramatizes the main character's choice to live (*Lawrence: Novelist*, 86–90). Secor has picked up on Leavis's positive view of Fanny's choice and demonstrated the way Lawrence's language works to create a mood that moves from deadly familiarity to fresh, new possibilities ("Language and Movement," 395–400). Widmer, against whose stance Secor is arguing, sees the tale as another example of a character's fortunate fall into amoral, asocial eroticism. Harry's very dullness on an intellectual or social level assures his physical, sensual richness. Fanny's fate is to succumb to the imperative of Eros (*Art of Perversity*, 124–26). Cushman agrees ("Achievement of *England, My England*," 32). Here, as elsewhere, I find Widmer too ready to spot an

extremely attractive Eros. Lawrence suggests (a) that Fanny has no viable alternatives and (b) that Harry's eroticism, like the harvest festival, is only a qualified success.

45. "Tickets, Please" was also published by *Strand* in April 1919; with minor revisions, such as changing John Raynor's name to the more obvious John Thomas, it was collected in *England, My England*. No manuscripts have been found.

46. I am emphasizing the balance Lawrence creates between psychic energies men and women share; Wheeler sees a fine balance in the tale also, though between the two poles of the mother-infant unity ("'Cunning in His Overthrow,'" 242–50). For a brief consideration of the way setting helps to dramatize the theme of lawlessness leading to bleakness, see Lainoff, "Wartime Setting," 649–51). Cushman sees the women as the forces of Eros. That seems to me to deny the basis of their conflict with John Thomas ("Achievement of *England, My England*," 31).

47. "The Mortal Coil" was published by *Seven Arts* in 1917 and collected in *Phoenix II*. The only manuscript material that has survived is an eight-page typescript at the Humanities Research Center. It constitues the first part of the tale up to the lieutenant's comment that he will become a waiter. Even where words have been left out, one finds no marks or alterations. With corrections, it parallels the published version.

48. Moore states that the tale is based on an incident that occurred to Frieda's father (*Priest of Love*, 142). Even before Lawrence wrote it in 1913 or 1914, he said it had been on his mind (CL, 229).

49. See for example Mellow, "'The Captain's Doll': Its Origins and Literary Allusions," 227.

50. I am studying "The Mortal Coil" within the context of the 1913–1914 and 1916 fictions. Another perspective on the tale is provided by looking at it as a forerunner to "The Captain's Doll." (See n. 49, above.) As my discussion of both stories indicates, I disagree with Mellow's view that Friedeburg is transformed into a conquering Hepburn while Marta metamorphoses into a passive Hannele.

51. In studying "England, My England" and "The Mortal Coil" as stories written during the war which break with the thematic tendencies of the period, it is important to notice that, within the 1915–1916 stories, these two alone locate their action in a military setting. A pattern emerges here and in the stories to follow. Each time Lawrence explicitly incorporates the war into a story, he tends to urge a basic incompatibility between men and women, a need for men to withdraw

into something not complementary but counter to their relationships with women.

Chapter 6

1. For a good biography of this eccentric patroness of the arts see *Mabel*, by Hahn. See also Luhan, *Lorenzo in Taos*, for Mabel Dodge's view of the years Frieda and Lawrence spent in and about New Mexico.

2. Apart from the general leadership questions raised by all the fiction of these years, no tales speak to *Kangaroo* in any significant way.

3. Cushman has recently argued that *England, My England* is "Lawrence's most outstanding accomplishment as a writer of short stories." It is a unified collection of works characterized by its focus on the war, its tendency to use and then subvert myth and fairy tale, its insistent ambiguity, and its tone of sardonic comedy ("Achievement of *England, My England*," 27–38). My reading of specific stories occasionally disagrees with his, but, more important, I am studying the stories as they came, from early to mid- to postwar, rather than as they stand in the collection of 1922. Our different organizations lead to slightly different generalizations about the body of work.

4. See Janice H. Harris, "Moulting of *The Plumed Serpent*," 154–68.

5. A sixteen-page holograph and twenty-six-page corrected typescript of "Wintry Peacock" exist, the first in a private collection, the second unlocated. The Humanities Research Center owns four pages of corrected proof sheets. Sagar reports that these proof sheets, received by Lawrence from *Metropolitan* in July 1921, were heavily revised (*Lawrence: A Calendar*, 112–13). The texts in *Metropolitan* (August 1921), *The New Decameron* (vol. 3, 1922), and *England, My England* show only one minor difference, the deletion of the word "also" from the last sentence in the *England, My England* text.

6. The significance of Joey and his bedraggled friends has been seen differently: Widmer equates the wintry peacocks with the female forces in the tale, though he then says they do not provide a satisfactory image (*Art of Perversity*, 111). As I do, he finds the tale shallowly misogynist.

7. The essay was entitled "Autobiographical Fragment" by MacDonald, editor of *Phoenix*. Sagar more appropriately calls it "A Dream of Life" (*Life of D. H. Lawrence*, 207, 217). A curious blend of social criticism and dreamscape, it was written in 1927, after Lawrence's

last visit to England. It is unfinished and reads like a variation of the theme of resurrection Lawrence was exploring in May 1927, in "The Escaped Cock"/"The Man Who Died." It also has echoes of the utopian vision found in *The Plumed Serpent*.

8. Lawrence expresses the idea often; in a letter to Gordon Campbell in December 1914, he writes, "All vital truth contains the memory of all that for which it is not true" (*CL*, 300).

9. See Ruderman's detailed description of the three main texts of 1918, 1919, and 1921 ("Tracking Lawrence's *Fox*," 207–21). The 1918 text of "The Fox" is in a private collection but has been published in Lawrence, *Lawrence Miscellany*, ed. Moore, 26–47. The 1919 version is found in *Hutchinson's Magazine*, November 1920. Eight corrected galley sheets for this version are in a private collection. In a letter to Curtis Brown in December 1921, Lawrence says "Nash's Magazine" published the first part of "The Fox" story. Roberts reports that no version of "The Fox" shows up in the one magazine title he found resembling Lawrence's reference, that is, *Nash's Pall Mall Magazine* (*Bibliography*, 342). The 1921 version is available in manuscript at the Humanities Research Center as well as in the published volumes *The Ladybird*, *The Captain's Doll*, and *Four Short Novels*. Ruderman has also tracked down much of the biographical background of the tale. While some of her proposed prototypes are convincing, others, such as Frieda, seem so broadly and generally influential that "prototype" appears at once too weak and too strong a word ("Prototypes," 77–98). Readers interested in the film version of "The Fox," produced by Raymond Stross and directed by Mark Rydell may want to consult Thomas Sobchack, "'The Fox': The Film and the Novel," 73–78. Sobchack finds the film lacking Lawrence's subtle ambiguities. In Sagar's *Lawrence Handbook*, David Gerard lists films and sound recordings related to Lawrence (449–54).

10. Lawrence, *Lawrence Miscellany*, ed. Moore, 46.

11. Ruderman, Pritchard, and Cushman mention but do not develop the relationship between these two tales. See, respectively, "Prototypes," 91; *Lawrence: Body of Darkness*, 140; and "Achievement of *England, My England*," 27.

12. "You Touched Me" was originally called "Hadrian." No manuscript materials exist. It was published under its present title in *Land and Water* in April 1920, and collected, without changes, in *England, My England*. Tennessee Williams and Donald Windham wrote a play based on the tale, which was produced on Broadway in 1945 (Roberts, *Bibliography*, 338).

13. Draper, *D. H. Lawrence*, 124. Lerner disagrees, stating that if

at first the tale looks like a nasty plot, careful reading will show that the unconscious needs of both Hadrian and Matilda have "outwitted" the dreary house (*The Truthtellers*, 206–07). Lerner goes on to contrast Lawrence's subtlety in the tale with Tennessee Williams's vulgar adaptation. Cushman offers still a different view, seeing the tale as sardonic, mocking Lawrence's own belief in the power of touch ("Achievement of *England, My England*," 36).

14. No manuscripts of "Monkey Nuts" have survived. First published in *Sovereign* in August 1922, the story was collected with no changes in *England, My England*.

15. See Harrison, *The Reactionaries*. An equally interesting, though brief, look at the reactionary tendencies in many modern writers is Lerner's analysis in *The Truthtellers*, 230–33. Drawing partly from Trilling's ideas in *The Liberal Imagination*, Lerner observes that the modern, liberal view of humanity is unable to discuss the irrational or mysterious qualities of the psyche, the very forces that are often of deep interest to the artist.

16. A demonstration of these points may be found in Janice H. Harris, "Sexual Antagonism," 43–52.

17. Leavis was one of the first to explore the fine dramatic ironies and the comedy in "The Captain's Doll." See his *Lawrence: Novelist*, 197–224; and *Thought, Words and Creativity*, 92–121.

18. Exploring the literary background of the story, Mellown sees Hannele as typical in a different way. See Mellown, "'The Captain's Doll': Its Origins and Literary Allusions," 226–35. He cites "The Mortal Coil," Gerhart Hauptmann's play *Hanneles Himmelfahrt* (*The Assumption of Hannele*), and general legends of Alexander the Great as literary background for the tale. Understating the comic tone, the strength of Hannele's resistance, and the carefully ambivalent conclusion, Mellown sees Hepburn as developing from the puppetlike Friedeburg of "The Mortal Coil" into a conquering male, a savior. Hannele, he argues, develops from the aggressive Marta into "Lawrence's ideal moon woman, the passive creature who honors and obeys her male" (229).

19. A seventy-seven-page holograph of "The Captain's Doll" is in a private collection. The corrected typescript, owned by Bucknell University, has only typographical corrections; it comprises the published version.

20. Dawson demonstrates the influence of Dr. Trigant Burrow's theory of self-image on Lawrence's portrayal of Hepburn's plight ("Love among the Mannikins," 137–48). Developing a theme found in many of his later works, Lawrence shows Hepburn as attracted to and repulsed by

the doll-like image of himself he encounters through Hannele and his wife. The frightening alternative is an image of an "organismic self," dynamic, fluid (close perhaps to the "theatre of desires" Leo Bersani writes of in *A Future for Astyanax*) and able to honor the changing selves of Hepburn. Dawson's analysis, while very useful, does not sufficiently account for Hannele's need to change nor for that awkward word "obey" in Hepburn's closing vision. While the tale is not a leadership tract arguing starkly for male supremacy, one cannot avoid the fact that it is exploring leadership issues, among them, obedience.

21. Lawrence, *Four Short Novels*, 266.

22. In my emphasis on Hannele's powers of opposition and the tale's open ending, I see the tale as "male supremacist" only in the most qualified of terms. For a different view, see Rossman's "'You Are the Call and I Am the Answer,'" 296–97.

23. Gurko, who sees "The Fox," "The Ladybird," and "The Captain's Doll" as Lawrence's "most brilliant single assemblage of tales," does not view the men as static ("Lawrence's Greatest Collection," 173). He sees the men in each as initially reduced by their respective emblems but growing in freedom and selfhood. To me this is an accurate description of "The Captain's Doll" but not of the other two.

24. The corrected typescript of twenty-nine pages, and hand-written "tail" are at the Humanities Research Center. Ruderman's careful description of the texts in "Tracking Lawrence's *Fox*" notes several articles on the tale that include inaccurate textual information (see n. 9 above).

25. Both Ruderman ("Tracking Lawrence's *Fox*") and Rossi ("Lawrence's Two Foxes," 265–78) see Grenfel as becoming simply more cunning. Ruderman correctly criticizes Rossi's contention that Banford was more benign in the first version than in 1921; Lawrence added benignity to her in his 1921 text, thereby heightening the tale's dramatic tensions.

26. Gregor, "'The Fox': A Caveat," 10–21. Gregor suggests that Lawrence's 1921 additions may have begun with the explanatory passages that follow upon Banford's death. The typescript shows that they begin much earlier, with Henry's proposal. The phrase, "man alive," comes from Lawrence's essay, "Why The Novel Matters," *Selected Literary Criticism*, 102–08.

27. Critics specifically emphasizing the mythic dimensions are Vickery, "Myth and Ritual," 79–82; Gurko, "Lawrence's Greatest Collection," 173–82; Moynahan, *Deed of Life*, 196–208; and Allen, *Short Story in English*, 109. Draper, in *D. H. Lawrence*, finds Henry lively,

necessarily ruthless (126). Ruderman traces the devouring mother motif as well as the dying England perspective in "'The Fox' and the Devouring Mother," 251–69; in "Lawrence's 'The Fox' and Verga's 'The She Wolf,'" 153–65; and in "Tracking Lawrence's *Fox*," 207–21. In an interesting examination of March's male and female tendencies and needs, Brayfield argues for Banford being the exclusively female side of March ("Lawrence's 'Male and Female Principles' and the Symbolism of 'The Fox,'" 41–52). She is one critic who sees the closing as truthtelling, if not coherent, in its ambivalence. For views of March as Persephone or a Sleeping Beauty, see Gurko and also George Ford, *Double Measure*, 101–2. George Ford only briefly discusses "The Fox," giving it a generally negative evaluation. Praising what they see as conscious ambiguity in Lawrence's ending are Fulmer, who wrestles with the point behind Henry's killing the fox ("Significance of the Death of the Fox," 275–82), and Ruderman in "Lawrence's 'The Fox' and Verga's 'The She Wolf,'" 153–65.

28. Finding difficulties with characterization are Rossi, "Lawrence's Two Foxes," 265–78; Draper in a partial recantation of his views in his book (*D. H. Lawrence*), "Defeat of Feminism," 186–98; and Davis, who sees the tale as an exercise in obliterating the female. It all makes more sense, Davis argues, if we see March as male along with Henry ("Chicken Queen's Delight," 565–71). Shields analyzes narrative tone in "Broken Vision," 353–63. Wolkenfeld contends that the tale's contradictions may come from Lawrence's growing criticism of the original version's Sleeping Beauty myth ("Sleeping Beauty Retold," 345–52).

29. As Spilka writes in "On Lawrence's Hostility," Lawrence is not describing impasses in "The Fox", he is prescribing doctrines (195). My point is that the doctrines contradict each other, as do the scenes and image patterns.

30. Millett, *Sexual Politics*, 266. Core writes that female friendships become Lawrence's "ideal metaphor for sterility and willful self-exclusion from all possibility for redemption" ("'The Closed Door': Love between Women," 129). In "Feminism and Literature," Florence Howe agrees; women in Lawrence must never like or trust other women (265). For Lawrence's curious link between homosexuality and "the ghoul of work," see Wilt, *Ghosts of the Gothic*, 254–55, and for a more general discussion of lesbianism, see 269–76. Wilt concludes that one rent in Lawrence's "often admirable feminism" is his inability to imagine adult relationships between women (275). Two critics view the possibility of friendship between women in more positive terms. See Blanchard, "Mothers and

Daughters," 75–100; Blanchard, "'Real Quartet' of *Women in Love*," 199–206; and Spilka, "Lessing and Lawrence," 218–40.

31. Millett, *Sexual Politics*, 239–40.

32. Hardy argues that Lawrence's feminism can often be seen more clearly in his poetry than in his fiction ("Women in D. H. Lawrence's Works," 90–122).

33. Cavitch, *Lawrence and the New World*, 30.

34. See chapter 5 for a discussion of "The Thimble." Scott has written an account of some of the reading and thinking that went into Lawrence's revisions ("'Thimble' into 'Ladybird,'" 161–76).

35. The New York Public Library owns a 108–page holograph of "The Ladybird." It is too fragile to be copied, however, and I was unable to see it. Finney, who did examine the text, writes that the published version is missing 2 pages. The gap comes between the count's words "'to destroy the world of man. Ah God.'" and "'Ah God. Prisoner of Peace.'" Finney prints the missing pages, which do not discernibly forward the argument between the count and Lady Daphne but do introduce the curious image of her as an "aching lily root" longing for the count's hammer and fire. ("Two Missing Pages," 191–92).

36. See Cowan for a study of the particular kind of Dionysian force the count represents ("Lawrence's Dualism," 73–99). Cowan sees Basil as a slain Apollo, the count as Dionysian in both his destructive and creative energies, and Daphne as the prize to be won and the recipient of the goods that attend the count's victory. Moynahan comes closer to my own response to the count when he calls him "a lineal descendant of Dracula." Moynahan sees the tale as stylistically "Lawrence's ugliest" (*Deed of Life*, 178). For a contrasting view of the style in the tale, see Engel, "Continuity of Lawrence's Short Novels," 93–100. Engel finds the count a more "intellectual, varied, and charming" character than Hepburn of "The Captain's Doll" and sees the style of "The Ladybird" as admirable because the "exact weight of meaning [is] unfixed" (96). As my discussion indicates, I see confusion where Engel sees a "complex fluency of style."

37. In Lawrence, *Four Short Novels*, 90. Further references to this work appear in the text.

38. Cavitch offers a good discussion of the tone of *Aaron's Rod* in his *Lawrence and the New World*, 108–10.

39. See Lawrence, "A Paris Letter," *Phoenix*, 121.

40. After almost a year in New Mexico, Lawrence and Frieda had parted angrily in August 1923. Frieda sailed from New York to England and Lawrence traveled back across the United States into Mexico. In

England, Frieda saw their old friends and her children. In particular, she saw Murry. Traveling together on a train to Germany in September, she proposed that they have an affair. He apparently turned her down at the time, but it was clear to them both, and to Lawrence when he arrived in England in early December, that the attraction was mutual. It is difficult to say whether Lawrence knew Murry's basically loyal stance. Their years of difficulty as friends and coworkers suggest that Lawrence would have hated either situation, Murry accepting Frieda's proposal or him turning her down out of loyalty to Lawrence. In urging Lawrence to come back to England, Murry had promised him a voice in Murry's journal, the *Adelphi*. Murry soon withdrew the invitation. In returning to England, Lawrence had hoped to attract some of his old friends to his old dream, a Rananim in the new world. That failed. Aside from the Honorable Dorothy Brett, no one wanted to go. His three months in Europe were, as Moore says, "wretched" (*Priest of Love*, 380). See also Nehls's *Lawrence: A Composite Biography*, vol. 2, 295–302. Cowan has carefully documented the biographical references in Lawrence's anti-Murry tales (*Lawrence's American Journey*, 45–50). The reader should also consult Frieda Lawrence's letter to Murry in *"Not I But the Wind . . . ,"* 141. See also Murry's recollections in Lea, *Life of John Middleton Murry*, 118; and in Murry, *Reminiscences*, 168–70. Both Green (*The von Richthofen Sisters*, 243–44) and Lucas (*Frieda Lawrence*, 255) confirm Cowan's statement that Murry and Frieda did have a brief affair in 1930, after Lawrence's death.

41. In a wide-ranging study, Merivale has traced the use of the Pan myth, mainly in English and American literature, between 1890 and 1926. Her chapter on Lawrence emphasizes his development in using the mythic figure, culminating in Pan's powerful presence as god and goat, beautiful and terrible, in the fiction of 1924–1926. See *Pan the Goat God*, 194–219.

42. Lawrence's letter to Willard Johnson (CL, 767) provides valuable background to "The Last Laugh." Sagar records a twenty-four-page holograph and twenty-one-page corrected typescript of the story, both in a private collection. Along with the other two Murry tales, he mailed "The Last Laugh" to Pinker on April 4, 1924. It was first published in *The New Decameron*, vol. 4, March 1925. In collecting the tale for *The Woman Who Rode Away*, Lawrence made no changes.

43. See Cavitch, *Lawrence and the New World*, on Lawrence and Hawthorne, 92–93.

44. For background on the relationship between Brett and Murry, see "Dorothy Brett's Letters to S. S. Koteliansky," ed. Zytaruk,

240–74. Lawrence assumed, apparently incorrectly, that Brett and Murry's relationship was platonic.

45. Baim offers a slightly different reading, stating that James and Marchbanks are ambivalent—divided in themselves—whereas the policeman stands for law, order, restraint. Marchbanks can see only the lasciviousness (the goat) in Pan and thus is doomed; James of course believes and is saved. But the policeman is crippled and made into the devil he already is ("Second Coming of Pan," 98–100). Baim misses, I believe, the sympathy the young policeman evinces for the search. On a different point, the Jewishness of the waylaying woman briefly raises an issue. Her ethnic designation can be evidence of Lawrence's anti-Semitism. See Clarke, Kermode, and George Ford, "Critical Exchange," especially 57–58. However, given the content of Lawrence's letter to Johnson, it seems more likely that he is linking Marchbank's refusal to follow Pan with his Judeo-Christian inclinations. It was Jesus, Lawrence wrote to Johnson, who had killed Pan.

46. Cowan, *Lawrence's American Journey*, 61.

47. Merivale disagrees, finding the tale muddled in its logic. In her view, it never rises above an attack on Murry (*Pan the Goat God*, 207–13).

48. "Jimmy and the Desperate Woman" was probably written in January or February 1924, after Frieda and Lawrence left England for brief stays in Paris and Germany. *Criterion* published it in October 1924, and it was collected in *The Woman Who Rode Away*. As with "The Last Laugh," a holograph and typescript are in a private collection. The magazine and collected texts are the same.

49. Cowan, *Lawrence's American Journey*, 56.

50. Widmer, *Art of Perversity*, 144.

51. There are two holographs of "The Borderline," both in a private collection. One is fifteen pages, one twenty-five. The longer reads like the collected version up to page 17 and then is entirely different (Sagar, *Lawrence: A Calendar*, 203). The change in ending, however, does not relate to the difference between the magazine and collected versions, for Sagar speaks of both holographs as "early." The conclusion we find in *Hutchinson's Magazine* and *Smart Set* (both September 1924) is nearly twice as long as the one in *The Woman Who Rode Away*. In receiving proofs for that volume in 1928, Lawrence found the last section of "The Borderline" missing. He added the truncated ending one finds in the *The Woman Who Rode Away* and in the Compass edition (Sagar, *Lawrence: A Calendar*, 169). In discussing the forthcoming Cambridge edition of the short stories, Black briefly

compares old and new endings, finding the new "artistically inferior" ("Works of D. H. Lawrence," 52). I find that both endings conflict with the expectations set up by the tale's beginning.

52. Other critics point to the break that occurs here, but find no loss of power. Cowan sees the tale as moving from realism to allegory when Lawrence introduces the cathedral; he reads the tale as a study of paired oppositions, with Katherine gradually pulled toward the right set of beliefs and actions (*Lawrence's American Journey*, 55). Hudspeth similarly emphasizes duality in the plot, tracing the tale's key movement from a state of confused male-female identities, to a spot of confusion (the "unreal" city of Strasbourg), to an ending that establishes correct dualities. To him it is a beautifully designed tale with a "genuine, satisfactory emotional resolution of the human duality of man and woman" ("Duality," 55). Perhaps my main disagreement with Cowan and Hudspeth rests on their not accounting for the lack of male-female dualities within each character. Rossman has recently analyzed Lawrence's extreme chauvinism in *The Boy in the Bush*, written approximately three months before "The Border Line." The verbal echoes between the two works are striking (Rossman, "*The Boy in the Bush* in the Lawrence Canon," 185–94).

53. Lawrence, "A Letter From Germany," *Phoenix*, 107–10.

54. Scott sees the awareness of both the negative and positive effects of Germany's withdrawal from the rest of Europe as the key focus in the tale. Germany's barrenness is posed against her revitalized fierceness. The latter is contrasted with Britain's nullity ("Lawrence's Germania," 156).

55. Sagar records an unlocated holograph of forty-five pages described by Tedlock; a corrected typescript of forty-eight pages is at Yale University (*Lawrence: A Calendar*, 265). That typescript shows isolated word changes in Lawrence's hand and a fairly thorough rewriting of several passages in which the woman's captor speaks to her of the sun and moon. The *Dial* text honors all of Lawrence's corrections and additions. The collected versions (*The Women Who Rode Away* and the Compass edition), however, ignore many spelling corrections (for example, Lawrence consistently corrects sarape to serape) and honor most but not all of his interlinear revisions.

56. Hough, *The Dark Sun*, 140–46; Leavis, *Lawrence: Novelist*, 342–43; Draper, *D. H. Lawrence*, 135–39; Cowan, *Lawrence's American Journey*, 70–78; Allen, *Short Story in English*, 100–1; Scholes in correspondence with this author, October 1973; MacNiven, "Lawrence's Indian Summer," 42–46. In his book, Draper expresses reservations

about the moral dimensions of the tale but feels that those dimensions are successfully held at bay by the conception and style. His discussion offers an excellent analysis of the style. In his subsequent article, "The Defeat of Feminism," Draper develops his initial reservations, reading the tale now as finally contradictory and confusing (186–98). Cowan's analysis is particularly useful in its drawing together of the many sources and rites that inform the tale. He traces, for example, Lawrence's use of Christian, Celtic, and Aztec beliefs in the journey, sacrifice, and fertility rites the woman undergoes.

57. West, "The Short Stories," 215; Moynahan, *Deed of Life,* 178; Widmer, *Art of Perversity,* 29–35; Rossman, "'You Are the Call and I Am the Answer,'" 298–300; Hardy, "Women in D. H. Lawrence's Works," 96; Millett, *Sexual Politics,* 376–86. In a good discussion of the place of primitivism in Lawrence, Widmer sees the confusions created by scenes and authorial intrusion but also emphasizes the tale's powerful ability to capture "self-destructive longings" (34). Millett's scathing analysis raises good points. One problem with her attack, however, is that it concludes her chapter on Lawrence. She makes no mention of his going on to write "St. Mawr," for example. Hardy draws an important parallel between the woman in the tale and the speaker of Lawrence's moving Ship of Death poems. Rossman's analysis comes closest to my own, emphasizing contradictions within the tale itself as well as its place in Lawrence's leadership fiction.

Chapter 7

1. The Humanities Research Center owns a twelve-page holograph of "The Overtone"; the University of New Mexico has a corrected carbon typescript of five pages. The holograph constitutes the published text, with isolated sexual lines deleted. In the holograph, when the husband asks the wife to make love with him, she says "'You wouldn't have me if I don't want to.'" That line is dropped from published text as is his reply, "'Do have me. . . . Have me then without taking your clothes off.'" Later, when the three characters discuss Pan, the holograph reads "'But the fauns and satyrs are there—you only have to look under the surplices that all men wear nowadays.'" The published text replaces "look under" with "remove." Catherine Carswell dates "The Overtone" in late 1923 (see Roberts's *Bibliography,* 164); Sagar's date of April 1924 is supported by Lawrence's letter to Selzer in April

(*Lawrence: A Calendar*, 135). The story was first published in the posthumous collection *The Lovely Lady*.

    2. Merivale, *Pan the Goat God*, 214.

    3. To Merivale, the solution is artificial, proposing a symmetrical polarity that is impossible and born of Elsa's naiveté (*Pan the Goat God*, 215). I find it espousing a refreshing complementarity in contrast to the oversimplified polarity of the three tales immediately preceding.

    4. Sagar records two holographs, both destroyed in a fire that consumed the home of Maria and Aldous Huxley. In a private collection there is a corrected typescript of 183 pages. "St. Mawr" was published in 1925 in England with "The Princess," in America alone. Critical debate on the tale's merit has been lively. Leavis opened it with sweeping praise as he judged it parallel in intention but superior to Eliot's "Waste Land" (*Lawrence: Novelist*, 225–45). Disagreeing with Leavis and criticizing sloppy style, flat characterization, and inaccurate observation are Liddell, "Lawrence and Dr. Leavis," 321–27; Hough, *The Dark Sun*, 182–83; Vivas, *Lawrence: The Failure and Triumph of Art*, 151–65; and Lerner, *The Truthtellers*, 185–91. In response, Leavis's sense of the story's power and structural soundness has been extended by several analyses of Lawrence's use of irony, myth, and purposeful ambiguity. See the replies to Liddell from Craig, Roberts, and Thomas in *Essays in Criticism* 5, no. 1 (January 1955): 64–80; see also Wilde, "Illusion of *St. Mawr*," 164–70; Cowan, *Lawrence's American Journey*, 81–96; Gidley, "Antipodes," 25–41; Ragussis, "False Myth of *St. Mawr*," 186–96. While the latter four critics disagree on the tale's structure (Is dualism the key or is the tale continually undercutting any easy certainties?), Blanchard looks at the valuable relationship between Lou and her mother ("Mothers and Daughters," 91–95) and Moynahan draws links between the two groups of "outsiders" in the tale—the Celts and the women—and judges the tale as "the stoutest blow Lawrence ever struck for women's liberation" ("Lawrence, Women, and the Celtic Fringe," 132–34). My own discussion draws together the emphases on Lawrence's ambivalence and feminism in the story. Still another important aspect of the work—the variety and complexity of the Pan allusions—is examined by Merivale, *Pan the Goat God*, 203–04.

    5. See Wilde, Gidley, and Ragussis for good analyses of ways Lawrence builds ambiguities into the nature of the beautiful marigold stallion (n. 4 above).

    6. The Humanities Research Center owns a fifty-one-page holograph of "The Princess." A comparison of it with the magazine and

collected texts shows no changes. Lawrence wrote the tale in September 1924, finishing it in early October. It was published in three installments in the *Calendar of Modern Letters*, in March, April, and May of 1925. That spring it was also published in England with "St. Mawr."

7. Carswell, *The Savage Pilgrimage*, 211–14.

8. For an opposing argument see Travis, "Lawrence: The Blood-Conscious Artist," 174. Travis sees "The Princess" as a lopsided, narrow story, sharing the same assumptions and motifs as "The Woman Who Rode Away" and "The Daughters of the Vicar." Although she discusses tone when she analyzes "Daughters of the Vicar," she does not discuss it in comparing the two American tales. In my view, the shift of tone is a crucial aspect of Lawrence's intentions.

9. In tracing Lawrence's reversal of both the Sleeping Beauty myth and the monomyth, which Joseph Campbell describes as "separation—initiation—return," Cowan offers valuable commentary on the psychological dimensions of the princess's father fixation (*Lawrence's American Journey*, 65–70). I would add that Lou Witt's ability to take from her mother what she needs and reject what will hamper her provides a clear, contemporary contrast to the Princess's fixation. Story speaks to story.

10. In seeking out the symbolic level of the tale, MacDonald sees Romero and the princess as simply antithetical, Romero as fire, the princess as ice, each doomed because each repels the other ("Images of Negative Union," 289–93). Along the same lines, Travis argues that Romero is a representative of blood consciousness, the princess a figure of mental consciousness. The impossibility of their mating mirrors the impossibility of their creator ever moving beyond a simplistically dualistic approach to human complexity ("Lawrence: The Blood-Conscious Artist," 174).

11. Spilka, *Love Ethic*, 41–42.

12. While giving an interesting account of the Crosby's purchase of the "Sun" manuscript, Moore implies that the initial version done at Spotorno in 1925 was a fuller and more sexually explicit text than the one published in *New Coterie* (Autumn 1926) and collected in *The Woman Who Rode Away* in May 1928 (*Priest of Love*, 443). In examining Lawrence's correspondence with Nancy Pearn, who was his contact at Curtis Brown, Sagar offers a different description of what happened. On April 1, 1928, Lawrence asked Pearn if she had his original manuscript. She wrote back, April 13, "No, alas. Couldn't you rewrite it for Harry Crosby." If one carefully reads Lawrence's letter to Crosby, one may

suspect that Lawrence did indeed rewrite, expanding and revising the tale for Crosby's collection of manuscripts and for his Black Sun edition of the tale. Lawrence writes to Crosby, "'Sun' is the final manuscript, and I wish the story had been printed as it stands there, really complete" (Sagar, *Lawrence: A Calendar*, 148). Three manuscripts exist, two of which are at the Humanities Research Center. The third, a corrected typescript, is in a private collection. One of the manuscripts at the Humanities Research Center is a holograph, one a typescript. Sagar's view asks that the reader alter normal expectations and see the typescript as coming before the holograph. My comparison will be between the typescript version, available in CSS and the holograph, available in the Black Sun edition and at the Humanities Research Center. See also n. 14 below.

13. Spilka suggests that "Sun" and "St. Mawr" register Lawrence's own lapsed confidence in the masculine ideal of the postwar years. He "knows in his bones" that he cannot win the battle of the sexes with the crude chauvinism of the leadership work. Thus for a time, the men disappear and the women worship sun and landscape ("On Lawrence's Hostility," 197). I would agree and emphasize an implication in Spilka's comment. In "St. Mawr" and "Sun," Lawrence has again set a woman at the center of the work and identified his own search for something to believe in with his heroine's.

14. Ross, "Lawrence's Second 'Sun,'" 1–18. Finney responded to Ross's article, arguing that Ross and Sagar have no cause to doubt that the Black Sun version was the original, unexpurgated text. For his view and Ross's reply see Finney and Ross, "Two Versions of 'Sun,'" 371–74.

15. Humanities Research Center manuscript of "Sun," 41. Also Black Sun edition, 36.

Chapter 8

1. Arguing for a decline in Lawrence's late tales, for example, are Hough, Moore, Delavenay, Pritchard, and Cavitch.

2. For works that deal specifically with Lawrence's sojourn in America, see Clark's *Dark Night of the Body*, Cowan's *Lawrence's American Journey*, and Cavitch's *Lawrence and the New World*.

3. See Hamalian, *Lawrence in Italy*, for a detailed account of Lawrence's Italian footsteps.

4. Hopkin's memories are recorded in Moore, *Priest of Love*, 421.

5. Lawrence's 1928 revisions of the tales collected in *The Woman Who Rode Away* were generally minor. Where significant, I examine them within analyses of individual tales.

6. "Mother and Daughter" is discussed below; "Rawdon's Roof" is baffling for several reasons, among them a discrepancy in texts. One, published in 1928 as the seventh of the Woburn Books (a series from Elkin Mathews and Marrot) follows a corrected typescript, now at the University of California at Berkeley. Another, published in *The Lovely Lady* and CSS, follows the same typescript but ignores Lawrence's penned-in corrections. Thus the more familiar version is the earlier, shorter, unrevised text. Equally important, both versions circle around a joke that goes nowhere, employ contradictory characters and narrator, and close with a denouement that mainly muddies the already murky waters. There are several manuscript items. Sagar records a twenty-one-page holograph in a private collection that follows *The Lovely Lady* text (*Lawrence: A Calendar*, 252). This may be the version Lawrence sent to Nancy Pearn in November 1927. In the same collection is a twenty-page, corrected typescript. According to Sagar, this latter follows the Woburn text through page 11, then deviates from both published versions. The University of California at Berkeley owns a corrected typescript of twenty-one pages. The Woburn text follows it closely.

7. The University of California at Los Angeles owns a thirty-page holograph of "Two Blue Birds"; Yale owns a twenty-six-page typescript. Lawrence made no changes between the texts. He mailed the tale to Curtis Brown in May 1926. *Dial* published it in April 1927, *Pall Mall* in June 1928, and Lawrence collected it in *The Woman Who Rode Away*.

8. Moore, *Priest of Love*, 418.

9. Rossman, "'You Are the Call and I Am the Answer,'" 317–20.

10. The Humanities Research Center owns a twenty-page holograph of "In Love," titled "More Modern Love." Yale owns a seventeen-page typescript titled "Modern Love." The ending in the holograph version differs from the typescript and published version. In the holograph, the clear resolution of conflict is checked by a concluding image. After the quarrel, Joe turns out the light and softly calls Hester's name. She does not reply. The reader's last image is of him stumbling around in the dark. While this original ending neatly visualizes the theme of sexual misunderstanding that runs throughout the tale, it also denies the recognition scene just preceding. With an eye perhaps on his magazine audience, Lawrence dropped the lights-out incident in the published text and closed with the couple's affirmation.

11. Kermode nicely summarizes Lawrence's attitudes toward

behavior such as Joe's as he paraphrases and quotes from Lawrence's late essays: "We live in a world of fake sexual emotion; only true sex can change it. 'When a "serious" young man said to me the other day: "I can't believe in the regeneration of England by sex, you know," I could only say, "I'm sure you can't." He had no sex anyhow. . . . And he didn't know what it meant, to have any. . . .' To such young people sex is at best the trimmings, thrills and fumbling. Real sex seems to them barbaric" (*D. H. Lawrence*, 144).

12. For an important discussion of the value and difficulty of tenderness in Lawrence's fiction, see Spilka, "Lawrence's Quarrel with Tenderness," 363–73.

13. The story looks back to Lawrence's stay in America two years earlier. Sagar reports that Lawrence mailed "None of That" to Curtis Brown in May 1927, telling him that it was based on fact. Although he usually mailed his tales soon after he wrote them, it is possible that "None of That" was done earlier. In *Lawrence: A Calendar*, Sagar mentions a "Venice story," written in September 1921. He offers no additional identification (113–14). The telling of "None of That" does occur in Venice. If the tale was written then, later revisions seem likely. The bullfighting passages in particular seem based on first-hand observations of Mexico. Lawrence's only comments on the tale come later, as when he writes to Dorothy Brett in November 1928, expressing his disgust that no magazine will publish it (see Roberts's *Bibliography*, 100). The newspapers will report the detail of any divorce scandal, they will publish his own frank articles, but no one will publish this tale of brutality. The tale came out as the one previously unpublished story in *The Woman Who Rode Away*. A thirty-three-page typescript is at the University of California at Berkeley. Between it and the version published in *The Woman Who Rode Away* there are minor changes, two in the interest of propriety. In the typescript, Cuesta speaks of Ethel's "'beaked gate'" and asks who would ever put his finger in it. In a change of tune, he then says he wants her, she is so rich and white and his member is so red. Both passages are dropped in the published version.

14. Meyers sees a very different meaning in the tale, arguing that the tale is "an allegory of Katherine Mansfield's seduction by the mysticism of Gurdjieff." Harry is J. M. Murry; Virginia is Katherine; Mrs. Bodoin is Mabel Luhan ("Katherine Mansfield, Gurdjieff, and Lawrence's 'Mother and Daughter,'" 44).

15. Lawrence sent the tale to Curtis Brown in June 1928. May seems the likely time of composition. *New Criterion* published it in April 1929; Martin Secker included it in *The Lovely Lady*. The Humanities

Research Center owns the forty-four-page holograph and eight pages of galley proofs. The University of California at Berkeley owns a thirty-four-page carbon transcript. Comparison of holograph, typescript, and published texts shows no revisions.

16. Blanchard argues that the tale is a coherent examination of a negative relationship between mother and daughter. She sees Lawrence as critical of Virginia's alliance with Arnault ("Mothers and Daughters," 95–97).

17. The Brewsters recall Lawrence reading the tale to them in manuscript during the summer of 1928 when they were together in Switzerland. Lawrence stopped reading just before the conclusion and asked the Brewsters how they thought the tale should end. They opted for an unhappy ending; Lawrence said that he had originally planned to follow that line but had reversed it. Relating this anecdote, Moore comments on the "sharp cruelties" in the piece, saying it is one of the "typical satirical pieces of Lawrence's last period, containing no strong feeling, no color, no glow, no music" (*Priest of Love*, 453). Lawrence sent the tale to Curtis Brown on July 26, 1928. It was first published in *Plain Talk*, February 1929, and collected with minor word changes in *The Lovely Lady*. The Humanities Research Center owns a seven-page incomplete holograph and a thirty-two-page complete one. The University of California at Berkeley owns a twenty-seven-page carbon typescript. The thirty-two-page holograph contains the original ending. Percy responds, "'She's perfect. Puts the final touch on life.'" "'Your life?'" asks Alice. "'Ay!'" says Percy. The Berkeley typescript contains the published "happy" conclusion, uniting Alice and Percy.

18. See for example, Pritchard, Moynahan, Spilka, Cavitch, and Williams. Pritchard and Cavitch state a minority view in finding *Lady Chatterley's Lover* regressive. They argue that in contrast to its surface argument, the novel dramatizes the withdrawal of two adults into a narcissistic, irresponsible, infantile sensationalism. Not only do Connie and Mellors lack interest and engagement in the world around them, they have no awareness of or concern for each other (Cavitch, *Lawrence and the New World*, 194–201; Pritchard, *Lawrence: Body of Darkness*, 186–95).

19. O'Connor, *The Lonely Voice*, 17–21.

20. Ibid., 18.

21. Moore, *Priest of Love*, 414.

22. Ibid., 415.

23. "Smile" was published in the *Nation and Athenaeum* and in the *New Masses* in June 1926; it was collected with no alterations in *The*

Woman Who Rode Away. Writing to Harry Crosby in 1928, Lawrence speaks of "Smile" as "a slight thing of four pages which I like" (*CL*, 1,051). Sagar records an unlocated, nine-page holograph (*Lawrence: A Calendar*, 256).

24. In *Lawrence's American Journey*, Cowan sees Matthew as ironically compared to Christ, Orpheus, and Hamlet and interprets the nuns as "the triadic image of woman in man's life"; he argues that the mythic dimension of the tale lifts it from the level of a simple attack on Murry (50).

25. Two holographs of "Glad Ghosts," one of nine pages and the other of seventy-eight, are in a private collection. Eighty-four pages of advance proof copy is in a different private collection. The other manuscript item is a corrected typescript of forty-eight pages, owned by Yale University. Comparison of the typescript and published texts shows no revisions. While Brett was typing the first version of "Sun" in December 1925, Lawrence wrote to her complaining of a cold, a desire to throw his pen into the sea, and an inability to get on with "Ghosts of Silence" (*CL*, 870). Nevertheless, by the end of the month, he had finished his tale, retitling it "Glad Ghosts." One month later, Brett had it typed and Lawrence sent it off, sure no magazine would print it. *Dial*, however, did publish it, in July and August of 1926; it was subsequently collected without revisions in *The Woman Who Rode Away*.

26. See Moore, *Priest of Love*, for his suggestion and Powell's comment (415).

27. Moynahan registers the same criticism in stating that "the lady ghost [is] too involved in problems of the life of the senses to persuade us that she is as other-worldly as the convention demands" (*Deed of Life*, 178). Allen is one critic, however, who puts "Glad Ghosts" on the same high level as "The Rocking-Horse Winner" (*Short Story in English*, 108).

28. Written at Spotorno, "The Rocking-Horse Winner" was sent to Curtis Brown on February 25, 1926. *Harper's Bazaar* published it in July; Asquith's *Ghost Book* came out in September, and the tale was later collected in *The Lovely Lady*. A thirty-page holograph is in a private collection. The University of California at Berkeley owns a carbon typescript. Comparison of the typescript and published texts reveals no revisions.

29. In this reading I am arguing that a key structural principle in the tale is the stand-off between competing fairy tales. E. San Juan, Jr., offers a different view, seeing the "dialectical interplay" between the fantastic and the worldly as a key dramatic tension. See "Theme *vs.* Imitation," 138.

30. Criticism of the tale has tended to emphasize one level over the others. While perceptively discussing the social and familial themes, Snodgrass concentrates on the psychological, particularly on the allusions to masturbation in Paul's pathetic rides ("A Rocking Horse," 117–26). Goldberg draws the reader's attention away from Snodgrass's Freudian reading to the social level by citing convincing parallels between Lawrence's tale and Dickens's *Dombey and Sons.* Both works constitute criticisms of a vast obsession with money, which each author saw as strangling all human emotions and love. Thus Paul's mother is as much a victim as Paul ("Lawrence's 'The Rocking-Horse Winner,'" 525–36). George Ford sent Goldberg an addendum by tracing other references to rocking horses in Dickens, noting their usual alliance with mechanical activity (Goldberg, "Dickens and Lawrence," 574). For a psychological reading that examines the mother in the tale, see Koban, "Allegory and the Death of the Heart," 391–96. Koban sees the tale as an allegory of death (both Paul's and his mother's) as well as a moral fable criticizing society. My own reading seeks to draw together these several emphases and urge their interdependence. Readers curious about the racing horses' names should consult Snodgrass, "A Rocking Horse," 121; and Fitz, "'The Rocking-Horse Winner' and *The Golden Bough,*" 199–200.

31. Lawrence, "Autobiographical Fragment," also referred to as "A Dream of Life," *Phoenix,* 817–36.

32. Finney describes the history of the tale and analyzes the revisions. ("A Newly Discovered Text," 245–52). As he notes, the holograph of "The Lovely Lady" is in a private collection. Three typescripts exist; the first, of forty-two double-spaced pages, is at Yale and constitutes the longer version. The second, of twenty single-spaced pages, is at the University of California at Berkeley and constitutes the condensed version as published in Asquith's *The Black Cap* and collected with the addition of three sentences in *The Lovely Lady.* The third is a fragment of two pages, 19 and 20, and is at the University of New Mexico. Finney argues that in condensing the tale Lawrence mainly cut passages of explanation and sermonizing; the final text still betrays Lawrence's anxiety to create a murder story with psychological significance but is less didactic than the original. He also comments on Lawrence's dropping the Garden of Eden and sun-storm imagery. My comparison of the texts indicates that Lawrence cut scene, imagery, and explanation, all in approximately the same proportion, resulting in a tale that is not only less didactic, but also clearer in characterization and imagistic design. A brief comment by Black sheds light on Lady

Cynthia's initial rejection. In his overview of the Cambridge edition, Black says Asquith "objected to the absence of a proper ghost and to the length of the original version" ("Works of D. H. Lawrence," 52). Black does not cite a source.

33. Lawrence, "Edgar Allan Poe," in *Selected Literary Criticism*, ed. Beal, 345.

34. The sun imagery is less developed in the second version of "The Lovely Lady" but more coherent. The sun is a source of energy but can be oppressive. Its oppressiveness is emphasized when Lawrence uses a rainstorm as backdrop for Ciss's triumph over her aunt. In the earlier version it is difficult to sort out the associations between the sun and storm, Ciss and Pauline. For an interesting discussion of sun imagery in this tale and others, see Wilt, *Ghosts of the Gothic*, 279–80.

35. I borrow this phrase from E. San Juan, Jr. ("Theme *vs.* Imitation"), who sees the dialectic between fairy tale and reality as characterizing "The Rocking-Horse Winner" (see n. 29). Here, as there, I am emphasizing the tension Lawrence creates between fairy tales.

36. Finney, "A Newly Discovered Text," 252.

37. Lawrence, "Edgar Allan Poe," in *Selected Literary Criticism*, ed. Beal, 345.

38. Lawrence sent his original version of "The Man Who Loved Islands" to Curtis Brown on July 10, 1926. *Dial* and the *London Mercury* each published it, in July and August of 1927 respectively. The tale was collected without revisions in the American edition of *The Woman Who Rode Away*, but due to Mackenzie's pressure it was excluded from the British. It was also collected in *The Lovely Lady*. Neither Tedlock nor Roberts records the existence of the tale's holograph version. Sagar has located it but references in his book are contradictory. In the "Calendar" section, which he wrote, he follows Tedlock and Roberts in stating that no manuscripts have surfaced. He offers a suggestion that Lawrence rewrote the tale in August 1926, after visiting the Isle of Skye, since certain descriptions refer closely to Celtic landscape (Sagar, *Lawrence: A Calendar*, 153). But in the "Manuscripts" section of Sagar's book, compiled by Vasey, Vasey records Bucknell University as owning a forty-four-page holograph, and Yale a thirty-page corrected typescript (*Lawrence: A Calendar*, 223). Vasey is correct. In examining the Bucknell holograph, I find no clear evidence to determine whether or not it is the original sent to Curtis Brown in July or a later rewrite. The descriptions of the islands are embued with fine localizing details, but Lawrence's imagination and sense of that country could have supplied the information.

In the main, Lawrence's holograph version is close to that published by *Dial* and collected in later volumes. The changes that he does make, on the holograph itself and between holograph and typescript, however, are interesting. On the holograph Lawrence deletes general philosophical paragraphs that try to explain in abstract terms the relativity of time and space. In their stead, he creates images of that relativity through Cathcart's specific nightmares. Comparing holograph and Yale typescript, one sees Lawrence now expanding passages. Additions occur throughout, often enriching a description but also elaborating on ideas. The key substantive change is a shift of attitude toward Cathcart's wife. In the holograph she is simply adoring, pathetic. In the typescript, her adoration carries the suggestion of a dogged, even shrewd capacity to manipulate Cathcart through her ostensible powerlessness. Between typescript and published versions there are no changes.

39. Moynahan offers an acute reading of "The Man Who Loved Islands." Especially good is his analysis of Lawrence's structural intricacies (*Deed of Life*, 186–96). My reading is indebted to his, though I emphasize diseased idealism as Lawrence's target rather than "the disease of human idealism" (188).

40. Toyokuni examines Cathcart's obsession with time, arguing that on the first island he wants time to be linear and rational; the seasonal cycles frighten him. The second island is midpoint and transitional. By the third island, Cathcart expresses a modern attitude toward time as a fixed fragment with no context, no unity ("A Modern Man Obsessed by Time," 78–82).

41. In "Malice in Paradise," Willbern emphasizes the effect of the narration as creating a "sense of union with an awareness of separation" (224). The two voices are alternately sympathetic or ironic. That yoking of contraries points to others, in particular the struggles of the islander against himself. The islands are himself, projections of his own mind, which he creates and then does battle with. In turn, the tale is an "aesthetic space" into which the reader can only project him or herself (235). For Willbern, the tale is finally about both the islander and reader's "search for significance which leads ultimately to an awareness of its absence" (235). Far from ending with a moral, the story ends with a blank silence, a fully realized ambivalence. For a different, also very good, study of the voices in the tale, see Squires, "Teaching a Story Rhetorically," 150–56.

42. Widmer, *Art of Perversity*, 16.

43. Ibid.

44. Willbern, "Malice in Paradise," 238–39.

45. Foreword to *Fantasia of the Unconscious*, in Lawrence, *Psychoanalysis and the Unconscious*, 57.

46. Cathcart's opposite is a character like Will Brangwen, a man who at fifty was as "unresolved as he was at twenty." Never quite able to create a stable identity, he is "a strange, inexplicable, almost patternless collection of passions and desires and suppressions and traditions and mechanical ideas, all cast unfused and disunited into the slender, bright faced man . . ." (*Women in Love*, 248). Cathcart is nothing but pattern and idea; Will is nothing but flux and reaction.

47. Widmer, *Art of Perversity*, 5.

48. Lawrence, "Review of *The Social Basis of Consciousness*, by Trigant Burrow," *Phoenix*, 382.

49. In arguing that Lawrence finally damns Cathcart for his islanding, I do not wish to minimize Lawrence's sympathy for his character's yearnings. When one hears echoes of Lawrence's Rananim in Cathcart's vision of a perfect society, one must disagree with Karl's early reading of Cathcart as a composite of all Lawrence hated ("Lawrence's 'The Man Who Loved Islands,'" 265).

50. A fourth work stands at the margin of this cluster. Written between "The Man Who Loved Islands" and "The Man Who Died," "The Man Who Was Through with the World" is clearly a spin-off of the former and prelude to the latter. One more satire on soulful hermitage, the story mocks the main character's search for solitude, his joy in the sun (that same sun which was Juliet's salvation in "Sun"), and his solemn attempts to meditate. The narrator sympathizes however with Henry's aversion to people. The target of the tale is quite specifically the Eastern monasticism and ideals Lawrence believed central to Buddhism. Lawrence did not finish the story—it lacks both ending and depth—but, approximately a month after laying it down, he returned to the problem of how one can and cannot withdraw from the world in his first version of "The Escaped Cock"/"The Man Who Died." "The Man Who Was Through with the World" was printed and discussed by Elliott, and is listed here in the bibliography under Lawrence. A holograph of ten pages and a carbon typescript of seven pages is at the University of California at Berkeley; the original seven-page typescript is at the Humanities Research Center.

51. Moore, *Priest of Love*, 454.

52. Apparently written in May 1927, "Things" had been returned to Lawrence by Curtis Brown in June. With no revisions, it was published in *Bookman* a year later, in *Fortnightly Review* in October 1928, and collected in *The Lovely Lady*. The Humanities Research Center

owns a nineteen-page holograph; a carbon transcript of sixteen pages is at the University of California at Berkeley; a typescript and two carbon copies, all of nineteen pages, are at the Humanities Research Center; and eight pages of corrected proofs are at the University of New Mexico. Comparison of holograph, typescripts, and published texts reveals no changes.

53. Lawrence, *The Escaped Cock*, ed. Lacy, reprints the several versions and provides a detailed analysis of the tale's history, texts, and analogies. As Lacy notes, Lawrence grudgingly acquiesced in 1930 to the title "The Man Who Had Died"—not "The Man Who Died"—but insisted that "The Escaped Cock" be the subtitle. In neither respect were his directions carried out (Lawrence, *The Escaped Cock*, ed. Lacy, 152). For the sake of clarity, I will refer to the first, shorter version as "The Escaped Cock," the later, longer version as "The Man Who Died." Readers interested in the several texts should consult Sagar's *Lawrence: A Calendar* (210–11) as well as Lacy's edition, because Sagar's more recent list indicates changes in the location of some of the manuscripts. In all, there are twelve manuscript items, five for part 1, four for part 2, and three for parts 1 and 2 combined.

54. Lawrence, *Collected Letters*, ed. Moore, includes a note referring to Brewster's memory of the tale's original inception (975). Lacy demonstrates that Brewster got many details wrong (Lawrence, *The Escaped Cock*, ed. Lacy, 136). In "The Christ Who Didn't Die," Thompson also warns against taking Brewster's account as an indication of the story's primary origin. He cites analogues to Lawrence's tale by Yeats, Wilde, Frank Harris, and especially George Moore as clear sources, arguing that the idea was very much in the air (19–30).

55. The majority of critics read "The Man Who Died" as a beautifully realized vision of resurrection and relationship. Criticism has divided not on the issue of quality but on the "heretical" nature of the work. Ledoux, for example, argues that Lawrence introduces the Isis/Osiris myth in order to revitalize and add to the Christian conception of Christ ("Christ and Isis," 132–48). Cowan, who offers a fine review of the way in which Christian and pagan allusions and myths are incorporated, notes that the context Lawrence employs gives the Biblical references an unorthodox meaning, but he too feels that the story infuses the Christian myth with new vitality ("The Function of Allusions and Symbols in D. H. Lawrence's *The Man Who Died*," 241–53). Lacy also emphasizes Lawrence's intention to fuse the myths

on which he was drawing (Lawrence, *The Escaped Cock*, ed. Lacy, 124, 128).

Arguing against the reconciliationists are critics such as Hough, Fiderer, and, more recently, Hinz and Teunissen. Hough (who finds the tale flawed) maintains that Lawrence's quarrel with Christianity is deep, determined, and founded mainly on his consistently locating human fulfillment here and now, on earth ("Lawrence's Quarrel with Christianity," 101–11). Fiderer examines the many antinomies in the work, concluding that its structure is dialectic, with a new synthesis born of the thesis and antithesis ("Lawrence's *The Man Who Died*." 91–96). Hinz and Teunissen, in a fascinating discussion of the tale's allusions to Asclepius, the Greek healer, and of its parallels with a phallic icon in the Vatican, support Hough's view and raise one of the issues I find troubling in the tale. They contend that Lawrence shows Christ awakening to a "pagan and elitist attitude toward regeneration," the attitude of Asclepius ("Savior and Cock," 287). On a slightly different issue, both Ledoux and Rossman ("'You Are the Call and I Am the Answer,'" 323) see Lawrence has having finally captured the ideal sexual relationship in the Christ figure's love of the priestess.

56. Gutierrez mentions the sharp class discriminations that mark "The Escaped Cock" as well as *Apocalypse* and *Lady Chatterley's Lover*, but he finds the unattractiveness of those discriminations assuaged by "the sensitivity, variety, and force of [Lawrence's] conceptions of immortality" (*Lapsing Out*, 41). I would be more inclined to agree if the stated intention of at least "The Escaped Cock" were not to show that "life bubbles variously." To me, Moynahan captures what is missing in "The Escaped Cock" when he praises "Odour of Chrysanthemums" in these terms: "the tale locates in the lives of working people . . . those irreducible human elements which define the characters' worth and dignity beyond the contingencies of class or system" (*Deed of Life*, 180). For a curious poem that echoes the class divisions of the tale, see Lawrence's "The Cross."

57. Widmer, *Art of Perversity*, 205.

58. A discarded conclusion to the early version underscores the above problems. In the manuscript, the man who died gives his apostles the slip and, next morning, does the same with his cock. The final paragraph reads:

And he went on. And he sojourned in many places. He healed some people, and some he left to die. And he knew strange men and commonplace men, and laughed at most women. But some women who had beauty for him and a gleam of the great day about them, and a freedom from the little day, and a true ring of life, he lay with them, and knew them. But the day came to go, and he married none of them.

So he grew old in the wonder of the world, and hid himself from public knowledge.

These lines are not in Lacy's edition but are in a typescript at the Humanities Research Center, 23. Feeling that his earlier desire to save all mankind was foolish, here the man who died saves arbitrarily or at least without explanation. Feeling that he had honored women too much, he now laughs at them, or most of them.

In many ways, the paragraph illustrates an equation made often in the tale: immortality is insouciance. Escapist, the man's insouciance is also unconvincing. For throughout the tale this man continually responds and ponders his responses. Spilka reads the yearning for insouciance differently, seeing Lawrence as able to imagine in the man who died "the purging of his own self-importance and self-will" ("On Lawrence's Hostility," 210). I recognize that as the intention but do not see it accomplished.

Another slight variation in the conclusion is found on the typescript at Tulsa (reprinted in Lawrence, *The Escaped Cock*, ed. Lacy, 154). On the typescript Lawrence pens in an answer to the question that concludes the *Forum* text, "From what, and to what, could this infinite whirl be saved?" Lawrence writes, "For the inner air is always within it, and out of the dust one can look at the freshness which is the Father, wherein the iris unfolds himself, and wherein my young cock has his kingdom, sometimes." The many conclusions to the tale as well as the tentativeness of the closing on the Tulsa typescript suggest that Lawrence was having trouble ending the piece. That trouble may speak in turn for difficulties Lawrence was having with the tale in general.

59. See Lacy's discussion of the links between "The Flying Fish" and "The Man Who Died" (Lawrence, *The Escaped Cock*, ed. Lacy, 129–130). Lacy is also good on the links between Lawrence's review of *Solitaria* by Rozanov and "The Man Who Died." In the main, he modifies Zytaruk's emphasis on the importance of that review (see Zytaruk, *Lawrence's Response to Russian Literature*, 163).

60. Lacy sees Lawrence's revisions as being more radical than I do. In his view, the first Christ is almost a satirical portrait of asceticism and puritanism; the second is a "truly mystic new man" (Lawrence, *The*

Escaped Cock, ed. Lacy, 146). I feel that the asceticism and puritanism remain.

61. For discussion of the Isis and Osiris myths and Lawrence's allusions see Lacy's discussion in his edition of Lawrence, *The Escaped Cock*, 124–26; Cowan, "The Function of Allusions and Symbols in D. H. Lawrence's *The Man Who Died*," 248; Ledoux, "Christ and Isis," 132–48; and George Ford, *Double Measure*, 108–9. Ford also discusses the man's parallels to Pluto as both a figure of death and rebirth.

62. Remarkably, critics have seen this scene as depicting "natural" and "spontaneous" sex, somehow paralleling the cock's robust mating. See, for example, Widmer, *Art of Perversity*, 208–9; and MacDonald, "Union of Fire and Water," 42. While I disagree with his view of the slave's mating scene, I find MacDonald's examination of the style of the story very helpful. He, too, suspects a "personal unresolved dilemma" in the tale's attitude toward the slaves (see n. 63 below).

63. I am emphasizing here that the positive view of the slaves corresponds to Lawrence's switch from the third person intimate views of the hero and heroine to the perspective of the omniscient narrator. MacDonald (n. 62 above) sees a contradiction in attitude toward the slaves but relates it to Lawrence's switch from close-up shots, conveying disgust, to distant shots, conveying beauty. The view of the slaves copulating, however, is both negative and distant. Also, the eye that sees them as lovely picks up small details that suggests medium distance, if not close-up.

64. Kinkead-Weekes argues eloquently for the same loss of contact and healthy conflict in *Lady Chatterley's Lover* ("Eros and Metaphor," 115–20). While I disagree with the application of his argument to *Lady Chatterley's Lover*, his description of Lawrence's shrinking concept of sexuality—which is intimate, interior, and private—and relationship—which reaches toward another and toward the world—seems fitted precisely to "The Man Who Died": "drama has virtually disappeared, no effective opposition or cross-criticism is permitted. . . . Process becomes programme" (118). For two critics who also see problems with the relationship between man and priestess, see Pritchard, *Lawrence: Body of Darkness*, 197; and Travis, "Lawrence: The Blood-Conscious Artist," 182–85.

65. In *John Thomas and Lady Jane*, Lawrence states with particular force Mellors's desire to be alone. Mellors "wanted no one to come near him, never any more while he lived. He had never, all his life, felt at ease and free with other people. . . . The one real gratification he had in life was in being alone, always alone" (86).

66. Several critics do see close parallels. For Weiss, "The Man Who Died" works as a "spiritual abstract" of Lady Chatterley's Lover, making its "anagogic level explicit" (Oedipus in Nottingham, 107). Spilka also draws correspondences, seeing "The Man Who Died" as dramatizing in mythic-social terms the vision that Lady Chatterley's Lover enacts in private terms (Love Ethic, 205–31).

Bibliography

Adelman, Gary. "Beyond the Pleasure Principle: An Analysis of D. H. Lawrence's 'The Prussian Officer.'" *Studies in Short Fiction* 1 (1963–1964):8–15.

Allen, Walter. *The Short Story in English.* Oxford: Clarendon Press, 1981.

Amon, Frank. "D. H. Lawrence and the Short Story." In *The Achievement of D. H. Lawrence,* edited by Frederick J. Hoffman and Harry T. Moore.

Baedeshwiter, Eileen. "The Lyric Short Story: The Sketch of a History." *Studies in Short Fiction* 6 (1968–1969):443–53.

Baim, Joseph. "Past and Present in D. H. Lawrence's 'A Fragment of Stained Glass.'" *Studies in Short Fiction* 8 (1971):323–26.

———. "The Second Coming of Pan: A Note on D. H. Lawrence's 'The Last Laugh.'" *Studies in Short Fiction* 6 (1968–1969):98–100.

Baker, P. G. "By the Help of Certain Notes: A Source for D. H. Lawrence's 'A Fragment of Stained Glass.'" *Studies in Short Fiction* 17 (1980):317–26.

Beauvoir, Simone de. *The Second Sex.* New York: Knopf, 1953.

Black, Michael H. "The Works of D. H. Lawrence: The Cambridge Edition." In *D. H. Lawrence: The Man Who Lived,* edited by Robert B. Partlow, Jr., and Harry T. Moore.

Blanchard, Lydia. "Love and Power: A Reconsideration of Sexual Politics in Lawrence." *Modern Fiction Studies* 21 (1975):431–43.

———. "Mothers and Daughters in D. H. Lawrence: *The Rainbow* and Selected Shorter Works." In *Lawrence and Women,* edited by Anne Smith.

———. "Portrait of a Genius and. . . ." *D. H. Lawrence Review* 10 (1977):277–85.

———. "The 'Real Quartet' of *Women in Love*: Lawrence on Brothers and Sisters." In *Lawrence and Women,* edited by Anne Smith.

Bloch, Ruth. "Untangling the Roots of Modern Sex Roles." *Signs* 4 (1978):237–52.

Boulton, James T. "D. H. Lawrence's 'Odour of Chrysanthemums': An Early Version." *Renaissance and Modern Studies* 13 (1969):4–48.

Brayfield, Peggy L. "Lawrence's 'Male and Female Principles' and the Symbolism of 'The Fox.'" *Mosaic: A Journal for the Comparative Study of Literature and Ideas* 4 (1971):41–52.

Brett, Dorothy. "Dorothy Brett's Letters to S. S. Koteliansky," edited by George J. Zytaruk. *D. H. Lawrence Review* 7 (1974):240–74.

Carswell, Catherine. *The Savage Pilgrimage: A Narrative of D. H. Lawrence.* 1932. Reprint. St. Claire Shores, Mich.: Scholarly Press, 1972.

Cavitch, David. *D. H. Lawrence and the New World.* New York: Oxford University Press, 1969.

Chambers, Jessie [E. T., pseud.] *D. H. Lawrence: A Personal Record.* London: Jonathan Cape, 1935.

Clark, L. D. *Dark Night of The Body: D. H. Lawrence's "The Plumed Serpent."* Austin: University of Texas Press, 1964.

Clarke, Colin. *River of Dissolution: D. H. Lawrence and English Romanticism.* New York: Barnes and Noble, 1969.

Clarke, Colin, Frank Kermode, and George Ford. "Critical Exchange on 'Lawrence Up-Tight.'" *Novel* 5 (1971):54–70.

Core, Deborah. "'The Closed Door': Love between Women in the Works of D. H. Lawrence." *D. H. Lawrence Review* 11 (1978): 114–31.

Cowan, James C. *D. H. Lawrence's American Journey: A Study in Literature and Myth.* Cleveland: Press of Case Western Reserve University, 1970.

―――. "D. H. Lawrence's Dualism: Apollonian and Dionysian Polarity and *The Ladybird.*" In *Forms of Modern British Fiction,* edited by Alan Warren Friedman. Austin: University of Texas Press, 1975.

―――. "The Function of Allusions and Symbols in D. H. Lawrence's *The Man Who Died.*" *American Imago* 17 (1960):241–53.

―――, comp. and ed. *D. H. Lawrence: An Annotated Bibliography of Writings about Him.* 1 vol. to date. DeKalb: Northern Illinois University Press, 1982–.

Cowley, Malcolm, ed. *Writers at Work: The Paris Review Interviews.* New York: Viking Press, 1957.

Craig, David, Mark Roberts, and T. W. Thomas. "Responses to Robert Liddell." *Essays in Criticism* 5 (1955):64–80. See also Robert Liddell.

Cushman, Keith. "The Achievement of *England, My England and Other Stories.*" In *D. H. Lawrence: The Man Who Lived,* edited by Robert B. Partlow, Jr., and Harry T. Moore.

——. *D. H. Lawrence at Work: The Emergence of "The Prussian Officer" Stories.* Charlottesville: University Press of Virginia, 1978.

——. "'I Am Going through a Transition Stage': The Prussian Officer and *The Rainbow.*" *D. H. Lawrence Review* 8 (1975):176–97.

——. "Lawrence's Use of Hardy in 'The Shades of Spring.'" *Studies in Short Fiction* 9 (1972):402–04.

——. "The Making of D. H. Lawrence's 'The White Stocking.'" *Studies in Short Fiction* 10 (1973):51–65.

Daleski, H. M. *The Forked Flame: A Study of D. H. Lawrence.* Evanston, Ill.: Northwestern University Press, 1965.

Davis, Patricia C. "Chicken Queen's Delight: D. H. Lawrence's 'The Fox.'" *Modern Fiction Studies* 19 (1973–1974):565–71.

Dawson, Eugene W. "Love among the Mannikins: 'The Captain's Doll.'" *D. H. Lawrence Review* 1 (1968):137–48.

Delany, Paul. *D. H. Lawrence's Nightmare.* New York: Basic Books, 1978.

Delavenay, Emile. *D. H. Lawrence: L'homme et la genese de son oeuvre, Documents.* Paris: Librarie C. Klincksieck, 1969.

——. *D. H. Lawrence: The Man and His Work: The Formative Years: 1885–1919.* Translated by Katherine M. Delavenay. Carbondale and Edwardsville: Southern Illinois University Press, 1972.

Draper, R. P. "The Defeat of Feminism: D. H. Lawrence's 'The Fox' and 'The Woman Who Rode Away.'" *Studies in Short Fiction* 3 (1965–1966):186–98.

——. *D. H. Lawrence.* New York: Twayne, English Authors Series, St. Martin's Press, 1964.

Ejxenbaum, B. J. "O. Henry and the Theory of the Short Story" (1925). Translated with notes and postscript by I. R. Titunik. Ann Arbor: Michigan Slavic Contributions, 1968.

Eliot, T. S. *After Strange Gods.* New York: Harcourt, Brace and Company, 1934.

Engel, Monroe. "The Continuity of Lawrence's Short Novels." In *D. H. Lawrence: A Collection of Critical Essays,* edited by Mark Spilka.

Englander, Ann. "'The Prussian Officer': The Self Divided." *Sewanee Review* 71 (1963):605–19.

Engleberg, Edward. "Escape from the Circles of Experience: D. H. Lawrence's *The Rainbow* as a Modern *Bildungsroman.*" *PMLA* 78 (1963):103–13.

Fadiman, Regina. "The Poet as Choreographer: Lawrence's 'The Blind Man.'" *Journal of Narrative Technique* 2 (1972):60–67.

Fiderer, Gerald. "D. H. Lawrence's *The Man Who Died*: The Phallic Christ." *American Imago* 25 (1968):91–96.

Finney, Brian H. "A Newly Discovered Text of D. H. Lawrence's 'The Lovely Lady.'" *Yale University Library Gazette* 49 (1975):245–52.

———. "Two Missing Pages from 'The Ladybird.'" *Review of English Studies* 24 (1973):191–92.

Finney. Brian H., and Michael L. Ross. "The Two Versions of 'Sun': An Exchange." *D. H. Lawrence Review* 8 (1975):371–74.

Fitz, L. T. "'The Rocking-Horse Winner' and *The Golden Bough*." *Studies in Short Fiction* 11 (1974):199–200.

Ford, Ford Madox. Foreword to *The English Review Book of Short Stories*, compiled by Horace Shipp. London: Samson Low, Marston and Co., 1932.

Ford, George. *Double Measure: A Study of the Novels and Stories of D. H. Lawrence*. New York: Holt, Rinehart, and Winston, 1965.

Friedman, Alan. "The Other Lawrence." *Partisan Review* 37 (1970):239–53.

———. *The Turn of the Novel*. New York: Oxford University Press, 1967.

Frye, Northrop. *Anatomy of Criticism*. Princeton, N.J.: Princeton University Press, 1957.

Fulmer, O. Bryan. "The Significance of the Death of the Fox in D. H. Lawrence's 'The Fox.'" *Studies in Short Fiction* 5 (1967–1968): 275–82.

Garcia, Reloy, and James Karabatsos, eds. *A Concordance to the Short Fiction of D. H. Lawrence*. Lincoln: University of Nebraska Press, 1972.

Gidley, Mick. "Antipodes: D. H. Lawrence's *St. Mawr*." *Ariel* 5 (1974):25–41.

Gissing, George. *The Odd Women*. 1893. Reprint. New York: AMS Press, 1969.

Goldberg, Michael. "Dickens and Lawrence: More on Rocking Horses." *Modern Fiction Studies* 17 (1971–1972):574.

———. "Lawrence's 'The Rocking-Horse Winner': A Dickensian Fable?" *Modern Fiction Studies* 15 (1969–1970):525–36.

Green, Martin. *The von Richthofen Sisters: The Triumphant and the Tragic Modes of Love*. New York: Basic Books, 1974.

Gregor, Ian. "'The Fox': A Caveat." *Essays in Criticism* 9 (1959):10–21.

Gullason, Thomas. "Revelation and Evolution: A Neglected Dimension

of the Short Story." *Studies in Short fiction* 10 (1973):347–56.
———. "The Short Story: An Underrated Art." *Studies in Short Fiction* 2 (1964–1965):13–31.

Gurko, Leo. "D. H. Lawrence's Greatest Collection of Short Stories: What Holds It Together." *Modern Fiction Studies* 18 (1972–1973):173–82.

Gutierrez, Donald. *Lapsing Out: Embodiments of Death and Rebirth in the Last Writings of D. H. Lawrence.* East Brunswick, N.J.: Associated University Presses, 1980.

Hahn, Emily. *Mabel: A Biography of Mabel Dodge Luhan.* Boston: Houghton Mifflin, 1977.

Hamalian, Leo. *D. H. Lawrence in Italy.* New York: Taplinger, 1982.

Hardy, Barbara. "Women in D. H. Lawrence's Works." In *D. H. Lawrence: Novelist, Poet, Prophet,* edited by Stephen Spender.

Harris, Janice H. "D. H. Lawrence and Kate Millett." *Massachusetts Review* 15 (1974):522–29.

———. "The Many Faces of Lazarus: *The Man Who Died* and its Context." *D. H. Lawrence Review* (forthcoming).

———. "The Moulting of *The Plumed Serpent*: A Study of the Relationship between the Novel and Three Contemporary Tales." *Modern Language Quarterly* 39 (1978):154–68.

———. "Sexual Antagonism in D. H. Lawrence's Early Leadership Fiction." *Modern Language Studies* 7 (1977):43–52.

Harris, Wendell V. "English Short Fiction of the Nineteenth Century." *Studies in Short Fiction* 6 (1968–1969):1–93.

Harrison, John R. *The Reactionaries: A Study of the Anti-Democratic Intelligensia.* New York: Schocken Books, 1968.

Hinz, Evelyn J., and John J. Teunissen. "Savior and Cock: Allusion and Icon in Lawrence's *The Man Who Died.*" *Journal of Modern Literature* 5 (1976):279–96.

———. "*Women in Love* and the Myth of Eros and Psyche." In *D. H. Lawrence: The Man Who Lived,* edited by Robert B. Partlow, Jr., and Harry T. Moore.

Hoffman, Frederick J., and Harry T. Moore. *The Achievement of D. H. Lawrence.* Norman: University of Oklahoma Press, 1953.

Hough, Graham. *The Dark Sun: A Study of D. H. Lawrence.* London: Duckworth, 1956; New York: Macmillan, 1957.

———. "Lawrence's Quarrel with Christianity: *The Man Who Died.*" In *D. H. Lawrence: A Collection of Critical Essays,* edited by Mark Spilka.

Howe, Florence. "Feminism and Literature." In *Images of Women in Fic-*

311

tion: *Feminist Perspectives*, edited by Susan Koppleman Cornillon. Bowling Green, Ohio: Bowling Green University Popular Press, 1972.

Howe, Marguerite Beede. *The Art of the Self in D. H. Lawrence.* Athens: Ohio University Press, 1977.

Hudspeth, Robert N. "Duality as Theme and Technique in D. H. Lawrence's 'The Border Line.'" *Studies in Short fiction* 4 (1966–1967):51–56.

―――. "Lawrence's 'Odour of Chrysanthemums': Isolation and Paradox." *Studies in Short Fiction* 6 (1968–1969):630–36.

Joost, Nicholas, and Alvin Sullivan. *D. H. Lawrence and the* Dial. Carbondale and Edwardsville: Southern Illinois University Press, 1970.

Junkins, Donald. "D. H. Lawrence's 'The Horse Dealer's Daughter.'" *Studies in Short Fiction* 6 (1968–1969):210–13.

Kalnins, Mara. "D. H. Lawrence's 'Odour of Chrysanthemums': The Three Endings." *Studies in Short Fiction* 13 (1976):471–79.

―――. "D. H. Lawrence's 'Two Marriages' and 'Daughters of the Vicar.'" *Ariel* 7 (1976):32–49.

Kaplan, Harold. *The Passive Voice: An Approach to Modern Fiction.* Athens: Ohio University Press, 1966.

Karl, F. R. "Lawrence's 'The Man Who Loved Islands': The Crusoe Who Failed." In *A D. H. Lawrence Miscellany*, edited by Harry T. Moore.

Kermode, Frank. *D. H. Lawrence.* New York: Viking Press, 1973.

―――. "Lawrence and the Apocalyptic Types." *Critical Quarterly* 10 (1968):14–38.

Kinkead-Weekes, Mark. "Eros and Metaphor: Sexual Relationship in the Fiction of D. H. Lawrence." In *Lawrence and Women*, edited by Anne Smith.

Koban, Charles. "Allegory and the Death of the Heart in 'The Rocking-Horse Winner.'" *Studies in Short Fiction* 15 (1978):391–96.

Lainoff, Seymour. "The Wartime Setting of Lawrence's 'Tickets, Please.'" *Studies in Short Fiction* 7 (1970):649–51.

Lawrence, D. H. *The Collected Letters of D. H. Lawrence.* 2 vols. Edited by Harry T. Moore. New York: Viking Press, 1962.

―――. *The Complete Short Stories of D. H. Lawrence.* 3 vols. New York: Viking Press, Compass edition, 1961.

―――. *England, My England and Other Stories.* New York: Seltzer, 1922.

————. *The Escaped Cock.* 1929. Critical Edition by Gerald Lacy. Los Angeles: Black Sparrow Press, 1973.

————. *The First Lady Chatterley.* Foreword by Frieda Lawrence. London: Heinemann Ltd., 1972.

————. *Four Short Novels.* New York: Viking Press, 1965.

————. *John Thomas and Lady Jane.* New York: Viking Press, 1972.

————. *Lady Chatterley's Lover.* 1928. Reprint. Introduction by Mark Schorer. New York: Grove Press, 1959.

————. *Lawrence in Love: Letters to Louie Burrows.* Edited by James T. Boulton. Nottingham: University of Nottingham, 1968.

————. "A Letter from Germany." In *Phoenix.*

————. *The Letters of D. H. Lawrence.* 2 vols. to date. Edited by James T. Boulton. Cambridge: Cambridge University Press, 1979–.

————. *Love among the Haystacks and Other Pieces.* Reminiscence by David Garnett. 1930. Reprint. Penguin Books, 1972.

————. *The Lovely Lady and Other Stories.* London: Secker, 1933.

————. *The Man Who Died.* See his *The Escaped Cock.*

————. "The Man Who Was Through with the World." Printed and discussed by John R. Elliot, Jr. *Essays in Criticism* 9, no. 3 (July 1959):213–21.

————. *A Modern Lover.* London: Secker, 1934.

————. "Morality and the Novel." In *Selected Literary Criticism.*

————. "A Paris Letter." In *Phoenix.*

————. *Phoenix: The Posthumous Papers of D. H. Lawrence.* Edited by Edward D. McDonald. London: Heinemann Ltd., 1936.

————. *Phoenix II: Uncollected Writing by D. H. Lawrence.* Edited by Warren Roberts and Harry T. Moore. New York: Viking Press, 1959.

————. "'Prologue' to *Women in Love.*" In *Phoenix II.*

————. *The Prussian Officer and Other Stories.* London: Duckworth, 1914.

————. *Psychoanalysis and the Unconscious.* New York: Viking Press, 1960.

————. *St. Mawr and The Man Who Died.* New York: Vintage Books, 1953.

————. *Selected Literary Criticism.* Edited by Anthony Beal. London: Heinemann Ltd., 1955; Viking Press, 1966.

————. *Sons and Lovers.* 1913. Reprint. New York: Compass Books, 1958.

————. *Sons and Lovers: A Facsimile of the Manuscript.* Edited by

Mark Schorer. Berkeley and Los Angeles: University of California Press, 1977.

———. *The White Peacock.* 1911. Reprint. Middlesex, England: Penguin Books, 1972.

———. "Why the Novel Matters." In *Phoenix.*

———. *Women in Love.* 1920. Reprint. New York: Viking Press, 1960.

———. *The Woman Who Rode Away and Other Stories.* New York: Knopf, 1928.

Lawrence, Frieda. *The Memoirs and Correspondence of Frieda Lawrence,* edited by E. W. Tedlock, New York: Knopf, 1964.

———. *"Not I, but the Wind. . . ."* 1934. Reprint. Carbondale and Edwardsville: Southern Illinois University Press, 1974.

Lea, F. A. *The Life of John Middleton Murry.* London: Methuen and Co., 1959.

Leavis, F. R. *D. H. Lawrence: Novelist.* London: Chatto and Windus, 1955.

———. "The Novel as Dramatic Poem." *Scrutiny* 17 (1950–1951):38–53, 203–20, 318–30; 18 (1951–1952):18–31, 197–210, 273–87; 19 (1952–1953):15–30.

———. *Thought, Words and Creativity: Art and Thought in Lawrence.* New York: Oxford University Press, 1976.

Ledoux, Larry V. "Christ and Isis: The Function of the Dying and Reviving God in *The Man Who Died.*" *D. H. Lawrence Review* 5 (1972):132–48.

Lerner, Laurence. *The Truthtellers: Jane Austen, George Eliot, D. H. Lawrence.* New York: Schocken Books, 1967.

Liddell, Robert. "Lawrence and Dr. Leavis: The Case of *St. Mawr.*" *Essays in Criticism* 4 (1954):321–27.

Littlewood, J.C.F. "D. H. Lawrence's Early Tales." *Cambridge Quarterly* 1 (1966):107–24.

Lodge, David. *The Modes of Modern Writing.* Ithaca, N.Y.: Cornell University Press, 1977.

———. *The Novelist at the Crossroads.* Ithaca, N.Y.: Cornell University Press, 1971.

Lucas, Barbara. "Apropos of 'England, My England.'" *Twentieth Century* 169 (March 1961):288–93.

Lucas, Robert. *Frieda Lawrence: The Story of Frieda von Richthofen and D. H. Lawrence.* New York: Viking Press, 1973.

Luhan, Mabel Dodge. *Lorenzo in Taos.* New York: Knopf, 1932.

MacDonald, Robert H. "Images of Negative Union: The Symbolic

World of D. H. Lawrence's 'The Princess.'" *Studies in Short Fiction* 16 (1979):289–93.

———. "The Union of Fire and Water: An Examination of The Imagery of *The Man Who Died*." *D. H. Lawrence Review* 10 (1977): 34–51.

MacNiven, Ian S. "D. H. Lawrence's Indian Summer." In *D. H. Lawrence: The Man Who Lived*, edited by Robert B. Partlow, Jr., and Harry T. Moore.

Martz, Louis L. *The Poem of the Mind*. New York: Oxford University Press, 1966.

McCabe, Thomas H. "Rhythm as Form in D. H. Lawrence: 'The Horse Dealer's Daughter.'" *PMLA* 87 (1972):64–68.

Mellown, Elgin W. "'The Captain's Doll': Its Origins and Literary Allusions." *D. H. Lawrence Review* 9 (1976):226–35.

Merivale, Patricia. *Pan the Goat God: His Myth in Modern Times*. Cambridge: Harvard University Press, 1969.

Meyers, Jeffrey. "D. H. Lawrence and Homosexuality." *London Magazine* n.s. 13 (1973):68–98.

———. "Katherine Mansfield, Gurdjieff, and Lawrence's 'Mother and Daughter.'" *Twentieth Century Literature* 22 (1976):444–53.

Millett, Kate. *Sexual Politics*. New York: Avon Books, 1969.

Moore, Harry T., ed. *A D. H. Lawrence Miscellany*. London: Heinemann, 1959.

———. *The Priest of Love: A Life of D. H. Lawrence*. Rev. ed. New York: Farrar, Straus and Giroux, 1974.

Moynahan, Julian. *The Deed of Life: The Novels and Tales of D. H. Lawrence*. Princeton, N.J.: Princeton University Press, 1963.

———. "Lawrence, Women, and the Celtic Fringe." In *Lawrence and Women*, edited by Anne Smith.

Murry, John Middleton. *Reminiscences of D. H. Lawrence*. New York: Henry Holt and Co., 1933.

Nehls, Edward, ed. *D. H. Lawrence: A Composite Biography*. 3 vols. Madison: University of Wisconsin Press, 1957–1959.

O'Connor, Frank [Michael O'Donovan]. *The Lonely Voice: A Study of the Short Story*. Cleveland: World, 1963.

Partlow, Robert B., Jr., and Harry T. Moore, eds. *D. H. Lawrence: The Man Who Lived*. Papers delivered at the D. H. Lawrence Conference at Southern Illinois University, April 1979. Carbondale and Edwardsville: Southern Illinois University Press, 1980.

Pascal, Roy. "Tense and Novel." *Modern Language Review* 57 (1962):1–11.

Phillips, Steven R. "The Double Pattern of D. H. Lawrence's 'The Horse Dealer's Daughter.'" *Studies in Short Fiction* 10 (1973):94–97.

Pritchard, R. E. *D. H. Lawrence: Body of Darkness*. London: Hutchinson University Library, 1971.

Ragussis, Michael. "The False Myth of St. *Mawr*: Lawrence and the Subterfuge of Art." *Papers on Language and Literature* 2 (1975):186–96.

Roberts, Warren. *A Bibliography of D. H. Lawrence*. 2nd ed. Cambridge: Cambridge University Press, 1982.

Rose, Shirley. "Physical Trauma in D. H. Lawrence's Short Fiction." *Contemporary Literature* 16 (1975):73–83.

Ross, Michael L. "Lawrence's Second 'Sun.'" *D. H. Lawrence Review* 8 (1975):1–18.

———. "The Mythology of Friendship: D. H. Lawrence, Bertrand Russell, and 'The Blind Man.'" In *English Literature and British Philosophy*, edited by S. P. Rosenbaum. Chicago: University of Chicago Press, 1971.

Rossi, Patrizio. "Lawrence's Two Foxes: A Comparison of Texts." *Essays in Criticism* 22 (1972):265–78.

Rossman, Charles. "*The Boy in the Bush* in the Lawrence Canon." In *D. H. Lawrence: The Man Who Lived*, edited by Robert B. Partlow, Jr., and Harry T. Moore.

———. "'You Are the Call and I Am the Answer': D. H. Lawrence and Women." *D. H. Lawrence Review* 8 (1975):255–328.

Ruderman, Judith. "'The Fox' and the 'Devouring Mother.'" *D. H. Lawrence Review* 10 (1977):251–69.

———. "Lawrence's 'The Fox' and Verga's 'The She Wolf': Variations on the Theme of the 'Devouring Mother.'" *Modern Language Notes* 94 (1979):153–65.

———. "Prototypes for Lawrence's 'The Fox.'" *Journal of Modern Literature* 8 (1980):77–98.

———. "Tracking Lawrence's *Fox*: An Account of Its Composition, Evolution, and Publication." *Studies in Bibliography* 33 (1980):207–21.

Ryals, Clyde de L. "D. H. Lawrence's 'The Horse Dealer's Daughter': An Interpretation." *Literature and Psychology* 12 (1962):39–43.

Sagar, Keith. *The Art of D. H. Lawrence*. Cambridge: Cambridge University Press, 1966.

———. "'The Best I Have Known': D. H. Lawrence's 'A Modern Lover' and 'The Shades of Spring,'" *Studies in Short Fiction* 4 (1966–1967):143–51.

———. *D. H. Lawrence: A Calendar of His Works, With a Checklist of the Manuscripts of D. H. Lawrence* by Lindeth Vasey. Austin: University of Texas Press, 1979.

———. "D. H. Lawrence: Notes from a Calendar of His Works." *Critical Quarterly* 21 (1979):31–36.

———. *The Life of D. H. Lawrence.* New York: Pantheon Books, 1980.

———, ed. *A D. H. Lawrence Handbook.* New York: Barnes and Noble, 1982.

Sale, Roger. *Modern Heroism.* Berkeley and Los Angeles: University of California Press, 1973.

San Juan, E., Jr. "Theme *vs.* Imitation: D. H. Lawrence's 'The Rocking-Horse Winner.'" *D. H. Lawrence Review* 3 (1970):136–40.

Schlauch, Margaret. "English Short Fiction in the 15th and 16th Centuries." *Studies in Short Fiction* 3 (1965–1966):393–434.

Scholes, Robert. *The Fabulators.* Oxford: Oxford University Press, 1967.

Schorer, Mark. Introduction to *Lady Chatterley's Lover.* New York: Grove Press, 1959.

———. "*Women in Love* and Death." In *D. H. Lawrence: A Collection of Critical Essays,* edited by Mark Spilka.

———, ed. *The Story: A Critical Anthology.* New York: Prentice-Hall, 1950.

Schreiner, Olive. *Women and Labour.* New York: Frederick A. Stokes, 1911.

Scott, James F. "D. H. Lawrence's Germania: Ethnic Psychology and Cultural Crisis in the Shorter Fiction." *D. H. Lawrence Review* 10 (1977):142–64.

———. "'Thimble' into 'Ladybird': Nietzsche, Frobenius, and Bachofen in the Later Works of D. H. Lawrence." *Arcadia* 21, Band 13 (1978) Heft 2:161–76.

Secor, Robert. "Language and Movement in 'Fanny and Annie.'" *Studies in Short Fiction* 6 (1968–1969):395–400.

Shields, E. F. "Broken Vision in Lawrence's 'The Fox.'" *Studies in Short Fiction* 9 (1972):353–63.

Shklovski, Victor. "La Construction de la nouvelle et du roman." In *Théorie de la Littérature,* edited by Todorov.

Simpson, Hilary. *D. H. Lawrence and Feminism.* DeKalb: Northern Illinois University Press, 1982.

Smith, Anne. "'A New Adam and a New Eve'—Lawrence and Women: A Biographical Overview." Introductory essay in her *Lawrence and Women.*

———, ed. *Lawrence and Women.* New York: Barnes and Noble, 1978.

Snodgrass, W. D. "A Rocking Horse: The Symbol, the Pattern, the Way to Live." In *D. H. Lawrence: A Collection of Critical Essays*, edited by Mark Spilka.

Sobchack, Thomas. "'The Fox': The Film and the Novel." *Western Humanities Review* 23 (1969):73–78.

Spender, Stephen, ed. *D. H. Lawrence: Novelist, Poet, Prophet.* New York: Harper and Row, 1973.

Spilka, Mark. "Lawrence Up-Tight or the Anal Phase Once Over." *Novel* 4 (1971):252–67.

———. "Lawrence's Quarrel with Tenderness." *Critical Quarterly* 9 (1967):363–77.

———. "Lessing and Lawrence: The Battle of the Sexes." *Contemporary Literature* 16 (1975):218–40.

———. *The Love Ethic of D. H. Lawrence.* Bloomington: Indiana University Press, 1955.

———. "On Lawrence's Hostility to Willful Women." In *Lawrence and Women*, edited by Anne Smith.

———. "Ritual Form in 'The Blind Man.'" In his *D. H. Lawrence: A Collection of Critical Essays.*

———, ed. *D. H. Lawrence: A Collection of Critical Essays.* Englewood Cliffs, N.J.: Prentice-Hall, 1963.

Squires, M. "Teaching a Story Rhetorically: An Approach to a Short Story by D. H. Lawrence." *College Composition and Communication* 24 (1973):150–56.

Stewart, Garrett. "D. H. Lawrence and the Allotropic Style." *Novel* 9 (1976):217–42.

Tedlock, E. W. *D. H. Lawrence, Artist and Rebel; A Study of Lawrence's Fiction.* Albuquerque: University of New Mexico Press, 1963.

———. *D. H. Lawrence Manuscripts: A Descriptive Bibliography.* Albuquerque: University of New Mexico Press, 1948.

Thompson, Leslie H. "The Christ Who Didn't Die: Analogues to D. H. Lawrence's The Man Who Died." *D. H. Lawrence Review* 8 (1975): 19–30.

Todorov, Tzvetan. *The Poetics of Prose.* Trans. by Richard Howard. Ithaca, N.Y.: Cornell University Press, 1977.

———, ed. *Théorie de la Littérature.* Paris: 1966.

Toyokuni, Takashi. "A Modern Man Obsessed by Time: A Note on 'The Man Who Loved Islands.'" *D. H. Lawrence Review* 7 (1974): 78–82.

Travis, Leigh. "D. H. Lawrence: The Blood-Conscious Artist." *American Imago* 25 (1968):163–90.

Van Ghent, Dorothy. *The English Novel: Form and Function.* New York: Rinehart, 1953.

Vickery, John B. *The Literary Impact of "The Golden Bough."* Princeton, N.J.: Princeton University Press, 1973. Reprinted and expanded from "Myth and Ritual in the Shorter Fiction of D. H. Lawrence." *Modern Fiction Studies* 5 (1959):65–82.

Vivas, Eliseo. *D. H. Lawrence: The Failure and the Triumph of Art.* Evanston, Ill.: Northwestern University Press, 1960.

Watt, Ian. "Serious Reflections on *The Rise of the Novel.*" *Novel* 1 (1968):205–18.

Weiss, Daniel A. *Oedipus in Nottingham: D. H. Lawrence.* Seattle: University of Washington Press, 1962.

West, Anthony. "The Short Stories." In *The Achievement of D. H. Lawrence,* edited by Frederick J. Hoffman and Harry T. Moore.

Wheeler, Richard P. "'Cunning in His Overthrow': Give and Take in 'Tickets, Please.'" *D. H. Lawrence Review* 10 (1977):242–50.

———. "Intimacy and Irony in 'The Blind Man.'" *D. H. Lawrence Review* 9 (1976):236–53.

Widmer, Kingsley. *The Art of Perversity: D. H. Lawrence's Shorter fictions.* Seattle: University of Washington Press, 1962.

Wilde, Alan. "The Illusion of *St. Mawr.*" *PMLA* 79 (1964):164–70.

Willbern, David. "Malice in Paradise: Isolation and Projection in 'The Man Who Loved Islands.'" *D. H. Lawrence Review* 10 (1977): 223–41.

Williams, Raymond. *The English Novel: From Dickens to Lawrence.* New York: Oxford University Press, 1970.

Wilt, Judith. *Ghosts of the Gothic.* Princeton, N.J.: Princeton University Press, 1980.

Wolkenfeld, Suzanne. "The Sleeping Beauty Retold: D. H. Lawrence's 'The Fox.'" *Studies in Short Fiction* 14 (1977):345–52.

Yarmolinsky, Avrahm. *The Portable Chekhov.* New York: Viking Press, 1969.

Zytaruk, George J. *D. H. Lawrence's Response to Russian Literature.* Paris and The Hague: Mouton Press, 1971.

———, ed. "Dorothy Brett's Letters to S. S. Koteliansky." *D. H. Lawrence Review* 7 (1974): 240–74.

Index